Reasonable Doubt

By

Rick Fɩ

GW00470499

DetectiveRyanTyler@gmail.com

This is a work of fiction. That means this book and all of
the incidents in it are purely figments of my imagination.
Any resemblance to actual persons, whether living or
dead, is purely coincidental. Although many of the places
and events in this book are based on actual places and
events, this is still a work of fiction. No inferences should
be made between the incidents in this book and any
actual incidences that may take place or have already
taken place in real life.

Part One

PROLOGUE

Heaving the backpack to the ground, Richard Frost sat on a log to catch his breath. Time was short, but he was exhausted and desperately needed a break. He took a great gasping breath that caught in his lungs. Coughing strenuously, he leaned forward, covering his mouth with his gloved hand, a habit ingrained in socially accepted standards, though there was nobody around to take offense. Getting the coughing under control, he looked down at the palm of the glove and paused for a moment staring at the blood splattered on it. Shaking his head, he wiped the glove in a patch of snow, spitting to clear his mouth before opening his water bottle and drinking the last drops.

He took just another moment, enjoying the solitude, the quiet and the beauty of the natural world surrounding him. This is what had sustained him throughout his life, what had allowed him to work so hard for so many years. Knowing the wilderness was always waiting had let him push through the long weeks, looking forward to the one day each week he always set aside to spend in the woods. He was sorry his life was coming to an end like this, but glad he'd found a small path to immortality in the backpack at his feet.

Standing at last, he suffered through one more coughing spell, saying a quick prayer that it was the last or that the next would hold off at least for a couple of hours. He still had a lot of work to do and darkness was fast approaching.

He grabbed the backpack and gingerly picked his way down the embankment to the place he'd chosen so carefully. He'd spent months looking for just the right spot. The conditions he'd set as the standard while searching for the perfect location had required a lot of thought. He had no idea how long it would be before *someone came looking for this cache, and it probably needed to survive years, quite possibly decades.*

He opened the backpack and then leaned into the concealed cavity, dragging out the titanium box, grunting under its significant weight. He felt another coughing spell coming on and he paused while he fought it down. The spells had recently become serious enough that he'd passed out on two occasions, unable to control his breathing, blood spraying in the air as he fell to the ground; a recurrence of that now would be disastrous.

After a brief moment, his lungs began to work smoothly and he said a silent prayer of thanks. The danger averted, he swallowed down the small amount of blood that had bubbled up from his ravaged lungs and then returned his attention to the box. He opened it and smiled at the sight; he'd worked hard his entire life and he never tired of looking at the fruits of that labor. He turned to the backpack and, reaching in, removed seven small objects, one at a time. Though small, the objects were heavier than they appeared to be. Each item was perfectly shaped, manufactured to be exact in size and weight.

He added the seven items to the box that already contained thirteen identical objects he had packed up on two earlier trips. He then pulled three small sacks from the backpack. The sacks were made of oilskin which he hoped would protect them for many, many years. He made sure they were closed securely and then piled them in around the twenty heavy objects, pushing the sacks down with his hands so the lid would be able to close securely. It was surprising even to him, a man used to dealing with items such as this, how small a box was required. Someday in the future, somebody would be surprised at how heavy such a small box could be.

Before he closed the lid, he removed a piece of paper from the backpack, the paper laminated and enclosed in a Ziploc bag. He placed it on top of the items in the chest, smiling at the thought of someone reading the words sometime in the future.

There was no point in locking the box, none at all actually, but old habits die hard, and Richard found himself fighting the urge to snap the padlock onto the reinforced clasp. He'd wanted the complex, secure lock when he originally had the box made, but it wasn't needed anymore. He would have given the padlock a symbolic toss into the lake but, being a lover of nature and a hater of those who would despoil it in any way, he turned and dropped the lock into the backpack instead. He would pack it out, along with any other evidence of his presence, just as he'd done his entire life.

He turned back to the box and, leaning down, put his entire body into it, shoving it back into the place he'd discovered, the place that would keep it safe for as long as necessary.

Moving all of the logs and sticks back exactly as he'd found them, he stood and surveyed the scene. There were definite signs that someone had been here...footprints and drag marks, vegetation crushed, a rock unearthed, but he wasn't worried about that. It was getting dark and it would snow tonight, covering all signs of his visit.

Richard Frost picked up the nearly empty backpack and slung it over his shoulders. This part of his life's journey was nearly over. He'd never see this place again, so he took just a moment to enjoy one last look around before he began working his way back to the path that led to his car.

The distance wasn't far but, in his weakened condition, it had taken him the entire day to make the three trips needed to carry it all here. He smiled to himself as he remembered a time when he would have carried a load like that in just one trip. He missed the days of his youth when nothing had seemed impossible and the world lay at his feet.

Richard worked his way down the slope, finding the trail and following it to his car, arriving right at dark. A few snowflakes began to fall as he unlocked the door. He got in and drove away and didn't allow himself the luxury of one final look back. The deed was done, the past was the past, and the future belonged to somebody else.

Chapter One

Eight years later

The killer, dressed all in black, looked down at the man tied to the chair. His expression reflected sadness mixed with satisfaction: sadness at what he'd had to do (killing someone was no small feat after all) and satisfaction at what he'd discovered just before he'd pulled the trigger.

The man in the chair moved just slightly, a twitch really, his head lolled over toward his right shoulder, his chin nearly touching his chest. He was dead already, though his body was still trying to fight that finality. The two bullet holes in his chest, a moment before gushing blood, were now releasing just a trickle.

After a few seconds, the man in the chair finally relaxed fully, his body sagging forward, the bonds tying him to the chair the only thing keeping him from falling to the floor. The killer lowered the gun. He was glad the man in the chair hadn't resisted too much, hadn't forced him to use measures he'd been willing to use but would have found distasteful in the extreme.

He knelt down and carefully placed the gun into the backpack he'd brought, a few tools rattling around inside as he did so. It wasn't until then, crouched on the floor by the dead man's feet, that he finally took the time to look at the piece of paper in his hand.

The man in the chair had hidden it, and the events tonight were a result of that unfortunate decision. Of course, he'd quickly revealed the location and a whole lot more when he'd realized his life was in danger. The decision to end that life had already been determined though. It was only the manner of his death that had been left up to him.

One side of the paper was covered with notes, painstakingly written; cross-outs littered the page, along with question marks, underlines, and circled words. This was all the work of the man in the chair, and the man in black took a moment to admire it.

"I couldn't have done it myself," he said quietly to the man in the chair, admitting it for the first time.

He flipped the page over and examined the words written there, words that he was intimately familiar with. The words printed on this page had consumed the last six months of his life, ever since he'd discovered them while reading an interesting news story online:

They say youth's folly is the pursuit of wealth,
It's the theif of that which is not slowed.
The most precious thing you own is your health,
And you'll need it to recover this lode.

Your search begins where rocks once grew,
And the music man, he spins through the night.

The pitcher's goal, in his name replaces two,
The Lincoln Logs of life must give him a fright.

Smog without air makes no sense at all,
But adding gold makes him mighty and great.
A place such as this, a home he might call,
'Lo he ignore the ghosts of those working the freight.

Protected from the Arctic's wet kiss you'll find,
As you begin the true quest from here.
The stalwart kid of course is kind,
But only trustworthy as far as the mirror.

Now a mile is the goal, are your legs burning yet?
Don't worry, you've nearly arrived.
A heavy load, a truly great get,
I was amazed at how they had thrived.

Go quickly now, for the end draws nigh,
All great adventures must come to a close.
The entrance you seek, low and yet dry,
The chest in a trunk, protected by a rose.

If you're persistent enough to have come this far,
The gold, I bequeath all to you.
A paragon of honor, I have no doubt that you are,
Though if not, this day you shall rue.

Seven stanzas, four lines per stanza with alternating rhymes. 230 words, 963 characters, 1166 characters counting the spaces, and one misspelled word. The man in black knew every single detail about this poem, inside and out. He'd studied it, dissected it, and examined it backwards, forwards, upside down and in a mirror. He'd looked up the definitions and synonyms and antonyms of every word. He'd changed every letter to its reciprocal number and tried to find meaning that way. He'd done research with cipher keys, trying to find hidden meaning in the text.

The only thing he hadn't known about this poem, and really the only thing that mattered, was what the poem meant.

That misspelled word alone had consumed the killer for weeks, trying in vain to figure out why just that one of all 230 words had been misspelled--every available hour of every day for weeks, just trying to unravel the meaning behind the spelling of that one word.

For this poem, and in particular for the solution now written on the back and divulged by the man in the chair, the killer had risked much, a calculated risk, but one with potentially dire consequences should he fail.

He carefully folded the piece of paper and tucked it away in a zippered pocket of his black leather jacket. He then bent down to the backpack and, opening a separate zippered compartment, began removing items and placing them on the floor. He had a lot of work still to do and time was short.

Two hours later, the killer looked out the back door, making sure there was nobody watching, and quickly walked through the rear alley. He cut across the golf course to his car which he'd left parked on a street, well away from the victim's house. Checking once more for any observers, he opened the car door and tossed the backpack inside. Getting behind the wheel, he drove through back streets, following a carefully planned route. As he approached his destination, he picked up his prepaid cell phone and hit a number that was programmed in.

The man with the scar on his face answered on the first ring.

"Go ahead and make the call," the killer said to the man with the scar on his face.

The phone went dead in his hand. He hit the button to lower the window on his side and carefully tore the phone apart, dropping the battery out first, then the SIM card, and then the two halves of the phone, the parts scattering behind him on the highway.

The deed was done, but the fun was just beginning. The man in black smiled to himself in the rearview mirror as he carefully turned off the highway and headed toward home.

Chapter Two

It was only 9:20am, but Franklin Daniel Richardson was already having a shitty day.

Pulling up to his office, his eyes scanned the street looking for a parking spot. He could have parked in the lot back on Hewitt Avenue, but he was boycotting it because he'd gotten in a fight with the lot attendant the previous week.

The lot was supposed to have in and out privileges, and he'd left for lunch. When he returned, a new lot attendant had wanted to charge him for another day, and nobody was going to screw Franklin Daniel Richardson out of eight bucks. He'd gotten in a screaming match with the lot attendant, got back in his car, and threw rocks and gravel at the stupid little shack they stand in as he burned out of there. His current stand was that he wouldn't be back unless he got a refund of the earlier charge and an apology. If history was any predictor, that stand would not be a lasting one.

Even if he hadn't been in full boycott mode, the lot was two blocks from his office, and it was currently raining. *Of course it was raining*, Franklin thought, it was always fucking raining here, especially in January. And naturally, when it wasn't fucking raining, it was fucking snowing.

Franklin hated the rain and he hated the snow, but what he hated most was when it was fucking raining or fucking snowing and he forgot his fucking umbrella.

His shitty day, of course, had nothing to do with the rain that was drizzling down. If he allowed the weather to significantly affect the quality of his day, he'd have blown his brains out years ago. You don't decide to live in the western part of Washington State if rain ruins your day, even though you may hate it.

No, his shitty day was a direct result of a conversation he'd been forced to have this morning with his bitch of an ex-wife who was trying to extort more money out of him. That phone call and the screaming match that ensued with the bitch, had made him late getting on the road to his office, which in turn had made him hit horrendous rush hour traffic, amplified in magnitude by the relentless rain.

Actually, "Bitch" was too nice a title for Erica. He had a different designation for her… a word he used with nobody else, of course, even though he secretly liked the word and mentally used it to describe a lot of people, both men and women, who pissed him off. He would never use the word out loud though. Except maybe on the rare occasion when his law school buddies got together for drinks and he tipped back a few too many. But there was no harm in yelling it out when he was with those guys; they understood him.

So, Erica had her own moniker, though he'd never actually worked up the courage to say it directly to her. It gave him great pleasure to sign off all text message conversations to her with, "C U Next Tuesday!!" even using the capital letters in "Next" and "Tuesday" in case she was too dense to understand the hidden context without them.

Erica never replied to those messages; she always let him get the final word in their text message battles, so Franklin couldn't actually be sure she did understand his intended message, or if she always thought he was trying to meet up with her next Tuesday.

His eyes continued to search for a parking spot as he turned up Oakes Avenue and approached the courthouse. He could have parked in the small lot right in front of his office, but he wouldn't allow himself that luxury. He was, unfortunately, a little cash tight at the moment, so his current mode of transportation was a thirteen-year-old Honda Accord that had seen better days. There was no way he was going to attract the type of clientele he hoped for—and by that he meant the rich kind with a bunch of legal problems—if this piece of shit Accord was the only vehicle parked in the space in front of his office.

As it stood now, Franklin's standard response to potential clients who asked, "How come there are no cars in the parking lot?" was to claim that his Tesla was currently charging at the Tesla service center down the street. The fact that there was no Tesla service center down the street didn't seem to be a point of contention for any of them.

A few months ago, he'd worked out a deal with a doctor who had an office one block over, to let the doctor park his Mercedes in the lot for free. For a few weeks, Franklin had had a great time claiming ownership of that car to anybody who asked. Then one day the doctor saw him pretending to get in the car while one of Franklin's potential clients took his own goddamn sweet time driving away after an end-of-the-day appointment. Franklin hadn't wanted to be seen walking up to his piece of shit Accord that he'd parked in a fortuitous spot on the street one door down from his office. The doctor and his Mercedes hadn't returned.

Franklin was usually in his office by 8:30am, and that meant he usually had a plethora of parking choices. But today he was late thanks to his C U Next Tuesday of an ex-wife, and now he couldn't find a goddamn parking spot.

Just as he was about to spin a U-turn and drive back to Hewitt Avenue, he saw the sweet sight of white back-up lights come on in one of the spaces reserved for courthouse parking.

Franklin hit the gas and stopped just short of the car preparing to back out. The jackass was taking his fucking sweet time, and Franklin impatiently thrummed his fingers on the steering wheel, muttering under his breath. When the car finally moved, Franklin flipped the driver the bird and then whipped into the spot, killing the engine just as his cell phone started to ring.

The caller ID showed his office number, and he knew his secretary was wondering why he was so late. He grabbed his briefcase off the passenger seat, looked around one more time in vain for his umbrella, then picked up his phone and hit the answer button.

"I'll be there in two minutes!" he shouted.

"There's a..." his secretary began, but Franklin had already hit the end call button.

Grabbing his Styrofoam cup of 7-11 coffee, he maneuvered himself out of the car, slamming the door shut with his foot and not bothering to lock it. He'd insured it to the hilt and having it stolen would be a blessing; the type of blessing he was actually considering manufacturing if it didn't happen on its own.

He eyed the sign that said he could park in that spot only for courthouse business and for no more than two hours. He shrugged. Technically, as a lawyer, he was always on courthouse business and he would come back and move the car before two hours had passed. He turned and rushed off to his office, trying not to spill his coffee or slip and fall on the wet pavement.

Chapter Three

Franklin's office was located at the corner of Wall Street and Oakes Avenue, a location he'd chosen very carefully three years earlier when he'd left the Prosecutor's Office after seven years of putting criminals away. He'd struck out on his own on the other side of the street or, as he liked to say, on the right side of the street, moving into the business of keeping criminals free.

Although his accountant could have told him that the criminal defense business was netting pretty significantly less than his salary would have been as a ten-year veteran of the Prosecutor's Office, Franklin wouldn't have listened. He knew he was just one O.J. Simpson level case away from achieving worldwide fame and fortune, and he wouldn't let the naysayers like his accountant and the ex-Mrs. Richardson ruin his dreams.

Franklin had chosen the location of his office based on a number of factors. The first had been that it was located very close to the courthouse. In Franklin's mind, proximity to the action equated to success and clients, and he wasn't going to locate his place of business in some fucking strip mall in the suburbs. Nope, he wanted his potential clients to walk out of the courthouse and see his sign before any other. His secretary could have told him that what he'd failed to take into account was that most criminal clients who are at the courthouse have already procured an attorney.

The next biggest factor in his choice of office location was the names of the streets. Appearances were everything and "Wall Street" invoked images of money and wealth, while "Oakes Avenue" invoked images of *old* money and wealth, as well as stateliness and confidence.

The official postal address of Franklin's office was 417 Wall Street, but he would never use such a pedestrian address on any of his correspondence. He'd had every letterhead and every business card in his office printed up with the address label reading *The corner of Wall Street and Oakes Avenue, in the heart of the Judicial District.*

Those were the words his secretary was directed to say when clients asked for the address, and Franklin had even tried to have the postal service recognize that description as his official address. He'd gotten into a heated argument with the postmaster when they'd insisted his address needed a street number. He'd threatened a bunch of legal actions against them and the old guy had thrown him out of the post office. Franklin still directed his clients to send things to *The corner of Wall Street and Oakes Avenue in the heart of the Judicial District,* and the mail always seemed to get delivered, so fuck the post office and fuck that old bastard of a postmaster.

Despite the fact that even Franklin would admit when pressed that the building his office was located in was a piece of shit, the third reason he'd chosen this location was the huge billboard in the front, the billboard that faced right at the courthouse.

Even though the rain hadn't slackened, Franklin couldn't help but stop for just a moment to admire his billboard. Measuring twenty feet long by twelve feet high, the bottom edge of which was fifteen feet above the ground, the thing was a true work of art.

Right after Franklin had taken up residence in this office, and before he'd even had a chance to attach his name to what had then been a shared space billboard, his landlord had come by with a representative from the City of Everett along with a work crew to tear it down. Franklin had thrown a fit, and the city representative had tried to explain to him that the billboard was in violation of the current city ordinances governing the size and location of advertorial billboards.

Franklin had immediately marched over to the courthouse and filed a motion for an injunction barring the construction crews from touching the billboard. The judge had signed off on the motion, granting a thirty-day reprieve until a hearing could be held, and Franklin had run back to the city representative and shoved the court order into his chest. The city rep had glanced at the order, shrugged, and left with his crew.

Franklin then negotiated a deal with the landlord where he bought the full rights to the billboard for the sum of $100 which he paid to the landlord in cash. The landlord, not collecting any advertising revenue from the billboard anyway and thinking Franklin was likely to lose his injunction hearing, was just happy to be out from the responsibility of renting and managing the damned space for the five tenants who shared the office building.

Franklin, of course, had no intention of losing the billboard hearing. He spent the entire thirty days looking up supporting case law involving grandfathering clauses, rights to advertising laws, city ordinance procedural laws, and everything else he could think of that even remotely resembled his case including, for some reason, case law on dog leash ordinances which had nothing to do at all with the issue at hand, at least not in the mind of the city attorney.

He'd then served a mountain of paperwork on the court and the city attorney and informed the judge he was going to need six days for witness depositions and planned to call at least a dozen to testify. The judge had called the city attorney into his chambers and asked him if he really cared about a fucking billboard that was quickly becoming a nightmare of epic proportions, and the city attorney decided he'd acquiesce to the judge granting a summary motion that the billboard was grandfathered in under the previous ordinances.

That was Franklin's first win, and he wasted no time having the billboard repainted. He had just hired Stacy, his secretary, and her first job was to go around and tell the other four tenants that the billboard space they'd previously enjoyed now belonged solely to the new attorney downstairs.

The billboard Franklin couldn't help but admire showed his picture on the left side, taking up nearly 25% of the huge space, his smile beaming down for all to see. Next to that was his slogan: *The other FDR may have given you the New Deal, but THIS FDR gives you the BEST DEAL!!*

If Franklin ever had the inclination to conduct a survey, or even an informal poll, he likely would have learned that the vast majority of his clientele didn't have a clue who *"The other FDR"* was or even what *"The New Deal"* was. It didn't matter, though, because Franklin wouldn't have cared either way. The sight of his smiling face looking out toward the Snohomish County Courthouse twenty-four hours a day, seven days a week, always served to cheer him up, even when he was having a shitty day like this.

Chapter Four

Detective Monika Sodafsky took a sip of her coffee while she stared at her partner over the rim of the cup. Detective Bruce Norgaard was currently engaged in trying to maneuver a huge spoonful of scrambled eggs onto the edge of a toasted cinnamon-raisin bagel that was smothered in cream cheese. She watched as he pushed the scrambled eggs into the cream cheese with his plastic spoon, the cream cheese bulging out around the eggs. A large glob of it fell off the bagel and was about to land in his lap when he whipped the spoon down and caught it. He licked the cream cheese off the spoon and then bit off a huge chunk of bagel, cream cheese, and scrambled eggs.

"You're disgusting," Monika said to him, setting her coffee cup down on the table and pulling off a small, bite-sized piece of her blueberry muffin, popping it into her mouth.

Bruce shrugged and chewed rapidly until he had made enough room in his mouth to be able to speak.

"It's all about ratios, Monika. You see, every item on this plate is, by itself, inedible." He paused while he finished chewing and then swallowed the food in his mouth. She was grateful for that, at least; his habit of talking while he was chewing was enough to make her not want to eat her own breakfast.

Bruce continued. "Take this bagel." He pointed down at his plate. "This thing is just barely edible. Sure, it's got cinnamon in it, which is delicious, and raisins, which are great, but they're all mixed in with dough that was made in some factory in massive quantities by some minimum wage worker using the cheapest ingredients they can bulk buy. Then the cream cheese. Sure, it's a type of cheese, which automatically makes it delicious, but you can't just grab a spoon and start eating cream cheese out of a container. That would be socially unacceptable."

Monika arched her eyebrows. Bruce actually cared about whether or not something was socially unacceptable?

"Then we get to the eggs. Look around this place." He waved his hand toward the kitchen of the deli where they were eating. "Who the fuck knows what happens back there? When do you think an inspector was last here checking on the sanitation conditions? Probably never. Then you have the fact that these scrambled eggs are made from some kind of dehydrated powder with God only knows what's in it. The guy back there adds water and cooks it on a stove and then serves it to us calling it eggs, because if he called it rehydrated, yellow, egg-like powder with monosodium glutamate and a touch of cockroach carcass nobody would buy it."

"So why in the world are you eating it then?" she demanded.

Bruce smiled. "For two reasons. Number one, I'm a cop. I don't make enough money to go to the nice restaurants and eat the good food. And number two, when you put them together in the right proportions, it's delicious!" He spooned up another heaping load of rehydrated egg-like powder, balanced it on the cream cheese smothered bagel, and took another huge bite.

"Delicious!" he mumbled around the mouthful of food.

Monika sighed and ate another small bite from her muffin. As disgusting as the eating habits of her partner were, he actually managed to stay somewhat trim and in decent shape. In fact, he wasn't bad looking and in another time in her life, she might have been interested in some kind of romantic involvement with him. As it was, though, she was entirely focused on her career.

Monika Sodafsky was thirty-five years old and had been a cop for ten years now. She loved being a detective and she loved working in homicide, the pinnacle of detective work, in her mind. She'd never been married and wasn't planning on getting married for some time. Companionship was great and she missed it sometimes, but her career came first.

She sipped her coffee and tried to tune out the sound of Bruce eating as she stared out the window at the rain coming down. She had worked hard to get to where she was, and relationships were often distracting. In fact, her motto was *Comfort is the enemy of success*. She usually applied that motto just to her work, but she had come to realize that it applied to her personal life as well.

She had been in exactly three serious relationships in her life. The first had been during college at the University of Washington where she had dated the same guy for her entire sophomore and junior years. He'd been a soccer player and had decided not to return for his senior year, instead opting to try to make it as a professional. He'd wanted to continue dating, but they both knew it wasn't going to work and they'd called it off.

The second serious relationship had been during her rookie year as a police officer. She'd begun dating another recruit from her same academy class. She thrived during her field training period, the time after a cop graduates from the police academy when they ride with a training officer to learn how actual police work is done. Her boyfriend, Nate, didn't thrive. In fact, he struggled and, after six months of field training, he was fired by the department.

She still would have tried to make that relationship work, but Nate was threatened by her success in the same arena as his failure. She'd tried to make it easy on him, commiserating with him about the bad luck he'd had in training officer assignments and trying to make up complaints of her own in an attempt to sympathize with him. The problem was, Monika loved her job and she loved the Snohomish County Sheriff's Office. Coming home every day after Nate was fired and trying to pretend she'd had a terrible day became a chore. It brought her down and she knew it was affecting her career.

That was the first time she realized that relationships are bad for a career. She did some soul searching and came to the conclusion that in order to be everything she wanted to be as a cop, she had to lose the baggage. The baggage in this case had a big tag on it that read *Nate*.

After a nasty breakup, she spent three years being single before giving a relationship one more try, this time with a prosecuting attorney named Jacob who had hit on her relentlessly for months. She had finally acquiesced to his date requests and they'd gone out for the next three months.

The only reason Monika considered this a serious relationship was because she'd told Jacob that she loved him. It hadn't been true, but what do you say when a guy says, "I love you"? "Thank you. That's really sweet of you," just doesn't cut it. So she'd said, "I love you too," just like a good girlfriend was supposed to do. A month later, he'd begun talking to her about moving in together and him taking care of her. He was surprised and hurt and angry when she broke up with him. She tried to explain that she'd made the decision to work on her career and that the relationship was doing nothing but interfering with that. He'd made a bunch of accusations that there was another guy (there wasn't, of course) and had actually cried when she started to leave.

To Monika, that was a manifestation of weakness, something she despised in a man. She knew that some women thought a man crying meant that he was sensitive and that it was a redeeming quality, but Monika didn't see that at all. *She* certainly didn't cry, almost never anyway, and she could only look at Jacob with contempt when she saw the tears.

That had been nearly five years ago, and since then she'd never been happier. She still dated; after all, a girl needs to get laid on occasion, but she never allowed herself to develop an emotional attachment to anybody.

This policy had been very beneficial for her career. She'd made the rank of Master Patrol Deputy after five years on the road, the minimum amount of time required to achieve that rank, and had then moved into Investigations. She'd planned on just a short stint there before testing for Sergeant and moving back to patrol, but she'd discovered she loved being a detective. Moving into Major Crimes two years before, she had been the lead detective on eight homicide cases, nine if you count the case she'd pulled just yesterday morning, and so far, she'd achieved a conviction on 100% of them.

The homicide case she'd pulled yesterday didn't seem like it was going to be the one that would break her perfect record, though she knew better than to give voice to that opinion, lest her words come back to haunt her.

Bruce Norgaard had been assigned to assist her with this one, a random draw in the rotation that all detectives go through. It wasn't a bad draw either; as detectives go, Bruce was a great one, despite his questionable eating habits. He was intelligent and inquisitive and, unlike a few others in the division, he wasn't lazy. Monika despised laziness and couldn't stand anybody who thought it was even remotely acceptable, especially in this business.

She glanced at Bruce who was just finishing his last mouthful. She hadn't wanted to try discussing the case with him while he was eating, knowing that food in his mouth wouldn't have kept him from talking, but now seemed like a safe time.

"Now that you're done poisoning your body, can we talk about the Conner case?"

Bruce smiled. "You have my undivided attention."

Monika pulled a manila folder from her leather detective's bag on the floor and opened it up. Normally they would have gone back to the office before discussing the case, but they were alone in the café, the owner and cook out of earshot behind the counter. As long as she wasn't worried about anybody overhearing confidential information, she preferred to work away from the office as much as possible.

"Any luck with the trace on the 911 call?"

Bruce shook his head. "Nothing. Comes back to a throw-away, phone appears to be turned off, and the cell company isn't able to track it. Activated with a prepaid credit card that wasn't ever used anywhere else. I pulled the tape; it should be at the office later today."

She pursed her lips. The Conner homicide case had originated as a 911 call at 4:15am from someone requesting an ambulance. The person, a male voice, had called from a cellular phone, given the address and said someone was hurt, and then hung up. The 911 operator had attempted to call back, of course, but no call was ever able to get through, as if the phone had been destroyed right after the call was made. That possibility made Monika despise throwaways. They were cheap and could be purchased at any number of stores, could be activated using prepaid credit cards that could be bought for cash at many places, and could be deactivated by doing nothing more than removing the battery and throwing them away. They are impossible to trace as long as the person using them knows what they're doing.

The 911 call was recorded, of course, so they had a taped copy of the caller's voice, but that was useful only if they had something to compare it with.

In this instance, the 911 operator had dispatched the fire department to the address given. They'd arrived to find the door unlocked and nobody answering their hails. They'd entered the house, discovered the body lying on the floor, checked for a pulse, and then backed out, trying not to disturb anything. Textbook on the part of the FD, and she appreciated the job they'd done.

They had then notified dispatch of their discovery and dispatch had sent the cops. That could sometimes be a disaster, but the patrol sergeant on duty that morning had been a good one. No cops had entered the house; they'd simply secured it, and closed the street in front of it; easy enough to do as it was a quiet neighborhood street with ample detours around it. Then they'd strung up about a mile of crime scene tape. Crime scene tape was cheap and, as far as Monika was concerned, you could never string too much. It's easy to make a crime scene smaller, it's tough to make one bigger.

Monika had been first up on the rotation board and she'd received the call at 4:30am from the detective sergeant in charge of major crimes. She'd been on-scene and had taken charge of it from the patrol sergeant by 5:00am.

This case had immediately taken a turn toward the interesting side for Monika when she had leaned down to examine Conner's body and seen a redness and swelling around his wrists that would indicate he'd been tied up. Not that there were any uninteresting homicide cases, but it was rare to find a victim who'd been tied up and then executed.

One of the first things she'd done after checking Conner's body for any immediate clues had been to position herself in the spot she thought the shooter would have been standing based on the location of the body. She had then mimicked shooting a gun and gone looking for shell casings. If the shooter had used a revolver, the shell casings would have stayed with the gun, but if he'd used a semi-automatic, the casings would have flown. She knew very well the randomness that can happen as a shell is ejected from the chamber of the gun, and that randomness is amplified whenever those casings are going to land on a hard surface, such as the hardwood floors in the dining room where Conner had been shot.

Conner had been shot twice, so there were two chances for a shell casing to skip away and not be found. Monika hadn't been hopeful but had been pleasantly surprised and excited to discover something glinting in the floor-mounted heater vent when she'd shined her flashlight down there. She'd waited for the crime scene guys to arrive, hardly able to contain herself. It was all worthwhile when they finally removed the louvered vent cover and a beautiful, shiny, brass shell casing was sitting right there in the trap. Not only had the casing been found, the latent print guy had been able to pull a near perfect print off it.

The print on the shell casing wasn't as unusual as it might at first seem. She would have bet her next paycheck on the print being a thumb from the right hand, based on the fact that 90% of people are right-handed and the only really effective way of loading a semi-automatic pistol magazine is to press it down into the clip using the thumb of your dominant hand.

The great thing about a shell casing is that, when you find the gun from which it has been ejected, you can usually match the casing to the gun based on the strike of the firing pin on the primer, as well as the marks on the rim caused by the ejector as it gets forcefully pulled out of the firing chamber. Every gun is slightly different, so the marks they make during the violent explosion and extraction process involved in firing a shot are all different enough to be identifiable. That alone was reason enough to be excited about finding the shell casing; the thumb-print was just the icing on the cake.

Cop movies and TV shows always make it seem as though finding a fingerprint gets you an identification on a person almost immediately, but it doesn't usually work that way. A large percentage of the population has never been fingerprinted, so "negative returns" are more common than the public would probably believe. Monika hadn't dared to hope for a good return when the latent print guy pulled the print and sent it off to the FBI database, which is why, when the print returned with a match in less than forty-five minutes, she'd been ecstatic.

At that point, she'd been at the homicide scene less than two hours and she already had a solid suspect.

Chapter Five

The door to Franklin Richardson's office was made of glass, but the top half was plastered with a slighter smaller version of his billboard, which gave a semblance of privacy to the interior and also conveyed openness and trust, he hoped. On the bottom half of the door were the words, *Franklin Daniel Richardson, Esq.* and under that, *Attorney at Law*. The redundancy of using the abbreviation for *Esquire* as well as the more commonly used *Attorney at Law* was not lost on Franklin. However, he felt *Esquire* was important for the image he wanted to portray and *Attorney at Law* was important for the idiots he usually represented who would typically be impressed by the formal title, albeit oblivious to its significance.

The door tended to stick which is why, as Franklin pulled it open and began to step into his office, the door was suddenly wrenched from his hand, pressured back toward its closed position by the malfunctioning piston rod designed to make it close automatically. The door struck him in the shoulder causing his coffee cup to jerk in his hand, and hot coffee to spill down the front of his rain-soaked suit jacket.

"Goddammit!" he shouted, whirling around and drawing back his foot as he prepared to kick the insubordinate door.

"Excuse me, Mr. Richardson?" The voice of his secretary caused him to freeze mid-kick. There was only one reason she would call him Mr. Richardson.

He lowered his foot and turned slowly around to see his secretary, Stacy Wright, looking at him and cocking her head toward another person who was sitting in one of the two reception area chairs and staring his way.

"Mr. Richardson, this is Mr. Whittaker. He stopped in this morning to talk to you about representing him."

Stacy was looking at him with her eyebrows raised and when Franklin looked back at her, she lowered her gaze to where her hand was resting on the counter, all five fingers moving up and down. This was a code they had worked out, and it was based on the type of vehicle the client had arrived in. This gave Franklin an idea of how much time or energy he should spend on the client. One finger meant the client had arrived on a bus or a bike and one finger was, unfortunately, what Franklin was used to seeing. Five fingers meant drop everything and put on your fucking professional face because the money truck has just backed in and the driver wants to know where to dump the cash.

Franklin turned back to the potential cash cow. "Good morning, Mr. Whittaker," he said, tossing his coffee cup in the garbage and walking up with his hand extended. "I'm so sorry to be late this morning. I forgot to plug my Tesla in to the supercharger in my garage last night so I had to drop it off at the service department up the road. Anyway, they were apparently out of loaners and I had to wait for them to drive me back here."

Whittaker continued to stare at him, and Franklin dropped his hand taking the opportunity to look him over. The first step in his appraisal, of course, was the shoes: Burberry leather wingtips, and nice ones too, probably close to a thousand bucks. Working upward, he saw a good Italian suit. He couldn't identify the brand but quality stands out regardless. The ensemble was completed with an Ermenegilda Zegna tie. A few thousand bucks all together, along with the nice car that Franklin had somehow missed, but Stacy had apparently seen in the parking lot.

Hopefully this guy had killed the Pope.

Whittaker was shorter than Franklin, probably about 5'8", and slight of build. He appeared to be in his early thirties, but his light brown hair was already showing serious signs of thinning on top, the hairline receding far back on each side.

"Please call me Ron and excuse me for not shaking hands," he said, stiffly. "I've been fighting a cold and I'd rather not spread it around."

"Understandable, understandable of course, and no offense taken, none at all!" Franklin beamed at Ron as he glanced back at Stacy, trying to confirm she was holding five fingers on the counter. Stacy wiggled all five fingers again and gave him a thin-lipped smile.

"So, Ron Whittaker, what brings you in to see me? How can I help make your day better today?" he asked, continuing to give Whittaker his best billboard smile as he inwardly prayed, *Don't say you want help with your will, don't say you want help with your will.*

"You're a criminal defense attorney, no?"

"I absolutely am, the best in the business too!" Franklin replied, his grin getting even wider still.

"I think I may very soon find myself in need of your services. Is there somewhere we can talk privately?" Ron asked, looking skeptically around the small, dingy space.

Franklin's office consisted of the entryway, which he called his reception area, and his personal office, a small space through a door in the back wall. The reception area housed Stacy's desk and the two client chairs, as well as one of those water stations where the guy comes in the truck and replaces the bottle. Franklin had it set to be replaced just once a month which was the minimum order you could make. A few times a week he would bring some milk jugs full of water from his apartment and pour them into the bottle before Stacy got to work. The bottle was currently empty because he'd forgotten the milk jugs yesterday, and the fight this morning had made him forget them again.

He shook off all thoughts of C U Next Tuesday while he tried to keep his mind on his soon to be new client.

"We'll go to my office," he said. "Anastasia, will you please run down to Starbucks and get my usual, and something for you Mr. Whittaker?"

Stacy glared at him for his use of Anastasia. Her full legal name was Stacy, but Franklin had told her Stacy was just a little too low-rent sounding for any of their four- or five-finger clients. Stacy had tried numerous times to get him to call her Stacia as a compromise, but every time he'd said to her, "You don't cross the train tracks halfway, that's how you get hit by a train, Anastasia." She still didn't know just what that meant.

"Nothing for me, thanks; I'm in a bit of a hurry here," Ron Whittaker replied, glancing at his wristwatch.

"Of course, absolutely, right this way sir." Franklin led the way to the door set into the back wall. He unlocked it with a key on his key ring and walked in ahead, chatting the entire time.

"I apologize for the state of my office. We're currently in a transition phase expanding and remodeling the building, so I'm stuck using this tiny little office for now. I keep telling the construction crews that I'm going to take a break from my important criminal work and go into civil litigation with them if they don't get my suite of offices done soon, but of course that's an empty threat and they know it. Litigators of my caliber do NOT move into civil litigation, you know what I mean?" He turned around at his desk and looked back at Whittaker winking conspiratorially.

Ron Whittaker sighed. "Mr. Richardson, can we cut the bullshit?"

Franklin's smile faltered. "What do you mean?"

"I mean that you are a two-bit criminal defense attorney who spent more time on the probation list at Washington State University than most frat house party planners. You barely passed the LSAT, you would have been thrown out of Gonzaga Law school had your father not made a sizable campaign contribution to the Governor, and you're currently under investigation by the Washington State Bar Association for shady marketing practices. You don't own a Tesla, in fact, you've probably never even seen a Tesla, and you're currently two months late on the mortgage on your shitty condo."

"I've seen a Tesla," Franklin muttered, the smile now gone completely from his face.

"Despite all of this," Whittaker continued, "I still think you have potential to be a good defense attorney and I want your help." He sat down uninvited in the chair and Franklin followed suit, dropping into his own chair after a moment of stunned silence.

77

"Can I count on you to drop all the bullshit and the salesmanship so that we can talk business?"

Franklin stared at him for a second and then nodded abruptly.

"Good!" Whittaker clapped his hands. "Then let's talk business. The night before last, my best friend in the world was murdered." Whittaker looked down at his hands, picking at one of his fingernails, and then looked back up. "The police notified me of his death yesterday morning. I was devastated of course."

He paused for a second and rubbed at the corner of his eye. Franklin took the opportunity to grab a yellow legal pad and a pen from his desk drawer. "Why did the police choose to notify you? Wouldn't they notify his family and the family would notify you?" he asked.

Whittaker nodded. "An astute question. I didn't think about that until after they'd left. I was in shock as I'm sure you can imagine."

"Where were you when they notified you?"

"I was at work."

"Okay, and where is that?" Franklin scribbled a few notes on the pad of paper.

"I work for Puget Sound Aerospace in the Defense and Security Division."

Franklin frowned. "So they came there just to notify you that your friend had been murdered?"

"Yes. It actually didn't strike me as odd in the moment because my friend worked there as well, in the same division as me."

"Let me just say that I'm sorry to hear of your loss." Whittaker acknowledged the condolence with a nod. "What was his name?" Franklin asked.

"Ron Conner. Ronald James Conner was his full name." Franklin wrote down the name.

"Best friends, both named Ron and working together in the same job, huh?" he asked with slight grin.

Whittaker gave a small grin himself, a faraway look in his eye. "Yup. We met in grade school and became best friends right then. Having the same name tends to do that, you know."

"Where did he live?"

"You know the Walter Hall Golf Course?" Franklin nodded. "He owns a house right on the golf course."

"And, excuse me for this, but is that where the murder occurred?"

"I guess so. They told me he'd been found murdered in his home."

"Okay, so were these Snohomish County Sheriff's Office detectives who came to talk to you?"

Whittaker nodded. "I think so. I didn't really pay too close attention to where they said they were from."

Franklin jotted down some more notes. "So, you're here because you're suspicious about the motives of the detectives who were telling you about Ron while you were at work?"

Whittaker sighed. "Let me see if I can help you understand better why I think I'm here. My company works with the United States Department of Defense. We operate as a liaison between them and companies like Boeing who build and manufacture the planes that Defense orders. Because of this I hold a top-secret security clearance and our company has very stringent security in place."

"I see. It wasn't that simple for them to come notify you?"

"That's right. They came to talk to me under the pretense of notifying me about the death of my friend, but it took pulling some serious strings just to get into the building to see me. I think they might suspect I had something to do with Ron's death."

"Do you have any idea why they might think that?"

Whittaker shook his head. "None at all."

Franklin leaned back in his chair and put the end of the pen in his mouth, chewing on it and thinking, then asked, "What questions did they ask you?"

Whittaker crossed his legs and leaned back as well. "First, they told me about his death. I was stunned and wasn't sure I even believed them in the beginning. I hadn't seen him at work that day and in retrospect, that was a little unusual, but I didn't have any indication at the time that he was absent."

"What time was this?"

"Early in the day, probably around 9:30 or 10am."

Franklin jotted that down. "Okay, please continue."

Ron Whittaker continued his story, telling Franklin that the police detectives had asked him a bunch of questions about when he'd last seen Conner and when he'd last been to his house. "At the time, I just assumed they were looking for any information I might have that would help them identify a suspect. Thinking back, I think they were actually looking at me *as the suspect*."

Just then there was a knock on the door and Stacy walked in carrying a large Starbucks cup. She set it on the desk. "Let me know if you need anything else, Mr. Richardson."

"Thank you, Anastasia, that will be all for now." She frowned at him and walked out, closing the door behind her.

"You sure you don't want anything?" he asked Ron.

"I'm sure. So, what do you think? Do I need to hire an attorney?"

What Franklin was really thinking was, *Why me?* But he certainly wasn't going to give voice to such a self-defeating thought. Instead he nodded.

"I think that would be a very good idea. You know, Mr. Whittaker, you don't have to be guilty of a crime for that crime to have a drastic negative effect on your life. Just the suspicion of guilt can have serious consequences."

Ron was already nodding before he finished. "I know that, and that's why I'm here. I also have to think of my security clearance. They yank those things for almost any reason at all, and they're nearly impossible to get back once you lose them."

Franklin didn't know anything about Defense Department security clearances but he nodded knowingly anyway. "Yes, yes, indeed. So, here's what I think we need to do. You put me on retainer right now and then go about your business without worrying about anything. I have some police contacts and I'll see what I can find out, see if you're actually on their radar. In the meantime, you don't talk to anybody with a badge. I don't care if it's a kid wearing a Marshall of Tombstone badge and carrying a cap gun; if you see a badge, the only word that comes out of your mouth is *Lawyer*, understood?"

"Yes. Do you have a card?"

Franklin handed him a bunch of them. "You feel free to hand these out like candy, okay? If a cop even looks in your direction, you hand him this card and tell him to contact me."

"Somehow I knew I could count on you, Mr. Richardson. Should we talk money then?"

Hells yeah we should, Franklin thought. He loved it when the client brought it up first. "That seems like a reasonable next step," he replied.

"What is your hourly rate?"

This was a good question. Franklin's hourly rate was whatever he thought the client could afford and Ron Whittaker looked like he could afford a bundle. Of course, he didn't want to chase him away either.

"My rate is $200 per hour for my time, $100 per hour for a research assistant should I need to prepare for trial, and all rates double for actual court time," he sputtered out, and then held his breath waiting.

"Will you take a check?" Whittaker asked without flinching.

Damn it! I didn't shoot high enough! "Of course. I usually like to get at least ten hours up front. Of course I'll refund you should anything..."

Whittaker interrupted. "I'm going to write this for $10,000 just to make sure we have enough. If that runs out, you just let me know and I'll get you more."

For three seconds, Franklin felt that his heart had actually stopped. *Ten grand?* He kept his face impassive. "That will be just fine. You can make that out to FDR Law." Franklin had enough problems with the IRS already; this was one account he was definitely going to have to run legitimately as opposed to the cash payments he often received. Those went right into his pocket because *Fuck the IRS.*

Whittaker finished filling out the check, signed it with a flourish, handed it to Franklin and stood up. "Thank you, sir, for your time. I'm sure I'll be in touch soon." He turned and walked out the door.

Franklin leaned on his desk and controlled his breathing as he heard Whittaker say goodbye to Stacy. As soon as he heard the front door close, he bounced out to the reception area and handed her the check.

"Get this over to his bank right fucking now and have them convert it into a cashier's check. I want to know right now if it's any good and I don't want any stop payments." Stacy nodded, staring at the check with her mouth open. "Then go straight to our bank and deposit it. Our health insurance check is hitting today and unless you want to pay for your next PAP smear out of pocket, you'd better beat it there."

Chapter Six

Ronald Joseph Whittaker had been the holder of a Top-Secret security clearance from the U.S. Department of Defense for the last six years. He'd been fingerprinted for that clearance, and those fingerprints had been submitted to the FBI which had dutifully entered all of the information into their extensive database. He'd also had a DNA cheek swab done as part of the process, so they had that as well if they needed it.

Monika knew that back before 9/11/2001, her request would have returned no information. Rather, it would have resulted in a phone call from the FBI or the Defense Department demanding to know why she was running the prints for a holder of a Top-Secret clearance without divulging the name of the holder of that clearance.

Since the fiasco of 9/11, things had changed, and the FBI had been ordered by the federal government to extend full support to local law enforcement agencies to the best of its ability, in the interest of information sharing and full cooperation. This had been determined to be the best way to combat terrorism. What that meant was that instead of an angry phone call and no information about the return of the print, she had received the information on the print and *then* the angry phone call.

In another first for her, the print had returned with Whittaker's full information, including his current employer, a private company called Puget Sound Aerospace, and an urgent message to contact the nearest FBI or Defense Department office if this was a criminal inquiry.

Knowing that she had to make that call as soon as she "officially" saw the message, and knowing that the FBI would likely be calling her as soon as they got curious enough, she made a deal with the fingerprint tech. If he would play dumb and hold the FBI off for as long as he could, she would agree to have a drink with him. He jumped at it.

Monika had then found Bruce and they'd driven to the offices of Puget Sound Aerospace. They had another stroke of luck when, upon entering the lobby and approaching the security podium, she had received a call from her boss, Detective Sergeant Meyers, who told her they had found information in Conner's house that identified his workplace as the very place they had just entered.

This gave them a good reason for being there, aside from talking to the only suspect they had. Monika showed her badge and then asked for Conner's supervisor, a guy named Gerry Gresham. Gresham expressed shock upon hearing of the death of his respected employee. After asking the appropriate questions to establish that was her only reason for being there, Monika asked if she could speak with Whittaker.

Gresham seemed surprised, but hadn't asked for the reason. He'd approved them for one-hour visitor passes, accompanied them up the secure elevator, and shown them to Whittaker's office.

Monika was a student of psychology and she was good at identifying the traits humans tend to exhibit when they are being deceitful. Despite those qualifications, she hadn't noticed anything other than the expected shock, anger, and sadness when she notified Whittaker of Conner's murder.

Unbeknownst to Ron Whittaker, and to Bruce Norgaard for that matter, Monika had activated the recording feature on her brand-new iPhone 6 and had discreetly placed the phone upside down so the screen didn't show on Whittaker's desk while they talked. After leaving the offices of Puget Sound Aerospace, she sent the audio recordings to Bruce who took them up to the tech guys to get an analysis done on Whittaker's voice.

"Any info yet on that voice analysis for Whittaker?" she now asked Bruce who was eyeing the deli counter as if thinking of ordering more food.

"Yeah, two things. First off, the tech guy compared the recording of Whittaker with the recording of the 911 call. He says it's definitely not the same...two different people."

Monika frowned. That complicated things. So far everything had been coming together like it was going to wrap into a nice tight package that she'd be able to deliver to the prosecutor's office with a flourish. The addition of a third party made things a little murkier.

"How about the tone, inflection, that sort of thing?"

Bruce pulled his notebook from his jacket and looked at his notes. "The guy told me that based on the computer analysis, he thinks there was genuine emotion and surprise during the initial conversation. He also ran it through a stress analyzer. The results were inconclusive."

This was another disappointing finding. The Voice Stress Analyzer, or VSA, could have told them if Whittaker was lying when she asked him questions such as, "When did you last see Mr. Conner?" An inconclusive finding meant the recording probably wasn't clear enough to pick up the slight tremors and modulations the machine needs to detect the minute levels of stress present when someone is lying.

None of it could have been used in court anyway; voice inflection technology is imperfect and the science is untested and inadmissible. Still though, it would have been nice if it had pointed to Whittaker as a suspect. An FBI guy named Agent Carson called before lunchtime yesterday, and Monika's fingerprint guy stalled him for as long as he dared. By 6pm that evening, she had no choice but to call the guy back. Of course, he wanted to know why they were running fingerprints of a guy with a Top-Secret clearance. She told him that Whittaker's prints had been found at the scene of a homicide, but that he wasn't an official suspect yet. She then asked for some time before the FBI let Whittaker know he was being looked at. Agent Carson said that he would have to open a case report on his end but, as long as she kept him informed of any pertinent information discovered in regard to Whittaker, he could hold off on contacting him.

"Okay," she said to Bruce, looking at the next item on her list. "Let's talk about Whittaker's trash cans."

Chapter Seven

Gerald Gresham, who much preferred Gerry, was pacing his office and fuming. He rarely allowed himself the luxury of anger these days--not since his doctor had told him that at the pace he was going, he was destined to die of a heart attack before he turned 50.

Now he had lots of stress relievers to help him control his anger. Squeeze balls all over his spacious office, Yoga three times a week, walking every day during lunch; these normally all helped keep his blood pressure down and his heart rate steady.

Not today though.

Everything had actually started yesterday when the two police detectives showed up in the lobby with the shocking news that Ron Conner had been murdered. Gerry had been devastated. Ron had been his employee first, but also his friend. Gerry and his wife, Jessamyn, had had Ron over to the house for dinner on multiple occasions, and they'd been out together numerous times as well. Not only were they close outside of work, Gerry had just offered Ron a big promotion, one that would have had the two of them working side by side every day building this company into one of the major players in the Defense Industry. Ron had accepted, and the announcement had been planned for next week.

Although Gerry was upset and hurt by Ron's death, the position was still open and still needed to be filled. Last night he'd reluctantly made the decision to promote Ronnie Whittaker. Ronnie couldn't hold a candle to Ron in terms of intelligence and ability, but there was no other option now that Ron was dead.

The reason Gerry was fuming was that it was now 10am and Ronnie had still not appeared for his work day which was supposed to start by 8am.

Gerry set the start of the day as 8am but, in reality, he expected the top echelon of his department staff to be there even earlier. Their one customer, at least as far as his department went, was the United States Department of Defense, headquartered at The Pentagon. Those guys started work at 9am sharp, east coast time, which equated to 6am here in Everett, Washington. Gerry was here at 6am every morning, and Ron Conner had also always been here that early. Ronnie, on the other hand, was usually here by 7:30 or 8am, but rarely earlier than that. And today he was still absent at...Gerry checked his watch: 10:06am.

On top of that, Gerry had received a very disturbing call an hour ago from an Admiral on the J3, the Operations Directorate of the Pentagon. The Admiral told him they had received a notice from the FBI that Ronnie was potentially the subject of a police investigation. They'd wanted information that Gerry hadn't been able to provide and he'd promised to get back to them with some answers.

Gerry's secretary had called Ronnie's cell phone at least three times already this morning, to no avail. One key employee dead and another missing and possibly in danger of losing his security clearance. This was turning into a bad week.

Gerry took a seat at his desk and forced himself to take deep breaths. He picked up two of the stress balls that were supposed to calm him down and began rolling them around in his hand. He needed to take his mind off the issues with Ronnie. Selecting a file from his desk, he tried to focus on work.

The file contained the specification requirements for a new type of aircraft The Pentagon was trying to procure. Boeing had won the contract for the jet, a long-range, supersonic, hunt-and-kill aircraft that was neither fighter nor bomber, but rather a hybrid of the two. This jet would be capable of climbing right to the edge of space. Its purpose was twofold: be able to fire a missile that could target and destroy an enemy satellite in orbit at altitudes of up to 200 miles, and be able to target and shoot down an enemy ICBM. Intercontinental Ballistic Missiles had been thought of as a significantly reduced threat until the maniac in North Korea had begun developing them again. The U.S. was trying to adapt to that new threat, the most credible one in recent times.

In order to accomplish these two tasks, the jet would basically need to be one big-ass fuel tank with wings. It had to be able to climb to an altitude of 180,000 feet before firing its missiles, basically making it a space ship.

The paper he currently held was a letter from the Boeing Vice President in charge of Defense and Aerospace that said the jet they had under production right now would likely be able to reach an altitude of only 150,000 feet, essentially making it useless for the purposes the Defense Department needed. This was Gerry's top priority right now. Puget Sound Aerospace was the liaison between Defense and Boeing, and he was not looking forward to telling The Pentagon that Boeing was unable to fulfill the specs of the contract.

Gerry needed Ron to help him figure this out, and with Ron dead, he really needed to be able to count on Ronnie. If Defense pulled the contract from Boeing, which they were almost sure to do, it was going to cost PSA tens of millions of dollars in fees and incentives.

Just then, Gerry's phone buzzed.

"Mr. Gresham?" his secretary's voice came through the intercom speaker. "Security just called; Mr. Whittaker is in the elevator and headed up."

"Thank you, Linda," he said, relieved yet angrier at the same time. He glanced at his watch: 10:25am. "Please notify his secretary that I want to see him the minute he arrives."

Gerry ended the call and leaned back in his chair, thinking about what he was going to say when Ronnie arrived. He needed to be firm, to tell him exactly what he expected from someone about to be promoted to a position where he would make a lot more money and have a lot more responsibilities. On the other hand, he also needed to be sensitive. He knew that Ronnie and Ron had been very good friends, even better friends than he and Ron had been. A period of mourning was in order, and he'd have to be careful about how he balanced this conversation and tempered his expectations.

Five minutes later, Ronnie had not appeared in his office. He reached down and buzzed his secretary.

"Linda, where's Ronnie?"

"I don't know Mr. Gresham. I told his secretary to send him here immediately. I'll try her again right now."

Gerry disconnected the phone. The anger that he'd managed to control earlier was coming back and he was beginning to get a headache.

He opened his desk drawer and picked up another folder, opening it and looking at the piece of paper inside. This document was one that he hadn't known what to make of when he'd received it a week before. It was a letter from PSA's Chief Financial Officer.

Meant to be informational only, it had nonetheless alarmed Gerry when he'd read it, but he'd not yet decided what it meant or if he should do anything about it. In any other company, this information would have been considered private and he'd have never known about it. But in a company where all of the executives held Top Secret or higher security clearances, there were different rules in place. Any sort of abnormal behavior had to be reported, and this letter certainly pointed out some abnormal behavior.

His phone buzzed again.

"Umm, Mr. Gresham? I'm sorry sir, but Mr. Whittaker said no."

"Excuse me? What do you mean?"

Linda paused for a second. "Well, sir, I buzzed his secretary and conveyed your message. She kept me on the line, and I heard her tell Mr. Whittaker that you wanted to see him right away. He said no."

Gerry was in shock. "You heard him say no?"

"Yes sir. He yelled it. That was it, just, *No*."

Gerry disconnected the phone without saying anything. What the fuck was going on with Ronnie? He stared at the file from the CFO a moment longer, and then abruptly grabbed it off his desk and stormed out of his office, passing Linda without a word and turning down the hallway toward Ronnie's office. He was going to get to the bottom of this.

Chapter Eight

Detective Bruce Norgaard reached back into his folder and handed another sheet of paper over to Monika.

"Jackpot," he said with a smile. He waited for her to see it, wanting to witness the expression on her face.

Monika's jaw dropped. "Are you fucking kidding me?" she exclaimed, looking at Bruce.

"Keep reading."

The document Monika was looking at was a report typed up by a junior detective who had drawn the fun duty of sorting through Ron Whittaker's trash. The previous day, after leaving the offices of Puget Sound Aerospace, she and Bruce returned to the crime scene for a few hours and then drove over to where Ron lived.

She'd had no real reason for driving by at that time other than Whittaker's house was only a ten-minute drive from the victim's, and she wanted to get a look at where their only current suspect spent his time.

They'd driven by the front of the house, an upscale, ranch style place in a nice neighborhood inside the city limits of Mukilteo. As they drove by, they watched to see if there were any signs of anybody else living there. Not seeing anything of interest, they made one more pass by the front and then turned down the alleyway that ran behind the house. As they passed by the back of

Whittaker's house, Monika noticed his trash cans sitting by the curb.

"You think today is garbage day?" she'd asked Bruce.

"I don't see cans out at any of the other houses," he replied, motioning her down the alley with his hand.

Monika thought about it for a minute and pulled as far to the right as she could, still partially blocking the alley but out of sight of Whittaker's house in case anybody was home. If this wasn't garbage day, then why were his trash cans out at the curb? Of course, garbage day could have been the day before and he might not have brought them in, or it could be the next day and he'd brought them out early for some reason.

She glanced over at Bruce. "Didn't you tell me once that you always wanted to be a garbage man?"

He just looked at her and sighed. "You have some gloves at least?"

She opened the glove box (because where else would you keep gloves?) and handed him the box of latex gloves she kept there.

Monika watched the rear-view mirror as Bruce nonchalantly strolled back toward the garbage cans. He took a quick look around and then opened the lid of the first can, the recycling bin. He quickly closed it and then opened the lid of the smaller garbage can. She watched him look around one more time and then quickly reach inside, grab two closed Hefty bags of garbage, and walk back to the car. Monika hit the trunk release button, and Bruce threw the two bags into the trunk along with the disposable gloves, slammed the trunk closed, and got back in the car.

The Supreme Court had long before ruled that once you put your garbage out at the curb, you no longer have a right to privacy, nor is that garbage protected by the fourth amendment against unlawful search and seizure. Basically, if you throw it away, it can be taken by anyone else, even a cop.

More than one case had been solved because a dumb suspect attempted to discard evidence by throwing it in the trash, thinking that once it got mixed together with the trash of a thousand other households, it could no longer be tied to him. Even that wasn't necessarily true, but if something was found in your trash can before it got to the dump, things were even easier.

Monika hadn't held out much hope of finding anything; in fact, it was nothing but a spur of the moment decision to grab the trash and probably a waste of time. Looking at the report, she could hardly believe their luck.

"You're telling me they actually found strips of duct tape in the trash can?"

Bruce nodded. "Yup, and that's not all. They found hairs stuck to the duct tape. Look at who the lab says the hairs belong to."

Monika had already looked. It was almost unbelievable, and she sat there a moment in stunned silence. The hairs had been examined under a microscope. They belonged to the victim, Ron Conner.

"So, what now, boss?" Bruce asked with a grin, knowing what the answer would be.

"Let's go find a judge," she replied.

Chapter Nine

Gerry Gresham blew by Whittaker's secretary who glanced at him but didn't say a word, suddenly finding the monitor on her computer to be completely compelling. He wrenched open the door to Ronnie's office, walked in, and slammed it behind him. Ronnie didn't even bother to look up. His eyes were focused on his laptop computer screen, as his hand worked the mouse.

"Do you mind telling me just what the fuck is going on, Ronnie?"

Ronnie held up his hand, his eyes still focused on his computer screen. "Not now, Gerry."

Gerry stood there a moment in stunned silence, staring at Ronnie, unused to such impertinence and insubordination. Puget Sound Aerospace was not the type of company where employees acted in this manner toward their supervisors. Founded by a retired Air Force General, it was more of a quasi-military structure, and this type of behavior was almost unheard of and never tolerated.

Because he'd never before experienced this kind of insubordination, Gerry wasn't sure how to respond. He tried to think of how best to deal with it and eventually decided there must be something severely wrong for Ronnie to be acting this way. Perhaps a softer approach would work better. Gerry walked up to Ronnie's desk and sat down in one of the chairs, staring at Ronnie and waiting for him to finish whatever he was doing on his computer.

After an uncomfortably silent couple of minutes, Ronnie finally looked up.

"What do you need, Gerry?"

"I don't know. Maybe you can start by telling me why you were so late today."

"I had things to do--important things, the details of which are none of your business."

Gerry felt the anger stirring inside him, threatening to boil over, and he fought back the urge to explode. Instead, he held up the manila folder he'd brought with him.

"Okay then. Maybe you can explain this."

Ronnie sighed and took the folder from Gerry's hand. He opened it, glanced briefly at the letter from the CFO inside, then closed it and handed it back.

"So what? That's none of your business either, Gerry."

"None of my business? Ronnie, you cashed out your 401k--your retirement, your future. You paid a huge penalty, and you sent a red flag right up the chain with regard to your security clearance."

"I'll deal with my security clearance when that time comes, Gerry. Now, if you don't mind, I have a lot to do."

Gerry sat in stunned silence for a moment, trying to come up with something to say. It had to be Ron's death that was making Ronnie act this way. Then again, he'd cashed out his 401k days before Ron's murder, so something must have been affecting him before that. Whatever it was, Gerry hadn't noticed it until today.

He decided to try a different approach. "You know, I've been considering you for the director's job that's open."

"Bullshit." Ronnie's reply was abrupt and said with a smirk. "You were giving that job to Ron, we both know that. Hell, the people in the mailroom know it."

"Ron was the frontrunner, true, but with his death, you're now a shoo-in to get it..." he trailed off.

"Fuck that job Gerry, and fuck you."

That did it. Gerry could no longer control the anger that now roiled up. He felt his face reddening, his nostrils flaring. "You will NOT talk to me like that. I don't know who you think you are or what the hell has gotten into you...," he began. Ronnie cut him off.

"Did you know that Ron was fucking your wife?"

Gerry froze, staring at him without moving. What was this bullshit? What kind of angle was Ronnie trying here?

Ronnie laughed at his expression. "Yup, that's right buddy. Sweet little Jessamyn, the Princess of PSA, was screwing your good buddy, Ron. Didn't you ever wonder why she always wanted you guys to hang out with Ron? Didn't you ever wonder why Ron never minded being the third wheel? How many times do you think she gave him a hand job under the table while the three of you were out to dinner? Didn't it ever strike you as odd that he never brought a date with him on those outings? He wasn't the third wheel, buddy, you were."

Gerry didn't move, staring at Ronnie, his mind blank, his consciousness receding to a dark place. A small part of him tried to bring himself back, but it was too late. The stress balls, the yoga, the breathing exercises, everything he'd ever tried to keep his heart in check was forgotten. He felt the shooting pain starting in his chest and immediately spreading to his right arm. He grabbed at his chest, his eyes bulging, staring at Ronnie, his face darkening as he began to twitch.

Still sitting, Ronnie calmly reached for his phone and pressed the button for his secretary.

"Anne, call an ambulance please. I think Mr. Gresham is having a heart attack."

Chapter Ten

Franklin sighed and lowered the phone to his chest, looking up at the ceiling and shaking his head. His previous indiscretions were coming back to bite him and at the absolute worst possible time. He put the phone back up to his ear.

"... and she's my sister, Frank. How could you have treated my sister that way?"

Franklin hated to be called Frank. Frank was the name he'd been born with, but he'd legally had it changed as soon as he'd turned eighteen. Who would want to be called Frank? It conjured up images of hotdogs and that stupid *There's Something about Mary* movie with that retard yelling out, "Frank and beans, Frank and beans!" all the time. Who would want to be associated with that? Of course that movie did feature Cameron Diaz and she was smoking hot back in the day.

"Are you even fucking listening to me, Frank, you douchebag?"

"I'm listening, Jackie, and all I can say is I'm truly sorry. I tried to make it up to her; I sent her flowers for God's sake!"

"Yeah, a month later, after I made you do it!"

Jackie launched into a whole new tirade, and Franklin tuned her out. He just had to get through this painfulness, then hopefully he'd be able to get some information about his new client. Jackie was the executive assistant in the Snohomish County Sheriff's Office Major Crimes Unit. That meant she saw every case file that came through.

Back when Franklin worked for the Prosecutor's Office, Jackie had been the contact at Major Crimes for any information requests. Franklin had dealt with her on a daily basis. One day he'd been in her office picking up a follow-up report from one of the detectives, and had happened to see a picture of Jackie and her sister on her desk. The sister, Meg, was a hottie, and Franklin had pestered Jackie relentlessly until she'd set them up. Looking back, it probably would have been a good idea to at least call Meg the next day, especially after she'd put out. Of course, she put out on the first date so how was he to know that someone that slutty would be upset by not getting a call? You'd think she would have been used to it.

He suddenly realized Jackie had stopped talking and he had no idea what she'd last said.

"Look, Jackie. You know I'm a good guy. I just really screwed up here and I'm sorry. I feel terrible, honestly. I don't know what else I can do."

Jackie sighed. "What is it you want, Frank?"

Franklin smiled. That wasn't too unpleasant. Relationships were important in this business, especially this one, and it appeared he had salvaged it without too much damage.

"I have a client; his name is Ron Whittaker. I just need to know if you guys are looking at him for anything."

"What case would it be in regard to?"

Franklin looked down at his notes. "A homicide investigation; victim's name is Ron Conner."

Jackie laughed. "This is a brand-new case, Frank. You know I can't divulge information about an active case, especially a homicide opened just yesterday!"

"Jackie, please. I'm begging you. I'll call Meg and I'll take her out on the town. I'll be the best date she's ever had, and I'll call her every day after just to tell her how beautiful she is. I just need this one thing from you. Please."

Jackie sighed. "I'll tell you what. I'll help you if you agree to not do any of those things. If you agree to forget her name completely and never call her."

Well that was disturbing, Franklin thought. Why wouldn't she want him dating her sister?

"That hurts, Jackie. I thought you liked me."

"Do we have a deal?"

"If you think that's what's best then we have a deal." Franklin gave himself a mental high-five. This had worked out better than he thought it would.

"Okay. I can tell you, just between you and me, we are not looking at your client at all. I have a list of every person of interest in the Conner case and there's no Whittaker on the list."

"Jackie, you are a lifesaver. I don't know how to thank you. I owe you big for this one."

"Just remember your promise and stay away from my sister!"

* * *

Jackie hung up the phone and glanced down at the search warrant affidavit she'd just been handed by Detective Sodafsky. Monika had given Jackie a copy to keep with the case file on her way out the door to go find a judge. The affidavit was for a search warrant for the residence of one Ronald P. Whittaker. Jackie smiled as she placed the copy in the case file.

Fuck Franklin Richardson, that douchebag.

Chapter 11

The Honorable Neil Chapman, Superior Court Judge for Snohomish County, sat at the desk in his chambers reviewing the affidavit he'd just been handed. He'd been hearing motions all morning in a variety of cases, which basically meant trying to keep long-winded attorneys from droning on all day attempting to influence his ruling. He had one of the best efficiency ratings in the county court system. This was mainly because he could smell bullshit whenever it appeared in his courtroom, and he didn't put up with it, hastily shutting down attorneys whenever they tried to pass it off.

It was just before a scheduled break when the two detectives came into the courtroom and passed a message on to his clerk, Linda Gruber, asking for a moment of his time to review a search warrant affidavit.

Judge Chapman knew he had a reputation for being a "police friendly" judge and he was fine with that reputation. The police had a tough job to do, but he balanced things by not being afraid to call out an officer when they showed up with incomplete or poorly written affidavits.

He demanded professionalism, thoroughness, and integrity in every affidavit he reviewed. On more than one occasion, he'd sent officers back to their computers to rewrite them. He would give them a lot of leeway on the probable cause side, as long as the affidavits were well written and articulate. All affidavits had to be approved by a prosecuting attorney before they were presented to the judge, at least in felony cases. This one, in particular, had been approved by Dana Porter who Chapman knew to be a superb litigator. Ultimately, she would have to defend the probable cause behind the warrant, and if she was okay with it, it was likely very well-founded.

Chapman also knew the two detectives in his office. They'd both appeared in his courtroom on multiple occasions to testify in cases, and he had a lot of respect for both, Detective Monika Sodafsky in particular. She had impressed him greatly the first time she'd been on the stand in his courtroom when an extremely enthusiastic defense attorney grilled her about a piece of evidence in a murder case. Detective Sodafsky had handled herself incredibly well, remaining calm, composed, and professional, even when the defense attorney began questioning her ethics and attacking her personally. It had been Chapman who had stepped in and stopped the aggressive questioning, admittedly a little later than he normally would have. He'd sort of been curious to see how well she was going to handle it, and she'd done beautifully.

Now she was standing in front of his desk, arms crossed as she coolly and patiently waited for him to finish reading the affidavit. Detective Norgaard, on the other hand, was pacing nervously. Chapman glanced up at him over the pages of the affidavit.

"Detective Norgaard, did you write this affidavit?"

He stopped and looked at him. "No sir, Detective Sodafsky wrote it."

"Then would you mind relaxing a bit and having a seat?" He motioned to the chair in front of the desk. "You're making me nervous."

Norgaard apologized sheepishly and sat down. Sodafsky just smiled and remained standing.

"Detective Sodafsky, has ballistics determined what caliber round was used during this shooting?" Chapman asked.

She shook her head. "No, sir, that report will take a while to get."

"Okay, but the casing you found at the scene was from a nine millimeter, correct?"

"Yes sir."

"So, do you mind explaining to me why you have written here that you want to search for and seize all firearms on the premises?"

She nodded. "Well, sir, we don't know for sure if the cartridge we found was the one used in the actual shooting. We think it probably was, based on the location where we found it and based on the scene in general, but just in case he used a different gun, we want to cover all bases."

"Unfortunately, that sounds suspiciously like a fishing expedition. I think you know how I feel about those."

"Your honor, I'm certainly not trying to go fishing. I think our probable cause here is rock solid, and I want to be thorough."

Judge Chapman considered for a minute. Although he was pro police, he was also a staunch supporter of Second Amendment rights and he wanted to make sure he balanced that well.

"I'll tell you what. I'll approve the seizure of any *nine millimeter* pistol you find, but you're not to seize any other calibers of guns. You can document them and, if probable cause exists down the road to seize any of those, we'll talk again."

Monika nodded. That was a fair compromise and she actually would have been surprised if he'd approved it as is. She always shot for the moon with these and was happy if she achieved only orbit.

"I see also that you want to search and seize any vehicles you find. I won't approve that, but if you change it to say any vehicles that are registered to Mr. Whittaker, I'll be good with that."

"No problem, your honor."

Chapman handed the affidavit back to Monika.

"When are you planning to serve the warrant?"

Warrants typically remained valid and could be served for ten days after they were approved.

"Immediately, your honor. This afternoon, hopefully. I want to be there inside the house when Mr. Whittaker gets home from work."

Judge Chapman smiled. "Okay, make those two changes and then bring it back. If I'm in session, just hand it to the clerk; she'll know to interrupt me so I can sign it right away for you."

"Thank you, your honor."

On the way out of the courthouse, Monika pulled out her cell phone and called Sergeant Myers.

"Two small changes and then it's approved," she said when he answered. "Let's get the entry team assembled and ready to go. I'd like to serve this thing right away."

Chapter 12

The man with the scar on his face reclined the driver's side seat of his Chevy Caprice and adjusted his body, trying to make himself comfortable. He'd been sitting here for two hours, waiting for something to happen, and he really needed to pee.

He'd brought along an empty bottle just for this purpose, but now he was reluctant to use it. He'd had mixed results in the past peeing into a bottle while sitting in his car. It required a bit of a balancing act, along with a good amount of dexterity and bladder control. The key was to not allow your bladder to get too full before you emptied it. If your bladder was too full, the bottle, which needed to be tipped at a severe angle while you peed, would fill too quickly and you'd have to exercise a great deal of control to cut off the stream at just the right time.

That kind of bladder control was a young man's game, not meant for a man in his forties.

He felt that he'd waited too long. He'd missed the optimal bottle-peeing window, and he now feared the urine spillage that was certain to happen. Not knowing how long he would be sitting here today, he decided he would have to leave his car.

The man with the scar on his face had been hired for some odd jobs before, and he rarely questioned them. This one was even more unusual though, not because of the job itself, but rather because of the amount of money the man who'd hired him had offered.

When he'd met the guy in the parking lot of the Kmart store just last week, he'd fully expected the guy would want the usual: "Follow my wife around and see who she's fucking." He'd been surprised by the actual request, as well as intrigued. His job as a private investigator was typically boring, when he worked at all. He didn't like to do too much in the effort department; as long as he had enough money to pay his rent and buy a few cases of beer each week, he was happy.

The man who'd hired him had offered $2000 for a simple job. The man with the scar would have done it for half the amount, and that's what was so intriguing about it.

The pressure in his bladder was getting worse, and he glanced again at the bottle. He was going to have to find somewhere to go and then hope he was able to get back to the car in time.

He raised his seatback up and started the car, putting it in drive and leaving the neighborhood where he'd been parked on the street, trying to remain inconspicuous. Turning right onto Harbour Pointe Boulevard, he drove a few blocks and pulled into the gas station on the corner. As he got out of the car and turned to go into the store, he warily eyed the two Snohomish County Sheriff's Office patrol cars parked in the lot of the church across the road.

The man with the scarred face cajoled the clerk into letting him use the restroom and then walked back out to his car. As he reached to unlock the door, he let his gaze wander over to the church parking lot again. The two Sheriff's Office cars had been joined by three more patrol cars, as well as three unmarked cars that were clearly cop vehicles. The trunks of two of the patrol cars were open, and the deputies were pulling tactical vests on over their uniforms and loading the pockets with magazines and flexible handcuffs. He stopped for a minute, watching as two of the deputies loaded rifles, checking the actions before locking them back into holders in their cars.

He got into his car and started it, but decided to sit there and wait. A few minutes later, another unmarked car with exempt plates drove in, a good-looking woman in a suit driving, with a black man, also dressed in a suit, sitting in the passenger seat. They pulled up to the other cops, said a few words, and then they all got into their vehicles.

The man with the scar on his face put his car in drive and pulled onto the street as the woman he assumed was a cop activated the blue and red lights of her unmarked car, pulled onto Harbour Pointe Boulevard and waited for the rest of the caravan of cop cars to pull out behind her. She shut off her emergency lights and headed east. The man with the scar pulled out behind the police caravan, following them as they all turned into the neighborhood he'd been parked in just a few minutes earlier.

Two of the patrol cars turned off from the caravan and headed toward the alleyway that ran behind the houses. The rest of the vehicles accelerated toward the house the man had earlier been watching, screeching to a halt a few doors down. Car doors opened and deputies formed a tactical line before moving as one up the street and onto the porch.

The man with the scar pulled to the side of the road, well back from the action and picked up his cell phone. He pulled up the number of the man who'd employed him and hit the call button as he watched the deputies knock on the front door. He could hear them shouting, even from a block away, "Police with a search warrant, come to the door!"

The man who'd hired him answered the phone just as a deputy wielding a ram smashed open the front door, falling aside as the rest of the stack of officers rushed into the house. The female detective casually and nonchalantly followed them inside.

"It's happening," the man with the scar said to the man on the phone.

"Thank you." The phone went dead, and the man with the scar made a U-turn and headed home. His job was done for the moment.

Chapter 13

Franklin Richardson was on the phone in his office ordering a new suit from his tailor. He'd had the foresight to have the salesman come to his office and take his measurements some time before, knowing that, even though the designer suits they sold were expensive, he would have the resources to own one someday.

It was this optimism; this irrational but unwavering faith that good things were bound to happen for him that had sustained him for his whole life. It was this conviction that led him to quit his dead-end job at the prosecutor's office and had driven him to leave his ball-and-chain of an ex-wife when she wouldn't stop complaining about the extreme salary cut he'd realized when he struck out on his own. The fact that he'd shortly before begun an affair with Stacy had made the decision to leave a lot easier.

This enduring faith in his imminent success was coming to fruition right now. Ron Whittaker walking into his office was the moment he'd been waiting for and, even though Stacy had tried to caution him, had tried to quash his dreams and his faith with her naysaying, Franklin knew this was his moment in the spotlight.

Stacy was sure that even though the check had cleared, Whittaker would come strolling in at any moment, fire Franklin, and demand his money back. Franklin made the mistake of telling her what Jackie had told him--that there was no current investigation focusing on Whittaker. Stacy had stormed around the office, crying doom and demanding he exercise financial responsibility. He'd finally had to send her out to get lunch just so he could have some peace and quiet while he ordered his new suit.

The new suit, along with three new shirts, three new ties, and a new pair of shoes came to a total of $2600, and Franklin happily paid an extra $200 to get a rush job done on the order. He'd just hung up the phone when Stacy returned with lunch.

She walked into his office and dropped two sacks from Taco Bell on his desk.

"What is this crap? I thought I told you to get sushi?"

"Sushi's expensive, and I told you we need to budget and be careful with the money. You're not going to go off spending it all on shit we don't need; I'm going to make sure of that."

She sat down in the chair in front of his desk and began to pout.

"You have to start making better financial decisions, Franklin. You've missed three of my paychecks in the last six months and I can't live this way!"

She managed to work up a tear as she quietly pouted in the chair. Franklin came out from around the desk and knelt down next to her.

"Baby, look, just keep the faith a little longer, I'm begging you. This is the big one. I can feel it! This is the one that's going to put us on the map, that's going to take us all the way to the big leagues!"

Stacy sniffed quietly as Franklin brushed her hair back from her face. He always tried to use the pronoun *we* when he talked about the future of the company. He couldn't afford to have her quit. Not only could he get away with occasionally not paying her, she was also easy on the eyes. Franklin's conviction was that having a good-looking girl at the reception desk would bring in a higher class of customer. Plus, she would sometimes sleep with him--the main reason to keep her around.

The chime on the front door suddenly sounded, and Stacy wiped the moisture from her eye, bounded out of the chair and pushed Franklin aside as she stepped out of his office, blocking his view and calling out, "Oh, Mr. Whittaker, how nice to see you again!"

Franklin swore under his breath and jumped up, grabbing the Taco Bell bags off his desk and stuffing them into the wastebasket next to it. He whirled around the desk and picked up the phone, settling into his seat.

Covering the mouth of the phone, he called out, "Please show him in, Anastasia." He straightened his suit jacket and waited for Whittaker to walk into his office before pointing at the receiver and mouthing, "Police." He then motioned Whittaker to the chair in front of the desk.

"I see. Okay, well that's good to hear. Thank you very much, detective. Yes, I appreciate that. Okay, good day."

Franklin looked up at Stacy standing in the doorway and slicing her finger across her throat, giving him a death stare. He ignored her and returned his attention to Ron Whittaker.

"Mr. Whittaker, I'm glad you stopped by! I've spent the entire day on the phone with my police contacts getting information for you."

"Then I guess you know that they just raided my house," Whittaker answered, calmly.

Franklin's smile withered. "Wait, what?"

"The police just raided my house. They're in there right now, searching for evidence, and presumably looking for reasons to arrest me." He stared at Franklin who seemed to have lost his ability to speak. "I'm guessing you already knew that, though, from all your police contacts."

Franklin recovered his composure and sputtered, "Well, I had been told they were going to hold off, but I guess my guys had some bad information. They're usually spot on." He mentally cursed Jackie at the Sheriff's Office, promising himself that he would get his revenge for this.

Whittaker shrugged. "Well, either way, the cops are there now, and I think you need to go out there and see what they're up to."

Franklin gaped at him a moment. On one hand, he was relieved Whittaker wasn't here to fire him. On the other hand, this entire scene was so strange. Whittaker was too relaxed and unperturbed, and that made Franklin's bullshit sensors tingle.

"Are they going to find anything at your house that we need to be worried about?"

Whittaker shook his head. "Not that I know of. But let me ask you this: have you ever seen the police move so fast on something if they weren't confident they had the right guy?"

"Not that I can think of," Franklin replied.

"So, if the cops are so sure they've got the right guy, and I know I didn't kill Ron, then I can only imagine that they must have found something that makes them *think* I killed him. That's what I need you to find out."

Franklin nodded. "Okay, I can do that. I need you to sign this." He pulled a contract from his desk. "This explains that you're officially hiring me to represent you, outlines my rates, and shows that you've paid a retainer of $10,000."

He placed the contract and a pen in front of Whittaker who quickly signed it with a flourish, not even bothering to read it. This was Franklin's favorite type of customer, and he was now regretting that he hadn't snuck in some kind of clause to double his fees for some made-up reason.

"You understand, if they do find enough evidence somehow, they're going to be issuing an arrest warrant for you?" he addressed Whittaker.

Whittaker nodded. "I'm aware of that and I'm prepared for it. However, I really don't want to be arrested today, so I'm going to stay at a hotel tonight, just in case. If you think they're going to arrest me, you'll let me know and we'll figure it out from there." He pulled a card out of his pocket and handed it to Franklin who saw his cell phone listed as well as his home address.

"Let me ask you something," Franklin said, placing the card in a manila folder along with the retainer contract. "Most people would be freaking out right now. Hell, I think even I would be freaking out. Why are you so relaxed?" He still wanted to ask why Whittaker, a man who was obviously of some means, had hired Franklin to represent him for an issue that clearly had enormous ramifications. Franklin was confident in his abilities, but he could also have moments of introspective honesty, and Whittaker was not the type of client he was used to representing. He was actually surprised that Whittaker didn't already have an attorney; his type typically did. He wasn't prepared to potentially open Whittaker's eyes with such a question though.

"I may appear relaxed on the outside, but I assure you, Mr. Richardson, I'm as nervous as anybody would be on the inside," Whittaker replied. "I have faith in the criminal justice system, however, and I have faith in your abilities as a defense attorney. If the police think I killed Ron, they are wrong, and justice will prevail, I'm confident of that."

Whittaker's calm demeanor and confident attitude was contagious, Franklin thought. He stood up, and Whittaker followed suit. "Well, Ron," he said. "You can absolutely count on me to help you out of this jam. You've hired the best in the business, sir!" he added, with a huge grin on his face.

Whittaker nodded. "I have no doubt of that. Please call me tonight and let me know what you've learned."

"I will, right away. Your case is my number one priority. You can count on that!"

Whittaker turned and headed out, while Franklin grabbed his briefcase and his overcoat. It was time to start earning his fee and paying for his new suit.

Chapter 14

Monika Sodafsky stood in the middle of the living room of Ronnie Whittaker's spacious Mukilteo home and surveyed the scene. She and Norgaard, along with two other detectives from the Major Crimes Unit, had been searching the house for nearly an hour and they'd found only one thing of interest. That item was *very* interesting though, and she was sure, based on the unusual item, they were going to find even more. They'd elected to perform the search systematically, starting in the front rooms of the house and working their way back to the bedrooms where the other three detectives were currently searching.

Monika walked slowly through the mess they'd made of the house--couch cushions flipped off, chairs overturned, books pulled off shelves and stacked on the floor. They didn't try to make a complete disaster of the house in these cases, but it was difficult to perform a thorough search without causing a considerable mess.

She returned the chairs back to their previous positions and stacked the cushions back on the couch while she tried to think of any places they could have missed, any secret hiding places Whittaker might have. She walked over to her bag and selected a small contraption with a lightbulb on the top and two prongs sticking out the sides, and began plugging it into the outlets. She watched for the lightbulb to turn on in each of the outlets, testing for any false outlets that were unpowered and might indicate a secret compartment in the wall.

Not finding anything, she moved into the kitchen, tapping the floor with her heels as she walked, listening for any sounds that were different and might indicate a hidden floor compartment. As she began testing the outlets there, Bruce Norgaard yelled at her from the back bedroom.

"Monika? You're going to want to come back here."

Monika tested the final outlet in the kitchen and then walked back to the master bedroom where Norgaard was standing by the walk-in closet with a dark backpack in his hand.

Norgaard clicked on his flashlight and shined it inside so she could see the semi-automatic pistol in the bottom of the bag.

"Nine millimeter?" she asked.

"Sure is," he replied with a grin, "Beretta 92FS."

"Where was it?"

Norgaard pointed into the closet. "The backpack was buried in the bottom of the laundry hamper, under a bunch of dirty clothes, I might add." He made a face.

Monika frowned. "Shine the light in there again. Let me see if I can get the serial number without touching it."

Bruce again illuminated the gun, and Monika, squinting, wrote down the serial number from the pistol. "There's a magazine in there too, and it looks like a spent shell casing." She pushed on the side pocket. "Some other stuff in here too. Let's get it bagged." Bruce turned off the flashlight and set the backpack down.

Monika walked back into the living room and sent an evidence technician to the bedroom to log and bag gun and backpack. The gun wasn't exactly smoking, but if this wasn't the weapon used in the Conner murder, it was a hell of a coincidence. It was all coming together smoothly, and that was causing Monika to hear warning bells in her head.

She'd rarely seen a case where the evidence lined up as neatly as this, and Ronnie Whittaker was supposed to be smart. *Why would someone so supposedly smart hide a backpack full of evidence in the laundry hamper?* she thought to herself, crossing her arms and frowning. It didn't feel right.

"Monika?" Bruce called. "I think I found something else."

She walked back once again to the bedroom. Bruce was holding a pair of black tennis shoes, examining the bottom of them.

"Take a look at this," he said. "Remember that little bit of dried mud we collected from the dining room at Conner's house?"

Monika nodded. They'd found a small amount of mud on the floor and, not seeing any mud in Conner's yard, they'd decided to collect it in case it was something brought to the scene by the killer.

Bruce pointed to the bottoms of Whittaker's shoes which were covered in dried mud. "I think we can have the lab match this up with that stuff we found at Conner's. When I collected his garbage yesterday, I think I remember seeing a big muddy patch on the path from the back door to the alleyway."

"Nice job," Monika replied. "Let's bag these up and then let's take a sample of the mud from the backyard. Maybe we'll get lucky and all three will match."

Norgaard nodded and handed the shoes to the evidence guy who'd just finished bagging the gun and other items from the backpack.

Monika strolled through the other two bedrooms, checked on the detectives who were searching there, and then wandered back out to the living room just as her cell phone began ringing.

"Sodafsky," she answered, not recognizing the number.

"Afternoon, Detective. It's Agent Carson, FBI."

Shit, thought Monika. The cat was about to be out of the bag. "Hey, Agent Carson, thanks for calling. I was just about to call you."

"Oh yeah? Well, good timing then. How are things looking with regard to Ronald Whittaker?" he asked.

"Well, it's starting to look like he's going to become an official suspect in this homicide. I'm probably going to be talking to the prosecutor this afternoon about issuing an arrest warrant."

"Well, damn," he replied. "We're going to have to pull his Top-Secret clearance in that case."

"Is there any way you can do that without telling him why?"

"I can do that for any reason I want, and I don't have to tell him anything," he answered.

"Can I ask you to keep the reason to yourself for a bit then?" Monika replied. "I'd really hate it if he decided to run or something before we can execute the warrant."

Agent Carson told her it was no problem and that he'd keep everything quiet. He would go to Whittaker's office himself and make sure nothing was said. Monika thanked him and hung up.

Just then the front door of the house opened and a uniformed deputy poked his head in. Monika had deputies stationed at both the front and the rear of the house. They had a description of Whittaker's car which was missing from the garage. Their orders were to stop anybody approaching the house and to identify them, detaining Whittaker if he arrived.

"Hey, Detective, sorry to bother you," the deputy said. "There's a guy out here who's demanding to talk to you. I told him to leave but he's refusing. Says he's Whittaker's attorney."

Chapter 15

Anne Fowler was worried. Unable to focus on anything, she was getting almost no work done. But then again, she wasn't sure what she'd be doing even if she could focus.

Bad things had started happening the day before when the police had come to the office with the shocking news that Ron Conner had been brutally murdered in his home the night before. Anne had been sickened. Conner's secretary, Mary Barnes, had been inconsolable; she'd felt dizzy and had been driven to the hospital where she'd been sedated. She hadn't returned to work today and, quite honestly, Anne wasn't sure where she'd go if she did return. If your boss gets murdered, do you still have a job?

The police had come into Mr. Whittaker's office and asked to speak to him, flashing their badges at Anne. They'd been professional and nice, and the female detective had assured her they would find Mr. Conner's killer.

Then, this morning, Mr. Whittaker had arrived at his office hours late for work and with no explanation for his absence. He'd barely said "good morning" to her before shutting his office door. She'd interrupted him with the news that Mr. Gresham wanted to see him right away and he'd told her, "No."

She'd been in shock; nobody said no to Mr. Gresham.

When Mr. Gresham had come storming down the hall, Anne had been terrified. He was angrier than she'd ever seen him, and even on his good days he was unpleasant, at least to her and to the other secretaries she spoke to in the lunch room.

He had been in Mr. Whittaker's office for just five minutes when Mr. Whittaker had told her to call an ambulance.

The ambulance crew arrived with PSA security officers, and they'd taken Mr. Gresham out on a stretcher, oxygen mask on his face, his arms strapped to the sides of the gurney. He hadn't been back, though the rumor was that he was recovering in the hospital from a minor heart attack and that he'd be okay.

Mr. Whittaker had watched them wheel Mr. Gresham out, a blank look on his face. He'd then taken a call on his cell phone and gone back into his office, coming out a minute later with his coat and briefcase. He'd said nothing to her on his way out except that he wouldn't be back to work that day.

Anne had sat at her desk for the last few hours, trying to stay busy, but unable to get her mind off everything going on. She couldn't imagine how things could possibly get worse. And then a few minutes ago, security had shown up with the big boss, the one from the seventh floor who never, *never* came down to the sixth floor. They'd locked Mr. Whittaker's office and confiscated her key. The boss then told her she could leave for the day and that she was officially on paid administrative leave until she heard from him. He'd warned her not to contact Mr. Whittaker and to report back to him if he attempted to call her. She'd then been escorted out.

On her way out, she saw security sealing Mr. Conner's office, and she'd overheard one of them say to the other that the FBI was on its way.

So Anne Fowler was worried. If Mr. Whittaker lost his job, she was probably going to be standing behind Mary Barnes in the unemployment line.

It was hard to believe that when she woke up yesterday morning, she'd thought her life was going great.

Chapter 16

Franklin paced back and forth on the street outside Whittaker's house as he waited for the lead detective to come out and talk to him. He warily eyed the deputy who was leaning against his patrol car, staring at Franklin with a smirk on his face. This was the one he thought of as *semi-retarded asshole*. The other deputy was standing on the front porch chatting with someone inside. That one was *less retarded asshole*.

For appearances' sake, Franklin had parked his car a block away. When he ambled up the street, he'd expected the deputies to treat him with a measure of respect. He'd given them his card and identified himself as Whittaker's attorney, then attempted to walk up to the front door. "Semi-retarded asshole" had stuck out one big, gorilla-like arm, and pushed him in the chest. He'd looked at him and simply said, "No."

Franklin didn't like being told no, and he had every right to be present at his client's home while the search warrant was being executed. He told "semi-retarded asshole" that he was not going to be tyrannized, and that if he didn't let him through, he would have his badge before the end of his shift.

That's when Franklin made his first mistake of the day.

He tried to push by the deputy and continue up to the house. For a moment, he thought he'd won, and he turned his back to the deputy and started for the steps. That's when "semi-retarded asshole" had simply said, "Excuse me, sir?"

Franklin had turned around to find "semi-retarded asshole" holding a small black and silver object with a blocky-looking plastic piece on the end of it. There was a curious red light coming from the object, just under the blocky-looking plastic piece. Franklin looked down to see the other end of that light focused in the form of a red dot in the middle of his chest.

"This is a Taser, sir. It fires two metal darts that will go through your suit as if it was paper and stick into your flesh. The instant they embed themselves into your flesh, this part of the Taser," "semi-retarded asshole" motioned to the pistol-like object he was holding, "will send an electrical pulse through the wires. That pulse will contain 50,000 volts of electricity."

"Now, sir, you are certainly more than welcome to continue walking up those steps, but if I were you, I would instead walk over to the grass. You see, I'm afraid that the human body is unable to maintain any kind of muscular control when it's lit up by 50,000 volts. You will fall immediately to the ground, and the concrete you're currently standing on is not very forgiving."

Franklin froze, unable to look away from the red dot on his chest. The deputy simply shrugged.

"Your call, sir."

Franklin carefully and slowly began walking back toward "semi-retarded asshole", keeping his hands slightly raised and walking past him, back out into the street. He then looked at the other deputy, "less-retarded asshole", and asked him, "Would you mind asking the lead detective if he'll come talk to me? Please?"

"Less-retarded" had heaved his rather sizeable bulk off the front of his patrol car where he'd been leaning, watching the show with an arrogant grin on his face. He waved his hand at "semi-retarded", who flipped a switch and placed the Taser back into the holster on his belt.

"I'll go ask if they want to talk to you," he said and started up to the porch.

So now Franklin was waiting, which he hated, in violation of his constitutional right to represent his client, which he hated even more, and it was starting to rain again, which he hated absolutely. He was pacing back and forth, eyeing the semi-retarded, quick drawing, asshole deputy, and plotting his revenge.

Finally, the front door to the house opened fully, and a good-looking female wearing a nicely-tailored, high-quality suit, along with a badge and a gun attached to the belt of the suit, came strolling down the walkway toward him.

"Hi, I'm Detective Monika Sodafsky with the Sheriff's Office," she said, her hand extended. "Who are you?"

Franklin let his eyes wander up and down her trim, tight figure and then shook hands with her. She was a beauty, and this was someone he could work with. He stood to his full height and cleared his throat, straightening his tie.

"It's a true pleasure to meet you. My name is Franklin Richardson, senior partner at FDR Law, and I've been retained to represent Mr. Ronald Whittaker." He handed the cute detective his business card.

"Do you have some kind of proof that you're representing Mr. Whittaker?" she asked, a pleasant look on her face.

Franklin pulled a manila folder from his briefcase and handed it to her. It contained the retainer contract Ron had signed that morning. Monika gave it a quick glance and then handed it back to him.

"Please come on in," she said pleasantly. "I've got a copy of the search warrant inside, and I guess we'll give you the return of service copy instead of leaving it." She glanced at her watch. "Will Mr. Whittaker be joining us?"

Franklin smiled at her. "Not at the moment, I'm afraid."

Monika led the way into the house and pointed to one of the chairs she had recently righted. "Please have a seat, Mr. Richardson. I want to remind you that we are serving a court ordered search warrant and that you're inside at my invitation. You're not to touch anything or leave this room."

She reached into her attaché case and pulled out a copy of the search warrant which she handed to Franklin.

He read over the search warrant carefully, blanching slightly when he saw the name of the prosecutor who'd approved the warrant, Dana Porter. He had a history with Dana Porter from when he worked at the Prosecutor's Office; he'd asked her out on dates numerous times and she'd turned him down each time. She'd actually filed a complaint against him, accusing him of unwanted advances and contributing to a hostile workplace. Unbelievable. He barely survived that complaint and was put on probation. His job had even been threatened by the elected county prosecutor. Dana Porter didn't like Franklin, and the feeling was mutual.

He was disturbed by the judge who'd signed the warrant, Neil Chapman. Chapman was well known for being tough on crime and for taking a personal interest in cases that involved him. He made sure these cases stayed in his courtroom. In theory, cases were supposed to be assigned randomly, but Franklin knew it didn't always work out that way. If a Superior Court judge wanted a particular case, he usually got it.

Detective Sodafsky excused herself and walked down the hallway, so Franklin took a moment to read the affidavit. He'd occasionally found warrants where the probable cause to issue them was incredibly weak. That was something you could attack in court, possibly getting everything the police found thrown out.

In this case, Franklin couldn't believe what he was reading. He'd rarely, if ever, seen an affidavit with more probable cause than this one. His client's fingerprint on the shell casing found in Conner's home was bad enough, but the duct tape in the garbage cans? What kind of an idiot was he representing?

His mind began to break down the evidence and form a defense. The garbage can thing was obviously an easy plant. Anybody could have walked down that alley and tossed the duct tape in Whittaker's trash can. The shell casing was more difficult, but he could establish that Conner and Whittaker had been close friends, maybe even the kind of friends who would go shooting together sometimes. It was easy to lose one of your expended casings, especially if you used Conner's dining room to clean your guns after you went shooting.

Franklin smiled and relaxed back in the chair. This affidavit was strong when the standard was *probable cause*, a standard that required a judge to say, *"Yeah, the information in the officer's knowledge would warrant a reasonable person to think a crime has been committed and this guy was involved."* It was, however, an entirely different matter when a case actually went to court where the burden of proof was *beyond a reasonable doubt.* That required a reasonable person to say, *"There is almost zero doubt in my mind that this guy committed this murder."*

They were going to need a lot more than an expended shell casing and some strands of duct tape in a garbage can to reach that level of proof, especially with Franklin D. Richardson arguing on the side of righteousness.

At that moment, Detective Sodafsky came back into the living room from down the hall, her arms full of plastic evidence bags, their tops sealed and the labels on the front filled out by the technician who'd processed them. She set the bags on the floor by the front door.

"What are those?" Franklin asked, eyeing the bags warily.

"Oh, just a few things we found," she answered, an innocent look on her face.

"Would you mind telling me what they are?" he asked suspiciously.

"Oh, sure, no problem. I was just about to list everything on the inventory report anyway, so we can do it together."

Franklin eyed her cautiously. She was acting much too confident and a bit duplicitous and he felt his concern growing.

Sodafsky pulled an inventory sheet that carbon copied in triplicate out of her attaché and moved over to the first bag.

"Let's see. In here we have a Beretta 92FS nine-millimeter pistol, serial number BER91146384." She wrote that down. "In this bag is a ten-round magazine for the Beretta 92FS nine-millimeter pistol, magazine containing eight rounds of silver-tipped, hollow point ammunition."

Sodafsky turned to Franklin. "There are two rounds missing from the magazine," she said helpfully, just in case Franklin couldn't subtract eight from ten.

"In this bag, we have a small, black, REI backpack which contains a pair of pliers, a utility knife, a large hunting type knife, a plastic bag, a carpenter's hammer, a pair of sheet metal shears, and a chocolate chip protein bar." She looked at Franklin again. "I guess whatever he was doing with those tools must have been hungry work!" She smiled at him. Franklin didn't return the smile.

Moving on, she picked up a smaller evidence bag. "This is a nine-millimeter shell casing, expended, originally located in the REI backpack alongside the tools." She wrote that on the sheet.

"In this bag is one pair of black, Nike athletic-type shoes, size 9, the soles of which contain bits of dried mud." She smiled at Franklin again. He was getting a really bad feeling in his stomach and was wishing he'd grabbed the bottle of antacid from the center console of his car.

"This bag," she said, holding up another small one, "contains a sample of mud we gathered from the backyard of the residence here. Never know when you might get lucky," she said, shrugging at him, a giddy look on her face.

"And then we have this one. Do you know what this is, Mr. Richardson?"

She held up a large evidence bag containing an empty plastic bottle of Vitamin water. The bottom of the plastic bottle was shredded, the shards of plastic expanded outward as if a firecracker had gone off inside it. The shards were slightly blackened. Franklin had no idea what it was.

"It appears to be an empty bottle, Detective. Didn't you get enough joy when you searched through my client's trash the first time?"

Monika smiled at him. "You know, the detective who found this didn't know what it was either. He was searching through Mr. Whittaker's recycle bin, the small one in his kitchen. I'm happy to report that your client is a conscientious recycler. Anyway, the detective had set it aside to place back into the bin when he got to the bottom. Luckily I happened to walk by and spot it."

"And just what is it that you think you've found?" Franklin asked her, his eyebrows arched.

Monika smiled that confident, smug smile. "A homemade silencer, of course."

Franklin looked at the evidence bag again, his heart rate increasing. He had a feeling his client was truly fucked and, in his mind, that was great news.

Chapter 17

When Franklin got back to his office, he parked in the parking lot in front of his door, something he never did and something that caused Stacy to stare at him open-mouthed as he walked in. He turned back to the door, locked it and then walked past her as he said, "Come in here."

Franklin set down his stuff and sat at his desk. Stacy came in, her arms crossed and a plaintive look on her face.

"I'm not in the mood for sex today, Franklin."

"This isn't about sex, Stacy. It's time for you to start helping me earn this retainer."

She relaxed and uncrossed her arms, returned to her desk for a notepad, and sat down in the chair in his office. He explained to her what the cops had found at Whittaker's, handing her the copy of the warrant and the inventory sheet for the file.

"We're closed for the day as of right now. I want you to do a full background check on Mr. Whittaker. I want to know everything about him--every arrest, every speeding ticket, what he eats for breakfast--everything. There's something wrong with this case, with the way he's acting, his whole demeanor and lackadaisical attitude."

Stacy was looking over the inventory sheet of the evidence from Whittaker's house. "Oh my God, baby. They're going to issue an arrest warrant for him."

Franklin knew that. They had too much evidence not to, and it was hard to imagine their investigation was pointing in any direction other than directly at his client's guilt.

"Do you have any contacts in the Sheriff's Office?" he asked, thinking angrily about Jackie again and how she had really fucked him over on this one.

"I do know one of the patrol deputies," she began. Franklin frowned and looked at her suspiciously.

"What? He's just a friend of my brother's, nothing more," she said defensively.

"Okay, well get hold of him and see if he can find out anything that we don't know already. We need ears into that building somehow. I have a feeling this case is going to end up at trial."

Stacy went back to her desk to start on the background checks, and Franklin picked up the phone. He needed to call Ron Whittaker and tell him what they'd found at his house. He also had to tell him that he was going to need more money since it looked like this case was headed toward an arrest. He then needed to call his tailor and order another suit or two. If he wanted to look good in court, he was going to need them.

Chapter 18

Dana Porter stood behind her desk and stared out the window of her first-floor office located in the Mission Building, part of the courthouse complex. It was a dreary day, typical for winter in western Washington, the dark, low-hanging clouds portending the onset of a premature dusk.

At 4:30pm, the mass exodus of the county complex had begun, most of the employees having started their days at 8am. Dana started this day at 7am, and it didn't appear that her personal exodus would be happening anytime soon, which was why she was wistfully staring out her window.

It would be nice if she could have a normal workday like the drones she was watching head to their cars on their way to their nice homes, to have a pleasant family dinner, maybe a glass of wine or two in front of the television, and then to their nice beds to get a regular night's sleep before doing it all over again.

She'd reached the point in her life where that was the dream, routine and humdrum, an ordinary life. These were the things she thought of when she envisioned her ideal future, and she envied those who were living that dream.

She'd actually been considering trying to sneak out early, calling her husband and seeing if he wanted to go catch a movie, maybe dinner. But then she'd received a phone call from Monika Sodafsky at the Sheriff's Office asking if she could come down.

The Sheriff's Office was on the fourth floor of the courthouse, so Monika should be walking in at any moment. Dana was hopeful the meeting would be quick, but since she'd just approved a search warrant for Monika that morning, she suspected that was the reason for her visit. If she wanted to meet up with her this quickly after serving the warrant, it was likely there was a problem.

There was a knock at her door and Dana turned away from the window as Monika let herself in, a manila file folder in her hand and a tired look on her face.

"Hi Monika. Come in. Have a seat." Monika sat in the comfortable chair in front of Dana's desk, yawning as she did so.

"Long day?" Dana asked.

Monika nodded. "Busy day for sure, I've hardly had a second to relax and I have a bad feeling it's just getting started. Might be a late night."

"The Conner case?"

"Yes. We served the warrant on the Whittaker place today."

"You didn't waste any time."

Monika shrugged. "Everything points right at him. We don't have any other suspects right now."

"How'd it go? Find anything worthwhile?"

Monika reached into the folder and pulled out a copy of the inventory sheet from the file folder. Wordlessly, she slid it across Dana's desk and waited.

Dana began scanning the document, skipping over the form stuff at the top that said the Sheriff's Office was seizing the below items as per the search warrant and listing the appropriate legal reasoning for the seizure. She got to the list of items and paused.

"Jesus."

Monika laughed. "Yeah. That's what everybody says. I don't think I've ever seen a more fruitful search in a case of this magnitude, have you?"

"Maybe a few times, but usually in those cases the suspect is caught before he can leave the scene of the crime, before he can get home and clean up, start getting rid of stuff," she trailed off, still looking at the inventory sheet. "What's this plastic bottle with the base exploded outward?"

"I think it's a homemade silencer for the nine-millimeter."

"How would that work?"

"Well, you stick the pistol barrel into the opening, and that keeps the expanding gases kind of contained. The majority of the noise from a gunshot is because of the rapid expansion of the gases as they exit the barrel. A conventional silencer works on that same principle. This is sort of a poor man's version, I guess."

"Would this actually silence the shot?" Dana asked, dubious that it could be that easy.

"It definitely wouldn't *silence* it, but it would *quiet* it pretty significantly. Hollywood always gets it wrong, you know. Silencers aren't meant to actually *silence* gunshots. In fact, most gun people prefer to call them "suppressors" because that's what they do--suppress the noise.

"Okay." Dana asked, "So would this do the job?"

I looked up some videos on YouTube about these types of silencers. They can be pretty dangerous if you don't know what you're doing; people blow their hands up and stuff like that sometimes. But they are effective if used correctly, for one shot anyway."

Dana frowned, trying to remember the info from the search warrant affidavit. "Wasn't Conner shot twice?"

"He was. We didn't find another silencer, so I'm going to guess that he anticipated having to shoot him just once and didn't really plan for the second shot."

Dana rocked back in her chair, thinking about this, trying to visualize the encounter as it might have happened. "Okay, so he shoots him once and that blows out the bottom of the silencer, then he realizes he has to shoot him again. Does he leave the silencer on for the second shot, even though it's already been used?"

Monika nodded. "I think so. It would still quiet the shot a little bit, not as effectively as for the first shot, but still quieter than without. Also, he was in the middle of the house; in the dining room and not close to any outside walls. This is an upscale neighborhood with nice, well-built houses; sound doesn't penetrate the walls very easily. If someone happened to be walking by on the sidewalk, they might have heard the second shot, but they certainly wouldn't have heard it from, say, inside the neighbor's house."

Dana considered that. "I wonder if we can test that somehow. We could fire a shot from inside his house and see if it's heard from outside. I'm guessing you spoke to the neighbors and they didn't hear anything."

Monika nodded. "Nobody heard anything, nobody saw anything." She shrugged. "Like I said, it's a nice neighborhood and it was late at night, probably two or three in the morning according to the medical examiner's preliminary report. People don't walk around outside in the winter at that hour in neighborhoods like that. He probably didn't even need to use any kind of silencer and it would have been fine."

"What about those containers of Thai food you collected from Conner's house?" Dana asked, thinking about the search warrant affidavit she had approved. "How do those fit into the story?"

"There were two separate containers of food that had been ordered from Satay Thai sitting on the counter. They were mostly eaten, just a little left in each one. One of our detectives went down and got statements from the restaurant manager and the delivery guy. They were ordered by the victim, Conner, at around 10:00pm and delivered at 10:45pm. Both of them were chicken Pad Thai." She paused and looked at her notebook before continuing. "The delivery guy didn't see anybody except Conner when he came to the door to pay for the food, but he did hear a male voice ask Conner if he had any beer. Conner shouted back that it was in the fridge, gave the delivery guy cash for the food, and the delivery guy left. He said there didn't appear to be any problems at the house at that time."

"What are we doing with the food then?"

Monika smiled. "We're going to get DNA off the chopsticks that were left in the food. Ideally, one of them comes back with Conner's profile and the other with Whittaker's profile."

Dana nodded her head. "Yeah that would be pretty strong. So, I assume you're here because you want to arrest Whittaker?"

"Well, I thought we should discuss it, but yeah, I think we might be there right now," Monika replied.

"Let's walk through this scenario for a minute here," Dana said, deliberately. "Whittaker decides he wants to kill Conner. We'll discuss motive in a minute, but let's start with the presumption that he has a reason for killing him."

"Okay, so he goes over to his house on Sunday night," Monika interrupted, "and I know you're going to ask, why does he decide to have dinner with him first?"

"Seems like that's something I'll have to address in court at some point, yes," Dana replied.

"My theory right now is that he didn't know at the time that he was going to kill him. He was prepared for that but didn't know for sure if he would have to. He needed to get over there at a reasonable hour for the sake of appearances, but didn't want any neighbors out and about who might hear something. He needed to stall until it got late before he taped him to the chair and then killed him."

"He didn't want to be knocking on the door at two in the morning but also didn't want to be shooting a gun at 10:00pm when people were still awake and might hear it," Dana summarized.

"Exactly."

Dana continued. "So, he goes over there with the intention of killing him, having planned it all out in advance, even thinking about the noise the pistol is going to make when he fires it and bringing along a plastic bottle to silence it."

Monika interrupted. "He may not have brought that along; he may have gotten it from Conner's house. We've got the lab guys looking for fingerprints right now, and for DNA on the mouth of it to see if we get a hit."

"Okay, so he either brings it along or he decides he needs to silence the gun when he actually gets there. He finds a bottle in Conner's trash and uses that. If we're going to presume that he planned this in advance, bringing tools with him, duct tape, that sort of thing, he probably brought the bottle as well, right?"

Monika shrugged. "Probably."

"Conner lets him in, they decide to order a late dinner, they eat, maybe sit around and have a few beers, then Whittaker conks him on the head, knocking him unconscious, tapes him to the chair, waits for him to wake up, questions him about something, and then kills him?"

"That's about the sum of it," Monika replied.

"So what were the tools for?"

"I think they were in case he didn't get the answers he was looking for."

"You think he brought these tools," Dana picked up the sheet and looked at it again, "the hammer and the pliers. You think he was going to torture him?" She raised her eyebrows and stared at Monika.

Monika raised her hands slightly. "I don't know. I can't figure out any other explanation."

"What about a motive?"

"We're still working on that. We've spoken with his boss, a guy named Gerald Gresham. Unfortunately he just had a heart attack, and he's recovering in the hospital, so we haven't had a chance to have a full conversation with him. He did say that Conner and Whittaker were up for a promotion to the same job and that he'd decided to give it to Conner."

"Did Whittaker know he wasn't getting the promotion?"

Monika nodded. "He did. Gresham said Whittaker confronted him about it the day he had the heart attack. He said Whittaker seemed angry but we didn't get any further before the doctor told us to end the interview. This was just about an hour ago, by the way."

Dana stood up again and walked back to the window, staring out. It was almost full dark, and the rush of people headed to their cars had ended. The few diehards who had chosen to put work before family, people like herself, were now beginning to walk to their cars with umbrellas to deflect the rain.

She turned back to Monika who was staring at her, patiently waiting. "How long will it be for ballistics to come back on the gun?"

"Probably three or four days at least. That takes us into the weekend, so probably Monday or Tuesday. It's the same gun though, Dana. I can feel it."

Dana nodded and leaned against the frame between the two windows of her office. "I know, and I'm sure you're right. How long for the DNA results?"

"That could be a month or more. We put in a rush request on it," Monika replied. "The good news is the FBI has his DNA profile on file; a cheek swab was part of his Top-Secret clearance. I think we'll be able to bypass the Washington State Patrol lab and get the FBI to process it. That should speed things up."

Dana chewed on the inside of her cheek, staring out the window. "I'm tempted to hold off on the arrest warrant for now. Have you tried to interview him?" she finally asked.

Monika shook her head. "He's already hired an attorney so I decided to wait."

Dana raised her eyebrows at this. "When did he hire an attorney?"

Monika shrugged. "The guy showed up at Whittaker's house today while we were serving the warrant." She glanced at the folder and picked out a business card. "Guy named Franklin D. Richardson."

Dana laughed. "Oh, I know Franklin. He used to work here. Did he hit on you?"

Monika smirked. "No, he was very polite. Maybe I'm not his type."

"Oh, you're his type," Dana said, shaking her head, "you have a vagina." She sighed. "Okay, well Franklin is a douchebag and he's a blowhard, but he's not an idiot. He's not going to let Whittaker talk to you except to maybe give a statement saying he didn't do it, but let's see what you can get anyway. Do you think he's a flight risk at all?"

If Monika thought Ron Whittaker was a flight risk, Dana would support the arrest, but otherwise she preferred not to. Once they arrested him, the clock started on his right to a speedy trial, and even though nearly every suspect waived that right, she preferred to play it safe, especially when waiting for DNA returns.

"I'm not too concerned about him fleeing," Monika replied, "He has no criminal record whatsoever, and he has a high-paying job, community ties, that sort of thing. Plus, he hired an attorney, so he must be thinking ahead to fighting this."

"I wonder how he knew you were serving the warrant," Dana mused.

Monika shrugged. "A neighbor perhaps? I don't know. His lawyer was there pretty quickly though, so he must have had him on retainer and ready to go."

Dana frowned. "From what I remember of Franklin, he isn't the type that someone with money would keep on retainer. That might be something we need to look into as well." She sighed, her mind made up. "Okay, we're going to wait for ballistics on the gun and lab results on this mud you found." She gestured at the inventory report, "And in the meantime, you'll see if you can get a statement from Whittaker, one way or the other, follow-up on the whole motive thing, talk to this Gresham guy and whoever else, and see if we can tie this all together a little more neatly before we proceed."

Monika stood up and nodded. "Sounds good. Thanks for being a sounding board for me; I know I'm a little premature."

Dana smiled and told Monika it was no problem at all. She escorted her to the door and went back to gather her things. Maybe she could still get out of here, call her husband, and salvage this night.

Chapter 19

Franklin woke up the next morning with a smile on his face, feeling better than he had in years. He had a real client and one who was truly fucked, something he'd been dreaming of for a long time. Fuck all the naysayers who'd thought it would never happen. Based on everything that he'd seen the police take from Whittaker's house yesterday, they would probably be looking to arrest him soon, and that meant tons of billable hours, many of them in court at double the rate. Today was going to be a good day.

He glanced over at Stacy lying in bed next to him, her long blonde hair spread across the pillow, her mouth open. She was naked, and Franklin lifted the covers just a little bit so he could look at her magnificent breasts. He felt a stirring in his loins and quickly lowered the covers again. As tempted as he was to go for a repeat of the previous night's bedroom escapades, he needed to focus today, and morning sex tended to make him lazy for the rest of the day.

So, instead of stroking her sumptuous body, he nudged her shoulder and said, "Stacy. Wake up."

Stacy opened her eyes partway, mumbled, "Not now," and turned away from him toward the wall.

"Get up," he said, grabbing her shoulder and rocking her body back and forth. "We have a big day, lots to do."

"Fuck you, Franklin, it's still dark out," she yelled, waving blindly behind her body in a feeble attempt to strike him.

Franklin laughed and jumped out of bed. "It's dark but it's morning, and we're getting an early start. Now hurry and get up. I'm jumping in the shower."

He turned on the overhead light on his way out, ignoring her shrieking protests, and headed into the hallway bathroom, the only one in his small, two-bedroom hovel. He couldn't wait for the day when he could get out of this crappy apartment, away from the food stamp abusing, lottery ticket buying, Olde English 800 swilling swine that infested this apartment complex and this area of town in general. He was better than this; he knew it, Stacy knew it, and soon the world would know it.

Win or lose, this was going to be a big case: lots of opportunities for media interviews, camera time, clever and witty statements such as, "My client, Mr. Whittaker, looks forward to the opportunity to clear his name, to defend his innocence in a court of law. He had absolutely no involvement in this heinous and despicable act, and we relish the chance to prove that to the world."

Franklin had called Ron Whittaker the night before when he returned to the office, and he let him know what had been seized from his house. Whittaker expressed outrage, vehemently declaring that he'd been set up, that somebody was framing him. Franklin listened politely (he'd heard it a hundred times before), and then commiserated with him, telling him he was confident that the issue of the evidence, despite its appearance, was far from a guilty verdict.

He'd then broken it to him that he was definitely going to need more money as it appeared certain this case was headed for court. Whittaker didn't hesitate before saying that he would swing by the office the next morning to drop off another check, and Franklin wanted to make sure he didn't miss him.

He finished his shower, then physically pulled Stacy from the bed and shoved her into the bathroom. He dressed in his best suit and his favorite red, white, and blue tie (because everybody loves a patriot), and impatiently waited for Stacy to finish dressing before hustling her out the door.

When they got to the office, he immediately sent Stacy out to get coffee, despite her protests that she hadn't had time to finish her makeup or do her hair. He reminded her that it was still dark and then told her to pick up a coffee maker and some ground coffee as well, thinking there were probably some long days coming.

Sitting at his desk, Franklin took a look at the results of the background check Stacy had done the night before. Ronald Peter Whittaker seemed like the picture of innocence. He'd never been arrested for a crime, had never had any contact with law enforcement, with the exception of a speeding ticket five years prior. He had good credit, a solid job where he made good money, filed his taxes on time every year; in essence, he was a model citizen. These were all good things, things that would work in his favor during a trial, things he could introduce to any jury should it get to that point.

Leaning back in his chair, Franklin picked up the inventory sheet from the search of Whittaker's house. Some of the items were not going to be a problem for him. The mud on his shoes, even if it did match the mud in Conner's house, was not an issue. It could be established that Whittaker and Conner were friends, and Whittaker was often at Conner's house. Any evidence that showed Whittaker inside the residence would be a similar issue unless it could prove he was there at the time of Conner's death, something that couldn't be done with fingerprints, DNA, or mud.

This pistol was a potential problem, assuming it was matched to the bullets that killed Conner. He made a note to have Stacy check the serial number and see if it was registered to Whittaker. He didn't know yet what they were doing with the tools from the backpack, but he'd deal with that during discovery, when the prosecution had to define the evidence they would be using at trial.

Stacy returned with two cups of coffee, and Franklin put her to work setting up the new coffee maker and then running the registration number from the pistol.

At 8:00am sharp, the front door opened and Ron Whittaker walked in. Stacy directed him back to Franklin's office and shut the door behind her as she left.

"Good morning, Ron," Franklin said, standing and offering his hand. Ron shook it this time. "How are you doing?"

Ron shrugged. "I'm okay. Nervous about everything they found at my house though. Do you think it's really bad?"

"Well, let's talk about it." He held up the list of items. "Let's start with the pistol. Do you own a Beretta 92FS?"

Ron nodded. "I do. I bought it maybe ten years ago. I don't think I've seen the thing in the last five years though."

"Where was it the last time you saw it?"

"I keep it on the top shelf of my bedroom closet in a shoebox. I couldn't tell you when it was last there, though; it might have been gone for years. Is that where they found it?"

"No, they found it inside a backpack in your laundry hamper," Franklin replied.

Ron laughed. "So they think I hid the thing in my laundry hamper?"

"That's where they found it, so I guess that's where they think you hid it."

"That's ridiculous. If I was going to hide a gun I just used to murder somebody, I would come up with a better place than that."

Franklin frowned. "So, if you didn't put it in your laundry hamper, who did?"

"I have no idea!" Ron exclaimed. "I'm not that great at keeping my doors locked. I live in a really nice neighborhood and we have virtually no crime, so I don't worry too much about it."

Franklin jotted down a few notes on his legal pad. "Okay, so let's talk about the mud on your shoes. Apparently there was mud at Ron Conner's house, inside his house, and they think the mud on your shoes might be the same mud."

"Well, I was at his house the day before he was killed, so it's possible it would have been from that."

"Is there anybody who could confirm that you were there the day before his death?"

Whittaker crinkled his nose and thought about it. "I waved to his neighbor when I was leaving, I don't know his name, but he would probably remember me. He was out checking his mail."

Franklin asked a few more questions, establishing which house the neighbor lived in and the time of day. He would be trying to track this neighbor down to confirm this.

"Okay," he said, "let's talk about the night Mr. Conner was murdered. Where were you that night?"

"I was home asleep."

"Start at the beginning. It was a Sunday night. You didn't work that day, right?"

Whittaker shook his head. "I didn't work. I watched football all day alone at my house. That evening, after the afternoon NFL games, I went to the grocery store and bought some stuff to make dinner--chicken, broccoli, some milk, I think some eggs for breakfast, and I think I bought a bottle of wine. I went home,

REASONABLE DOUBT | Rick Fuller

made dinner, watched the night NFL game, and then had some wine. I guess I was having a lazy day. I don't think I did anything else. I probably watched TV until 11:00pm or so, then went to bed."

"So you were alone all day?"

"Yes, and all night. I guess maybe the grocery store could verify I was there. I used my debit card for the groceries, so that will put me there."

"And other than the trip to the grocery store, you didn't use your car, didn't drive anywhere else all night? Didn't take an Uber, call a friend to come get you, didn't take a walk anywhere?"

Ron was shaking his head. "I didn't go anywhere. I may have talked to people, probably did, but don't remember for sure. I'm sure I at least had some text message conversations with people, but nothing after 11:00pm because I was in bed and asleep."

"What time did you get up the next morning?" Franklin asked, taking notes.

"Around 6:30am. That's what my alarm is set for. I might have snoozed for ten minutes or so though. I got up, I made breakfast, showered, shaved, and went to work. I was there by 8:00am, and the gate guards there can confirm when I came in; the key swipes from my security card will confirm it also."

"That's great, but the police think the murder occurred between 2am and 3am. Nobody can confirm your whereabouts at that time, right?"

"No," Ron replied, worriedly. "Is this a problem?"

"No, no, it's not. It would be nice if you had a tight alibi for that night, but you're not required to prove you weren't there, the state has to prove you were, so don't worry about that."

"Maybe the cell company can show that my phone didn't leave my house?"

Franklin nodded, impressed. He hadn't thought of that. Cell phones often pinged the nearest towers, even when they weren't active. At least he remembered reading that once. Most people also leave their GPS locators turned on all the time on their phones so that apps like weather and maps all work. He made a note to have Stacy check into that.

"Okay, let's talk about motive. The police are going to want to try to establish a motive for you killing Mr. Conner. Now, I'm not saying you did it," he added, holding up his hands. "We know you didn't do it, but let's just say for a second you had killed him. What reason would you have for doing it?"

"I wouldn't have a reason for killing him."

"Okay, let's say the State thinks you did. What reason are they going to come up with for you killing him?"

Whittaker paused for a minute, thinking. "Well, Ron was about to get promoted at work. Maybe they'll think I was jealous about that or something. I also knew he was having an affair with my boss's wife, so maybe they'll think I killed him because of that, like maybe I was jealous or something."

"Conner was having an affair with your boss's wife?" Franklin asked, incredulously. "Did your boss know about it?"

"Sure he did. I mean, he might say he didn't know about it, but he did. Also, I never even wanted the job that Ron was getting. I was offered it just yesterday by Mr. Gresham; he's my boss. He came into my office and offered me the job and I turned him down. He was so shocked by that, he actually had a heart attack right in my office."

Jesus, this was getting good. "Is he okay?"

Ron shrugged. "I think so. I'm planning to go in today so I'll know more when I get there."

Franklin nodded, jotting down all this information. If Ron Conner was having an affair with Gerry Gresham's wife, and Ron Whittaker knew about it, perhaps there was a love triangle thing going on, something he could work with in Ron's defense. It also made Gresham a bit of a suspect in Conner's murder, and he was going to have to see if the police were looking in that direction.

Chapter 20

"Do you have any suspects yet?"

"We're still pursuing a number of leads, and we aren't ready to narrow anything down to a single suspect at this point," replied Monika Sodafsky. She was standing on the steps in front of the courthouse and was surrounded by several news cameras and reporters. It hadn't exactly been an ambush; the news conference had been scheduled by the public information office of the Sheriff's Office. What was a surprise, though, was her involvement. Usually these things were handled by some camera-hungry lieutenant or captain, not by the lead detective.

When she arrived at work, she'd been told by Detective Sergeant Myers that she would be leading the press conference. She had almost no prep time and was trying to wing it the best she could while two supervisors and the public information officer nervously looked on.

"But you did serve a search warrant on a house yesterday, is that correct?" a reporter from Channel 5 shouted out.

"We did serve a search warrant yesterday, and we did recover numerous items of evidentiary value. We are not, however, prepared to discuss the identity of the person involved in that search warrant, nor are we prepared to disclose what we found at the residence."

"Do you anticipate making an arrest soon?" asked another reporter, Channel 4 this time.

"We'll be making an arrest just as soon as the evidence we gather supports an arrest. I would like to remind you that this is an active investigation, and everybody is entitled to due process and the presumption of innocence. Until we have enough probable cause for an arrest, we'll keep investigating and we won't rule out any possibilities."

More questions were shouted, but the public information officer stepped up to the microphones and gently nudged Monika aside.

"That's all we have for you folks for now. We'll have another news conference tomorrow morning at the same time or if we have a major break in the case. Thank you very much."

Monika was relieved and walked away. She snuck back into the courthouse, flashing her badge as she bypassed the metal detectors, and then took the elevator to the fourth floor where her office was located.

REASONABLE DOUBT | Rick Fuller

She was buzzed in through the secure door by the secretary. Walking to her cubicle in Major Crimes, she called across the room to Norgaard.

"You ready?"

"Sure." He stood and pulled on his suit jacket, walking over to her desk. "How'd it go?"

"Terrible. I hate that shit. Let's get out of here, back door."

They walked over to the staircase that led down to the secure back door, accessible only by Sheriff's Office personnel with a key card. Monika poked her head out the door and confirmed that all was clear, then walked quickly to her unmarked detective's car. Bruce followed her at a fast pace.

"Where we headed first?" he asked, getting in the passenger side.

"Hospital. Let's go see if Gerry Gresham can help us with some kind of motive." Monika started the car and pulled out, headed to Providence Hospital just a short way down the road.

When they got to Providence, they walked into the emergency entrance and straight up to Gresham's room on the third floor. Monika checked in briefly with the nurse on duty who told her Gresham was doing much better and visitation was fine.

When they walked into Gresham's room, he was sitting up in bed eating Jell-O and watching a home remodeling show on TV. He saw them coming in and immediately muted the volume.

"Good morning," he said, smiling at Monika.

"Good morning, Mr. Gresham. How're you feeling this morning?"

He nodded and motioned at his Jell-O. "Much better. I don't eat enough Jell-O for breakfast at home."

Monika laughed. "I don't think any of us do. We were hoping you were feeling well enough to answer some questions for us today, pick up where we left off yesterday."

"Absolutely," he replied. "Anything I can do to help bring down that son of a bitch, Whittaker."

Monika raised her eyebrows at this. "Did something new happen since we were here yesterday?"

"No, I just had time to think about things overnight." He paused for a minute as if collecting his thoughts, then continued. "He's the reason I'm in here. He's been acting strangely all week, and I went to see him yesterday morning."

Monika and Bruce took a seat while Gresham told them the entire story--how Whittaker had cashed out his 401k and retirement accounts, how when Conner had died, Whittaker had not seemed upset and how he, Gresham, had gone into Whittaker's office with the offer of the promotion Conner was supposed to have gotten. He told them how Whittaker had laughed at him and then had told him Conner was having an affair with Gresham's wife.

"That's the reason I had this heart attack, and it's not even true!" he said, angrily.

"No offense intended here sir, but how do you know it's not true?"

"I confronted my wife about it; she's been here almost the entire time I've been in here. I'd know if she was lying. She flat out denied it." He looked straight at Monika. "I think that bastard was trying to make me have a heart attack. He was trying to upset me enough to put me into a rage. Everybody at the office knows I've had some heart issues, knows I'm supposed to keep calm and on an even keel. Ron knew I was already upset when I came into his office, that I was upset about Ron Conner's murder and about him, Whittaker, being late that morning, and he intentionally provoked me, trying to put me over the edge."

Monika looked over at Bruce who just shrugged, jotting some notes down in his notebook. She returned her gaze to Gresham.

"What reason would he have had for intentionally upsetting you and trying to make you have a heart attack?" she asked.

"I think he killed Ron Conner. I think he was jealous that Conner was getting the job and I think he killed him. Then I think he turned his rage on me and tried to kill me too, just in a bit more natural way." He chuckled wryly. "What better way to murder someone with a bad heart than by making him have a heart attack?"

"So Whittaker knew that Conner was getting the promotion?"

"He wasn't supposed to know. It was supposed to be a secret, but after Conner's death, when Whittaker was the only candidate left for the job, I was going to give it to him. That was one of the reasons I went into his office yesterday morning--to tell him he was the frontrunner. When I told him, he laughed at me. He said he knew Conner was getting the job; he even claimed that everybody in the company knew about it. He said he wasn't taking a job I didn't want him for just because he was the only one left. That's when he told me the disgusting lie about Jessamyn."

"If he was planning to turn down the job, why would he have killed Conner? I mean, I get if he wanted to be the only candidate for it, he might kill him to get him out of the way, but why would he do so if he wasn't interested in taking the job?"

Gresham shrugged and picked up his Jell-O again, putting a spoonful in his mouth and thoughtfully chewing it before replying. "I think he was planning to kill Ron so he could get the job. Then I think he cashed out his retirement so that he could flee if he got caught and he'd have plenty of money. I think he was planning to get the promotion and then he'd put the money back into his retirement. Then I think he decided to reach even higher. If he could kill me, he might be considered as my replacement, an even bigger promotion for him. I don't have any other explanation for the way he acted yesterday."

Monika thought about this for a moment. It had some holes, some things that didn't quite add up, but it was an intriguing theory.

"Is there anybody who can corroborate any of this?" she asked. "Anybody who heard the argument, anybody he would have talked to who he might have told any of this?"

"You might talk to his secretary, Anne Fowler. I don't know if she overheard any of our conversation yesterday from outside his office, but she might have."

Bruce jotted down the name, and Monika chatted a little longer with Gresham seeking more information or people they might talk to. He gave her the name of the company's Chief Financial Officer who had processed Whittaker's retirement cash-out, and then they wished him well and left.

They had the germ of a possible motive, but more digging was needed.

"What do you think?" Monika asked Bruce on the way back to the car.

"The whole thing seems a little hinky. Gresham has a bone to pick, and it sounds like Whittaker has one to pick with him, too. I'm concerned that we might get in the middle of an office spat while we're trying to solve a murder."

Monika thought about that while they were walking to the parking lot. She turned to Bruce. "You ever hear the expression *The most obvious solution is usually the correct one*?"

"Of course. You think we need to stay focused on Whittaker?"

Monika nodded. "I do. Let's go see if he'll talk to us."

Chapter 21

"It's not going to happen, detective, uh-uh, no way, no how. Not in this lifetime." Franklin rolled his eyes at Stacy and made a circular motion with his forefinger at his temple. She smiled and licked her lips seductively which made him smile.

He was on the phone with Detective Sodafsky, and she had just told him she wanted his client to come in for a voluntary interview. Even though he thought it would be a nice opportunity to stare at her ass a little more, there was no chance he was going to allow his star client (and only client) to talk to the police. Zero. None.

"Look, we just want to get a statement from him, just a simple paragraph about where he was that night, what he did, if anything. Doesn't Mr. Whittaker want to help find his friend's killer?"

"Mr. Whittaker would really like it if the Sheriff's Office would focus their efforts on finding the *actual* killer as opposed to serving search warrants at his house and harassing him at his job, Detective Sodafsky," Franklin replied, winking seductively at Stacy who giggled.

"Mr. Richardson, you've seen the evidence we found at Mr. Conner's house. You know that we wouldn't be doing our jobs if we didn't follow through on that evidence. You're not going to tell me that we shouldn't be looking at Mr. Whittaker even a little bit, are you?"

"Umm, yes Detective, that's exactly what I'm going to tell you, because my client didn't do it! Ron Whittaker was best friends with Ron Conner. He did not kill him; in fact, he's devastated by Mr. Conner's death."

"Then why not give a statement?"

"I just gave you the only statement you're going to get from my client, Detective. He didn't do it. Look elsewhere or arrest him if you think you have enough."

"You saw the evidence we have, Mr. Richardson. You know we have enough to arrest him," Monika responded.

Franklin turned away from Stacy who was now running her tongue over the front of her teeth which was distracting him in a pleasant way, but at a bad time.

"Then why haven't you issued the warrant yet?"

Monika paused for a second and then sighed. "I guess you're not going to give me a choice. If you won't let me talk to him, let him clear his name on the record, then I just have to rely on the evidence." Franklin heard a very sad tone come into her voice. "I really hate ruining the life of an innocent man just because he's afraid to talk to me and tell me that he's innocent...," she trailed off.

Franklin could barely stifle a laugh. Monika Sodafsky thought she was playing games with an amateur. There was *never* anything good that could come from talking to the police when you were a suspect in a major crime, and Franklin had been around the block enough to know that. He made a motion for Stacy to leave his office. She pouted at him and he made the motion again. Stacy left reluctantly and closed the door behind her.

"How about if you and I meet up for a drink or two tonight?" he asked Sodafsky. "We'll chat about it, and then we'll see if you can get me to change my mind."

"Do you think maybe we can have sex afterwards?" she asked.

Franklin's jaw dropped a little. He was speechless. "Umm, I guess so, maybe."

Monika laughed at him. "Look, creep. I want to talk to your client, not have drinks with you. Are you going to let him make a statement or not?"

Franklin could feel his face reddening, his blood pressure rising. "No, he won't be making a statement. You can fuck off, detective," he spat out.

"Have a good evening, Mr. Richardson," she replied. "We'll be in touch tomorrow about that arrest warrant."

The phone went dead and Franklin spun around in his chair. He'd let himself get played and he wasn't happy with how he'd handled it. He had learned something about Detective Sodafsky though, and realized that she was not a bimbo to be trifled with. He would have to be very careful in his dealings with her going forward.

He hung up the receiver and called Stacy back into his office. They had a lot of work to do to start building a case for a client he was pretty sure was going to be arrested very soon.

Chapter 22

Monika and Bruce spent the next day trying to firm up the case against Ron Whittaker, while at the same time trying to rule out the possibility of any other suspects. They tracked down Whittaker's secretary, Anne Fowler, at her home in Snohomish and interviewed her. At first, she'd been unwilling to talk to them, stating she'd been ordered not to talk to anybody about Whittaker by the security department at PSA. Monika called her contact at the FBI who called PSA security and conferenced Monika in. She'd handed the phone to Anne who was told to cooperate fully with the police in their investigation into Whittaker.

After getting clearance to speak to them, Fowler was willing to help, but wasn't able to provide much that they could use. She told them that Whittaker had been withdrawn in the last week and that he'd spent much of that time out of his office, a behavior she claimed was unusual.

Monika asked her about the conversation Whittaker had with Gresham before his heart attack, but Fowler claimed she hadn't heard any of the actual conversation. She hadn't known there was a problem until Whittaker buzzed her and asked her to get an ambulance for Mr. Gresham.

After their mostly worthless interview with Anne Fowler, Monika called one of the technicians she was friendly with at the Washington State Patrol crime lab. They'd received the firearm she'd seized during the search of Whittaker's place, as well as the shell casings. He told her they'd done a preliminary match of the extractor marks with the rim of the shell casing, and he thought it was a very strong likelihood it would be the same weapon. They had to wait for the medical examiner to complete the autopsy and retrieve the bullet fragments from the victim's body before they could test fire the gun and make that comparison. He told her not to hold her breath though – the type of bullets that were in the magazine she submitted with the Beretta were the kind that were designed to disintegrate on entry into the body. He doubted they would get fragments large enough to compare.

Monika sent Bruce to the medical examiner's office to witness the autopsy that was scheduled for that afternoon, while she drove back to Whittaker's place to interview neighbors. Not one of the neighbors she talked to had seen Whittaker leave the house the previous Sunday. The houses in his neighborhood were pretty secluded, large lots and open spaces between them, with high fences where the houses were somewhat closer to each other. With that kind of arrangement, she realized there were very few opportunities for any of them to have seen anything, particularly in the winter when it's cold and raining and most people avoid going outside.

The day had been frustrating and mostly fruitless, she thought, as she headed back to the Sheriff's Office. Unfortunately, this was how major crimes investigations often went--long, tough days of unproductive interviews and futile driving around trying to firm up ideas and theories.

She spoke to Bruce on her way back. The autopsy had been completed and, like the lab guy had feared, the bullet fragments were all too small to be useful. The medical examiner said either one of the bullets would have killed Conner; two shots was overkill. Literally.

When she returned to the major crimes office on the fourth floor, most of the detectives had left for the day. The light was still on in Detective Sergeant Myers' office, though. He saw her walk into the cubicle farm and waved at her to come into his office.

"What's the latest?" he asked when she came in.

Monika plopped down in the chair in front of his desk. "Well, we have a possible motive, but it's sketchy." She filled him in on her interview with Gerry Gresham and her conversation with the lab guy at the WSP crime lab regarding the gun. As she was finishing her report, Bruce Norgaard walked in and sat down in the chair next to her.

He caught Sergeant Myers up on the report from the autopsy about the cause of death and the information that the bullet fragments found were too small to have value in a ballistics comparison.

"My instinct is that we should go ahead and make an arrest," Myers told them.

"Well, I agree, but I did talk to Dana Porter yesterday and she thought we should wait for the ballistics," Monika replied.

"Apparently there aren't going to be any ballistics, and the lab guy told you that the tooling marks were likely to be a match." Myers swiveled in his chair, chewing on the end of his pen and looking up at the ceiling. "There are a couple of problems with holding off on the arrest," he continued. "The first is that the media is swarming, demanding answers and demanding an arrest. The second is that I've got the lieutenant breathing down my neck wanting to know when we're going to make an arrest."

This was typical, thought Monika-- *office politics dictating the direction of a murder investigation.*

"And the third thing, the most important thing," Myers continued, "is, what happens if we hold off on the arrest and Whittaker kills again? Or he decides to run? We're fucked. We know we have probable cause for his arrest, and this is a big enough deal that I don't think we should be messing around. It could come back to bite us on the ass."

It was hard to argue with that kind of logic, Monika knew. There was a lot of potential liability in allowing a suspect to remain free when probable cause existed for his arrest.

"What about Dana Porter?" she asked.

Myers shrugged. "Call her up, talk to her, get her blessing if you can, but let's make the arrest either way--tonight if possible, tomorrow at the latest. I don't want this guy out on the street while we try to get ourselves to 100% when we don't need that to make the arrest."

"Okay, I'll give Dana a call right now and then we'll go see if we can find Whittaker," Monika replied.

She left Myers' office and went to her desk in the cubicle farm. Bruce followed and sat down at the desk next to hers while she called Dana Porter's office.

She got Dana's voicemail and glanced at her watch. It was 6 o'clock and she guessed Dana had probably left for the day. Pulling up her list of contact numbers for the prosecutor's office, she found Dana's cell phone number and called that.

"Dana Porter," she answered.

Monika identified herself and then went right into her reason for calling. Dana told her she was in the car driving home, and Monika said she would make it quick. She outlined the case again, just in case Dana had forgotten any of the details, and then told her what they'd found that day. She told her she was getting a lot of pressure to make an arrest and didn't think she was going to be able to hold off.

"Well, look," said Dana, "you have PC for the arrest, there's no question of that. The case isn't 100% but I see why you think Whittaker is the only possible suspect. If you want to make an arrest, then make it. I know you don't need my blessing to do so, but you have it. I just need to make sure you're going to be able to help me firm up a few of the things we're missing or lacking, such as the motive."

Monika thanked her and hung up the phone. Turning to Bruce, she said, "I know it's late but you want to come with me?"

Bruce grinned. "Of course I do. Are we going to call his attorney and let him know?"

"Let's go see if we can find him at home first. I don't like that scumbag attorney and I'd love to go around him."

She poked her head into Myers' office and told him Dana had given her blessing for the arrest. Myers gave her the thumbs up, and she and Bruce headed down to her car.

When they got to Whittaker's neighborhood, she pulled right up to the front of his house, not bothering to be deceptive, figuring they might as well approach this thing head on. Bruce walked around to the back of the house, in case Whittaker decided to flee, and Monika knocked on the front door.

No light came from the windows she could see, and there was no answer at the door. She walked down the front porch trying to peer into the windows through the blinds that were drawn, to no avail. After ringing the doorbell and knocking a few more times, she called Bruce on the radio and told him to come back around to the front. The arrest was apparently going to have to wait.

On their drive back to the Sheriff's Office, Monika used her cell phone to call in to dispatch. She told the dispatcher what she wanted, and the dispatcher told her she would get it done right away.

Monika dropped Bruce off at his car and drove home for the night. Hopefully tomorrow would be a more fruitful day.

***

The man with the scar on his face was cooking dinner-- two hotdogs boiling in a pot on the stove and a can of baked beans just starting to simmer. He turned down the heat on both and pulled a plate out of the cupboard next to the stove. As he started to spoon dinner onto his plate, his police scanner crackled with a message that caused him to freeze.

Attention all units: prepare for a broadcast regarding probable cause to arrest for the crime of first degree murder.

The man with the scar set down the ladle he'd been using and waited. He'd listened to the scanner all day, and he suspected this was what he'd been waiting for.

Attention all units, continued the broadcast. *The Snohomish County Sheriff's Office holds probable cause for the arrest of one Ronald Peter Whittaker, date of birth 05/17/1978. Whittaker is thought to be driving a green Land Rover SUV, 2014 model, Washington license plate number AVO5627. Probable cause exists for the arrest of Whittaker for the crime of murder, first degree.*

He should be considered armed and dangerous. If located, immediately contact Detective Monika Sodafsky for booking instructions. Again, probable cause exists for the arrest of Ronald...

The dispatcher continued droning on, but the man with the scar tuned her out. He picked up his phone and dialed a number. When the call was answered, the man with the scar simply said, "The broadcast just went out. County wide broadcast for first degree murder."

The man on the other end of the line thanked him and hung up. The man with the scar turned off the police scanner and finished dishing up his dinner. He carried it into his living room to eat in front of the TV. That had been relatively painless, and part three of his job was complete. It would be quite a while before he was needed for the final part of his contract, and he intended to enjoy himself while he waited.

Chapter 23

Franklin Richardson glanced impatiently at his watch. It was only 7am, and he was tired. He'd gotten a call last night from Ron Whittaker, who'd told him he needed to be in the lobby of the Silver Cloud Inn no later than 7am. Franklin had bristled at the order originally, but had eventually realized that a smart lawyer didn't argue too much with his only client.

REASONABLE DOUBT | Rick Fuller

Whittaker told him to be on the lookout for any police officers that might be in the lobby or around the hotel and to notify him if he saw any. Franklin had obviously been concerned about this, but had simply agreed.

Now, as he looked around the lobby, he eyed a Hispanic gentleman suspiciously. He was sitting on the couch near the reception area, reading the paper. Franklin was distrustful of anybody who still read an actual newspaper, but finally decided the guy didn't have the look of a cop. He also seemed engrossed in the newspaper and wasn't looking around or watching the doors.

Just a few minutes after 7:00, the elevator doors opened, and Whittaker stepped into the lobby carrying a briefcase along with a manila envelope, thick with whatever was inside it. He was dressed in a nice suit, but wasn't wearing a tie which was, coincidentally, exactly how Franklin himself was dressed.

Whittaker walked quickly up to him and handed the briefcase over to him.

"Take this," Whittaker said, not even bothering with any good morning pleasantries.

"What's this, your porn collection?" Franklin asked, a grin on his face.

Whittaker didn't return the smile. "It's something I need my attorney to keep safe for me, in case I get arrested today. Do you think you can handle that?"

Franklin's smile disappeared. "Look, if this is something illegal, or some evidence or something about this issue, I can't take it. I could get in a lot of trouble, lose my license..."

Whittaker cut him off. "It's nothing like that. It's just a few important papers and documents that I need to keep safe, especially if I go to jail. These are things that I don't want left in my house if I'm locked up, okay? I need someone I can trust to keep them safe for me."

Franklin nodded. "Okay, I can do that. I'll put it in the safe in my office."

"Good," Whittaker said. "The briefcase is locked, and I expect it to remain that way. I also don't want you to let anybody know you have it, including your secretary, Stacy, who you, for some reason, call Anastasia. I'm assuming she has the combination to your safe?"

Franklin nodded, irritated at the inside information Whittaker seemed to know.

"Change it," he ordered. "Only you should have that." He pointed at the briefcase. "Have I made clear the importance of keeping this safe?"

"I think I get it, yes," Franklin replied, indignantly.

"Okay, let's go. We're headed to your office, I'll lead in my car, you follow in yours. Take this, too." He shoved the manila envelope into Franklin's hands.

"What's with all the subterfuge, Ron?" asked Franklin.

Whittaker stared at him. "The police are looking for me. They're going to arrest me today."

Franklin laughed. "I think I would know if they were going to arrest you, Ron. I have a lot of contacts in the police department and they would have let me know immediately."

Whittaker turned and walked out the door, calling back over his shoulder, "Well, they broadcast probable cause for my arrest, along with my description and that of my vehicle last night to every cop in the county. Perhaps you should reevaluate your contacts." He walked into the parking lot and got into his Range Rover, leaving Franklin standing there speechless.

Fucking Jackie Beatty, thought Franklin. This was all her fault.

***

They pulled in to the parking lot at Franklin's office and Franklin unlocked the door, letting Ron inside. It wasn't quite 8am and Stacy hadn't arrived yet. Franklin got the coffee maker going and told Ron to make himself comfortable in his office.

Once the coffee was ready, Franklin brought a steaming cup to Ron and sat down behind his desk.

"Okay Ron, I have a plan," Franklin began.

"Yes, you're making a plan and God is laughing," answered Ron.

"Never mind. Look, here's what we're going to do. In just a little bit here, you and I are going to go over to the Sheriff's office and I'm going to turn myself in. I just need to know one thing and I need you to drop all the hubris and all the pretension and I need you to give me a completely honest answer. I want to talk to the Franklin Richardson who drives a ten-year old Honda Accord, not the Franklin Richardson who pretends to own a Tesla."

Franklin lowered his gaze and nodded, feeling properly chastised. He wasn't sure how Ron Whittaker was able to make him feel this way every time they met, but he didn't like it. He seemed to feel cowed and emasculated when Whittaker looked him in the eye and demanded things of him. He wondered if it was just the money that Whittaker represented or if there was something else, some character flaw of his that guided his demeanor in these meetings.

"Okay," he answered. "What's the question?"

"It's Friday, and I have no desire to spend the weekend in jail. If I turn myself in this morning, can you get me a bail hearing today after booking?"

Franklin nodded. "That much, I assure you, I can do. As I'm guessing you already know, since you seem to know everything about me, I spent a few years in the prosecutor's office. I know most of the clerks over there, and I can get you on the docket for a bail hearing today." He paused for a second, thinking and then added, "You're undoubtedly going to be arrested for first degree murder, though, Ron. The judge is probably not going to grant you bail."

Ron nodded. "That's why you and I are going to discuss right now how you're going to get me released. The first thing I need you to do is to take my briefcase over to your safe and lock it up in there."

Franklin nodded, carried the briefcase over to the safe, dialed in the combination and opened the door. The briefcase was a standard size, with a combination lock on each of the clasps, and he wasn't sure it would fit inside the safe. Luckily it slid in perfectly with no room to spare, and Franklin found himself wondering how Ron had known the size of his office safe. He seemed to know a disturbing amount of personal information about Franklin.

"Let's get that combination changed while you're in there. You and me, Franklin, we're the only ones who are going to know this combination, okay?"

Franklin sighed and nodded. "What do you want to make the combination?"

The safe accepted a six-digit number as the combination, and Ron had the number ready to go, further reinforcing the idea that he'd somehow known exactly what type of safe Franklin had in the office. He was really having a bad feeling about this relationship.

He finished changing the combination, locked the safe, and returned to his desk.

Ron took a sip of his coffee, peering over the rim of his cup. "Why don't you open that envelope I gave you and take a look at the contents? Then we can get started on our plan."

Chapter 24

Detective Monika Sodafsky was in a great mood this morning. She'd just given a press briefing downstairs on the steps of the courthouse, announcing that they had a suspect in the Conner homicide and that they expected to make an arrest today. She refused to give them Whittaker's name and refused to confirm that Whittaker was the subject of the BOLO that had gone out the night before. Some of the reporters had apparently picked up this information on their police scanners. Her refusal to confirm that intelligence, she knew, would just lead them to speculate and put more pressure on Whittaker, wherever he was.

She'd had patrol units checking Whittaker's house and sitting on the end of his street throughout the night. He hadn't returned home. This morning, she called the security podium in the lobby of Puget Sound Aerospace and spoke to the supervisor. He'd told her that Whittaker's security clearance had been revoked and that he hadn't showed up for work the day before. He assured her that Whittaker wouldn't be allowed into the building, and that if he showed up, they would call her immediately.

Monika was in a good mood simply because she felt they had the right guy, and the case was well on its way to being solved. The longer Whittaker remained on the loose, though, the faster her good mood was going to disappear.

"Maybe we ought to check with that attorney of his, this Richardson guy," suggested Bruce Norgaard. They were sitting in the cubicle area of Major Crimes, discussing the best way to go about tracking down Whittaker.

"I called him first thing this morning. There was no answer," Monika replied. "Maybe we should swing by his office and see if he's in."

"It might be a good idea to start thinking about having Whittaker's passport blocked, maybe checking with Port of Seattle Police at SeaTac to see if he's trying to fly, calling Border Patrol and letting them know, too, in case he tries to drive to Canada."

Monika nodded. If Whittaker found out he was officially wanted, he could be in Canada in less than two hours. She hesitated to take those steps without an official arrest warrant, but notifying the airport police and the Border Patrol involved just a couple of phone calls. Those calls might end up saving her a very big headache later.

She was reaching for the phone on her desk to make the calls when it beeped and lit up, the intercom feature activated from the receptionist in the Sheriff's Office lobby.

"Detective Sodafsky?" came Betty's voice over the phone's speaker.

"Yes, Betty?"

"There are two gentlemen here to see you, Ronald Whittaker, and his attorney, Franklin Richardson. He says he's here to turn himself in."

Monika looked up at Bruce and grinned. Today was definitely going to be a good day.

"I'll be right there," she replied.

Chapter 25

Franklin was in the court clerk's office, and he was beginning to sweat. Things were not going well.

"Bail hearings happen the next day, Franklin, not the same day," announced the clerk, a woman named Judy whom Franklin knew from his time as a prosecutor. He was wracking his brain trying to remember if he'd ever done anything to Judy or anybody she knew and he couldn't think of anything. Thank God.

"Bail hearings happen at 11:00am every day, Judy. It's only 9:30 right now. All I'm asking is that you put my client on the list for this morning's hearing. It's Friday for crying out loud, if he doesn't get on the list today, he'll have to wait until Monday; that's not right!"

Judy sighed and turned to her computer, typing for a minute. "He's not even listed on a booking sheet, Franklin. There's nothing I can do."

"He's being booked right now, Judy. I promise you, he'll be in the system in just a few minutes; can you please just put his name on the judge's calendar for the 11:00am hearing?"

When Sodafsky had come out to the lobby earlier with that other detective, Franklin and Whittaker were waiting for her. Sodafsky had acted professionally, bringing Whittaker back into the office with Franklin following, and agreeing not to handcuff him while she processed him. They escorted him into a back office where they fingerprinted him and took his booking pictures. Sodafsky then told him she was required to handcuff him for the walk across the street to the jail for his booking. Franklin asked if she could at least handcuff him in front of his body, using his jacket to cover the handcuffs to avoid any embarrassment. Sodafsky agreed and thanked Whittaker for being cooperative. Franklin was even more attracted to her than he'd been before.

Now he was doing his best to fulfill his promise to Whittaker and get him on the calendar for the bail hearing today. If Ron ended up having to spend the weekend in jail, Franklin could only imagine how quickly he would be getting fired. Of course, he thought there was a good chance Ron would be spending the weekend in jail anyway: it was tough to get bail in a felony case of this magnitude.

Franklin gave Judy the best wounded puppy-dog look he could muster, hoping that it would be enough. She stared at him a moment and sighed.

"Okay." She typed some more at her computer. "His name is on the docket. I need you to check back in with me by 10:30 so I can attach the booking report information and get him brought over here before the hearing starts."

"Thank you, thank you, thank you, Judy! You are the best! Can I kiss you right now? Please? Just a little one?" Franklin leaned forward over the counter, causing the other clerks to glance up.

Judy laughed and pushed him back. "Get out of here. Come see me before 10:30!"

"I will, I promise." Franklin started to leave, then turned back. "Hey, what judge is doing the bail hearings this morning?"

Judy turned to the computer. "Judge Neil Chapman, courtroom five."

Crap, thought Franklin. Chapman was the one who had approved the warrant. It looked like he was going to be involved in every step of this case. Franklin knew he had better make a good first impression since he and Chapman were going to be seeing a lot of each other in the near future.

Chapter 26

"Your Honor, the State intends to file a charge of first degree murder against Mr. Whittaker, as well as other felony charges, possibly including kidnapping or unlawful imprisonment. These crimes will carry a maximum penalty of life in prison without the possibility of parole. I don't think I need to tell you the danger that Mr. Whittaker represents to the public, not to mention the risk that he might choose to flee in light of the penalty he's facing. We would request that you do not assign bail in this matter and that the defendant remain incarcerated until trial."

Jason Garvey was the prosecutor assigned to the bail hearings this morning, and Judge Chapman was only partially listening. He was busy reading the booking sheet on the defendant, Ronald Whittaker. He remembered the name from the search warrant he had approved only a few days earlier. The detectives had moved quickly, apparently, if Mr. Whittaker had already been booked and was in his courtroom.

Chapman hadn't yet had an opportunity to review the return of service from the search warrant, and now he jotted a note to himself in his folder reminding himself to take a look at it.

Looking up, he took his first close look at Whittaker's attorney, Franklin Richardson. Richardson looked vaguely familiar, but Chapman couldn't remember where he'd seen him before. Ron Whittaker was seated next to Richardson, wearing the orange jumpsuit of the Snohomish County Jail, and shackled to the chair. A corrections officer stood nearby and watched over him with his ever-present scowl.

"I'm generally inclined to agree with the State in matters of significance such as this. Mr. Richardson, do you have anything to add that might be relevant to this before I make a ruling?"

"I do, Your Honor," Richardson said, standing. "If it please the court, my client, Mr. Whittaker, called me this morning and told me he had heard the Sheriff's Office was looking for him and that they were planning to arrest him. He came directly to my office, and together we walked over to the Sheriff's Office where Mr. Whittaker turned himself in. Your Honor, Mr. Whittaker has no intention of fleeing. He is innocent of these charges, and he looks forward to the opportunity to defend himself against them."

Richardson reached down to a paper on the desk in front of him and picked it up, handing it to the court clerk who passed it on to Chapman. "I know that this court has the ability to look up Mr. Whittaker's criminal record for itself, but I took the liberty of printing it out. As you can see, Your Honor, Mr. Whittaker has a spotless record. He's never been charged with any crime, never been arrested, and in fact, until yesterday, he held a Top-Secret government clearance, a clearance that was revoked solely because of the charges he's facing today, outrageous charges of which he's innocent. In fact, judge, Mr. Whittaker's only contact with the police in the last decade was a single speeding ticket."

Richardson walked back to the defense table and continued. "Mr. Whittaker is a valued and trusted member of this community. He owns a home in Mukilteo, he works at Puget Sound Aerospace here in Everett, or at least he did before these charges were filed and his security clearance was revoked because of them. He has no intention of going anywhere, Your Honor."

Richardson reached into the manila envelope on his desk and pulled out a passport, holding it up for Chapman. "Your Honor, the moment Mr. Whittaker found out the police were looking for him, he came to me. He brought me his passport, which he is willing to surrender, and he brought me the means to post bail." Richardson pointed to the envelope. "He's more than willing to submit to electronic monitoring as well. Mr. Whittaker intends to fight these charges, Your Honor, and to regain the liberties that have been unfairly stripped from him today. He's not going anywhere."

Chapman thought that was pretty fairly put and turned back to Garvey. "Mr. Garvey?"

Garvey hesitated a moment which Chapman thought was fairly telling. It appeared that he'd even been swayed by Richardson's impassioned plea.

"If the court is considering bail in this case, we would request that it be a significant amount, Your Honor. A million dollars at least."

Chapman turned back to Richardson. "What's in the envelope you brought, Mr. Richardson?"

Richardson picked up the envelope. "Your Honor, this is $250,000 in certified cashier's checks that Mr. Whittaker is prepared to post with the court today."

Chapman nodded, thoughtfully. A defendant willing to post $250,000 in cash was probably a better risk than one who posted a million-dollar bond which typically required only $100,000 to acquire. In addition, the lack of any kind of criminal record and a willingness to turn himself in showed a respect of the law that would seem to indicate to Chapman that Whittaker was probably not a threat to the community.

Chapman's job was to balance a defendant's presumption of innocence with a responsibility to the community. That responsibility was twofold: to keep members of the community safe from those who would do harm, and to make sure a defendant showed up in court to answer the State's charges.

He didn't see a reasonable expectation that either of these issues would be compromised by granting bail.

"Okay. I'm going to accept the bail amount of $250,000 in certified checks from Mr. Whittaker, along with the surrender of his passport to the clerk of the court. I'm also going to order electronic monitoring at Mr. Whittaker's expense, and I'm going to order that he not be allowed to leave Snohomish County without prior approval." Chapman banged the gavel on the block. The court clerk handed him the bail sheet, he signed it and passed it back to her.

"Call the next case, please."

Chapter 27

The processing and paperwork took a few hours. Nothing moves quickly in the court system, but Franklin got this matter fast-tracked, and he was proud to be standing at the exit of the jail waiting for Whittaker's release at 2:00pm.

The door opened, and Whittaker came strolling out, wearing the suit he'd worn when they turned him in at the Sheriff's Office just a few hours earlier.

"How's it feel?" Franklin asked, proudly, as Whittaker walked over to him.

"Which part? The part where I was strip searched in front of an audience, or the part where my dignity was ripped from me while shackled to a chair wearing an atrocious orange jumpsuit in front of the media and the world?"

Franklin's smile faltered, and then Whittaker grinned.

"Just kidding, buddy. You did well in there. Very good indeed. I'm free and you came through with your promise to get me in front of a judge today, which I'm very happy about."

Franklin felt relieved, and he clapped Whittaker on the back. "So what's next?"

"Let's go to your office and have a chat. We have a lot of work to do."

They turned down Wall Street and headed toward Franklin's office building.

"When will my arraignment date be?"

The arraignment happened after the prosecutor filed formal charges. By law, official charges had to be filed within 72 hours of the bail hearing, which meant Monday morning, and the arraignment, the court hearing where the defendant would hear the charges, the potential penalties, and enter an official plea, had to occur within fourteen days. Franklin passed that on to Whittaker as they got to his office.

"Okay, so we have a week, maybe two, before the arraignment?" Whittaker asked, walking inside and smiling at Stacy who was sitting at the reception desk.

"Yes, I would expect it to happen toward the end of the week after next."

"And then they have to bring me to trial within ninety days, correct?"

The Sixth Amendment of the Constitution guaranteed a defendant the right to a speedy trial. It stipulated that an incarcerated defendant had to be brought to trial within sixty days, and a defendant out on bail had to be brought to trial within ninety days. The defendant could, however, waive that right and almost always did.

"Technically, yes," Franklin answered, walking into his office and sitting behind his desk. "But don't worry about that; we'll waive your speedy trial rights, and you can expect not to be in court for a year or more. We'll be filing motions and fighting to exclude evidence; it will take a long time."

"No. We won't be waiving speedy trial."

Franklin frowned. "That would be highly unusual and not at all recommended."

"Why not? Why don't I want to get my name cleared as soon as possible?"

"We need the extra time to prepare a good defense. Look, witnesses change their minds when a lot of time passes; they forget things, hell, sometimes they die before they can testify! Taking more time is a benefit to us."

"The extra time also helps the prosecution build their case, right?" Whittaker asked.

"Technically, yes, but I'm telling you, it helps us more than it helps them."

Whittaker shook his head. "I've lost my security clearance, I'll probably be getting fired today. I've handed you all the money I have, both to post the quarter million in bail, and the other $100,000 I gave you for my defense. No, I need to get to trial quickly. We're not going to waive my Sixth Amendment rights."

In addition to the ten certified checks for $25,000 each that were in the manila envelope Whittaker had given Franklin this morning, there had been four others, made out to FDR Law, each for $25,000. It was more money than Franklin had ever seen at one time, and Whittaker had already told him that if he got him out on bail today, he could deposit all of them in his account to use as prepayment for his defense. That was one (or four!) of the reasons he'd been so motivated this morning.

In addition to that, Whittaker had also promised Franklin that he would double his courtroom rate if he could get him released. That meant he would be paid $800 per hour for court time, a mind-boggling amount. Whittaker had been prepared to blow Judge Chapman if that was what it took to get him to set bail. Thank God it hadn't come to that.

"Ninety days takes us to mid- or late April. The trial will be over by mid-May at the latest. That's perfect timing." Whittaker mused.

"Perfect timing for what?" Franklin asked.

"Never mind," Whittaker said quickly, shaking his head.

Franklin looked at him suspiciously, wondering what the timeframe meant and why mid-May was important.

"Forget I said that," Whittaker continued. "We have a lot of motions I'm going to want you to file and a lot of things to discuss. We have only ninety days to prepare. Let's get to work."

Part Two

Chapter 28

Judge Neil Chapman entered the courtroom and heard his clerk, Linda Gruber call out, "All rise!" He walked over to his high-backed leather chair and lowered himself into it, adjusting his robes so he wasn't sitting on the folds as he did so. He'd long ago learned that comfort was the most important thing in a trial that was going to require him to sit here for the next three weeks, maybe longer. He hadn't gotten to the point of no return that some colleagues had; they wore black sweat pants that looked like dress pants under their robes, but he did recognize the need for comfort.

Linda was finishing her standard statement: "Snohomish County Superior Court is now in session, the Honorable Neil Chapman presiding."

For some time during his career, Chapman loved that everybody stood when he entered or left the room. He secretly reveled in the implied respect that had come from that attention, from being the focal point in the room. A judge in his courtroom was about the closest thing to royalty this country has. His powers are very nearly absolute and, in Chapman's younger years, he'd enjoyed the glory of wielding those powers. That was nothing more than a level of extreme immaturity, though. He'd long since come to the understanding that with those powers came a great responsibility. He also understood that it was not respect for the person that garnered the attention; it was respect for the position. The person was required to *earn* the respect that the office signified, and Judge Chapman strived at every opportunity to be the kind of judge that the robes, the office, and the people demanded.

"Please be seated," he ordered and waited for the commotion of a hundred people sitting to die down. He spoke into his microphone, listening to the echo of his voice, making sure he could be heard throughout the courtroom.

"In just a minute I'm going to call the case on the docket here, but I want to first take a moment to remind everyone here that this is a court of law. The proper administration of that law, and of justice, is my primary focus." He took a moment to look around at the spectators before continuing. "I know that we have a lot of media in the room, and I'm going to allow that for the time being. If there are any issues, any outbursts, any gimmicks, anything that disrupts this trial in any way, I will order the bailiff to clear this courtroom first of the miscreants involved, and then of all spectators if need be, to see that justice is served without incident or delay. Have I made myself clear?"

He waited as a chorus of, "Yes, Your Honors" and nodding heads swept softly through the room. He then looked down at his docket sheet.

"Okay, we're about to begin the State versus Ronald Peter Whittaker. I'll read the charges in this case." He picked up the sheet and read from it. "Charge one is Murder in the First-Degree. Charge two is Unlawful Imprisonment."

He set the sheet down and looked at the prosecutor. "Mrs. Porter, is the state ready to begin?"

"We are, Your Honor," replied Dana Porter.

Chapman looked at Franklin. "Mr. Richardson, is the defense ready?"

Franklin stood up. "We are, Judge."

"Okay." Chapman looked over at the bailiff. "Please show the jury in."

The bailiff opened the door to the jury room and the jurors began filing in, twelve primary jurors and three alternates, all looking curiously, first at Ron Whittaker, and then out at the media, then the prosecutor's table, and lastly at Judge Chapman, before finally sitting down.

Chapman knew they were all feeling a little nervous and a little anticipatory. He'd interviewed enough jurors, been through enough post-trial jury polling and questioning, to know that the reaction was standard and normal. It was his job to relax them, not to the point that they didn't feel the burden of what they were here for, but to a level where they understood their duty and were comfortable with it.

He began with his normal jury instructions, reading off the sheet in front of him, though he knew them by heart. It was important that he get every one right, that he not miss a step, not just for his own personal sense of responsibility, but because if he did miss a step and a conviction was ruled, it would be grounds for the defense to request, and almost certainly to be granted, a mistrial. So, much like the veteran cop, who knows every word of the Miranda warnings by heart, but still reads them to the suspect off the laminated card, Chapman read the instructions off the sheet in front of him.

It took him a solid ten minutes, after which the jurors' attention was beginning to wander, a sign that they had begun to relax, something that was good in the long run. Chapman felt that he'd adequately stressed to them the importance of paying attention to every bit of evidence, not drawing conclusions from things that weren't said, or that were ordered stricken from the record and, in particular, not assuming or inferring anything that wasn't specifically entered as sworn testimony.

"Council," he finally addressed Dana Porter when he finished, "does the State wish to present an opening statement?"

Dana stood at her desk. "We do, Your Honor."

"Very well, please proceed."

Chapman sat back in his chair and watched as Dana approached the jury, smiling at them and addressing them in a smooth, confident voice. He'd seen her in action several times, and he thought she was a star in the Prosecutor's Office. She was good looking, smart, eloquent, and formidable; he would hate to be a defendant in a case she was prosecuting. Also seated at the prosecution table was a deputy prosecutor named Jason Garvey who Chapman only knew from the bail hearing months prior. He had put up only a half-hearted fight during that bail hearing, but Chapman figured if Dana had chosen him to assist her with this prosecution, he was probably a good attorney overall.

It was expected by the system in general, and by himself in particular, that prosecutors in his courtroom, as representatives of the State, refrain from inflammatory and abusive argument, maintain their objectivity as agents of the court, and behave at all times in an exemplary and professional manner. Dana Porter was a walking personification of those ideals, not something he could say about every prosecutor that came through his courtroom.

He listened now to her opening statement, watching as she captured the jury's attention. She spoke slowly and softly, her eyes moving back and forth among the fifteen jurors; all of their eyes followed her.

"May it please the court: members of the jury, welcome, and thank you for being here. January 3rd, 2016 was a normal Sunday in the life of Ronald Conner. He held an important position for our nation's security and defense, a position that required him to have a Top-Secret security clearance; a position that required him to work sixty hours a week, sometimes more, doing a job that helped to ensure the safety of this nation. Sunday was his day of rest, the only day he allowed himself to take a break, to watch his beloved Seattle Seahawks play football; to relax and unwind from the stress of his long work week. It was also a day when he spent time with friends and with family, enjoying the fruits of his labor, much like you and I do."

"It was a rainy day, the kind of day where you long to spend your time on the couch, in front of a warm fire, ordering takeout and just relaxing, knowing that the next day your long work week will begin again. We are going to show you evidence that will prove to you that on the night of January the 3rd, 2016, the defendant, Ronald Whittaker, went over to Mr. Conner's house at around 10:00pm. Mr. Whittaker left his phone at home, knowing that it could be tracked by finding out what cell phone towers it was pinging at the time. He knocked on Mr. Conner's door and Mr. Conner, thinking that Mr. Whittaker was a friend, a good friend...a lifelong friend actually, willingly let him into the house. Once inside, Mr. Whittaker and Mr. Conner ordered food, takeout from the Thai restaurant down the street. They ate the food, after which, Mr. Whittaker overpowered Mr. Conner, striking him on the head, knocking him unconscious, and then duct taping him to a chair. Hours later, he shot him," she paused, staring at the jury, her eyes wide, an expression of disbelief on her face, "not once, but twice. BAM! BAM! Two shots to his best friend's chest."

She turned and walked away from them, in the direction of Ron Whittaker who was sitting comfortably in his chair, a relaxed look on his face.

"Now, you're probably wondering why Mr. Whittaker would be so upset with his lifelong friend that he would do such a horrible and despicable thing."

Dana stared at Ron Whittaker for a moment, and Chapman tried not to smile. It was a brilliant show, and the jury was all ears, their eyes leaving Dana to flick momentarily in the direction of Whittaker before returning to Dana.

"He did such a thing for just one reason: Jealousy." She turned quickly back to the jury, a look of disbelief on her face. "Yup, that's right, jealousy. You see, Mr. Conner was about to get a promotion at work. He was about to get a job that would pay him a lot more money, that would, in fact, make him Mr. Whittaker's direct supervisor. It was a job that Mr. Whittaker himself had applied for, had dreamed of attaining for a long time. And Mr. Whittaker was angry. So angry, in fact, that he chose to kill Mr. Conner rather than allow him to be promoted into that coveted position."

Chapman tuned Dana out a bit, still listening in the background as she continued telling the jury how the evidence was going to point at Whittaker and only at Whittaker and how she was going to prove the State's case.

Chapman took a moment to study Ron Whittaker. He had seen the entire spectrum of emotions from defendants during his years of presiding over cases such as these. Some couldn't handle the pressure; they broke down or they got angry at the words being hurled in their direction. Some remained calm on the outside, simply stirring in their chairs or looking away from the prosecutor or the witnesses testifying against them. Most of them were terrified on the inside, though, and if you knew what to look for, it showed. It was a rare defendant indeed who appeared like Ron Whittaker looked now.

He was calm, and Chapman didn't think it was an act. He had a slouch that couldn't be faked, a relaxed posture that, were it any more exaggerated, might have approached insolence. He was looking curiously at Dana Porter as she gave her elegant opening statement, his full attention on her as if he was merely a spectator hanging on every word, waiting for a conclusion that would have no impact on him personally. If his demeanor were an act, then he was a brilliant actor. Somehow Chapman didn't think Franklin Richardson was a good enough coach to have been able to instruct Whittaker to that extent.

Someday, perhaps, somebody would study defendant posture and expression during a trial and figure out what the guilty looked like and what the innocent looked like. There were lots of studies about how best to appear to a jury, but none that he was aware of that actually dissected the moments of pure honesty when the defendant was certainly not acting, to see how the guilty and innocent differed.

He refocused on Dana as she concluded her opening statement.

"Every bit of the evidence, ladies and gentleman, points directly at Mr. Whittaker. Every bit. Not even the tiniest shred of evidence points toward any other person. Ron Whittaker and Ron Whittaker alone carefully planned and executed this heinous and despicable act, and we will show you exactly how and why he did it. Thank you."

She turned and walked back to the prosecution table; all eyes followed her until she sat down, took a sip of water and looked at her notes. Judge Chapman turned to the defense table, "Mr. Richardson, does the defense wish to make an opening statement at this time?" It was up to the defense to make their statement now or wait until the State had presented its entire case. Most attorneys chose to try to counter the State's powerful opening argument with one of their own right away.

Franklin Richardson was apparently in that group. "We do, Your Honor," he replied, standing.

"You may proceed."

Chapman watched curiously as Richardson stepped out from behind the defense table, his hands empty, his gaze focused on the jury members. One of Chapman's fears when dealing with unknown defense attorneys was the distinct possibility of a future appeal on the grounds of incompetent counsel, should they lose and their clients get convicted. Every defendant is constitutionally entitled to a rigorous defense from a competent attorney, and Chapman knew this was Richardson's first murder trial. He'd looked carefully into Richardson's background during the motion phase of the trial, prior to jury selection. Richardson had the credentials (just barely) to serve as Whittaker's defense attorney, despite his lack of experience. Not for the first time, Chapman wondered why Whittaker, a man who had the resources to post a quarter of a million dollars in bail, had chosen to hire an attorney with such a cavernous gap in experience level.

Richardson walked up to the jury box and stood there looking at the jurors. Just as the silence was starting to become uncomfortable, he smiled warmly.

"Ladies and gentleman of the jury, welcome and thank you for being here. My name is Franklin Daniel Richardson, and I have the honor of representing Mr. Ronald Whittaker, a man I've come to know quite well over the last few months. It's my sincere hope that over the coming weeks, you will have the opportunity to know Mr. Whittaker as I've come to know him, to see him as the sincere, honest, and principled man that I know him to be."

Franklin turned then and motioned toward Whittaker who still sat relaxed in his chair with his hands folded in his lap.

"Ron Whittaker, ladies and gentlemen, is an innocent man--not just because the Constitution demands that he be presumed innocent, but because he is, in fact, innocent. Ron Whittaker is a man who is grieving. He's a man who, over the last few months, has had an incredible and nearly unbearable strain put on his life, on his health, and on his happiness. You see, on January 3rd of this year, Ron Whittaker had his best friend taken from him--his lifelong friend, a man he'd known since the first grade, a man he'd lived with in college, took vacations with, spent weekends and evenings with, and even worked with."

"Ron Whittaker lost his best friend in the early morning hours of January 4th, but that was just the start of his problems. Before he could even begin the grieving process, he suddenly found himself having to defend against a first-degree murder charge. Not only had he lost his best friend, but the police unexpectedly decided he was responsible for that death. Ron Whittaker is an upstanding citizen of this country, so trusted, in fact, that he held one of the nation's highest security clearances."

"Ladies and gentlemen, you'll notice I said *held* and not *holds*. That's because that Top-Secret security clearance, a clearance that only a very few people in the country have the privilege of holding, along with his job and livelihood, was yanked from Mr. Whittaker the minute it was found that he was even a *suspect* in this terrible crime."

He looked at the jury members plaintively, making sure they all took note of the wounded look on his face. "There is no due process, folks, not when it comes to the government and their revocation of a security clearance. In the span of just a few days, Ron Whittaker went from being a successful, trusted, productive member of society, to an outcast, a man who lost his job, his trustworthiness, and his ability to make a living, not to mention his lifelong best friend."

Judge Chapman listened to Richardson's opening statement and felt encouraged. He was doing well so far, leading the jurors along a path to a conclusion where they felt empathy toward the defendant, a solid start to any defense. He had done a fair job of humanizing Whittaker, unraveling the villainous veil that Dana Porter had tried to wrap him with, and Chapman was happy to see it. His job was to ensure a fair trial, and having the two attorneys near the same plane, ability-wise, would help with that.

Richardson continued. "Now, folks, you're going to see the prosecution present an enormous amount of evidence that is going to seem to point right at Ron Whittaker." He shrugged, looking directly at Dana Porter. "Some of the evidence we're going to show you will actually exonerate Mr. Whittaker. Some of it we'll show you is meaningless, and some of it we're going to show you was planted." He paused a long moment, staring at Dana Porter and allowing that last word to sink into the minds of the jurors.

He spun around and looked back at the jury. "Now, the prosecution is going to tell you that any claim that Mr. Whittaker was framed would be ludicrous. And if Mr. Whittaker were a normal person, ladies and gentlemen, they might be right. He's not, though. Ron Whittaker is a genius. His IQ level is so high, in fact, that if you were to gather 1,000 random people in a room, there is a very good chance that he would be the smartest person in that room."

Richardson paced back toward the jury box and lowered his voice slightly, causing them to lean in. "Mrs. Porter, the esteemed prosecutor, will tell you that, on one hand, Mr. Whittaker carefully planned this murder, spent a great deal of time mapping it out before putting it into motion. On the other hand, she's going to show you all of the evidence he left behind, evidence that points directly at himself. What I would like you folks to do is to remember; the entire time you're hearing all the evidence that seems to point directly to Ron Whittaker, that he is one of the brightest geniuses in this country. A genius who, according to the prosecutor, carefully planned the heinous murder of his best friend and yet somehow left all this evidence pointed right at himself." Richardson finished with a disbelieving look on his face, shaking his head and scoffing slightly. The jury members were now looking right at Dana Porter, gauging her reaction, and that, Chapman thought, was a good sign for the defense. This would have seemed to Chapman to be a good time to quit, but Richardson continued.

"Folks, the Bible says, in the Book of John, chapter 8 verse 32, *"And you will know the truth, and the truth shall set you free."* At the end of this trial you will know the truth. And, armed with that truth, it is our sincere hope that you will set Mr. Whittaker free, that you will set him on the path where he can begin to rebuild the life that has been torn asunder by this awful murder and the stain on his reputation that this trial is. Thank you, ladies and gentlemen."

Richardson walked back to his seat, and Chapman winced a little. The last few lines there were terrible. Invoking a Bible verse would tend to be polarizing at best. If the jury members were religious, they would either appreciate the verse or be offended that he was using it to play on their beliefs. If they were not religious, they would lose respect for Richardson for using religion as a crutch in his statement. It's always a better idea to play toward the middle ground of juries than it is to lean on the fringes where some might find offense.

Still, it was a decent start to the trial and, overall, Chapman was encouraged. He waited for Richardson to sit down at the defense table and then he looked over at Dana Porter.

"Mrs. Porter, is the State ready to proceed?"

She stood. "We are, Your Honor."

"Very well, you may call your first witness."

Chapter 29

"The State calls Detective Monika Sodafsky."

One of the courtroom deputies opened the back door and walked out, returning just a moment later with Detective Sodafsky in tow. During pretrial motions, Judge Chapman had excluded all potential witnesses from the courtroom until after their testimony had concluded, a standard practice but one that required the witnesses to wait around in the hallway, an exercise in tedium and patience at best.

Monika took the stand, raised her right hand, and swore to tell the truth, the whole truth, and nothing but the truth, so help her God. She was dressed in a dark suit: slacks and jacket, over a white shirt. Her detective's badge was pinned to her belt, and her Glock firearm was just visible behind the cut of her jacket, the perfect look for this case and one that Dana had requested of her.

The lead investigator was always one of the most important witnesses in the prosecution's case, and the badge and gun were subtle reminders to the jury that this was a police officer, a trusted member of society and one whose integrity was without question. That approach might not work for many juries in many areas of the country, but Dana had managed to get this jury stacked with citizens of above-average intelligence, citizens with above-average incomes, who lived in nice neighborhoods—the kind of citizens who had an appreciation for the police and for law and order in general. She still couldn't believe her luck with this draw. It was tough to get a *jury pool* of the caliber she had in general. And then the moron at the defense table had decided to use a bunch of his peremptory challenges, the free challenges that both sides got to eliminate jurors for any reason whatsoever without having to state a legal cause, to eliminate jurors who had seemed to be of below-average intelligence, jurors that Dana would have used her own peremptory challenges for.

She had been barely able to contain her delight every time that sleaze ball, Richardson, had stood up and challenged a juror that she thought was perfect for the defense, a juror who lived life near the poverty line and was much more likely to have had a negative experience with the police or believe the police capable of framing a citizen.

With some juries, Dana would have requested the lead detective to conceal their badge and gun, but not with this jury. This jury was much more likely than most to appreciate what that badge and gun symbolized.

Dana started by having Monika walk her through what she'd found when she first arrived at the homicide scene. Monika discussed the positioning of Conner's body, how he'd been lying on the floor at the foot of one of the dining room chairs.

Dana had blown up one of the crime scene pictures of Conner's body, and she now introduced it as State's exhibit one, having her assistant place it on an easel where the jury could see it. Using a laser pointer, Dana directed the beam toward the photo.

"Can you tell me if you noticed anything unusual about the victim's body?" she asked Monika.

"Yes, I did. I noticed that his wrists appeared to be red and swollen."

"Did you take a closer look at them?"

Monika nodded. "I did. I leaned in close and could see that it appeared there were patches of hair missing from his wrists and that the skin was clearly inflamed in a circular area across the upper part of the wrists."

Dana had State's exhibit two, a close-up photo of Conner's wrists, brought out and set up on the easel. She directed the laser pointer to the inflamed area of Conner's wrists.

"Detective Sodafsky, as a detective, what did these marks mean to you?"

Out of the corner of her eye, Dana saw Franklin stir a little at the question, and she smiled slightly. Her goal with her first witness in a case was always to see just how far the defense attorney would let her go before objecting to the questioning. Objections to questioning had to be handled carefully; too many of them that were borderline, and both the judge and the jury would begin to tire of them. Everybody wanted to hear the story and if you spent too much time interrupting that story for chippy reasons, you would lose credibility. On the other hand, you also need to make sure the other side was staying within the rules, and Dana's question was phrased in a very marginal way.

"They told me it was likely the victim had been restrained before his death."

"And what did you think had been used to restrain him?" Dana asked.

"Objection, Your Honor," Franklin finally interrupted, standing up. "Unless Mrs. Porter is willing to establish that Detective Sodafsky is some sort of bondage expert, this question calls for some serious speculation."

The courtroom tittered at his usage of the term "bondage expert"; even most of the jury members were smiling, and Dana mentally gave him credit for it. Not only had he correctly objected to her intentionally marginal question, he'd done so in a way that made the jury like him.

"Sustained," Judge Chapman replied.

Dana moved on smoothly, rephrasing the question. "Did you *see* anything that would lead you to a conclusion as to what had been used to restrain him?"

This was marginal too, but Franklin remained seated as Monika talked about the small bits of gray tape she had recognized as duct tape, that she had noticed on the bottom side of the arms of the chair behind the Conner's body.

Dana then walked Monika through her observations, starting with the two gunshot wounds in Conner's chest, and then her finding of the empty shell casing in the heater vent. She brought out several more large photos and marked them as State exhibits, showing the location of the heater vent in relation to the body, and showing the shell casing itself in its resting place in the vent.

Dana led Monika through her finding of the shell casing, establishing how she'd used her experience with firearms to predict the trajectory of the empty shell casing as it exited the gun, and how she'd discovered the casing itself. By the time she was finished and preparing to move on to the actual collection of the casing, it was a little after noon. The initial proceedings and the opening statements had taken most of the morning, and now Judge Chapman interrupted her.

"Let me stop you there, counselor. It's getting into the afternoon here, and I'd like to stop for lunch if this would be a good spot."

"Absolutely, Your Honor, this is a fine spot," Dana replied.

"Okay then, we'll take a lunch break now. I will remind the jurors that you're not to discuss the case in any way amongst yourselves or with any other party. We'll reconvene at 1:30pm sharp." He banged his gavel and stood up, his court clerk also stood and announced, "All rise."

Everybody waited until the jury members had filed out and Judge Chapman had left through his chamber door. Dana gathered up her papers, taking care to keep them all in order as she filed them into her briefcase. Deputy Prosecutor Jason Garvey gathered his things as well and then asked her, "Want to grab lunch?"

"Sure," she replied, "let's see if Monika wants to go as well I'd like to talk to her about this afternoon's testimony."

Chapter 30

Franklin exited the courthouse with Ron Whittaker and watched Dana, Jason, and Monika crossing the street toward the Fireside Café.

"Come on," he said to Whittaker. "I've got Stacy ordering us lunch at the office."

It wasn't raining, for once, and they quickly walked the two blocks to Franklin's office in silence, each lost in his own thoughts. Franklin's thoughts were consumed by the unusual nature of this relationship with Whittaker, and he meant to get to the bottom of it, preferably at lunch.

The culmination of his concerns had come during *voir dire*, the jury selection process. Franklin had his own idea of how a jury should be chosen, and he'd spent a lot of time studying the process. Even though this was his first murder trial as a defense attorney, Franklin knew what a friendly jury looked like, and this jury was not one of those.

He'd hoped to be able to use his expertise in studying the *voir dire* process to make a statement, to impress his client. Instead, he'd been censored even in that endeavor. Whittaker had given him the list of questions that he'd wanted asked on the jury questionnaire. Not included in that list of questions had been anything about objectivity or anything about bad experiences with cops or the court system, standard things to ask in any meaningful questionnaire. What had been included? A goddamn riddle. In one fell swoop, Whittaker had destroyed Franklin's entire game plan in his one area of expertise.

Whittaker wanted him to ask questions about education level and income, which was fine, but then he wanted him to eliminate anybody who hadn't graduated high school and anybody who didn't make at least $70,000 per year, which was just insane. It was pretty universally accepted that the higher the jurors' education levels, the more of a proponent they were of the rule of law. Prosecutors wanted smart people; the defense typically wanted dumb people who would make a ruling based on emotion. This applied even more when your entire case was built on the most ludicrous defense in the world, the, "Somebody else did it and they're framing me" defense.

At no point had Franklin been a proponent of these strategies. He wanted to attack the evidence. He told Whittaker that being friends with Conner had a plethora of benefits that would destroy the State's case against him. Who could say that he hadn't been out shooting guns with his best friend at some point and that the shell casing hadn't rolled into the heater vent months or years earlier? Who could say that the mud from his shoes came at the time Conner had been killed instead of the day before or the week before?

Whittaker asked him what his plan was for the fact that the bullets had been fired from the gun owned by him, the gun found in his closet, and Franklin told him that a vigorous cross-examination of the forensic technicians could well find holes in their testing process or in their results. Whittaker had laughed at him.

At the very least, he expected Whittaker to take advantage of his jury expertise, but he hadn't. Whittaker had instructed him, nay, *demanded* of him, to use all of his peremptory challenges on anybody with a known low IQ, anybody who didn't make a high salary, and anybody who was unable to solve the stupid fucking riddle.

Four fathers, two grandfathers, and four sons go to a theater to watch a movie. What is the minimum number of tickets they need to buy?

Whittaker provided him that riddle, told him to ask it on the juror questionnaire, and then told him to use his first peremptory challenges on anybody who didn't know the answer. He hadn't made Franklin come up with the answer (thank God), but simply told him that anyone who didn't give the answer *four* didn't belong on his jury.

Franklin didn't understand any of this, but he meant to get some answers.

He held open the door to his office and stepped aside to let Ron in. Stacy wasn't back with lunch, so Franklin turned on the lights and invited Ron back into his office.

"Let's have a chat about how the case is going so far," he said, as he settled behind his desk.

"Okay. I think it's going great. I think you gave a good opening statement, and I think the jury really likes you, mostly because you haven't said much." Ron winked at him, but Franklin wasn't in a joking mood.

"There were three spots in her testimony this morning where I would have objected if you hadn't instructed me not to. I don't understand this at all."

Whittaker had worked out a system where if Franklin wanted to object to a question, he would tap Whittaker on the leg, and Whittaker would then either shake or nod his head to let Franklin know if he was allowed to object. It was atrocious; a lousy, rotten way to run a case, and it didn't even work very well. By the time he tapped him on the leg and got the approval, the witness was likely to already be answering the question.

"What would have been the point of objecting to her questioning this morning?" Ron asked.

"We could have made her ask less leading questions, made her work harder to get information to the jury, and maybe even made it impossible for her to get some of the evidence into the record."

Ron chuckled. "Dana Porter is going to get the evidence into the record, Franklin. She's going to get every bit of it in there one way or the other, you better believe that. And I don't care if she does. The evidence is irrelevant. All you're going to do by objecting is piss off the judge, piss off the jury, and waste everybody's time. We won't be objecting to anything else that Detective Sodafsky has to say unless the line of questioning is completely ridiculous and a serious violation of court rules. It's possible we won't be objecting to anything the State has to present with *any* of its witnesses."

"I don't understand," Franklin replied.

"You don't need to understand, Franklin. Don't fight me on this. It's *my* life on the line here, and I want this case run *my* way. You don't need to do anything except follow my plan, follow my instructions, sit back, and make your $800 per hour. You do want to keep making $800 per hour, don't you?"

"Of course I do," Franklin muttered.

"Good! Then just relax, have fun, and maybe learn a little something along the way. *Listen to advice and accept instruction, that you may gain wisdom in the future.* That's from the Bible, Proverbs 19:20," Ron replied.

Another fucking bible verse, Franklin thought. It had been Ron who had asked him to put that bible verse in his opening statement, something he had been completely opposed to. "Are you at least going to share our defense strategy with me at some point in time? Maybe tell me what kinds of questions I'll be asking the defense witnesses?" he asked.

"Soon," Ron replied with a smile.

"Fucking fantastic," Franklin snarled, still stewing. He sure was glad Whittaker was having a good time, despite the unsettling prospect of spending the rest of his life in prison. He would have considered approaching the judge and attempting to withdraw as counsel, just on principle, but there were three major problems with that. The first was that Stacy would have killed him. The second was that passing on a job that was going to make him tens of thousands of dollars with very little actual work was against his religion. And the third was that Judge Chapman almost certainly wouldn't have let him withdraw. Defendants did have a right to run their own defense, after all, and there was no law that said they had to listen to their attorney, even if they were paying them a small fortune in fees.

Stacy finally arrived, carrying a bag of takeout from the sushi restaurant down the street. She unpacked the bags on the desk and passed out the orders to the two men; she pulled up a chair and started setting out her own order.

"Thanks for picking up lunch, Stacy," Ron told her.

She smiled. "Of course! We'll be doing this every day unless you want to do something different."

"No, I think it's a great idea to meet for lunch each day, maybe for dinner too."

Franklin watched the exchange with a sour feeling in his stomach. He really hated where all of this was going. He hated being told what to do in an arena where *he* was supposed to be the expert, and he didn't like the way Ron was looking at Stacy and talking to her.

Something needed to change.

Chapter 31

Judge Chapman called the court back to order for the afternoon session, and Dana announced she was ready to continue her direct examination of Monika Sodafsky.

Franklin and Ron arrived at the defense table in plenty of time for the start of the afternoon session, and now Franklin poured a cup of ice water and sat back in his chair. He wished the water was vodka or scotch or even goddamn Boone's Farm for fuck's sake, anything to take the edge off the way he was feeling about Ron Whittaker and his self-destructive methodology of running his own defense. Franklin was in a terrible spot; on one hand, he needed the money, on the other hand, he thought there was a really good chance he'd come out of this trial looking like an incompetent boob.

For the time being, he'd decided he had no choice but to take a 'wait and see' approach. Ron was sitting comfortably in his chair, a yellow legal pad on his lap and a pen in his hand, waiting for the testimony to start so he could take notes that he'd then give to Franklin to use during his cross-examination. Franklin was the figurative trained monkey, sitting on the sidelines and waiting for instructions.

Monika retook the stand and Judge Chapman reminded her that she was still under oath. Dana remained seated at the prosecution table for this round of questioning.

"Okay, Detective Sodafsky, what happened after you found the shell casing in the heater vent?"

Sodafsky gave a long narrative with only a few interruptions from Dana to clarify points. Franklin had to admit that Sodafsky was smooth and articulate, going at just the right speed through the crime scene, building a chronology that the jury could easily picture and follow. She was a great witness for the prosecution, and he could understand why Dana enjoyed using her as the State's primary witness.

Sodafsky testified that she had waited for the evidence technician to bag the shell casing and had it sent immediately to the county crime lab for a fingerprint extraction.

"And were they able to extract any fingerprints from the shell casing?" Dana asked her.

"Yes, they were able to pull a right thumb print from the side of the casing."

"Were they able to get a match on that thumbprint from the FBI database?"

"Yes, they were," Monika replied.

"And whose thumb print was it?"

"It was the defendant's thumbprint. Ronald Whittaker's."

Out of the corner of his eye, Franklin saw the jury members all turn and look directly at the defense table, right on cue, just as expected. Dana paused for a moment, purportedly to study her notes, but in truth, to allow the evidence to sink into the minds of the jurors. The defendant's thumbprint was found on a shell casing at the scene of a murder by shooting. Gasp!

Franklin would have yawned at the tedium of the act, had there not been twelve sets of eyes boring holes into his client seated right next to him. He wanted to turn and scream at them, "What the fuck did you think she was going to say, that it was somebody else's thumbprint?" but he stifled the urge.

He was glad to see that Whittaker had stopped his notetaking and was sitting still, a serene look on his face and in his demeanor. The last thing you want to be doing when the jury is focusing on you is frantically scribbling notes on your notepad. Well, maybe crying was the *last* thing you wanted to be doing, but scribbling notes was bad too.

Finally, after what seemed like an eternity, Dana looked up and continued with her questioning.

"We'll come back to the shell casing shortly, but let's move on for now. After you sent the shell casing off to the lab, what did you do next?"

Monika moved on from her narrative about the heater vent and discussed the bits of dried mud she'd seen on the dining room floor.

"Did you think the mud could have come from the shoes of the victim, Ron Conner?" Dana asked her.

"No, I didn't."

"Why not?"

"Well, for one thing, Conner wasn't wearing shoes, he was wearing only socks. For another, I had seen several pairs of shoes near the front door, and none of them appeared to have any mud on them."

"These were Conner's shoes near the front door with no mud on them?"

Franklin was furiously tapping Whittaker wanting to object to this question that clearly called for speculation on Sodafsky's part. How could she possibly know if the shoes by the front door all belonged to Conner unless he had put a tag on them that said, "These are Conner's shoes."

Nevertheless, Whittaker just shook his head, continuing to jot down notes and refusing to allow Franklin to interrupt and object to the question. Franklin burrowed into his chair, fuming at his forced incapacitation.

Sodafsky confirmed the shoes were Conner's, and Franklin saw Judge Chapman glance his direction. He gave Chapman a small, tight smile to hide his irritation. It wasn't a terrible breach to allow a leading or speculative question, but it was unusual, and he knew Chapman was likely starting to question his competence.

"After you had the evidence technician collect the dried mud fragments, what did you do next?" Dana asked.

"I moved into the kitchen and began looking for evidence there."

"And did you find any evidence in the kitchen?" Dana prodded.

Sodafsky explained that sitting on the counter near the sink were two cardboard containers of takeout food from Satay Thai, a restaurant close to Conner's house. Dana asked her to describe them, and Monika testified that they were mostly white, with a picture of the storefront at Satay Thai, along with the restaurant name. Dana brought out another blown-up crime scene photo and introduced it into State's evidence. The photo clearly depicted two takeout containers on the counter, a set of chopsticks protruding from the top of each container.

"Why did you feel this was important evidence?" Dana asked.

"Well, by all appearances, Mr. Conner lived alone, yet there were two containers of food which indicated to me that he'd had a guest over for a meal, probably for dinner. I suspected by then, and it was confirmed later, that Mr. Conner had been killed late that night or in the early morning hours, so this was likely the last meal he'd eaten."

"Detective Sodafsky, did you think at the time that you might find evidence in these containers that would further help identify your suspect?" Dana asked.

"I thought there was a very good chance the murderer had eaten from one of those containers and that we might be able to find evidence of that."

"And did you?"

"I had the crime scene guys bag up the food containers and the chopsticks, labeling each so we'd know which chopsticks came from which container of food. I then asked them to submit the chopsticks for DNA testing to see if we could identify a specific individual."

Dana pulled two sheets of paper from her file folder, introduced them as State's evidence, and then passed them up to Monika.

"Detective, I have here the lab results from the DNA testing that was done on the two sets of chopsticks you submitted. Can you tell me what they say?"

Monika glanced at the sheets, though she was obviously very familiar with what they said.

"One of the sets of chopsticks contained saliva which had distinct DNA markers identifying it as that of the victim, Mr. Ronald Conner. The other set of chopsticks had distinct DNA markers, also from saliva, identifying it as that of the defendant, Mr. Ronald Whittaker."

Dana did her cute pause again, looking down at her notes and allowing the jury to process this important new fact. Not only was Whittaker's thumbprint found on the shell casing, his DNA was also found in a food container located in Conner's house.

This new evidence was not nearly as significant as the thumbprint, Franklin knew. For starters, the defense was going to establish (at least he hoped they were), that Conner and Whittaker had been best friends. Best friends sometimes have meals together, so placing Whittaker at the scene of the crime was not too damaging. Franklin did have a copy of Dana's expected witness list, though, and he knew she planned to call the delivery guy from the Thai restaurant. His testimony would really begin to seal up a tight timeframe that would establish Whittaker's presence at the scene in close proximity to the time of the murder, which was circumstantial evidence, but very damaging nonetheless.

When Dana finished with her questions about the food containers, Judge Chapman called for a quick recess.

Franklin remained seated next to Whittaker as the courtroom cleared out. When there was nobody left within earshot, he turned toward him.

"I'm getting really frustrated here, Ron."

"Well, don't be," Whittaker replied.

"I can't just sit here like this. I'm feeling completely incompetent, and the judge is looking at me like I'm an idiot!"

Ron turned toward him, an angry look on his face. "I'm not going to keep having this conversation with you, Franklin. This is my call. I don't want to hear anything more about it. If you don't want to represent me, the judge will be back in a few minutes and you can tell him then. If you do that, get Stacy on the line and make sure she has a refund check ready for me for the unused balance of my retainer." He looked directly in his eyes. "Is that what you want to do?"

Franklin grumbled and spit out, "No."

"Good. Then let's hear no more of this. I'm going to use the restroom." Whittaker stood and walked out of the courtroom, leaving Franklin to stew alone. He needed to get over it and keep reminding himself how much money he was making.

It was the knock on his reputation that was the hardest thing for him, though. He sat there with his head hanging down before he eventually decided he had to let that go and stick with his lifelong mantra, *"Worry about the future when the future is the present."* With that in mind, he leaned back in his chair and closed his eyes, picturing all the ways he was going to spend the money he was earning.

Chapter 32

As Judge Chapman called the courtroom back to order, Dana couldn't help but think that, so far, things were going swimmingly. Other than the one objection Franklin raised early in her direct examination of Detective Sodafsky, he sat there silently. There were a couple of times she thought he was going to object, (a couple of times he *should* have objected, quite honestly), but he continued to sit there quietly and let her ask her leading and speculative questions. She was thrilled with the amount of latitude he was giving her and, if he allowed it to continue, it was going to make her job so much easier, particularly when she got some witnesses on the stand who weren't as easy and comfortable as Monika Sodafsky was.

She continued her direct of Monika, walking her back into the dining room scene and having her describe the body, its positioning, the two bullet wounds, as well as Conner's overall appearance, all backed up with the blown-up crime scene photos she continued to introduce into evidence.

She had Monika describe the chair sitting behind the prone body of the victim. Monika described the bits of duct tape residue on the bottom sides of the arm rests and on the back sides of both of the wooden legs on the front of the chair. She described the slatted back of the chair and, backed up again with photos, showed how one of the bullet fragments had nicked one of the slats on its way through before becoming embedded in the wall.

Most of the other bullet fragments had remained in Conner's body, and Monika talked about the location of the two entry wounds in his chest cavity, along with the exit wound in his back, showing how she had determined Conner was seated in the chair when he was murdered.

At the end of her questions regarding Monika's observations of Conner's body and the chair, Dana turned toward Judge Chapman.

"Your Honor, I'm reaching the end of my questions regarding the crime scene itself, and I'll be moving on next to the sequence of events that occurred after Detective Sodafsky left the crime scene. I noticed that it's almost 5:00pm and I wanted you to know this might be a good time to break for the day."

Dana knew that Chapman typically liked to hear testimony pretty late into the day during major cases, but that he also didn't like to stretch the attention span of the jurors on the first day. Most of them would have had trouble sleeping the night before the first day of a big trial, and they would be getting tired now. He preferred to build them toward the long days slowly.

She was also hoping he would call it for the day because of where she was in her testimony. If she continued now, she would end up having to stop right in the middle of important testimony about the search warrant Monika had served on Whittaker's house, and she didn't like to split testimony in unnatural spots.

"Thank you for the notice, Mrs. Porter. We'll go ahead and knock off right here for the day, and we'll reconvene tomorrow at 9am. I do want to advise everyone here that we will rarely be quitting early like this moving forward. I want this trial to conclude within three weeks, so be prepared for longer days in the future. I'll remind the jury members again that they aren't to speak to anybody about this case in any way, including each other. I'll also ask them to refrain from watching or reading any news stories about this case. Thank you for your attention today. You're excused."

He waited for them to file out and then continued, "Court is dismissed. I'd like to see both counsels in my chambers for a few minutes."

Everyone stood as Chapman left the courtroom, and then Dana gathered up her papers. She told Jason she would see him in her office when she was finished speaking with Chapman, and she walked to the clerk's door that led to chambers. Franklin arrived at the door at the same time.

"After you, Mr. Richardson," she said, smiling at him and motioning him to go ahead.

"Oh no, Dana, I insist, after you," he replied, leering at her.

She shuddered with revulsion at the suspicion that he wanted only to stare at her ass as she walked in front of him, but she proceeded through the doorway anyway. Working her way back toward Chapman's chambers, she studiously attempted to ignore the sound of his breathing as he followed behind her.

Dana knocked on Chapman's door and entered when he called out. He had already removed his judicial robes and was seated behind his desk looking at some paperwork.

"Please have a seat," he said, motioning to the two comfortable leather chairs in front of the desk.

"I want to talk about a couple of things," he said when they were both seated. "The first is the timeline of the State's case-in-chief. Mrs. Porter, you originally gave me an estimate of eight or nine days for your direct examination, including Mr. Richardson's anticipated cross examination, and I want to make sure, seeing how it seems you're going to spend two full days with Detective Sodafsky, that we're still on that timeframe."

"We are, Your Honor. Detective Sodafsky's testimony is the bulk of the State's case, and we should have no trouble getting everybody else's testimony in five or six days."

He nodded. "Mr. Richardson, do you still anticipate just two or three days for the defense's case?"

"I do, Your Honor."

"Okay, great. Next, I want to discuss the substance of the questioning I heard today. Mrs. Porter, your questions were often borderline, and Mr. Richardson, I'm concerned with your apparent indifference toward those fringes. There were times that I wanted to object for you. Is there a reason you'd like to share as to why you seem to be so apathetic toward your client's rights?"

This was a real rebuke coming from Judge Chapman, Dana knew, not just toward Franklin, but indirectly toward her. She decided she would have to stop pushing the envelope to the extent she'd been doing. A small part of her admired Chapman for his circuitous but effective method of admonishing her while giving the outward appearance of condemning Franklin alone.

Franklin meanwhile, Dana noticed, had turned red. He sat up straight and seemed to struggle with something he wanted to say, before eventually simply replying, "I'll be more aware moving forward, Judge."

Dana realized that there was more going on than Franklin was willing to say. The cynical part of her suddenly wondered if perhaps he was setting up a future appeal based on ineffective assistance of counsel should she receive a conviction. She wouldn't have thought Franklin Richardson, with his extreme hubris, would have found the humility to set himself up as such a complete failure that way. The very idea he might be capable of such a duplicitous act was enough to make her realize she needed to be exceedingly careful of the way she prosecuted this case going forward. From here on out, she would play it straight and avoid trying to get away with anything borderline.

Chapman nodded and thanked them both for their time. He dismissed them, and Dana noticed a real change in Franklin's posture as he slunk out the door, not bothering to give her his normal lust-filled ogle. She shook her head in disbelief and headed to her office to prepare for the next day's continuing testimony.

Chapter 33

The next morning, Franklin awoke early and was in his office by 7am. He had contractors arriving today to begin a long overdue expansion project on his offices. He'd managed to lease the two offices on either side of him, negotiating a great deal with the building owner who'd been wanting to evict both tenants anyway, but hadn't wanted to do so without other tenants to occupy the space. Franklin offered to pay for a remodel of the entire suite of three offices, combining them into one large, modern space that was more than three times the size of his current space, in exchange for a simple doubling of his lease amount with a five-year contract.

The remodel work was going to cost him somewhere between $40,000 and $50,000, depending on how elaborate he decided to get, which was a great bargain. He'd already earned nearly half that amount against the retainer from Whittaker, and he estimated he'd be bringing in around $35,000 per week in fees for the next few weeks. That made this deal a no-brainer.

With a new suite of offices, completely modernized, spacious, and professionally decorated, he expected to have as many customers as he could handle. The sounds of hammers and saws from next door made him happy, and the fact that he was wearing one of his new suits, the expensive suits that fit him perfectly, made him even happier.

On top of that, he spoke with Whittaker last night after the first day of the trial, and Whittaker shared with him some of the notes he'd taken during the testimony of Detective Sodafsky. He showed Franklin the direction he wanted him to take with his cross-examination, the points he wanted him to make and the questions he wanted asked. Although he refused to elaborate on the overall plan, Franklin was astute enough to recognize the beginning of *some semblance* of a plan at least, and that alone was enough to brighten his day.

At 8:30am sharp, he grabbed his briefcase, gave Stacy a kiss on the cheek, and headed up to the courthouse, whistling as he walked along. As he approached the entrance where the metal detectors were set up, he saw a gorgeous, young blonde in a tight skirt that emphasized her ample curves walking toward the administration building next door to the courthouse. He stopped and stared as she crossed in front of him, heedless of the distasteful looks his slack-jawed gawking was causing.

"Do you ever feel any shame?" he heard, turning to see Ron Whittaker standing beside him, watching the hottie as she entered the building.

"Man, did you see that little piece? My God. I would give my left arm for just a sniff of that beautiful vagina. Just a sniff, that's all and whack..." He mimicked cutting off his left arm with his right hand.

"Seems like a reasonable trade," Whittaker commented.

"Hey, you know how it is buddy!" Franklin smacked him on the back in a chummy way. "We spend the first nine months trying to get out of the vagina and the rest of our lives trying to get back in. Am I right?" he laughed loudly and looked for confirmation from Ron.

"Are you ready for today?" asked Ron, not even bothering to humor him with a smile.

This fucking guy, thought Franklin. *He's full of humor when he should be serious, and then when it's reasonable to relax a little and have some fun, he gets all serious. Three more fucking weeks. That's all I have to put up with this bullshit for is three more fucking weeks.*

"You better believe I'm ready for today," Franklin exclaimed, forcing a smile. "We're going to fucking kill it in there today. I can't wait for my cross of that twat detective--wipe the smug look off her face for once."

"Just make sure you stick with the script," Ron replied seriously. "Nothing more, nothing less. You do not have my permission to adlib; you do not have my permission to expand the questioning beyond the scope I've given you. I'll be giving you a few more instructions as her testimony continues today, so make sure you get a recess before your cross so we can go over those things as well."

Franklin felt all of his earlier jocularity disappearing. Things had been going so well, but here he was, back in his role as Ron Whittaker's trained monkey. He nodded curtly and turned to walk toward the courthouse.

"One more thing," Ron called out from behind him.

"I know," replied Franklin, not bothering to turn around. "No objecting to any of Dana Porter's questions."

He walked glumly into the courthouse.

Chapter 34

Judge Chapman called the court to order and looked around.

Everyone seemed to be present, and he asked both Porter and Richardson if they were ready to proceed; both answered affirmatively. He ordered the jurors into the courtroom and welcomed them warmly.

He then turned back to Dana Porter. "Mrs. Porter, you may proceed."

She stood at her table. "If it please the court, the State would like to recall Detective Monika Sodafsky to the stand."

Chapman waited until Sodafsky had taken a seat and then said to her, "Good morning, Detective Sodafsky."

"Good morning, Your Honor," she replied.

"I would like to remind you that you are still under oath from yesterday."

"Yes, sir."

"Okay then." He looked at Dana. "Counselor, you may proceed."

Chapman listened attentively as Porter recapped where Sodafsky had left off with her testimony yesterday. She then began leading her through the events that followed her initial investigation at Conner's house. Sodafsky testified that she and her partner on this case, Detective Bruce Norgaard, drove to the offices of Puget Sound Aerospace to talk to Conner's boss, Gerald Gresham. She testified that before leaving for the PSA offices, they received confirmation of the fingerprint return, identifying the print on the shell casing as Ronald Whittaker's.

"Is it unusual to receive a return on a fingerprint so quickly?" Dana asked her.

Sodafsky nodded. "A little. It happens that quickly sometimes, but rarely. In this case, Mr. Whittaker was the holder of a government Top Secret security clearance, and so his profile was prominent."

Dana continued with the questioning, walking Monika through her notification to Gerald Gresham and her initial interview with Ron Whittaker in his office.

Judge Chapman was happy to see that every one of Dana's questions was phrased appropriately, that she had stopped trying to push the envelope as she had been doing yesterday. He had hoped she would see the underlying implication of his probe of Richardson in chambers after court last evening and that she would make the changes he was currently observing. The last thing he wanted, the last thing any judge wants, is to have to declare a mistrial or open himself up to a valid appeal because of something he could have controlled.

He was still unsure about Richardson's competency as a defense attorney for a case of this magnitude. He had little doubt Richardson was an adequate attorney when it came to a misdemeanor charge like shoplifting or driving under the influence, maybe even in some assault or burglary felony charges. He wasn't at all sure about his proficiency in a case of this significance though. He knew Richardson didn't have the experience to litigate this case; that much he could look up in court records. What he'd seen of Richardson during pretrial motions had only served to amplify his concern.

There were a number of evidentiary items in this case that Chapman himself would have sought to exclude if he were the attorney for the defense, and Richardson had not done so. The warrantless search of Whittaker's garbage cans that resulted in the police locating the duct tape with Conner's hairs stuck to it should have been a no-brainer, for example. Chapman probably would have ruled against him on such a motion; the Supreme Court had clearly ruled that warrantless garbage can searches outside of the curtilage of a home were proper, after all.

A competent attorney, however, might have argued how far curtilage extended. The courts defined curtilage as the area around the home but they left an exact definition open for fairly broad interpretation. Richardson could have and should have, in Chapman's mind, argued that the garbage cans were within the curtilage of the home and not subject to a warrantless search. He would have lost his motion, since the garbage cans had been very near the public roadway of the alley behind his house, but the lack of even an attempt at such an obvious motion was disturbing.

The only item in fact, which he'd sought to have excluded, had been a videotape of the defendant's vehicle taken from a security camera on the night of the murder. That videotape had not been taken from a city-operated street camera, but rather from a warehouse located on the edge of Paine Field Airport.

How Dana Porter or her investigators discovered the footage, Chapman had no idea, but it was an impressive find. The routes Whittaker could have taken from his home in Mukilteo to Conner's home on Walter Hall golf course were numerous, and many of those routes traveled through industrial areas. Porter would have had to have people drive all the obvious routes, look for cameras, then stop and ask to see footage from the night of the murder, and then look at all the cars that passed by during a pretty significantly long time period.

It was incredible that they found it.

However, Richardson filed a motion to have that videotape suppressed, and he eloquently argued his case. He declared that there was no way to identify the vehicle in the video definitively as Whittaker's. The camera picked up only the first five numerical characters out of seven on the license plate, and it hadn't picked up the driver at all. Dana argued that a license plate search of the State of Washington's database found that the only 2014 Land Rover starting with those five characters was the one registered to Ronald Whittaker, and that the videotape clearly showed a 2014 Land Rover. Richardson argued that the video wasn't clear, was in black and white, which made the color and even model of the vehicle somewhat indiscernible, and that it couldn't be stated with 100% accuracy that the zero in the fuzzy license plate wasn't actually an "O". Dana hadn't done a search to see if any Land Rovers contained an "O" instead of a zero in that spot, and

Chapman had ruled in favor of the defense that the video was inadmissible as evidence.

In truth, though he would never admit it out loud, he'd done it simply to balance what he felt was an inequitable ability level in the caliber of the two attorneys, in addition to his disagreement with Richardson's refusal to file any other motions questioning the prosecution's evidence or their witnesses.

Now he found himself wondering if he'd have to make any further balances during the trial just to ensure fairness to the defendant.

As Detective Sodafsky continued to testify about her initial interview with Ronald Whittaker in his office, Chapman took some time to look at the defendant and examine his demeanor.

Whittaker appeared relaxed and at ease. He was sitting in the defense chair, next to his attorney, leaning back slightly with one leg crossed over the other. Though he was staring intently at Detective Sodafsky as she testified, his expression and body posture conveyed a sense of nonchalance and serenity. Although Chapman envied Whittaker's ability to convey such a bearing during a time when he should have been experiencing extreme stress, it concerned him.

One of the other things that bothered Chapman about Richardson and his defense roadmap was his decision not to waive his client's right to a speedy trial. In very nearly 100% of cases of this magnitude, the defense chose to waive speedy trial. Preparing a solid defense for a trial that would last an estimated three weeks of dense testimony from dozens of witnesses, as well as hundreds of items of evidence, was close to impossible. Although that applied both ways, the prosecution typically benefited from a quicker trial for a number of reasons.

The first was that they were usually able to employ as many attorneys as needed for all the preparation. The county prosecution budget was pretty significant, and they were already paying all the salaries of the attorneys and the investigators; they simply had to divert whatever resources were needed to be ready for trial.

The second, and probably most important reason a quicker trial benefited the prosecution, was that witnesses' memories were still fresh. The longer a case takes to come to trial, the more likely it is that a witness could forget an important fact. Maybe the witnesses would change their minds about testifying, or maybe they would die before the trial. Chapman had seen all three of those things happen, and it was nearly always a benefit to the defense when they did.

The only time he'd ever seen a major case not get extended beyond the speedy trial requirement was when the defendant was in jail. Even then, they usually waived speedy trial, and that was a testament to the importance of doing so. They usually figured it was better to sit in jail for a year than to take the much greater risk of being there the rest of their lives.

But Whittaker had been out on bail, for crying out loud. He had his freedom, and he still chose not to waive his right to a speedy trial. Chapman wasn't sure if Whittaker had insisted on that or if Richardson had just not been competent enough to insist that time was the defense's friend, but it was yet another source of concern to him as the trial judge.

Porter finished with Sodafsky's testimony regarding her interviews with Gresham and Whittaker in the offices of Puget Sound Aerospace, and was preparing to move on to her drive by Whittaker's residence and the search of the garbage cans. Chapman decided this was a good spot to take the midmorning break.

He ordered a fifteen-minute recess and excused the jury before going back into his chambers. His goal during these breaks was to use the restroom, refill his coffee cup, and to do some stretching exercises. These trials were long and arduous, but he'd been through enough of them to know the best way to survive.

He was looking forward to the end of Porter's direct examination of Sodafsky, hopefully before lunch time, and then Richardson's first attempt at a cross examination.

Chapter 35

Monika Sodafsky was exhausted, and she'd already decided she would use the upcoming lunch break to find a dark hole in her office and take a nap.

The week prior to the trial had been spent in consultation with Dana Porter, preparing for her lengthy testimony as the State's chief witness. She'd also been forced to work on several other major cases at the same time, including another homicide she'd drawn a few weeks before. As the lead detective on that case, she'd had several interviews to conduct this past weekend, including a stressful interrogation of the main suspect in the case.

The worst part of the other case was that the victim was a child, always the worst possible assignment for a homicide detective. Emotionally draining in addition to the physical strain from the long hours, Monika was finding it difficult to get up in the morning and prepare for this trial.

All day yesterday she spent the breaks from her testimony up in her office, checking on the status of the child homicide, following through on leads and assigning work to the detectives assisting her. Finally this morning, Detective Sergeant Myers had told her to focus only on the Whittaker case and her testimony today. She was hoping that meant she would be able to sneak in that nap during lunch.

Despite her emotional and physical exhaustion, she knew this case was going well, although she was also aware that the direct examination was the easy part. If she could get that nap in, she'd be ready for the grueling second part of her testimony, the cross-examination.

Before the break, she testified about her trip to Puget Sound Aerospace and her conversations with Gresham and Whittaker in their offices. She hadn't mentioned the recording she made of her conversation with Whittaker because Dana Porter decided the information didn't help the prosecution's case. She put a line in her report about making the recording, though, and the detective who ran it through the Voice Stress Analyzer wrote a report for the case as well, so she suspected Whittaker's attorney would have something to say about it during the cross exam.

For now, Dana was asking her about her trip to Whittaker's and her decision to confiscate his garbage.

"Detective, were you aware of any legal precedent that would allow you to remove somebody's garbage from their garbage cans without a search warrant?"

Dana had discussed this with her and told her she felt it was important to establish that this seizure was perfectly legal, just in case somebody on the jury decided it was a breach of Whittaker's rights.

Monika nodded confidently. "Yes; it's been well established by the Supreme Court that garbage placed out on the curb is in no way protected by the Fourth Amendment which protects against illegal searches and seizures."

"Now, you didn't search through the garbage from the cans yourself, is that correct?"

"That's correct."

"So, how did you find out what was in the garbage?"

Monika explained that Detective Norgaard coordinated the search of the garbage and that he reported back to her that only one item of evidentiary value had been found in the bags. She waited for Dana to prompt her by asking what that item was, and then she explained the crumbled wads of used duct tape that had contained hairs purported to be from the victim.

During testimony, Monika saw several of the jury members turn their heads from her to look directly at Ron Whittaker. He didn't appear to be phased; the calm expression he had for the entire case so far never left his face.

After a few more questions regarding the duct tape, Dana shifted the questioning to the search warrant for Whittaker's house. Monika knew Dana would be calling Detective Norgaard to the stand to discuss the actual collection and search of the bags of garbage, since he was the one who had took them while Monika waited in the car, and he was the one who coordinated the search of the trash bags.

"Is this a copy of the search warrant you served on the residence of Ronald Whittaker, located at 4214 Sunset Drive in Mukilteo, Washington?" Dana brought the copy up to Monika, and Monika confirmed that was the warrant that she served.

"And this warrant gives you the power to seize any nine millimeter firearms, as well as any potential evidence pertaining to the homicide involving Ronald Conner, is that correct?"

"Yes, it is."

"Can you tell the court what you found when you entered the house?"

Monika walked through her service of the search warrant, starting with the fruitless search of the living room and dining room, before getting to the discovery of the plastic bottle with the bottom blown outward. Dana told her in advance that, since Monika wasn't an expert on firearms, she wasn't going to be able to testify that it was actually a silencer.

"Was there something unusual about this plastic bottle that caused you to collect it as evidence?" Dana asked her.

"Yes, the bottom of the bottle had been blown out and there appeared to be a black residue on the inside part of the plastic."

Dana walked over to the evidence box and removed the bag with the bottle in it, which Monika confirmed was the bottle she'd collected.

Dana told her they would be coming back to the bottle with another witness at some point, and she then moved on to Bruce Norgaard's discovery of the gun in the master bedroom closet. From the confused frowns on the jury members' faces, it was apparent to Monika that they didn't understand the significance of the plastic bottle as a silencer for firing shots in a residential area. When they did get it, after whatever expert she'd lined up testified about it, they were going to be in for a shock at the meticulous planning that had gone into this murder.

"Just to be clear, Detective Norgaard discovered the gun in the closet, but you saw it as well with your own eyes?" Dana asked, as Monika snapped back to the present.

"Yes. Detective Norgaard called me to the master bedroom and showed me a backpack he found in the closet."

Even Monika recognized that this wasn't a good answer; she couldn't testify as to where Norgaard found the backpack because she wasn't in the room when it was found. Whittaker's attorney remained seated, though, and Dana moved on, requesting State's exhibits fourteen through twenty be brought into the courtroom.

When the box was brought in, she walked over and picked up a clear plastic evidence bag containing a black, REI backpack. "Is this the backpack that Detective Norgaard showed you when you got to the bedroom?"

"It appears to be the same one, yes."

"Okay, and can you please tell the court what you found inside the backpack?"

Monika described how Norgaard shined his flashlight into the backpack and she saw a firearm she recognized as a Beretta 92FS nine-millimeter pistol. She told the jury she saw the magazine for the firearm at the bottom of the backpack and noticed that it contained just eight rounds of its maximum capacity of ten.

"Were you able to note the serial number of the pistol at that time?"

"Yes, I was."

Dana removed a pistol from the evidence box, the slide locked open and the breach secured with a plastic and metal strap that rendered the pistol inoperable. She brought the pistol over to

Monika and asked, "And is this the firearm that was in the backpack?"

Monika looked at the firearm and compared the serial number to her memory of the one that had been in the backpack. This was all a tedious exercise, obviously, as every single person in the courtroom knew it was clearly the same firearm or the prosecutor wouldn't be showing it to them. They also knew that, at some point, some ballistics technician would be up there where Monika was currently seated, testifying that he'd fired test rounds from the weapon and it was indeed the same weapon used to commit the murder of Ronald Conner. It was an exercise in tedium, certainly, but a necessary path to showing the elements of the crime and eventually getting a conviction.

Knowing this was coming, Monika had, just this morning, memorized the serial number from the notebook she'd kept during that investigation, and she confirmed it was the same firearm.

Dana walked her through the discovery of the single empty shell casing before moving on to the shoes in the closet that had dried mud on the bottom. Monika talked about her suspicion that the mud might be related to that on the floor in Conner's house, and how she directed the gathering of the sample from Whittaker's back yard.

Judge Chapman interrupted and asked if Dana was close to a natural breaking point, and Monika took that opportunity to surreptitiously glance at her watch. It was 12:20pm, and she was sincerely hoping she'd be able to get to that nap. She could feel herself struggling not to yawn, and she was feeling loopy.

Dana told Chapman she'd be completely finished with Monika in fifteen minutes, and Chapman told her to finish, which made Monika extremely happy. She sat up straighter and shook off the fatigue.

Dana spent the next fifteen minutes taking her through the remainder of the evidence, including a brief accounting of the ballistics report that showed the firearm found in Whittaker's closet was the one used in the homicide. That brought her to the arrest and booking of Whittaker for first-degree murder.

Dana had previously told her she was going to end her direct with the arrest and booking and she would have a DNA expert testify later about the DNA results, since the decision to arrest had been made prior to those returns.

Finally, Monika heard the words she'd been dying to hear all morning.

"No further questions, Your Honor."

Judge Chapman thanked Dana and asked Whittaker's attorney if he was going to have any cross-examination for her. He stood slowly and answered that he did have some questions, which was no surprise. Chapman advised that they would break for lunch and start back up at two o'clock.

That gave Monika enough time to get up to her office, nap for an hour, grab something to eat and still get back in time for the afternoon session. Feeling incredibly relieved, she headed up to her office on the fourth floor to find a dark closet and something soft to lie on.

Chapter 36

Franklin, despite his frustration with his client, was thrilled to be allowed to finally do some lawyer work. Other than his opening statement to the jury the other day, he'd effectively looked like a complete nitwit, sitting quietly next to his client as if he was nothing more than a mute observer.

Now, as he prepared for his cross examination of Detective Sodafsky, he realized that the truth of the matter was that he was nothing more than Whittaker's lapdog. There were a lot of questions he would have liked to have asked the detective, a lot of her testimony that he would have been thrilled to challenge, but Whittaker was going to allow him to question her on only a few things.

Franklin wasn't sure if he had a complete genius for a client, or if Whittaker was a self-destructive moron, hell bent on spending some quality time taking Bubba's cock up his ass while he stamped out license plates at Walla Walla State Prison. By all appearances thus far, things were leaning toward the "cock in ass" conclusion.

Judge Chapman called the afternoon session to order, and the jury members filed in, looking fat and content after their free lunch. This reminded Franklin of another problem: not one of the jurors was even remotely good looking. Actually, thinking about it, he realized that was a good thing. Normally he enjoyed strutting his stuff and showing how good he was at the lawyer thing when there was a hottie in the jury box. At least there was nobody up there he wanted to bang bearing witness to his forced trial impotency.

Franklin suddenly realized that the courtroom had grown silent, and Chapman was staring at him. He'd just told him to proceed with his cross, and Franklin was so engrossed in his personal thoughts that he missed it.

Clearing his throat, he grabbed his notepad, stepped in front of the defense table, and put on his most engaging smile.

"Thank you, Your Honor. I have just a few questions for the witness." He looked at the jurors. "I don't want to take up any more of the jury's time than absolutely necessary."

"Please get to it then, counselor," Chapman ordered.

Franklin nodded and turned to Sodafsky who, he noticed, appeared to be much more awake and alert than she'd been this morning. "Detective Sodafsky, good afternoon. I want to talk to you just a little bit about some of the things you testified to yesterday, about when you first arrived at Mr. Conner's house."

Sodafsky nodded and Franklin continued. "I want to jump right ahead to when you found the shell casing in the heater vent. Did it appear to you as if this shell casing had been placed in the vent, or that it had fallen in there accidentally?"

Sodafsky frowned for a minute and then replied, "Well, I don't know that I'd know the difference."

"Okay, so as far as you know, the casing might have been placed in the heater vent as opposed to falling into it?"

"As far as I know, it could have been," she conceded.

Franklin glanced at his notes and then turned to Chapman. "Your Honor, can we bring up the photo of the dining room? I believe the one I want is State's exhibit four."

The court deputy brought up the correct exhibit, placing it on the easel. Franklin grabbed a laser pointer from his table and directed the beam at the heater vent grate, set into the floor against the wall, approximately three feet from the corner of the room.

"This is the heater vent where you found the shell casing, correct?"

"That's correct," replied Sodafsky.

"What made you decide to look into the heater vent for the shell casing?"

"Well, I tried to position myself like the shooter would have been positioned, and then I mimicked holding a gun like so," she lifted her hands up to chest level, arms extended as if holding a pistol. "Once I did that, I realized that if it had been a semi-automatic, the shell casings would likely have been ejected in an arc in the direction of the heater vent."

"So you walked directly over there and looked in the vent. Was the shell casing hidden, or was it clearly visible?"

"It was clearly visible once I looked down into the vent," she replied.

"So the heater vent was the only possible place that a shell casing could have landed in that room?"

"I suppose it could have fallen behind the leg of the dining room table there," she answered, pointing at the picture on the easel again, "but I thought at the time that the heater vent was the most likely spot for a shell casing to end up and not be noticed by the killer."

"Did it ever strike you as odd that the killer didn't follow that same thought process and find the shell casing himself?"

"Objection, Your Honor," Dana Porter said, standing up. "Calls for speculation."

"I'm not asking the witness to speculate about anything, Judge," Franklin replied. "I'm asking if she herself ever thought it was odd that the killer didn't find a shell casing that had landed in a most obvious location and wasn't purposefully hidden in that obvious location, but was visible to the detective when she walked over and looked down."

Judge Chapman glared at Franklin who had taken the opportunity to present his argument against the objection, and had clarified the testimony while doing so.

"Overruled; the witness may answer."

Franklin smiled and turned back to Sodafsky.

"No, it didn't strike me as odd."

Franklin scoffed, an expression of disbelief on his face. "Well why not?"

Monika shrugged. "I thought maybe the killer was in a hurry, maybe it was dark in the room at the time, maybe he just didn't think to look in there."

"But you thought to look in there. In fact, that was the first place you looked, correct?"

"Correct."

"Okay. Now, when you had the thumbprint submitted for testing, did the results give you the age of the thumbprint?"

"I'm sorry, the *age* of the thumbprint?" Sodafsky asked, a confused look on her face.

"Yes, the age. Did it tell you how old the print on the shell casing was?"

"No. I don't think we asked the lab to age the print," she replied. "It's not an exact science, and there's a pretty big error rate when they do so."

"So then you don't know if the thumbprint on the shell casing had been on there since the night of the murder or if it had been placed on that shell casing months or even years before that night, is that correct?"

"That's correct," Monika replied, somewhat reluctantly.

Franklin walked back to the defense table and sat down, looking again at his notes for a minute and then turned back up to Sodafsky.

"Detective, I want to talk for a minute about the mud you found on the floor. Now this mud was in the dining room only, correct?"

"That's the only place we saw any significant amount, yes."

"So you didn't find any in the living room? The kitchen? The entryway? The doorstep?" he asked, pausing for Monika to answer "No" each time.

Dana stood. "Your Honor, I believe the witness has established that the only place mud was found was the dining room. Does Mr. Richardson intend to exhaust the witness by listing every possible place in the house where the mud was *not* found?"

"Get to the point please, counselor," Chapman concurred.

"My question, detective," Franklin continued, "is: didn't you find it odd that there was mud only in the dining room and not anywhere else?"

"No, I didn't. I figured the dining room was where they had spent the most time and that it was the most likely place for the mud to have fallen off."

"Hmm, okay," Franklin replied, allowing his facial features to show his skepticism. Sometimes you could convey more to a jury with your face than with your voice.

"You don't think that the suspect levitated to the dining room, do you?" he asked.

"Objection, Your Honor." Dana stood up, shooting an angry look at Franklin. "Is Mr. Richardson really going to show such a lack of respect with his questions?"

Franklin stood as well. "I'm just trying to find out from the detective why she didn't think it odd that there was no mud anywhere else in the house."

"She answered that already, Mr. Richardson. Objection is sustained; move on," Chapman ordered.

Franklin sat back down, satisfied. Sodafsky didn't answer the question, but the jury knew where he was headed with it and he knew they understood the point he was trying to make.

"Let's move on to your conversation with Mr. Whittaker when you first came to his office and notified him of Mr. Conner's death. Did Mr. Whittaker seem upset when you told him?"

"Objection, calls for speculation," Dana said, standing.

Chapman considered for a good five seconds before replying, "I'll allow it."

"Yes, he appeared to be upset," Monika answered.

"Did you record your conversation with him?"

Monika nodded. "Yes. I recorded it on my iPhone."

"Did Mr. Whittaker know you were recording him at the time?" Franklin asked.

"Well, I didn't tell him I was recording him."

"Your Honor, I would like to play the recording Detective Sodafsky made and enter it into evidence as defense exhibit one."

"Objection, Your Honor, this is outside the scope of a cross examination," Dana declared.

Franklin had been expecting this objection. During a cross examination, he was allowed only to clarify testimony given during the direct examination, not to open up new testimony. However, he felt this was a part of the testimony Sodafsky had given about interviewing Whittaker in his office and, even though Dana hadn't specifically introduced the audio recording, it did fall into the same argument.

He voiced that argument to the objection, and Chapman again agreed with him. "Overruled," Chapman replied. Dana sat down and looked slightly frustrated which made Franklin smile.

Chapman then had the deputy set up the recording and play it over the speakers in the courtroom so everybody could hear it. It took fifteen minutes to play, and the jurors all heard Whittaker express his grief, stating, "Oh my God, I can't believe it." On the recording, Monika asked him a few questions about how well he'd known Conner, and Whittaker answered that he'd known him his entire life, and that they'd been best friends. Franklin imagined he could hear grief in Whittaker's voice and hoped the jury heard that as well.

When the recording finished, he looked at Sodafsky again. "Detective, what was your purpose in recording this conversation?"

"We had already received a return on the fingerprint on the shell casing and found it to be Mr. Whittaker's print, so he was an early suspect."

"But what was your plan for the actual recording once you made it?"

"I wanted to have our tech guys run it through the Voice Stress Analyzer," she replied, hesitantly, seeing where the line of questioning was headed.

"And what does the Voice Stress Analyzer do?" Franklin asked.

"It helps us determine if a suspect is lying."

"And when you asked Mr. Whittaker where he was at the time of Mr. Conner's murder, and he answered that he was at home all night, what did the Voice Stress Analyzer say about that answer?"

"The results were inconclusive."

"So then he wasn't lying?" Franklin prodded.

"It was inconclusive," Monika repeated.

Franklin decided that was good enough, and he didn't need to press it. "You had another reason for making that recording, didn't you, Detective?" This was a leading question, but Franklin knew that leading questions were allowed in cross examination, though not in direct examinations.

"Yes. I wanted to compare it to the 911 call that had been received."

"This was the anonymous 911 call that sent the paramedics to Conner's house originally?" Franklin asked.

"Yes."

"And did you compare the voice from the 911 call with Mr. Whittaker's voice on your recording?"

Monika nodded. "Yes, and it wasn't the same voice." She jumped the gun with that answer, responding to the question he planned to ask next, but Franklin didn't mind.

"Interesting. Okay, let's move on to the search warrant you obtained for Mr. Whittaker's house. I have one clarification I'd like you to make on this. During your search, did you find any food containers in the house?"

"Any food containers?" Monika asked, confused.

"Yes. You mentioned the food containers from Mr. Conner's house, but did you find any takeout containers in the garbage or in the fridge at Mr. Whittaker's house?"

Monika thought about it for a minute, her brow furrowed. "I do remember seeing a takeout container in the refrigerator."

"Do you remember if it was from the same restaurant as the takeout containers located at Mr. Conner's house?"

"Well, I remember that the container appeared to be of the same type, but I don't know for sure it was the same restaurant," Monika replied.

"Okay, but the container shows a picture of the front of the restaurant, correct?"

"Yes, that's correct."

"So the container wouldn't likely be from any other restaurant except Satay Thai, the same restaurant that the food at Mr. Conner's house came from; would that be an accurate statement?"

"Yes, it would," replied Monika.

"Do you recall if there were any used chopsticks in that takeout container in Mr. Whittaker's refrigerator or anywhere in his house for that matter--the garbage, the sink, anywhere?"

"Not that I recall," she replied.

Franklin nodded. "Thank you. No further questions, Your Honor."

Chapman looked at Dana and asked, "Redirect?"

After Franklin's cross-examination, the prosecutor had the opportunity to re-question the witness, but had to limit the scope of those questions to just the things Franklin had brought up during his cross.

Dana stood up, remaining at her table. "Detective Sodafsky, you testified that you didn't have the age of the thumbprint on the shell casing tested. Did it matter to you how old the print was?"

"No, it didn't."

"Why not?"

"Because the person whose thumbprint was on that shell casing was the most likely suspect in this murder, regardless of when the thumbprint had been left there," Monika replied.

"Had you ever met the defendant, Mr. Whittaker, before the day you interviewed him in his office?"

"No, I hadn't."

"So when you testified that he seemed upset, you didn't have any metric on which to base that observation, right? You'd never seen Mr. Whittaker upset, happy, bored, sad, no baselines whatsoever, correct?"

"That's correct."

"The Voice Stress Analyzer showing inconclusive, that could still mean he was lying, correct?"

"Yes, that's correct."

"Nothing further, Your Honor." Dana sat back down in her chair.

Franklin was annoyed at the last question and once again annoyed that Whittaker wouldn't let him object as, in his opinion, it called for a conclusion the detective wasn't qualified to give. She certainly hadn't been qualified as an expert in the science of voice stress analyzing.

Judge Chapman looked at him and asked if he would like to re-cross examine. He glanced sideways at Whittaker who subtly shook his head.

"No, Your Honor," Franklin replied, happy with his performance on the cross, but still frustrated overall.

Chapter 37

After the afternoon break, Dana had a decision to make. She asked Judge Chapman how late he planned to go, and he told her until at least 6:00pm. That meant she had to decide on the length of time she would need for her next witness, the goal being to complete their testimony during the afternoon session. Whenever she could help it, she preferred not to have a witness's testimony extend into the next day. She wanted the jury to have a complete picture of a testimony when they went to sleep at night, and not have only a partial story. She had no choice with Detective Sodafsky, since her testimony took more than a day to complete, but she did have a choice here.

Looking at the expected testimony times on her list, she decided to call the fingerprint technician from the Sheriff's Office, Royce Barham.

After he was sworn in, Dana walked Barham through his credentials, establishing him as an expert in fingerprint identification and processing, a designation that would allow her to solicit his opinion in those matters. Typically in courtroom proceedings, only someone who has been certified as a subject matter expert can offer an opinion.

After Dana submitted Barham to the court as an expert in fingerprints, Judge Chapman asked Richardson if he had any objections; he stated that he didn't.

Dana then walked Barham through his collection of the fingerprint on the shell casing, as well as many other fingerprints that he'd collected throughout the house. He identified numerous fingerprints belonging to the suspect, Ron Whittaker, and Dana had another exhibit introduced that showed where all of Whittaker's fingerprints had been located.

By the time she finished with Barham, it was nearly 6:30pm, and Judge Chapman asked Richardson how long he would need for his cross examination.

Dana happened to glance over as Whittaker handed Richardson the notepad he'd been scribbling in. Richardson glanced at it and then replied, "I have only one question for the witness, Judge."

"Okay, proceed then," Chapman replied.

Dana couldn't believe that Richardson was going to ask only one question on his cross of the fingerprint guy, but she wasn't at all surprised by the question itself.

"Mr. Barham, what was the age of the thumbprint you pulled from the shell casing?"

Dana knew Barham hadn't aged the print; as Monika had testified, aging prints is an inexact science, and it doesn't matter how old it was. Whether Whittaker had loaded the gun the night of the murder or a month prior to it, it was still his thumbprint on the shell, and it put him on the scene with the murder weapon.

Barham, who hadn't been in the courtroom during Sodafsky's testimony, seemed surprised by the question. He replied that he hadn't tested the print for age because he hadn't been asked to.

"No further questions, Your Honor," Richardson said, sitting back down in his seat.

Chapman dismissed the jury with his usual admonishments and then recessed the court until nine o'clock the next morning.

Dana sat at her table as the courtroom, including Richardson and Whittaker, cleared out. She was thinking about what she'd seen at the defense table. Her assistant prosecutor, Jason Garvey also remained seated, and she turned to him.

"Did you see Whittaker hand Richardson his notepad when Chapman asked if he wanted to cross examine Barham just now?"

Garvey shook his head. "No, I wasn't looking over there."

Dana thought about that, a contemplative look on her face. "Tomorrow, I'd like you to watch the defense during my questioning, especially as I'm drawing to a close with any particular witness. I think Whittaker might be leading the case prep over there."

Garvey raised his eyebrows. "Really? That seems like it would be an awful decision. Of course, his attorney is Franklin Richardson. I would imagine he thinks he can't do any worse than Richardson himself would do."

"Maybe," Dana replied. "It makes me a little nervous though. Keep an eye out tomorrow, I want to know what's going on."

Garvey left and Dana remained seated at the table, alone now in the courtroom, thinking about the case.

On the surface, it seemed that it was going well. Her direct examination of Detective Sodafsky had been great, with no interruptions by Richardson for the vast majority of it. She admitted that he'd done a great job with his cross-examination, making a lot of subtle points that she suspected he would be coming back to during the defense case. She thought that she'd done a good job of combatting some of them during her redirect, though.

Based on Richardson's cross, she thought she knew the direction the defense was taking. The part that worried her, though, was that she had no idea what his questions about the takeout food in Whittaker's refrigerator were all about. She didn't like not knowing the answers to questions like that, and she hated not having any idea where a defense attorney was trying to head with his questions.

She had told Jason Garvey to go home, but suddenly she picked up her phone and gave him a call.

"I need you to review all the photos from the search warrant they served at Whittaker's place," she told him when he answered. "I need to know if there are any pictures of the takeout food in his fridge, the food that Richardson was asking Monika about on his cross."

Jason told her he would take care of it, and she hung up. She had a bad feeling about that question, but she didn't quite know why.

***

The man with the scar on his face walked into the parking garage and got in his car. His job during the trial was to be present during the last hour of testimony each day and he'd just left the courthouse. He was watching for just one thing, and he'd not yet seen it after two days of testimony. When he did see it, if he saw it, he had his instructions, and they were fairly straightforward. He would accomplish them easily enough and he actually hoped he would see what he was looking for sooner rather than later. The quicker he could wrap up this job and get his final payment, the better.

Chapter 38

On Wednesday morning, Judge Chapman called court to order at nine o'clock sharp. Usually by day three of a trial like this, he would have had to spend some time getting the attorneys in line, threatening them to behave and to stop pushing edges, and making them play nice with each other. He didn't seem to need to do that for this case though. Although he appreciated not having to play referee too much, he suspected that was because of Franklin Richardson's inexperience, and that part worried him.

Richardson had done well on his cross of Sodafsky, but then had asked only one question of the fingerprint tech and hadn't objected a single time in all of yesterday's testimony. If that continued today, Chapman was probably going to have a word with him again to make sure he understood his responsibility to ensure a fair trial for his client.

"Mrs. Porter, you may proceed," he told Dana, getting the ball rolling for the day.

She stood and announced, "If it please the court, the State calls Lawrence Gunby to the stand."

Chapman knew that Lawrence Gunby was the State's witness from the county crime lab, who was in court to testify about Conner's hairs being found on the duct tape recovered from Whittaker's garbage cans. He also knew that this was the part of the case where tedium and boredom was most likely going to set in. The lab part was always technical and often difficult to follow as they talked about their testing methods and their findings. He knew it was difficult for he himself to follow and stay focused in these testimonies, let alone the jury members.

Dana Porter began in typical fashion by asking him questions about his background and training, attempting to establish Gunby's bona fides as an expert. If she wanted him to be able to testify as to his opinion in the evidence, it would require a ruling from the court that Gunby was an expert, and this part alone was often very tedious and thorough.

Franklin Richardson surprised Chapman by standing up suddenly.

"Your Honor, if I may, I would just like to know what the point of this testimony is."

Dana seemed surprised, and Chapman couldn't blame her. He was surprised too.

"Umm, the point of this testimony is to establish Mr. Gunby's training and education to certify him as an expert," she answered.

"Establish him as an expert in what field?" asked Richardson.

"In the field of forensic hair microscopy and trace evidence matching," Dana replied. "Your Honor, what is this?" she asked, confused about the timeliness of the objection.

Chapman was confused as well. "Mr. Richardson?" he asked.

"If it please the court, the defense will stipulate that Mr. Gunby is an expert in those fields."

Well, this is a nice change of pace, Chapman thought. Stipulating to Gunby's credentials was going to save a good amount of tedious testimony. It was also a good move by Richardson because it didn't allow Dana to build up Mr. Gunby to the jury, making him seem like some sort of superhero whose testimony couldn't be called into question.

"Okay, the court certifies that Mr. Gunby is an expert witness," he said. "Please proceed."

Dana returned to her table, picked up another notepad and then began asking Gunby about the duct tape he had received from the scene of the crime. She walked him through his opening of the sealed package, establishing chain-of-custody and that nobody had tampered with it. She then had him begin talking about his extraction and testing of the tape itself.

"How many hairs did you observe stuck onto the duct tape?" she asked.

"My initial examination observed approximately thirty individual hairs stuck mainly in two distinct places on the duct tape."

Dana then had a blown-up picture of the wad of duct tape brought up, set on the easel, and introduced as a State exhibit. She handed Gunby a laser pointer and asked him to identify where on the duct tape, which was wadded up into a pretzel-like mess, he had noticed the hairs.

Before he could continue, Richardson stood again. "Your Honor, once again, I'd like to know the point of this presumably lengthy testimony."

"Judge, is the defense's plan to interrupt my examination all day to ask what the point is? It should be evident to Mr. Richardson that the point is to establish that the duct tape was used to restrain Mr. Conner before his murder," Dana announced, clearly annoyed.

Chapman looked back at Richardson. He was slightly annoyed, too, and was considering calling both counselors to a sidebar.

"Your Honor, once again, in the interest of expediency, the defense will stipulate that this wad of duct tape was used to restrain Mr. Conner in the chair. We'll stipulate that the duct tape matches that of the remnants found on the underside of the arms of the chair, and we'll stipulate that the hairs stuck to the duct tape belonged to Mr. Conner. Anything to keep this case moving, judge, and to keep the esteemed members of the jury from falling asleep."

A light wave of laughter rippled through the court, humor not shared by Chapman nor by Dana Porter.

"I'm going to ask the jury to please return to the jury room for a moment. I will ask that you not discuss the case while we're in sidebar." Chapman motioned to the bailiff who escorted the jurors out of the room. Once they were gone, he turned back to Richardson.

"Mr. Richardson, do you mind explaining what's happening here?"

"Your Honor, we aren't going to be moving with a defense that Mr. Conner was not restrained before his murder, nor are we going to try to claim that the duct tape found in my client's garbage cans was not the duct tape used to restrain him. My goal here is to simply save the court an enormous amount of time by not making everybody listen to pointless testimony that we aren't going to argue against."

"Mrs. Porter?" Chapman asked, loath to pass on the opportunity to speed up a trial if both sides agreed.

"It's certainly unusual, Judge, but we'll agree as long as I can have Mr. Gunby present his final conclusion."

He looked back at Richardson.

"As long as that final conclusion is nothing more than that the duct tape was used to restrain the victim, then we're fine with that."

Dana nodded and said it was.

"Okay," Chapman said, "let's proceed then."

Richardson and Porter returned to their places, and Chapman had the jurors brought back in. They entered with envious looks on their faces as if they thought they might have missed something important while they'd been excused. Chapman waited for them to be seated and then nodded for Porter to continue.

"Well, Mr. Gunby, it appears that the defense has agreed to stipulate to most of your testimony here, so I guess I'll just ask you, what was the final result of your testing and what were your findings?"

Gunby seemed surprised, but answered, "The final result was that the hairs on the duct tape matched exactly to Mr. Conner, and the duct tape remnants found at the crime scene were a perfect match to the sample submitted."

"So, in your opinion, the duct tape found in Mr. Whittaker's garbage can was the same duct tape that was used to restrain the victim prior to his death."

"Yes, that's correct," Gunby replied.

"Thank you, Mr. Gunby. Nothing further, Your Honor."

"Very well," Chapman said, thrilled to see it wasn't even 10:00am yet. "Any cross?" he asked Richardson.

"Just one or two questions, Your Honor," Richardson said, rising at his table. "Mr. Gunby, did you find any fingerprints anywhere on the duct tape?"

"No, I did not."

"Any evidence of DNA that was not that of the victim, Mr. Conner?"

"No, I didn't perform any DNA testing on the tape itself."

"Nothing further." Richardson sat back down.

Chapman asked Dana if she had any redirect and she declined. He thanked and excused the witness and then asked Dana if she was ready for her next witness.

"Your Honor, I expected this testimony to take us to lunch, so I'll need a few minutes to locate my next witness. I know she's close but probably not in the courtroom at the moment."

"Okay," Chapman said, "we'll take a fifteen-minute recess and when we start back up, we'll go right to lunch time, so make sure your next witnesses are close." Just in case we have any more surprises like this, he didn't have to add. He dismissed the jurors and put the court into recess, slipping back into his chambers to refill his coffee cup and relax.

Chapter 39

Franklin Richardson figured that his antics this morning had cost him at least $2400 bucks. He'd saved the court an estimated three hours of testimony, maybe more if you included a normal and standard cross examination. Now, Whittaker wanted him to pull another stunt that was going to cost him another few thousand bucks. At this rate, he would end up having to reconsider the condo he'd been looking at, the one that overlooked Puget Sound near the Mukilteo ferry terminal and leased for around three grand per month. He'd planned to obtain a two-year lease on the place and to spend another fifteen-grand furnishing it to his newly eclectic tastes.

If Whittaker kept insisting he stipulate to the State's witnesses, those plans were going to vaporize quickly.

"Why don't we just stipulate to the State's entire case?" he asked. "Better yet, why don't you just plead guilty, and we'll get right on to the sentencing phase? Hey, here's a better idea: why not just stipulate to life in prison? Let me get the bailiff over here, he can just drive you straight to Walla Walla."

"Bailiff!" he called, waving his hand in the air. The judge, jury, and prosecutors were all gone from the court room, but there were a number of observers still seated behind them, including some members of the press.

"Knock it off, Franklin," Whittaker hissed.

He waved the bailiff off. "Never mind, sorry," he said. The bailiff frowned at him and returned to his station.

"Keep your fucking voice down and listen to me," Whittaker ordered. "If I was guilty of this, then I would plead guilty, but I'm not. So get that out of your head. I know where we're going with our defense and if you haven't figured it out yet, then you're stupider than I thought." He nodded over to the empty prosecution table. "I'm pretty sure Mrs. Porter has figured out what our defense is going to be; please tell me you have too."

"I know what our defense is," Franklin answered, defensively. He put a knowing look on his face to hide his unease. He had only a vague idea of Whittaker's defense plan, an understanding that it was going to revolve around the idea that he'd been framed for the murder, but he couldn't comprehend the entirety of the plan. And Whittaker refused to share it with him, instead making snide, underhanded remarks that Franklin should have figured it out for himself.

"Good. Then you know that none of this testimony matters. By stipulating to it all, we curry favor with the jury and with the judge, and we gain latitude in future questionable actions. Surely you see that?"

Franklin nodded. He did understand that in general, but without the big picture, he had trouble seeing the future benefit to what seemed to be an undermining of universally accepted sound strategy. He also could foresee his inability to purchase a boat he'd had his eye on, a boat that was going to require an extra twenty-five or thirty hours of court time at eight hundred bucks an hour. A boat that just *poofed* from his imagination as Ron Whittaker outlined the plan for the next witness.

Dana and her prosecution team returned just as Whittaker finished enlightening Franklin with the plan for the next few witnesses on the prosecution witness list. A few minutes later, Linda, the court clerk entered and called the court to order as Chapman entered behind the bench.

"Is the State ready to proceed?" he asked Dana.

"We are Your Honor," she replied.

"Very well, bring in the jury please," he directed the bailiff.

Franklin watched them come in and noticed they looked very relaxed and interested. He had to hand it to Ron Whittaker: in most of the trials he'd witnessed (from the observer seats since he had never defended or prosecuted a trial of this magnitude), he'd seen the jurors beginning to look bored and distracted at this point in the testimony. He wasn't sure if that was good or bad, but he supposed they would soon find out. At the very least, this experience was going to show him the soundness or foolhardiness of the unorthodox strategy Whittaker was forcing him to employ.

"The State calls Julie Bowers to the stand," Dana said from the prosecution table.

Franklin watched as a cute blonde girl took a seat in the witness chair after giving her oath. He was even sadder now for what he had been instructed to do, as he would have liked showing off his litigating abilities to the little spinner, the first cute girl he'd seen in this trial thus far.

Whittaker nudged him and glared at him as if reading his mind. Franklin sighed and stood.

"Your Honor, before Mrs. Porter gets started here, I see from the witness list that Ms. Bowers is here as an expert from the Washington State Patrol crime lab in the area of mud analysis."

Chapman glanced at Dana and raised his eyebrows.

"That's correct, Judge. That is why she's here," Dana replied.

Franklin reluctantly continued. "Your Honor, I'm quite sure that Ms. Bowers is highly qualified in that department. We have faith that my esteemed colleague, Mrs. Porter, isn't going to try to put up an expert in front of this court who isn't in fact, an expert. Again, in an interest to save the jury some tedium, the defense will stipulate that Ms. Bowers is an expert in the field of mud analysis." He gave a little grin to Julie Bowers who smiled back and then looked down, shyly.

"Okay, if the State has no objection then, the court will rule that Ms. Bowers is indeed an expert."

Dana answered that they had no objection. Franklin remained standing.

"Did you have something further, Mr. Richardson?" Chapman asked.

"Yes sir," he said, hesitantly. "I'm guessing that the purpose of the lovely Ms. Bowers' testimony is to establish that the mud found at the scene of the homicide is the same mud that was found on the pair of shoes from Mr. Whittaker's closet. I'm also guessing that she's here to testify that the same exact mud was also found in the sample taken from the rear of Mr. Whittaker's property, near the alleyway."

Franklin glanced back at Whittaker, one final, silent plea to not proceed. Whittaker gave an imperceptible nod of his head. Franklin sighed. "Your Honor, the defense will stipulate that the mud from all three locations is the same."

Chapman sighed and seemed perturbed. "I'm going to excuse the jury again for a moment." He asked the bailiff to escort the jury back into the jury room with instructions again to not discuss the case. Franklin noticed that Dana was staring at him, her brow furrowed and a look of disbelief on her face as they waited for the jury to file out.

"Mr. Richardson, do you have any idea just what you're doing here?" Chapman asked him, quietly but vehemently once the jury had left and the door to the jury room was closed.

"Yes sir, I do. Again sir, we don't think Mrs. Porter here is going to be bringing in a witness that isn't credible and didn't do a thorough job. I also don't think she made any mistakes in her testing process; she seems very competent to me."

Judge Chapman sat back in his chair and glared at Richardson. "I'll tell you right now, Mr. Richardson, if this is in any way a subversive attempt to sabotage this case or to set up an ineffective counsel appeal, I will hold you in contempt."

"I assure you it's not, Judge. I know exactly what I'm doing, and I assure you that we will be mounting a very vigorous and compelling defense." He shrugged. "I'm simply trying to save the court some time and expense, but if you'd like to proceed with the testimony, I'm happy to withdraw our stipulation and proceed."

Chapman stared at him a moment longer and then turned to Porter. "Dana?"

She shrugged, "We're fine with saving the state money and time, Judge. As long as we can get the evidence into the record and the jury understands what it means that the defense is stipulating."

He took a moment and then finally nodded. "Okay, we'll proceed."

Chapman had the jury brought in, the looks on their faces conveying annoyance this time. He then looked at Julie Bowers. "Okay, Ms. Bowers, it appears that the defense is going to stipulate to your credentials and to your findings in the mud analysis. Mrs. Porter will ask a few questions of you to clarify your testimony and then we'll send you on your way." He nodded to Dana.

Franklin glanced toward Ron who smiled at him and nodded. He glared back in return.

Dana had the sample of mud from the crime scene, the sample from Whittaker's back yard, and the tennis shoes found in Whittaker's closet all brought in and introduced as evidence. She then confirmed with Bowers that all three were the samples she'd tested and found to match. She acknowledged that they were, and Dana announced she had nothing further.

Chapman asked Franklin if he had any cross and Franklin stood, taking just a moment to look at Julie Bowers who was staring right back at him, looking him in the eye. He wanted to wink at her, but he knew Chapman and most of the jury members were also looking right at him.

"No questions for the witness, Your Honor," he said, sighing and sitting back down.

Chapman excused Bowers who stepped down from the witness box and strode out of the courtroom. Franklin turned slightly to watch her leave. Bowers did not glance back at him as she walked out.

Chapman cleared his throat. "Please call your next witness, Mrs. Porter."

Chapter 40

"The State calls Mrs. Carmen Hermes," Dana declared.

Carmen Hermes was Ron Conner's housekeeper, and Dana hadn't been sure she was actually going to be calling her as a witness.

Carmen's English wasn't the best, and Dana didn't like to have to use a translator. It made for awkward testimony for the jury and often became tedious. Jason Garvey argued that they didn't need her testimony, and Dana had agreed originally. After Franklin's cross of Monika Sodafsky, though, where he had asked her if she thought the mud being found only in the dining room was unusual, Dana had decided that the best way to head off one possible line of defense was to call Carmen to testify.

The question had then become whether or not to use a translator. Carmen did speak some English, but the possibility of her misunderstanding a question and answering it incorrectly certainly existed without a translator. Jason had convinced her that if she was going to call Carmen to testify, she would have to use the court appointed translator.

As Carmen took the stand, Dana requested the judge call up the translator. She'd set this up in advance during pretrial hearings, of course, just on the chance that she would decide to use Carmen.

Chapman instructed the jurors that the translator would be used and informed them that the translator was certified by the court and would translate exactly what was said, avoiding any usage of inflection or words not present in the original phrases. He motioned for Dana to proceed.

Knowing how laborious this was and how tiresome it would become, Dana decided to dispense with the preliminary niceties she would normally employ.

"Mrs. Hermes, what is your occupation?"

She waited as the translator asked the question in Spanish, and then Carmen answered through the translator, "I'm a housekeeper."

"Were you the housekeeper for the victim, Mr. Ronald Conner, during the time period around the 3rd of January of this year?"

The translator asked the question, waited for the reply, and then answered, "Yes, I was."

"Do you recall the last date that you cleaned Mr. Conner's house?"

Another pause while the translation occurred before the answer, "Yes, I cleaned it that Sunday, the day before he was found murdered."

Dana painstakingly established with Carmen that she cleaned Conner's house every Sunday, usually starting at 10am and finishing by 3pm. Dana then brought out the crime scene photo that showed the mud residue in the dining room. She showed Carmen the picture and asked her if she had cleaned the dining room that day and if there was any way that mud would have been left there after she was finished with the cleaning process.

Carmen appeared upset and defensive by the question and answered that there was no way she would have left such a mess. She elaborated and declared that the mud could only have been deposited there on the floor after she had left the residence at 3pm. Dana thanked her and told Chapman she had no further questions.

"Cross, Mr. Richardson?" asked Chapman.

This time, Dana was watching as she finished with her direct, and she saw Whittaker hand Franklin the notepad he'd been scribbling notes on. She glanced over at Jason Garvey who nodded to her; he'd seen it as well. It wasn't a complete surprise considering who his attorney was, nor was it improper; however, it might change the way Dana was presenting the prosecution. She was now pretty sure that Whittaker was running his own defense.

Franklin glanced at the notepad and then stood up.

"Mrs. Hermes, how difficult would it be for someone to leave mud from their shoes in the dining room only, without tracking it through the rest of the house, without leaving any trace near the doorway or the living room?"

Dana was on her feet, objecting before Franklin finished the question, but he managed to talk over her, finishing it anyway.

"Your Honor," she said, exasperated. "This question calls for a conclusion that Mrs. Hermes isn't qualified to give."

Franklin shrugged. "Mrs. Hermes is a professional housekeeper, Your Honor. Who else but she would be qualified to tell this court whether or not someone could leave mud in the dining room without levitating their way there?"

Dana shook her head. This was bullshit. It didn't matter how Chapman ruled now; Franklin had made his point to the jury.

"Sustained," Chapman replied, glaring at Franklin. "The jury will disregard the question, and counsel will refrain from asking such questions in the future.

Dana sat down, frustrated. The old saying was true: you couldn't unring a bell. The jury had been instructed to disregard the question, but they'd still heard it and they were likely now wondering how mud could have gotten into the dining room without any getting on the floor in any of the rooms between the dining room and the door. Her decision to put Carmen on the stand had backfired without Franklin ever having gotten an answer to his improper question.

Poor Carmen was sitting there watching the exchange, doubtless confused about what was going on. Franklin shrugged and replied,

"Okay then, Your Honor, I guess we have no questions for the witness."

Judge Chapman, who understood what had happened, continued to glare at Franklin for a second longer, and then looked at Carmen. He thanked her and released her. Carmen waited for the interpreter to give her the news and then shuffled down from the witness stand. Chapman glanced at the clock on the wall and then adjourned court for lunch.

Chapter 41

For the afternoon session, Dana called Detective Bruce Norgaard to the stand. Detective Norgaard testified about confiscating the bags of trash from the trash cans and about the evidence he'd found during the search of Whittaker's house, including the backpack with the firearm, magazine, empty shell casing, and the muddy shoes.

Judge Chapman thought Dana did a good job of getting this testimony into the record during her direct examination of Monika Sodafsky, and he was a little surprised that she'd chosen to repeat it with Norgaard. He thought it was probably a sign that she was slightly uncomfortable with the State's case thus far.

Again, Richardson didn't object to any of the questions Dana asked or the answers that Norgaard gave, despite several of them being somewhat borderline. When it came time for his cross-examination, he told Chapman he did have a few questions.

"Detective Norgaard, when you obtained the bags of garbage from the cans, were the bags sealed in any way?"

"Well, they were closed by the drawstrings," he said after a moment's thought.

"Okay, they were closed, but were they inaccessible; could the insides of the bags have been accessed?" Richardson clarified.

"Yes, I suppose you could still access the inside of the bags."

"So there was no knot tied in them or anything that would stop anybody else from putting an object into the bag after it had already been placed in the can?"

"There was no knot in the top, no."

"So somebody could have come along at any time and placed an object, even the ball of duct tape, into the bags while they were sitting out there along the alleyway, is that correct?"

Norgaard shrugged. "I suppose so."

Richardson looked down at the notepad he always had with him during his cross-examinations. Chapman had seen Whittaker taking notes in that very notepad and saw him hand it to Richardson before his questioning each time. It was apparent that Whittaker was running his own defense, and Chapman suspected that might explain some of the odd behavior from Richardson. He considered asking him about it but decided that it wasn't relevant to a fair trial.

If Whittaker wanted to make the questionable decision to run his own defense, that was his prerogative.

"Let's talk about the shoes you found in the closet," Richardson said to Norgaard. "Were the shoes labeled in any way with Mr. Whittaker's name?"

"I don't believe so."

"So you didn't see his name written on the tag or inside the shoe; there was no sign attached to them reading, 'These shoes belong to Ron Whittaker'?"

"No," answered Norgaard.

"So you don't know for sure that the shoes actually belonged to Whittaker then, is that correct?"

"Well, they were in his closet, next to all the other shoes."

Richardson stared at him. "That wasn't the question, Detective. Was there anything, other than the fact that they were in the closet, that would lead you to believe they belonged to Mr. Whittaker?"

Norgaard seemed to struggle for a better answer, then eventually admitted, "No."

"I see." Richardson paced back toward his table then turned again. "So you must have submitted the shoes for DNA testing then? To make sure Mr. Whittaker's DNA was inside them?"

"I don't think we did," answered Norgaard. "We didn't doubt the ownership of a pair of shoes found in the closet of the suspect."

"Judge Chapman, I would request that you order the witness to please refrain from expanding on the answers and merely answer the questions he's asked." Richardson said loudly, his expression showing outrage at Norgaard's answer.

Chapman thought this was a nice play on Richardson's part, and he was correct; Norgaard's answer was inappropriate. "The witness will answer only the question asked of him and not expand on that answer with opinion or conjecture that's not requested," he said firmly to Norgaard.

"Thank you, Your Honor. Detective Norgaard, just to confirm, you didn't do any type of forensic testing whatsoever, DNA or otherwise, to determine that the shoes you seized as evidence actually belonged to Mr. Whittaker?"

"Not to my knowledge," answered Norgaard.

"Nothing further," Richardson stated, walking back to his table.

"Redirect?" Chapman asked Dana. If it were true that the detectives hadn't done any testing on the shoes themselves, it was somewhat damaging to the State's evidence. He couldn't really blame the detectives, though; he doubted he would have bothered with such a test in their positions.

Dana understood the damage as well and did her best to mitigate it. With a look of disbelief toward the defense and then turning to the jury with the same look, she shook her head sadly.

"Detective Norgaard, would you have any reason whatsoever to doubt that a pair of shoes found inside a person's closet, a person who lived alone and had no roommates, would belong to that person?"

"No, I would not," he answered firmly, though somewhat defensively, Chapman thought.

"Did you note the size of the shoes you collected as evidence from the closet?" she asked.

"Yes, I did; it's written on the inventory sheet," he replied.

Dana went back to her desk, found a copy of the inventory sheet and brought it up to Norgaard. "What size were the shoes?" she asked.

"They were size nine," he replied, reading off the sheet.

"And did you notice the sizes of any of the other shoes in the closet?" she asked.

"Yes, I did; they were all size nine," he replied.

"Nothing further, Your Honor," Dana said, sitting back at her desk.

Chapman thought once again that she'd done well in the redirect, but that Richardson, or Whittaker, or whoever was running the defense, had scored a point on this one. Reasonable doubt was a fickle thing, and the defense had definitely managed to instill some question of doubt about the shoes, along with some doubt about why the Sheriff's Office hadn't forensically tied the shoes to Whittaker. Of course, the jury may have decided that it was just a bullshit move on the part of the defense and that the shoes were obviously Whittaker's. It was tough to tell with juries.

Chapman dismissed Norgaard, and Dana Porter called Detective Rory James to the stand.

James was the detective who actually searched through the bags of trash and found the wad of duct tape with Conner's hairs stuck to it. Dana had pictures of the trash that she introduced as evidence, including a couple of pieces of mail that showed Ron Whittaker's name and address on them. James testified that the mail and the duct tape had been in the trash together, thereby establishing a nexus between the bag of trash, Whittaker's home, and the duct tape.

When she was finished, Richardson had just one question, again asking if the bags of trash were sealed in any way when James opened them to go through them. He admitted that the tops were open and, when asked, admitted that it would have been possible for someone else to have added the ball of duct tape to the trash bags after Whittaker had brought them out to the alley.

Richardson announced he had no more questions, and Chapman glanced at the clock. It was only 5:15pm, but was much too late to begin with a new witness. Besides, he knew from the witness list Dana Porter had submitted, that they were well ahead of schedule. He called for a recess for the day and gave his standard instructions to the jurors about not discussing the case.

He was pleased overall with the case, he thought, as he made his way back to his chambers and hung up his robe. It was going along smoothly and although the defense had seemed at first to have no clue which way they were going to go with their defense, he now believed they at least had a plan.

Whether or not it was a good one remained to be seen.

Chapter 42

W hen Franklin got back to the office that night he felt better than he had since the onset of the trial. Although Whittaker was still running things, Franklin could finally see the light, see the direction the case was going and see the defense that Whittaker was lining up.

He sat down in his chair and put his feet up on the desk. Stacy had already left for the night; Franklin texted her before leaving court and told her to go home. He hadn't seen her outside of the office since the weekend before the trial started, and he was enjoying the break. It had been too long since he had time for just himself.

He reached into the bottom drawer of his desk and pulled out a bottle of 12-year old Chivas Regal he'd had in there for months. He wasn't much of a drinker normally, but he was in a bit of a melancholy mood and this felt like a Scotch kind of evening.

Walking back out into the lobby, he found one of the paper coffee cups and brought it back to his desk. Normally he preferred his Scotch on ice, but neat would work in a crunch. Sitting back in his chair and throwing his feet back up on the desk, he sipped the Scotch and stared at the cabinet that held his safe.

The briefcase in his safe was bothering him, had been bothering him for the last three months since he'd agreed to hold it for Whittaker. That briefcase had lately become his own personal Tell-Tale Heart, seemingly thumping out its presence in Franklin's mind. The unknown quantity it contained was the vulture eye of the old man, and Franklin feared he would need to kill it to silence it. Killing it of course meant cracking it open and seeing what was inside.

He reached down and entered the code into the digital keypad on the safe door, his nerves calming slightly with just the sight of the leather briefcase. Pulling it out of the safe, he dropped it on his desk and leaned back in his chair again, sipping the Scotch and staring at it.

Over the last three months, he'd steadily graduated from doing nothing more than staring at the case on his desk, to actually trying to guess the three-digit combination of the lock. Knowing that there were exactly 1000 possible combinations, he realized that he could probably figure it out in a short amount of time, assuming the combination of both latches was the same. The problem was that he could only ever psyche himself up to attempt five or ten tries before he broke out into a sweat and put the briefcase back into the safe.

This time, he vowed not to try to open it. Instead he stared at it while he sipped his Scotch, his curiosity building as he tried desperately to quench it with the Chivas Regal. He had a moral and legal responsibility to act on his client's wishes...to protect the briefcase without violating the sanctity of its contents. It wasn't in him to suppress the urges he was feeling here, though.

Sighing, he took the case and stuffed it back into the safe, quickly slamming the door and hitting the lock button. Whatever was in that briefcase, whatever was so important to Ron Whittaker, was none of his business.

He finished the last of the Scotch in his cup and put the bottle back in his desk drawer. Grabbing his coat, he took one last look at the safe, the keypad still glowing green, which it would do for sixty seconds, beckoning him in the same fashion as the aliens in Stephen King's *The Tommyknockers*, soliciting him to come and enter the code, to make one more attempt to satisfy his desire.

Franklin turned off his office light and shut the door hard, cutting off the phantom calling of the briefcase. He walked quickly to the front entrance of his office. One thing for sure, he promised himself. If Whittaker was eventually found guilty, the first thing Franklin was going to do was come back here and crack that fucking briefcase wide open. Once he found out what was in it that was so fucking important, he'd toss the thing into Puget Sound. Maybe he'd stop hearing the goddamn siren calling in his mind if the briefcase was at the bottom of the ocean.

Chapter 43

On Thursday morning, Dana was running late. It was almost nine o'clock and she was still in her office trying to gather her notes for today's testimony. Franklin Richardson's little shenanigans with her witnesses had thrown her entire schedule out of whack, and she spent most of last evening and this morning on the phone trying to get the rest of her witnesses lined up.

She originally planned for Lawrence Gunby and Julie Bowers, her first two witnesses from the crime lab, to be on the stand for the better part of a full day each, counting cross-examination. Instead, they'd been up there less than an hour each, and now she was scrambling to get the people into court today and tomorrow who she'd originally told to expect not to be here until next week.

Luckily, the two witnesses she needed to testify next were able to make it up here today, saving her the hassle of rearranging the other witnesses, and potentially having to tell the jury a story out of sequence, never something that helped her cases.

Running down the hallway from her office, she skidded to a stop at the doors of the courtroom, took just a second to straighten her blouse and run her fingers through her hair, and then calmly walked in. She lucked out in that Judge Chapman was just walking in from the door to his chambers. He gave her a smile as she made her way to the prosecution table where Jason Garvey was waiting, a worried look on his face.

"I was just about to figure out how I was going to ask Chapman for a recess before we even started," he whispered to her.

She grinned at him. "I should have waited another few minutes. That would have been fun to see."

Garvey rolled his eyes good naturedly and turned away from her. Dana knew that Garvey was fully briefed and prepared on this case and that he would be perfectly capable of taking it over if she were somehow unable to appear one day.

Chapman called the court to order and asked for any motions. Not getting any, he asked the bailiff to bring in the jurors, and then he directed Dana to begin.

She stood. "The State calls Justin Caldwell to the stand."

Justin Caldwell was the firearms and tooling expert analyst from the Washington State Patrol crime lab who had looked at the firearm they had seized from the search of Whittaker's house. Dana spent the first thirty minutes going over his qualifications, training, and experience as a firearms and tool mark expert. She then asked him to outline the testing process he'd used for the two shell casings that had been submitted, the first from the heater vent at Conner's, and the second from the backpack in Whittaker's laundry hamper.

Using long and detailed language to describe the entire process, he testified that he'd compared the two shell casings using a high-powered microscope. He said he examined the firing pin marks as well as the tooling marks made by the ejector of the pistol and the slide mechanism as it passed over the shell during the firing process. He determined that both the submitted shell casings came from the same gun.

He then test fired the Beretta pistol that was registered to Whittaker and examined the shell casing extracted from the gun to compare it to the two submitted casings.

"What did you find when you examined this casing?"

"The firing pin marks were exactly the same, as were the ejector marks and the slide scrape marks."

"So what was your final conclusion then?"

"The shell casings submitted as evidence in this case were fired from the Beretta 92FS firearm that was submitted for testing."

"Thank you, Mr. Caldwell. I want to move on now to another item that you examined." Dana requested State's exhibit thirty-two, and the clerk handed her the evidence bag that contained the plastic Vitamin Water bottle that Monika Sodafsky had collected from the recycle bin at Whittaker's house during the search. Dana walked slowly back toward the witness stand, holding the bag up so that the jury could clearly see what was in it, before showing it to Caldwell.

"This is an item that was found in Mr. Whittaker's house, collected as evidence, and submitted to you for testing. Do you recognize it?"

Caldwell acknowledged this.

"As an expert in firearms, did this plastic bottle with the base blown out appear to have any relevance as an accessory to a gun?" Dana considered the phrasing of this question very carefully while preparing for this testimony. As a key piece of evidence for the State's case, she needed to make sure she could get an expert to testify that it was a homemade silencer for a pistol, without *leading* the witness to that conclusion. It was a narrow line to walk.

She rehearsed the testimony with Caldwell in the weeks before the trial, and he answered smoothly, saying that as an expert in firearms, he recognized the item as a homemade silencer for a pistol. He told the court that he had tested the residue on the bottom of the bottle and identified it as burned gun powder residue, supporting his conclusion that it was a type of silencer.

This testimony had taken nearly two hours, and Dana had originally been concerned that Richardson was going to try to stipulate to the evidence. Had that happened again, she had been determined to tell Judge Chapman that the State was not going along with the defense's game. By stipulating to the previous witnesses' testimonies, the game Richardson/Whittaker was playing was a risky one: they were allowing the evidence into the record unopposed, but were undermining her ability to prop up witnesses, her ability to make them into unimpeachable experts. She was willing to let him roll those dice a couple of times but not to make a mockery of the entire forensic portion of her case, particularly with regard to the silencer, which she felt was a key piece of the State's case.

The tooling expert from the WSP crime lab helped to tie Whittaker's gun to the homicide, something that she absolutely needed to establish before she could put that gun in his hands. The fragmenting bullets he used had made them indefinable and matching them to the gun impossible, which is why the shell casings had been invaluable pieces of evidence. She knew she was lucky to have them.

Now she had only to worry about Richardson's cross-examination and hope he wouldn't be able to discredit Caldwell in any way.

Richardson stood at his table when Chapman opened the floor for him to begin his cross. He looked down at the notepad that Dana again saw Whittaker hand to him, and then he looked up at the witness.

"Mr. Caldwell, thanks for being here. I, for one, was impressed with your testimony and with your ability to match the marks on the shell casings so carefully with the firearm that was used to fire the bullets from those shell casings. The only question I have for you, sir, is with all the testing you did, were you able to determine who actually pulled the trigger of the gun that ejected those shell casings?"

Caldwell frowned and shook his head. "No, I didn't receive any evidence that would enable me to perform a test like that."

"So you only know that the Beretta nine-millimeter firearm you received for the tests was the gun that fired the bullets from those shell casings, but you don't know who fired that gun?"

"That's correct," Caldwell replied, looking confused.

"Nothing further, Your Honor," Franklin replied, sitting back down at his desk.

Dana stared at Franklin with something approaching disbelief. His ineffectiveness in trying to suppress any of the evidence she was introducing was staggering. The game he was playing, admitting all the existing evidence but then presumably planning to claim that someone else committed the crime, was a foolhardy gamble, and apparently, he was going all-in on it. She couldn't see any other plan, couldn't anticipate any other course that he could take with his defense at this point. He had allowed too much evidence to be entered, and all of it pointed right at Whittaker. As much as she hated to even consider victory before she was even finished presenting the State's case, she couldn't see how this could work out well for the defendant. As she mulled over her thoughts, she began to have a bad feeling that she was missing something. Whittaker was too calm, too cool, still sitting there in that annoying relaxed posture he had every day.

As Judge Chapman was dismissing Justin Caldwell, Dana scratched a note on her notepad and slid it over to Jason Garvey.

What are we missing? THINK!!! He's too calm.

Jason read the note and then nodded to her, his gaze shifting over to the defense table as he leaned back in his chair. Dana hoped she was wrong, hoped the defense was just that bad, and her case was as solid as it appeared.

"Mrs. Porter, please call your next witness," Chapman ordered.

Chapter 44

"Full stack of pancakes, meat lover's omelet with Swiss cheese, side of bacon, side of sausage, coffee, and a large orange juice."

Ron Whittaker handed his menu to the waitress and noticed Franklin staring at him, a frown on his face.

"What?" he asked.

"Is somebody else joining us?"

Whittaker shrugged. "I'm hungry and I couldn't decide what I wanted. Seemed sensible to get some of everything."

"Steel cut oatmeal, an egg white vegetarian omelet, dry wheat toast, and coffee for me, honey," Franklin said to the waitress, handing her his menu and turning back to Whittaker. "You're buying."

"Am I not paying you enough, Franklin?" Ron asked, looking at him askew.

"My expenses are high. It costs a lot of money to run a blue-chip defense like I'm putting on for you."

Ron seemed to think that was hilarious, drawing stares from the other customers as he guffawed loudly.

"All right, settle down," Franklin admonished him. "What are we doing here, Ron?"

It was 10:30am on Sunday morning, and Ron had asked Franklin to meet him at the Blue Bird Café in Mukilteo for a late breakfast. Considering that Dana Porter had nearly wrapped up the State's case on Friday, Franklin hoped his client, who was tighter lipped than a whore at confession, was planning to finally discuss their defense strategy.

To the best of Franklin's knowledge, at this point the only people on the defense witness list were a guy from Verizon, who was going to testify that Whittaker's cell phone hadn't left his house that night, Whittaker's neighbor, who was going to testify that Whittaker always left the door to his house unlocked, and Whittaker's boss, Gerry Gresham, who also happened to be a witness for the State, obviously a bit of a conflict of interest. Needless to say, that made for a complete cluster-fuck of a defense strategy.

On Thursday afternoon, following the lunch break, Dana called to the stand a DNA expert from the FBI who tested the two sets of chopsticks found at Conner's house, discovering Conner's DNA on one set, and Whittaker's DNA on the other set. He also tested the mouth of the plastic bottle silencer and found Whittaker's DNA on that as well, which pretty much firmed up any loose strings in the State's evidence chain. All day Friday was spent on Dana's direct examination of the medical examiner who was on the scene of the murder and did the autopsy of Ron Conner's body. The ME testified that Conner had a contusion on his skull from a strike by a blunt object that likely would have rendered him unconscious. Then he tied together the duct tape evidence nicely by testifying that the marks around Conner's wrists had been caused pre-mortem and were the result of being duct taped to the chair. Lastly, he testified that the two bullets to the torso were the cause of death and that Conner died between the hours of 2:00am and 3:00am that Monday morning back in January. Naturally, Whittaker didn't allow Franklin to do any type of cross-examination on either the DNA expert or on the medical examiner.

Judge Chapman sent the court into recess for the weekend after the Medical Examiner's testimony; he then asked Dana how much longer she expected the State's case to take. She told the judge that at this time, they had only two witnesses left: the delivery guy from the Thai restaurant, and the two Rons' boss, Gerry Gresham. Dana expected the State to rest at the end of the day on Monday.

That meant that the defense needed to be prepared to present their case starting Tuesday. Which meant that Franklin was desperately hoping Whittaker was about to enlighten him on exactly what the defense case was going to be because, at this point, he didn't have a goddamn clue. Which was why he was thrilled to hear Ron's answer to his question of why they were meeting at the restaurant.

"We're here because I think it's time to fill you in on what we're going to be doing this week."

"You mean we're finally going to have the meeting that we should have had months ago?" Franklin asked sarcastically as the waitress brought over two mugs of coffee and set them down.

Ron opened a yellow packet of sweetener and stirred it into his coffee before replying. "There were a lot of options as far as direction we could have gone with my defense. I didn't see any point in burdening you with the minutiae of a defense strategy we might not even utilize." He took a sip of his coffee and set it back down. "I want to get this trial done quickly, and I needed your focus to be on the motions and pretrial details considering our time was so limited."

Franklin considered this and tried to quell his desire to ask questions. He had a plethora of them, starting with the biggest one which, in his mind, was why they had not waived speedy trial and taken a lot more time to prepare. He could understand the rush if Whittaker was in jail, but he was out on bail, and it didn't make any sense to hurry to trial. The other big question, of course, was the mysterious briefcase in his safe, but he knew Whittaker wasn't going to answer that one.

Franklin picked up his coffee cup and sipped at the hot drink, thinking about the motions Ron brought up. The only real motion he filed, the only one that required some preparation and some argument, was the one to quash the video the prosecution had of Whittaker's car from the security camera the night of the murder. It was obvious to him that if Whittaker's defense was that he was framed, the video was deadly to that defense; it countered his claim that he'd been home alone all that night. However, if Ron wanted to quash that piece of evidence, why not work on the rest of it as well? Why not work on arguing against as much of the evidence as he possibly could? It seemed to Franklin as if Ron *wanted* all the other evidence to point right at him, encouraged it all, and that made no sense to Franklin Richardson.

"Okay, so what is our plan then?" Franklin asked.

"We're going to start with your cross of both the Thai food delivery guy and Gerry Gresham. I'm going to have a lot of questions for you to ask them, so I need you to be sharp tomorrow."

"I'm always sharp, Ron. That's why you hired me."

Whittaker snorted. "I know, buddy. I'm just saying that tomorrow, you're going to get a lot of face time with the jury, so look your best."

Franklin nodded. "Dana is probably going to rest at the end of the day tomorrow, unless for some reason she decides to call another witness. That means we'll be presenting our case starting Tuesday morning. I'll also want to file a motion to dismiss at the end of her testimony. It's a standard motion at the end of the State's case, you know."

"As long as the motion is to dismiss with prejudice, that's fine."

With prejudice meant that the prosecution couldn't file the case again; it was effectively a ruling of not guilty. The judge would never make that ruling, but Franklin knew it was something the defense was expected to do anyway. The interesting thing to him was that Ron didn't want the case dismissed without prejudice which would have allowed the prosecution to charge him at a later date. Every step of the way, he seemed to be concerned with being charged later, from his insistence on all of the evidence being introduced to his refusal to accept any kind of plea bargain, to this, his insistence on only a dismissal with prejudice.

Before the trial started, Dana Porter came to Franklin with an offer of a lesser charge of second degree murder without a charge of unlawful imprisonment. Franklin brought the offer to Whittaker who laughed and summarily dismissed it. Dana then tried to negotiate further and offered to drop the firearm enhancement, an add-on at sentencing that would add up to five years to his prison sentence if he was convicted. Without the unlawful imprisonment charge, and without the firearms enhancement, Ron could be sentenced to only fifteen years and would be out in nine with good behavior. With all the evidence pointed right at him, it seemed like a good deal. Ron didn't think so. He insisted that he was innocent and that he wasn't going to spend even one year in prison for something he hadn't done. Franklin warned him that he was risking a life sentence, but Ron still didn't budge. Franklin asked him if he ever watched the Netflix documentary *Making a Murderer* which told the story of Steven Avery, currently doing life in prison for a crime that many people thought he didn't commit. A crime that many thought he was framed for. Ron said he hadn't seen it and he didn't care. He was innocent and he was determined to fight for an acquittal.

The waitress brought their breakfast over on a huge tray and began placing the plates on the table, using every bit of space to accommodate Ron's enormous order.

"Do we have witnesses? Any kind of actual defense we're going to present?" Franklin asked when the waitress had left.

Ron smiled as he began to dig into the pancakes. "We have a very good defense Franklin. A great defense actually, and you're going to love it."

As Ron started to outline the details of the defense they would be presenting, Franklin began to feel the months of accumulated stress start to melt away. He pounced on his food with gusto as he listened to Ron explain exactly what was going to happen. It was indeed a good defense, one that would stun the courtroom, and one that Franklin was going to greatly enjoy presenting.

Chapter 45

Across town on the first floor of the courthouse complex, Dana Porter was listening to music on the Pandora app on her phone and reviewing the transcripts of the testimony so far, making sure she hadn't missed any elements of the two crimes she had charged Ron Whittaker with, and confirming to herself that she was ready to rest her case after the last two witnesses took the stand on Monday. She popped the last piece of her poppy seed muffin into her mouth and took a sip of her Starbucks skinny vanilla latte, a staple of her mornings.

The office was quiet this morning, once again making her long for the simple days when she could actually take Saturdays off. She had to admit, though, as she snuggled her feet deeper into the slippers she always wore around the office on weekends, it was nice to be able to enjoy the solitude of a quiet office and to work without interruptions.

Just as she was thinking that, she heard the outer office door open and then close followed by the heavy tread of a man walking across the room toward her open door. She looked up as Jason Garvey gave the open door a courtesy knock and then strolled in, wearing a gray Washington Huskies sweatshirt and blue jeans, a file folder in his hand.

"Figured I'd find you here. You aren't answering your cell phone."

Dana had put her cell phone ringer on silent and had activated the *do not disturb* feature on her office line, experience telling her that even on a Saturday, disturbances were a fact of life in the busy prosecutor's office. She smiled and reached over to turn the music down on her phone which she had flipped upside down on her desk, just to make sure she couldn't see the silenced calls or text messages coming in.

"What did you find for me?"

Garvey walked over to her desk and slapped down the file. He settled himself into the chair in front of her desk, his leg draped casually over the armrest. Dana picked up the file and opened it, removing three color photographs that Jason had apparently printed off.

These were the photographs from the police crime scene technician who served the search warrant at Ron Whittaker's house. Dana went through all of the pictures taken months earlier when she was preparing for the case, and she remembered seeing a photo of the takeout container in Whittaker's fridge that was from the same restaurant as the takeout containers on Conner's kitchen counter, the ones that contained the chopsticks they processed to find both Conner's and Whittaker's DNA. At the time she was reviewing the case, the photo of the similar takeout carton had seemed to be irrelevant and coincidental, though she knew Monika had instructed the photographer to take the picture at Whittaker's house due to the coincidence that they both ordered takeout from the same restaurant. These pictures were what Dana remembered seeing during court the other day when Franklin Richardson did his cross-examination of Monika. She asked Jason to find the photos, which she hadn't collected as part of the court file originally.

She now flipped through the three photographs. The first showed the inside of the plastic garbage can under the sink at Whittaker's house. The second showed the entire inside of the fridge, with the takeout container from Satay Thai sitting on the middle shelf, and the last showed a close-up of the takeout container itself.

Now she looked up at Jason. "What do you think?"

He shrugged. "Like Richardson established, no chopsticks in the container and none in the garbage can."

"So what does this mean? He's going to claim that the chopsticks were taken from the takeout container in his fridge as part of the frame-up?"

"It appears that way." Jason raised his eyebrows and shrugged again. "Seems like a really shitty defense to me, but I guess if that's all you got, that's what you go with. Although, to be fair to him, there *were* no used chopsticks in the container or in the garbage can, so that might be the actual plan."

Dana stared at the photo of the takeout container, wracking her brain to come up with a better conclusion than what seemed obvious. It wasn't going to be too difficult for her to scuttle any defense claim that the missing chopsticks was important evidence. Lots of people eat Thai food with a fork and toss the chopsticks in a drawer somewhere or tell the restaurant to keep them. It was far more believable that one of those things happened than it was that a murderer stole the chopsticks from Whittaker's fridge with the sole intent of framing him. She had very little respect for Franklin Richardson after working with him for a few years here at the prosecutor's office, but she couldn't see how even he could believe this to be a solid line of defense in a case of this magnitude. He seemed to be playing Russian roulette with his client's freedom, and Dana had loaded the six-shot revolver with five bullets, planning to slide a shell into the sixth chamber on Monday. It didn't make sense for him to be that incompetent, and that continued to worry her.

"Is there a picture of the actual food in this container? We know the two containers at Conner's place were both chicken Pad Thai, was this one the same?"

Jason shook his head. "These are the only pictures of the container or of the garbage can. I don't think anybody thought to compare the actual food or to document what it was. I think Sodafsky ordered these pictures taken because the containers were the same and showed a connection. Even she wasn't sure if it was relevant at all."

Dana sighed. "Okay, well I guess we'll have to wait and see then." She gathered up the three photos and handed them back to Garvey. "Hang onto these. I don't know what they're planning, but I'd like you to keep thinking about it and let me know if you come up with anything."

Garvey stood up and told her not to work too late. He took the photos and left her office. Dana turned the music on her phone back up and refocused on the transcripts, the bad feeling in her stomach continuing to grow. She was sure she was missing something and she just couldn't figure out what it was.

Chapter 46

On Monday morning, Neil Chapman walked into the courtroom at precisely nine o'clock and called the court to order. His first step was to ask if there were any motions, and then to have the jurors brought in and welcome them back. He knew some judges questioned the jurors at this point, asking if they had read any news about the case or talked to anybody about it, but he didn't like to do that. He'd given them clear instructions on Friday that they were to come to him and let him know if they had accidentally or intentionally seen anything newsworthy about the trial, and so asking them in open court was tantamount to questioning their integrity, in his opinion. He had no intention of trying to put himself in a position where he would have to dismiss a juror in the middle of the trial.

The jurors settled in, the court called to order and ready to proceed, Chapman directed Dana to call her first witness of the day. She told him on Friday that she expected to wrap up the State's case today, a full two or three days sooner than expected, and Chapman was thrilled. It was unusual for a murder case to wrap up so quickly, but it was also unusual for the defense to be so ambivalent about the witnesses and the evidence.

Dana called Mr. Chayond Demir, the delivery driver for Satay Thai, to the stand. Chapman waited as the bailiff went into the hallway and then returned with Demir, a diminutive Asian who was dressed in black slacks and a polo shirt, a baseball cap in his hand as he approached the stand. His hair was mussed up from the hat he had apparently been wearing while waiting for his turn to testify. Demir appeared to be in his early twenties and seemed to be nervous, his eyes shifting around the courtroom as he took the oath and Chapman asked him to be seated.

Chapman knew that Dana was going to be good at handling a nervous witness, particularly her own witness, and he watched as she smiled kindly and asked Demir some simple questions about his background and his employment at Satay Thai, calming him down with her easy manner and soft spoken voice. Chapman was pleased to see that Demir spoke perfect English, avoiding the need for another interpreter. After Dana established that Demir was a delivery driver and a cook with Satay Thai for more than three years, and that his uncle was the owner of the restaurant, she began with the pertinent questions.

"Mr. Demir, on the evening of January 3rd, did you make a food delivery to the address of Mr. Ron Conner?" Dana read the address off her notepad.

Demir testified that he had made the delivery and that he was familiar with the address and with Mr. Conner, having delivered food there regularly over the previous three years. Dana walked him through the time of the delivery, establishing through records from the restaurant that the delivery was made at around 10:45pm and that it was two orders of food, both chicken Pad Thai.

"While making the delivery, did you see or hear any other people in the residence?" Dana asked.

"I didn't see anybody else, but I did hear a male voice ask if there was any beer. Mr. Conner yelled back that he thought there was beer in the fridge," Demir replied.

"How many deliveries a day would you guess you make?" Dana asked.

"Probably between five and ten myself," Demir replied, shrugging his shoulders.

"So how is it, with thousands of deliveries per year, that you remember the details about this one delivery?" Dana asked him. Chapman knew this was a question designed to head off Richardson's cross-examination which would surely call into question Demir's veracity considering the mundane job of making food deliveries that should be typically unmemorable. Of course, with this case, the cross might not be coming, so Chapman wasn't sure just how important it was for Dana to bother.

Demir testified that he remembered this one in particular for several reasons. The first was that he was on a first name basis with Ron Conner from all of the deliveries he made there over the previous three years, and the second was that he heard of the murder the next day, when the delivery was fresh in his mind. He reached out to Detective Sodafsky a few days later, after speaking to his uncle about the voice he heard in the background when he was making the delivery.

Dana thanked him and said she had no further questions. Chapman looked over at Richardson.

"Cross?" he asked, eyebrows raised, completely uncertain what to expect.

"Yes, Your Honor, a few questions," Richardson replied, standing up at the defense table.

"Mr. Demir, did you cook the food that you delivered to Mr. Conner's residence that night?" he asked.

"No, it was cooked by my uncle."

"Do you know what the order was though?"

"Yes, it was two orders of chicken Pad Thai."

"Were there any special instructions with either of these orders, any special way to cook them, any additions or subtractions from the normal way Satay Thai would have made these orders for any other customer?"

Demir frowned and shook his head. "No, I don't think so."

"Okay, Mr. Demir, well, let's just make sure, just so there's no question." Richardson asked for and received the State's evidence item number eighty-two, which was the order sheet for that delivery. Richardson asked Chapman if he could approach the witness, and Chapman approved him to do so. He walked up to Demir and handed him the order sheet for the delivery.

"If there was a modification to the order in any way, is this where it would be listed?"

Demir acknowledged that it would have been written on the order sheet by the person who took the call.

"And there are no modifications listed there, correct?"

"That's correct."

"Okay, so then the two orders that you delivered were standard orders of chicken Pad Thai, cooked just how they would be cooked for any other customer who ordered them, without modifications?"

"Yes, it would appear so."

Chapman glanced over at Dana Porter who had hastily picked up her notepad and was furiously scribbling something. She handed the notepad to Jason Garvey who looked at what she'd written and then looked at her and shrugged. Dana looked almost sick, her face visibly paling when she returned her attention to the witness stand. Richardson had moved on from the questions about the food.

"Mr. Demir, have you ever delivered food to the home of the defendant, Mr. Ron Whittaker?"

Demir nodded. "Yes, several times."

"So you've spoken with him quite a few times then?"

Demir acknowledged that he had.

"The voice you heard that night asking about the beer, wouldn't you have recognized it as Mr. Whittaker's voice if you've heard his voice quite a few times in the past?"

Dana stood and objected to the question, establishing that it called for speculation. Chapman looked at her briefly and considered her objection. It did call for speculation, but it was also along the lines of an observation. It could have been phrased better, but Chapman did understand the intention of the question and decided it was reasonable. "Overruled," he ordered. "Mr. Demir, you may answer the question."

"I didn't recognize the voice," he answered. Chapman saw several of the jurors raise their eyebrows at that.

Richardson said he had no further questions and he sat back down.

Chapman looked at Dana and asked if she had any questions for redirect. She stood up and answered that she did.

"Mr. Demir, the voice you heard asking for the beer. Was it close by the front door, like in the living area right there, or far away, like back in the kitchen?"

"It was far away," he answered.

"So the person asking was shouting then?"

"Yes, he was shouting."

"Mr. Demir, have you ever heard the defendant, Mr. Whittaker, shout at you from another room?"

Demir shook his head. "No, I haven't."

"Could you say with certainty, then, that the voice you heard was *not* that of Mr. Whittaker?"

"No, I couldn't," Demir answered.

"In fact, from the distance you heard the voice, would you be able to identify the owner of the voice if you did hear it again?"

"I don't think so," he replied, after some thought.

Dana said she had nothing further and sat back down. Chapman could see she was distracted; her questions on redirect and Demir's answers had seemed to be scripted, as if she'd anticipated Richardson's line on cross and had previously discussed it with Demir, preparing him for the questions. She was rattled about something though, Chapman thought, her calm demeanor gone and her agitation evident.

Chapman thanked Demir, dismissed him and sent the court into recess for an early lunch break.

Chapter 47

Dana Porter was furious. She thought she had just figured out what Whittaker's defense was going to be, and she'd walked right into the trap, something every prosecutor feared. Even though she told herself not to relax; not to be lulled into a false sense of security, she suddenly realized that she'd done just that. She was confident and sure, happy with the way she was directing the trial and happy with the failings of Franklin Richardson. She now realized that the confidence she tried to avoid was going to come back to bite her in the ass.

She was at her desk, spending the lunch hour in her office, her focus on the computer screen in front of her and the internet search she just entered.

"He's going to claim he's allergic to something," she said to Jason Garvey who was sitting quietly in the chair across from her.

"He can't just make that claim," Garvey said. "He has to back it up with something, has to have a witness and there isn't one on his witness list."

"You watch, he's going to call a doctor to testify, and that doctor will say he's allergic to something." She pointed at her screen where she'd just searched for Pad Thai ingredients. "Here it is, standard Pad Thai contains peanuts. He's going to have a peanut allergy, I fucking know it."

"He can't add a doctor to his witness list this late in the game," Garvey said, a frustrated look on his face.

"He can because he'll claim that the doctor is a rebuttal witness. He'll claim that he didn't know we were going to proceed with the food evidence and that he needs the doctor to rebut our claim that he was the other one to eat that food." Dana typed at her keyboard some more and then turned the screen toward Garvey. It was the online menu for Satay Thai and she clicked on the Pad Thai image. One of the ingredients listed on the description was peanuts.

"It might not be peanuts," Garvey said, his head hanging.

"It doesn't matter. It might be peanuts, it might be noodles, it might be the fucking metal wok they cook it in for all I know, but he's going to claim he has an allergy; he's going to get a doctor to back it up, and he's going to call in the restaurant owner to testify that the food he normally orders at his own house doesn't contain whatever ingredient he's allergic to. Then he's going to use our photos of his own takeout order from his fridge, the one that's missing the chopsticks, and he's going to claim that the entire thing is a fucking setup and that he was framed."

Suddenly she froze as something clicked in her mind. Something that had been bothering her from a week ago, during Richardson's opening argument. Something he'd said that she'd heard at the time that had seemed to be significant but that she'd ignored. Frantically, she grabbed her keys from where they were laying on her desktop and she unlocked the drawer of her desk. Inside it was the transcript of the first week of the trial that she had been studying on Saturday. She grabbed it and began flipping through the first few pages.

"Fuck me," she said softly.

"What?" Garvey asked, a plaintive note in his voice.

"Remember in Richardson's opening statement, how he emphasized Whittaker's intelligence?"

Garvey nodded. "Sure. What of it?"

Dana laughed, "All those peremptory challenges he used, we laughed at him because it seemed like he was using them on jurors who would be perfect for the defense." She shook her head, "He was stacking the jury with smart people--successful people, people just like his client."

"I don't understand," Jason said, slowly. "Why?"

"Because he's going to show them all the evidence against him and he's going to say, 'You guys are smart, but I'm even smarter than you. Would *you* leave this much evidence of a crime? Would *you* have left the murder weapon in your laundry hamper? If *you* wouldn't have done that, what are the chances that *I*, someone even smarter than you, someone the prosecution claims planned this crime in advance, what are the chances that *I* would have done that?' And they're going to buy it."

"But we talked about this," Jason said, a small whine coming into his voice. "We knew this was going to be his defense, we knew he was going to claim he was framed."

"Yeah. But we didn't know he'd have evidence to back it up. He left something behind as evidence that he could prove beyond a reasonable doubt didn't belong to him."

"The food. The allergy," Jason replied, putting it together.

"That's going to be the keystone of the defense, I guarantee it."

"So you think maybe he didn't kill Conner then?" Jason asked, still confused.

Dana laughed, "Oh he killed him, I guarantee you that. Remember the security camera footage that Richardson fought so hard to repress? It was the only piece of evidence he actually fought over. Remember how hard that was to find?" Garvey nodded his head. "We weren't even going to look for it," Dana continued. "Monika Sodafsky had checked all the city and state traffic cameras and Whittaker's car didn't appear on any of the ones between his house and Conner's. Then we find his car on that private security footage, and Richardson flips out and gets Chapman to repress it. That was the key piece of evidence and we didn't realize it."

She shook her head, thinking hard. "This isn't over. We're going to have Gresham on the stand right after lunch and we're going to show the motive." She looked at Jason. "I want you to head over to Satay Thai right now. Find out if the owner or any of the employees have been asked to testify for the defense. If so, find out when they were asked and find out what they're going to testify. We can still redeem ourselves, maybe."

Jason jumped up and grabbed his coat, heading out. Dana gathered her files and walked back to the courtroom. The afternoon session was about to start, and she had a case to salvage.

Chapter 48

"If Ron Conner was removed from the picture, who would have been next in line to get the director's job at Puget Sound Aerospace?" Dana asked Gerald Gresham, who'd taken the stand to start the afternoon session.

Gresham was dressed in an expensive suit and looked like he'd recovered nicely from the heart attack he had three months before, Franklin thought. Ron Whittaker told him about the heart attack, and about what transpired in the moments leading up to it. Franklin knew that the heart attack was caused by Whittaker telling Gresham about his wife's affair, and he wondered how Dana was going to handle that in her questioning.

"Ron Whittaker would have been next in line for the job," Gresham answered.

"In fact, even with Mr. Conner still alive, was Mr. Whittaker a contender for the job?"

Gresham nodded. "Yes, it was a very close contest between the two of them. I finally made the decision just a few days earlier that I was going to go with Ron Conner."

"Did Mr. Whittaker know you were going to be selecting Mr. Conner?"

"He wasn't supposed to know, but there was a leak."

"How do you know there was a leak?" Dana asked.

"Ronnie Whittaker told me directly on that Tuesday, after Ron Conner's murder, that everybody in the company knew Conner was getting the job. In fact, he told me that even the people in the mailroom knew Conner was getting it."

"Do you know the source of the leak?" she continued.

Gresham shrugged. "A few people were copied on the memo outlining my decision to promote Ron Conner: my secretary, vice-presidents and chief officers up the line. There could have been any number of sources for the leak."

"Let's talk about the days leading up to Mr. Conner's murder. Did you receive any notices that Mr. Whittaker was acting in a way that would cause you to have any concern about him?"

Gresham nodded. "I did. I received a notice from our CFO that Mr. Whittaker had cashed out his 401k and his other retirement funds the week before Ron's murder."

"And why was this a concern?"

Gresham chuckled. "Well, I would imagine it would be considered aberrant behavior in any company, but in ours it was particularly concerning. Mr. Whittaker held a top-secret clearance, and so non-standard behaviors, particularly of the financial variety, are always concerning, just for national security reasons."

"I'm not sure I understand," Dana said, a perplexed look on her face that Franklin knew was contrived.

"Somebody taking a retirement plan and cashing it out, liquidating assets in the amount of close to $400,000 in cash signifies a possible flight scenario. The concern would arise that the subject was fleeing the country with cash and national secrets and it would…"

"Objection, Your Honor, move to strike." Franklin was on his feet interrupting Gresham. "This is purely wild speculation on the part of the witness." This was the problem with the system that Whittaker had dreamt up, Franklin knew. By the time Whittaker frantically tapped him on the leg to object, Gresham had already spewed his rampant speculation, and the statement was out there for the jury.

"Sustained," ruled Judge Chapman. "The jury will ignore the question and they'll ignore the answer that Mr. Gresham gave; the reporter will strike both from the record."

Dana moved on smoothly, "Did you meet with Mr. Whittaker about this financial anomaly?"

Gresham nodded. "I did. I met with him on Tuesday, January 5th."

"What did he have to say about it?"

"Well, he told me that he had been planning to leave the company. He said he hated me, hated everybody who worked there and he had been planning to quit and take all of his money with him. I asked him why he felt that way, and he told me that he hated Ron Conner, that he'd hated him all his life and that there was no way he was going to work for him."

Franklin glanced over at Whittaker who seemed to be perturbed for the first time in the entire trial. A frown on his face, he was leaning forward and staring intently at Gresham. Franklin also noticed the jury members staring at Whittaker, their expressions more hostile than they'd been at any other time during the trial.

"Did he say anything else to you?" she asked.

"Yes. He spouted off a lie that my wife was having an affair with Ron Conner."

"What was your reaction to that?"

"Well, I had a heart attack. I had to be taken to the emergency room."

The courtroom stirred at that, loud whispers sounding from the crowd. Judge Chapman stopped Dana long enough to warn everybody to keep quiet. He then motioned her to continue.

"So, the cash out request for Mr. Whittaker's retirement fund came the week before Mr. Conner's murder?"

"That's correct."

"When Mr. Whittaker told you he'd cashed that because he'd been planning to quit, did he quit at that time?"

"No," Gresham replied, "he actually never did quit. He was put on leave and then terminated a month after he was arrested for this murder when the Department of Defense officially yanked his security clearance."

"Did you notice any change in Mr. Whittaker's demeanor in the week leading up to Mr. Conner's murder?"

"Yes, I did..."

"Objection, calls for an opinion," Franklin stood up, too late again as Gresham had already answered the question.

"I'll withdraw the question, Your Honor," said Dana, looking back down at her notes. Franklin suspected that Dana had figured out Whittaker was running his own defense and she'd decided to take advantage of the inevitable delay that occurred during the time it took Whittaker to notify Franklin to make an objection. Part of him hated her for it, while another part admired the new tactic she was taking. It was just underhanded enough for him to appreciate it.

"Mr. Gresham, did you discuss Mr. Conner's murder with Mr. Whittaker at all?"

"Yes, I discussed it with him when I went to his office that Tuesday, the 5th of January, to talk to him about the promotion and about the retirement cash out issue."

"What did you say to him about Mr. Conner's murder?"

"I knew he had been very good friends with Ron, so I told him I was sorry for his loss."

"What was his reply to that?" Dana asked.

"He laughed and told me Conner's murder was good for the company and it was good for me. That's when he told me that Conner was having an affair with my wife."

The courtroom exploded with noise again, and Dana walked back to her table. Franklin caught her eye as she walked by and also caught the small smile she gave him, a smile of triumph. He looked back over at Whittaker and saw his hand trembling as he wrote on the notepad.

"No further questions, Your Honor," Dana said as she sat down.

Franklin glanced at the Whittaker who pushed the notepad over to him. On it, he had written in block letters *ASK FOR A RECESS,* and he'd circled it several times.

Franklin stood up. "Your Honor, the defense would like to spend some time cross-examining Mr. Gresham, and we'd like it to be all in one session. If it please the court, we request the afternoon recess at this time.

Chapman granted the recess and dismissed the jury back to the jury room before ordering everybody back in twenty minutes.

Franklin and Ron stepped out into the hall and walked down the open staircase to the outdoor atrium where they found a quiet corner away from the smokers who had all congregated in one area to discuss how they were all going to die of cancer soon.

Franklin noted a look of fury on Whittaker's face. "What's going on?" he asked.

"He's fucking lying. Almost everything he just said in there was a lie. I should have fucking known it. I can't believe I didn't anticipate this."

"Whoa, slow down. What did he lie about?"

"Everything!" Whittaker shouted, throwing his arms in the air. "All that about me hating him and the company, me hating Ron, me wanting to quit, the promotion decision being a close call between Ron and me... He's trying to set me up, and I can't believe I didn't see this coming. I should have known better, that dirty motherfucker. I pushed him too far but I didn't see this..." he trailed off.

"Did you tell him his wife was having an affair with Conner?"

"Yes! That part I did tell him, and it's true; she was."

"Is there any proof? Anybody who can corroborate it?"

"Not that I know of, just his wife, Jessamyn. She's never going to admit it on the stand though."

Franklin thought about things while Whittaker paced back and forth, mumbling to himself. This was definitely a departure from the previous week when he seemed to be in complete control, composed and calm.

"Okay, relax for a second and take a deep breath," Franklin said to him. "I have an idea."

He outlined his idea for the cross-examination to Ron who smiled and visibly began to relax as Franklin laid it out. When he'd finished, Ron clapped him on the back.

"I knew there was a reason I hired you, Franklin. Thanks for calming me down. Let's go see if we can salvage this thing."

Chapter 49

"Your Honor, before you bring the jury back in, I know Mr. Gresham here," Franklin nodded toward Gerry Gresham who was already seated back in the witness stand, "is the State's last scheduled witness which means we'll be beginning the defense case-in-chief right after this. We'd like to file a motion to amend our witness list."

Dana frowned and stood up when Chapman looked in her direction. "This seems like an odd time to be submitting such a motion, Your Honor."

"I just want to give counsel as much time as possible to prepare, judge. We're going to want to add Mr. Whittaker's secretary, Anne Fowler, to our list, in fact; we're probably going to start with her, maybe even today, if we begin today."

"Your Honor, the State would be opposed to this completely. We can't possibly prepare for a new defense witness to testify this afternoon. The notice we're getting is too short," Dana replied.

Franklin raised his arms in an expression of innocence. "Ms. Fowler is simply a rebuttal witness, Your Honor. She overheard the conversation between Mr. Whittaker and Mr. Gresham and we need her to rebut his testimony today."

"Your Honor, this is wildly inappropriate, both for the purpose of timing in general and timing during this case. Why is Mr. Richardson discussing this before his cross-examination?" Dana didn't fail to notice the look that passed over Gerry Gresham's face when Franklin said that Anne Fowler had heard the conversation between him and Ron Whittaker. She suddenly felt a little ill again. Had Gresham been dishonest in his responses to her direct examination?

"I agree with Mrs. Porter, counselor. After your cross-examination, we're going to adjourn for the day. I'll hear your motions to amend your witness list after the State rests today, and you can begin the defense's case in chief tomorrow. You can submit the list of proposed witness amendments to Mrs. Porter tonight so that she can begin to prepare for them."

"Thank you, Your Honor," Franklin replied.

Dana noticed that Gresham shifted in his seat and suddenly looked extremely uncomfortable. She'd never heard of an attorney proposing such a motion in the middle of testimony, and she wondered if it was just Franklin's inexperience or some kind of subtle intimidation ploy he'd come up with. Frowning, she took her seat as Chapman ordered the bailiff to bring in the jury and seat them. He then ordered Franklin to begin.

"Mr. Gresham, I'd like to go over some of the testimony that you just gave and make sure that I understand it completely," Franklin began, dispensing with any pleasantries, Dana noticed.

"You testified that Mr. Whittaker told you he hated you, hated Ron Conner, and hated Puget Sound Aerospace. Were those the *exact* words he used?"

Gresham nervously chewed on his lower lip before replying. "Maybe not the exact words…"

Franklin snorted. "Well then, maybe you can share with the court what the exact words were?"

"He used some language I'd rather not repeat."

Franklin looked at Chapman. "Your Honor?"

Chapman looked down at Gresham and told him, "Mr. Gresham, we're all adults here, and I appreciate that you don't want to repeat language you find offensive, however, you're testifying under oath and you need to answer the question."

Gresham sighed. "He said, 'Fuck you, Gerry, and fuck this company.'"

Franklin stared at him, waiting. The pause continued for almost ten seconds before Chapman intervened. "Mr. Richardson?"

"Oh, I'm sorry, judge," he replied, theatrically. "I was waiting for Mr. Gresham to continue. I didn't hear the word 'hate' in there at all, nor did I hear anything about Mr. Conner." He looked back at Gresham. "Mr. Gresham? Earlier you testified that Mr. Whittaker said he hated you, hated the company, and, most importantly, that he hated Mr. Conner. Do you want me to have the clerk read back your testimony to you?"

Gresham glared at Franklin, and Dana could feel the pain in her stomach growing and starting to slide up her esophagus. She wondered fleetingly if she was getting an ulcer.

Gresham finally replied. "I may have misspoken earlier. I guess, thinking back now that you asked me for the exact words he used, I guess he never actually said the word 'hate'. I was mostly trying to convey the attitude he had, and Mrs. Porter never asked me for the exact wording he used."

Franklin, Dana noticed, had a look of disbelief on his face, and she couldn't blame him. "You may have misspoken?" he asked.

Gresham nodded. "Yes, I think I misspoke when I said 'hate'."

"Okay. What else did you misspeak about during your testimony?"

"Nothing!" Gresham insisted, loudly. A little too loudly, Dana thought.

"Mr. Gresham, was your wife," he looked at his notepad, "Jessamyn Gresham, was she having an affair with Mr. Conner?"

"No. Of course not," Gresham replied, indignantly.

"How do you know?"

Dana stood up quickly and objected. "Mr. Richardson is badgering the witness, Your Honor. I'll also object on the grounds of relevance."

"Your Honor, Mr. Gresham has testified under oath that Mr. Whittaker lied when he told him about his wife having an affair with Mr. Conner. The defense simply wants to know how it's possible for Mr. Gresham to know that his wife wasn't having the affair. We didn't introduce the statement into evidence, the State did."

Chapman took no time at all before announcing, "Overruled; please answer the question, Mr. Gresham."

"I only know because she told me she wasn't and I believe her," he answered.

"But Mr. Whittaker told you she was having an affair with Mr. Conner, and you didn't believe him; in fact, you called it a lie under oath in your testimony to this court. Did you misspeak again, Mr. Gresham, when you said he lied?"

"I was stating my opinion," Gresham said heatedly.

"Your Honor, as Mr. Gresham is not an expert on identifying lies and his opinion is not valid as testimony, I would like to request that Mr. Gresham's statements that Mr. Whittaker lied, and the one that declared that Mr. Whittaker said he hated the victim, the witness, and the company, all be stricken from the record and the jury be instructed to ignore them."

Dana Porter was struggling to hold her head up at this point. She'd been counting on Gerry Gresham as a key witness to establish motive, and Franklin, the supposed incompetent douchebag, was destroying him. She worked up the energy to tell Judge Chapman that the State didn't object to the statements being stricken and then barely listened as Chapman ordered the record expunged of those statements and the jury to ignore them. She listened with a growing sense of dread as to what else Gresham had lied about.

"So, Mr. Gresham, you also testified that Mr. Whittaker told you that Mr. Conner's death was good for the company and good for you personally, correct?"

"I think that's what he said, yes," Gresham replied, hesitantly.

Dana groaned almost audibly. She was just about to lose another statement, she felt, and with it, any chance to salvage Gresham as a witness.

"In fact, his death was good for you personally, wasn't it?" Franklin continued.

"I don't understand the question," Gresham replied.

"Well, it's just that if Mr. Conner was having an affair with your wife, then his death was quite convenient and good for you, wouldn't you say?"

Rage flooded Dana and she jumped to her feet. "Objection!" she nearly shouted. "Your Honor, this is surely badgering the witness; it's argumentative, and it's inflammatory, as well as beyond the scope of cross."

"The objection is sustained. The witness will not answer, the jury will ignore the question, and I'll warn counsel to keep the questions to the scope of cross-examination," Chapman replied, angrily.

Dana was pleasantly surprised to hear Franklin state that he had no further questions for *this witness*, saying the last two words with a marked note of venom and disgust. She could have complained to the judge about the theatrical tone but decided it would do nothing but make her lose credibility with the jurors.

As for the issue of credibility, Gresham had lost every bit of it, and Dana could see by the looks on the jurors' faces that, though they'd been ordered to disregard the question, they were clearly considering Gresham in a different light. Dana stewed for a minute, considering whether such a question could be grounds to request a mistrial. For Chapman to grant that, he would have to rule that the jury had been so prejudiced by the question that they couldn't possibly reach a fair verdict. It didn't seem that Chapman would entertain such a request with just that one example and asking for the mistrial would convey a level of insecurity and fear that she didn't want to project.

"Redirect, Mrs. Porter," Chapman ordered.

Dana considered for a bit before deciding it was best to cut her losses. "I have no questions."

"Very well." Chapman thanked Gresham and released him, then turned back to Dana.

"Mrs. Porter, call your next witness please."

Dana stood slowly, thinking hard about Gresham's testimony. His credibility had certainly been wounded, but it hadn't been destroyed and he'd still introduced enough with his earlier statements to establish a motive for Richardson to have committed the murder. She would be able to read back the statements from him that remained in the record during her closing arguments, something Franklin couldn't do with the statements that had been stricken. Her case was salvageable, as long as she was solid with her cross-examinations during the defense case and absolutely concrete with her closing arguments.

Finally, she looked up at Judge Chapman. "Your Honor, the State rests."

Chapter 50

Neil Chapman wearily shut the door to his private chambers and stripped off his robe. It was Tuesday night, and he'd spent the day hearing the first of the defense witnesses, with just one more day of expected testimony. If the defense rested tomorrow, he could hear closing arguments Thursday and send the case to the jury, giving them half of Thursday, and all day Friday to deliberate. He wasn't opposed to working them on Saturday either, if they were close to a verdict.

Chapman sighed and sat down in his comfortable leather chair, rocking back with his hands behind his head. Placing his feet on his desk, he closed his eyes, letting the stress of the day in court drain out of him.

The day before, after Dana rested the State's case, Franklin Richardson filed a motion to dismiss, claiming that the State had failed to prove their case beyond a reasonable doubt. This was a standard motion in criminal cases, and one that Chapman had only once seriously considered granting in his years of presiding over Superior Court cases. Only once before this case, that is.

When Richardson presented the motion, Chapman chose not to rule in his favor, dismissing the motion. However, it hadn't been a clear and easy decision for him. The evidence was flimsy, but it did all point directly at Ron Whittaker, and he felt it was enough to prove the State's case beyond a reasonable doubt. That being said, he didn't feel the defense was going to have too tough a job showing enough reasonable doubt to get an acquittal.

The prosecution should win somewhere around 95% of their cases in Superior Court, Chapman knew. This might seem like a ridiculously high number to the average person, but the average person forgets the simple fact that the prosecutors get to decide which cases they want to bring to trial. They don't have to bring to trial any case where they don't feel they have a near lock to get a conviction. In fact, as representatives of the people, they have a responsibility to *only* bring to trial those cases where they are completely confident they have the right suspect...that the defendant is guilty beyond any doubt.

This case had a pretty high likelihood, in Chapman's mind, of falling into the 5%. And it wasn't really Dana's fault. A lot of factors beyond her control had led to a case that, were she able to look ahead and see where it was sitting currently, she probably would have chosen not bring it to trial.

Richardson also presented his motion to amend the defense witness list. Dana argued against it, as expected, but the defense did have the right to bring rebuttal witnesses to refute the testimony that the State introduced. Chapman couldn't help but notice that Anne Fowler, Whittaker's secretary, was not on the new defense witness list like Richardson had said she was going to be when he originally stated his intent to add witnesses. Chapman was pretty sure that had been nothing more than a bluff aimed at Gerald Gresham, a bluff that resulted in his admissions that he'd "misspoken" during his earlier testimony. Chapman wasn't at all happy with those kinds of actions in his courtroom. He knew what had happened, and he knew that Richardson knew that he knew, but he decided it wasn't worth interrupting the trial for. He would likely have a discussion with Richardson about those actions after the trial was concluded.

Today the jury heard testimony from a neighbor of Ron Whittaker's who testified that he often watched over Ron's house when Ron left on vacation or took a weekend away. The neighbor testified that he would collect the mail, the newspaper, any packages, etcetera, and take them into Ron's house for him, and that he'd also water the plants and make sure everything was okay with the house in general. Richardson then asked if he had a key to Ron's house in order to facilitate all of this, and he testified that Whittaker always left the back door of his house unlocked.

This was the first testimony from the defense directly to the jury that Chapman knew was going to lay the groundwork for the defense that Whittaker had been framed. Easy access into the house was a key component of that.

Dana Porter asked the neighbor if he had any knowledge that Whittaker's house had been unlocked on the Monday morning following the murder of Ron Conner, when the killer would have to access the house to plant evidence. The neighbor said he didn't know that the house was unlocked for sure on that day. That would have been a good point for the State, but on re-direct, Franklin established with the neighbor that he'd *never,* in five years as Whittaker's neighbor and dozens of entries into the house through the back door, found the door to be locked. Point for the defense.

A Verizon Wireless manager was brought in and Franklin introduced documents into evidence via her testimony that showed Whittaker's cell phone had been pinging from the same tower, the one nearest to his house, throughout the night, starting with his return home from the grocery store at around 9:00pm, until he left for his office at around 7:40am Monday morning. Not only had the phone been pinging from the same cell tower, it had been connected to the Wi-Fi in Whittaker's house the entire time as well.

Dana skillfully asked if any calls, text messages, or other access to data requests were received by the Verizon tower during that period, and none had been. She then asked the manager if it was possible for someone to simply leave their phone in their home during that period without having to be there. The manager admitted that was possible, an obvious conclusion, but one that emphasized a key point to the jury that just because his phone was at his house, it didn't mean that Whittaker himself was there.

Richardson then brought in a Human Resources manager from Puget Sound Aerospace. He used her to introduce the results of the IQ test that Ron Whittaker had taken as part of his pre-employment screening process, an unusual test for a company to utilize, but one that PSA apparently employed for all of their new hires. The HR manager stated that the IQ test results were used in all promotion considerations at the company. Whittaker's test results were put on the screen for the jury to see that his IQ level was 163. Richardson then established with the HR manager that Whittaker's results were either the second or third highest results she'd seen in her capacity as HR manager, Ron Conner's being one of the higher ones.

Dana argued during pretrial motions against this defense witness, stating that her testimony was irrelevant to the case, but Chapman allowed it. He wasn't really in the business of denying a defendant access to any witnesses that they wanted unless the request was completely ludicrous, and he hadn't felt this one was. Dana chose not to cross-examine the HR manager, likely figuring there was no way to minimize the testimony that Ron Whittaker was smart.

The last witness Richardson put on the stand for the day had been his secretary, Stacy. She was a bit of a bimbo in Chapman's mind, but she served an important purpose for the defense. She testified that Whittaker came into the offices of FDR Law to retain counsel at 9:00am on Tuesday the 5th of January. Richardson didn't expand on the reasoning for this testimony, but Chapman knew he was using it to establish that Whittaker retained counsel prior to the police serving the search warrant on his residence late Tuesday afternoon. Everybody in the courtroom knew the underlying importance of this testimony, and Chapman was sure Richardson would bring it up in closing arguments: If Whittaker knew he was being looked at as a suspect as early as Tuesday morning, why would he have left all of that evidence in his house for the police to find late Tuesday afternoon?

The only obvious conclusions that could be drawn from that were: Whittaker was an idiot, something that had clearly been disproven with the IQ test results, or Whittaker was being framed.

On cross-examination, Dana managed to get Stacy to admit that the retainer contract itself hadn't actually been signed until Tuesday evening, after the warrant was served. It was about all she could do to minimize the damage of the testimony and it didn't do much; the time that he signed the actual retainer contract was much less important in the timeframe than when he had actually retained an attorney to represent him.

Chapman recessed the court after Stacy Wright's testimony, and Richardson told him he expected to call only two witnesses the next day, and then the defense would be resting. It was definitely unusual for a case of this magnitude to wrap up after less than two weeks of testimony, but Chapman wasn't going to complain.

He rubbed his temples as he relaxed his mind in the dark, quiet solitude of his chambers. He had a vacation coming up in just a few weeks, and this case was the last major item on his calendar before that time off. This case, then some easy motions the following two weeks, then he was off to Mexico for some much-needed rest and relaxation. He couldn't wait.

Chapter 51

Wednesday morning, Franklin called Anurak "Andy" Channarong to the stand to begin what he expected would be the last day of the defense's case-in-chief. Andy Channarong was the uncle to Chayond Demir, the delivery driver from Satay Thai restaurant. He was also the owner of the restaurant as well as the head chef and manager.

Franklin spent some time walking Andy through his experience as a chef and manager of the restaurant, and he established that he had opened the place slightly more than ten years prior. He then asked if Andy recognized the defendant, Ron Whittaker. Andy testified that he did recognize him, and that Whittaker had been a long-time customer of the restaurant. He also testified that he knew Ron Conner, that Conner and Whittaker came into the restaurant together on numerous occasions to eat, and that they both ordered food for takeout and delivery regularly.

Once Franklin had established all of that, he asked Andy Channarong if Ron Whittaker ordered his food in any particular way, if he had any special wants that he preferred. Channarong testified that Whittaker always insisted on no peanuts in his food. When Franklin asked if Andy knew why he requested his food that way, Andy told the court that Whittaker had told him he had a severe peanut allergy.

Franklin then had Andy go through the preparation of his restaurant's Pad Thai recipe, establishing that peanuts were a standard ingredient in that recipe. When asked if a customer could order Pad Thai without peanuts, Andy testified that when they got such an order, which happened fairly often, they had procedures in place to cook those orders separately. He talked about the training the order takers went through to make sure that any order modifications that were requested were clearly marked on the order form. Franklin then showed him the order form from Conner's delivery request from that January night, and Andy testified that the two orders of Pad Thai that went out to Conner's had definitely both contained peanuts.

The last thing Franklin did was introduce an order form from Satay Thai for a delivery to Whittaker's house on Saturday, the day before Conner's murder. That order had been for yellow curry, a dish clearly made without peanuts. Franklin introduced the pictures from Whittaker's fridge that showed the box from Satay Thai, and Andy had confirmed that box was from his restaurant. Franklin also managed to point out the missing chopsticks.

On cross, Dana attempted to establish that mistakes could have been made. She was able to get Andy to admit that in the ten years he'd been in business, the process had not been 100% error free. She also got him to admit that there had been times that an order had been returned when peanuts ended up in an order that wasn't supposed to have them, and that order-takers might forget to write a special request on the order form and then verbally tell the cook about the special request when they remembered later. She asked him if chopsticks from the delivery order in Whittaker's fridge could have been located anywhere else, like a drawer, and Andy had said that they certainly could be.

Franklin knew Dana was doing her best, but that it wasn't going to be good enough. The defense didn't have to *prove* the food delivered to Conner's house that night contained peanuts. They had to establish in the jurors' minds that it might have contained them, and he'd done significantly better than that. He knew the jurors would think it was highly likely that both containers of food had peanuts, and that was more than sufficient. Dana had previously introduced testimony that proved Whittaker's DNA had been found on one of the sets of chopsticks, chopsticks that were found inside a container of food that he couldn't possibly have eaten. And that had to be an issue for the jury, an issue they would have a tough time finding any explanation for, other than that Whittaker was being set up by someone who hadn't known or hadn't considered his deadly peanut allergy.

Now Franklin had only to medically establish the peanut allergy for his client, and he did that through Ron Whittaker's doctor, Rodger Tate. Dr. Tate testified that he had been Ron Whittaker's primary physician for the last fifteen years, and that Whittaker's records showed a peanut allergy that had been discovered when he was a child. Franklin led him through the different severities of peanut allergies that a person can have, and Tate told the jury that symptoms can range from itchiness and swelling of the skin to the rare but deadly anaphylaxis, a reaction that can impair breathing and send the body into shock, occasionally resulting in death. When Franklin asked, Dr. Tate testified that Whittaker's allergy was of the most severe variety, the potential for anaphylactic shock very high.

Dana took the opportunity on cross-examination to question Dr. Tate about someone with that level of allergy severity eating food that had been prepared next to peanuts. Tate admitted that he often counseled his patients against doing exactly that, but many disregarded his advice. He said he recommended that these patients always have epinephrine with them in the form of an auto injector.

Dana was able to get Tate to testify that it would be possible for somebody to intentionally eat a food laced with peanuts and avoid death by giving themselves a shot of epinephrine. She asked Tate if such a plot, to intentionally cause an allergic reaction in order to set up a scenario where someone would believe you couldn't have possibly been at a location, was possible with the self-administration of an epi-pen shot. Franklin objected to the question on the grounds that it was argumentative. Dana was trying to argue evidence through the testimony, but Chapman allowed the question. Dr. Tate admitted that it would be possible to set up such a scenario; his tone was one of disbelief that it would actually happen though.

On his redirect, Franklin established with Dr. Tate that such a scenario, set up by a defendant simply to frame himself, would be extremely dangerous to pull off. He managed to convey a sense of implausibility for that scenario.

Overall, Franklin was pleased with the last two witnesses for the defense. Dana had done her best to minimize the damage, but Franklin felt that the testimony had gone very much in his favor. When Chapman asked him to call his next witness, Franklin told him the defense rested.

Chapman recessed court for the day, and told the jurors that closing arguments would begin at 9 o'clock the next morning. Closing arguments were expected to take the better part of the day, and he told the jurors to plan to begin deliberations immediately afterwards and to be at the court until late into the evening.

Chapter 52

Dana Porter sat in her office chair, leaning back comfortably and swiveling it slowly back and forth as she stared out the window behind her desk. It was a rare Friday morning when she didn't have any work to do, and she wished she could go out and enjoy the rare late April sun. *April showers bring May flowers* was the famous saying. She had no idea in what area of the country that had originated, but in Washington, even sunny days in May were something to be cherished and enjoyed. In late April, these days were even more unique.

Dana could have worked on some cases that were coming up next or some of the motion hearings she had scheduled for the week after next, but what was the point? She'd blocked out three weeks on her calendar for this trial, and it had taken less than two, culminating yesterday in the closing arguments and the beginning of jury deliberations. Judge Chapman gave the jury the case at three o'clock yesterday, and they deliberated until nearly eight o'clock before calling it a night. They'd been back at it since nine o'clock this morning, which meant they had been deliberating a total of nearly seven hours.

She was well aware that deliberations could take days, sometimes even longer, but she was afraid of a very quick verdict. Typically, the longer the jury takes to deliberate, the better it is for the defense, but in this case, she thought time favored the prosecution. She knew that a quick decision, based on the strong case the defense had mounted, would probably be bad for her.

She closed her eyes, enjoying the sunlight on her face and thought about her closing argument. She'd done the best she could, recapping the strong evidence against Whittaker and trying to head off the defense that he'd been framed. She took no solace in the fact that she'd been right about the peanut allergy Whittaker had claimed. That should have been discovered by her or by her team before trial, and that misstep came back on her.

She was confident in the evidence, so much so that she failed to dig deep enough into the suspect, failed to anticipate his defense. She underestimated both Whittaker and Richardson. They had put on a brilliant defense, in retrospect, and she hated that she let them get the best of her. Part of it, she knew, was their decision to insist on Whittaker's right to a speedy trial. It was tough to prepare completely for a trial when you had only ninety days. The prosecutor's office gave her the resources she needed to prepare, so she could blame only herself, but it had still been difficult to anticipate everything. Not only that, Richardson filed virtually no pre-trial motions which meant she hadn't had a decent look into their defense strategy. Both the short time frame and the lack of motions should have worked against the defense. In every case she'd ever heard of, those things worked against the defense. Not this time though.

Part of the problem, she thought, was that the defense hadn't really had only ninety days to prepare for trial. In her mind, Whittaker was preparing for this trial for much longer than that. Dana was sure he planned this all very carefully, planned every detail of this scenario, and taken a huge risk. The problem was, she couldn't fathom what the reward was. What the hell did he have to gain for such a tremendous risk? His friend out of the picture? A promotion at his job? It didn't add up, and that bothered her more than anything. He'd been fired from his job, lost a security clearance that was going to be tough to get back, even with an acquittal. If there was an endgame here, it was lost on her.

A small part of her mind whispered that maybe Whittaker was actually innocent. That would explain all the nagging doubts, all the parts that didn't add up. But then she remembered the video that was suppressed from the evidence, the video that showed his car driving on the route to Ron Conner's late at night, well after he'd supposedly been in bed and asleep. Dana was sure she'd been played, the entire court had been played, but there was a piece missing, and she couldn't figure out what it was.

It wasn't over, she knew that. Juries could do just about anything they wanted, and the verdict could still very easily come back guilty. She did well with her closing argument, she knew that. She outlined all the evidence that placed Whittaker at the scene. His gun had fired the shots, his fingerprints were on the shell casings, mud from his shoes and his yard were in the dining room, the duct tape used to restrain Conner was in his garbage, the silencer in his recycle bin. She reminded the jury of the motive, the promotion at work that would have meant more money and more prestige, and his underlying resentment of Ron Conner. She then outlined a scenario to them, based on the defense strategy, that Whittaker intentionally placed evidence that would seem to exonerate himself, the takeout food from Satay Thai at the scene of the crime. She reminded them that Dr. Tate testified that Whittaker could have eaten the food with the peanuts, with an epinephrine shot to save his own life to seemingly give himself an airtight alibi.

It was the best she could do with what she had to work with.

Richardson's closing arguments were solid as well, she had to admit. He focused on Whittaker's IQ, just like she expected him to do. He focused on the fact that Whittaker hired him before the evidence in his house was located, when he could have simply disposed of the evidence instead of hiring an attorney. He brought up Monika Sodafsky's testimony that the shell casing in the heater vent had been easily located, and told the jury that if it had been so easy to locate, why hadn't the killer found it? The only explanation that made sense is that the killer left it there intentionally, just like the mud that "magically" appeared only in the dining room of the house.

He brought back in the pictures of the takeout food from Whittaker's refrigerator and showed the jury how there were no chopsticks with the food. He reminded them that Whittaker had ordered curry, a food that definitely didn't contain peanuts. He opened up the possibility with them that if someone wanted to frame Whittaker, taking chopsticks that were sure to contain his DNA and leaving them at the scene of the murder would be a great way to do so. The same applied to using Whittaker's gun to commit the murder. He reminded them of the testimony from the detectives who searched Whittaker's garbage and found the duct tape, that the bags of garbage had been accessible and that the duct tape could have been placed inside those bags, and he reminded them of the neighbor's testimony that Whittaker's back door was always left unlocked, the back door that led to the yard where the mud had been tested, the same mud that was found in Conner's dining room.

He then told the jurors that he knew a claim of framing was normally ludicrous and absurd. He told them he was terrified to proceed with that defense because he knew it sounded ridiculous. But what other defense could he possibly proceed with when the framing of Ron Whittaker was the truth and was supported completely by common sense in addition to the evidence? He then reminded each of the jurors that they themselves were smart, rational, and intelligent people, but that Ron Whittaker was smarter than they were. Would someone as smart as Ron leave all that evidence behind, easily discovered by the police, during a crime that he had allegedly carefully planned out? If the answer was no, Franklin insisted, then they had to look at why all that evidence had been left behind. If they couldn't see a reasonable doubt that Whittaker had killed his best friend for no reason other than jealousy, and had failed so miserably at covering up his tracks, then they were not reasonable people.

Dana smiled in spite of herself at Franklin's words, remembering that she told Jason Garvey that he would say exactly those things in his closing arguments. If only she could have found a way to combat the words that she had known were coming.

At that moment, her cell phone began vibrating. She didn't recognize the number.

"Dana Porter."

It was the court clerk. "Hi, Mrs. Porter, Judge Chapman asked me to give you a call. The jury has the verdicts."

Chapter 53

Franklin Richardson seated himself at the defense table next to Ron Whittaker and turned to him with a smile. Whittaker gave him a half-smile in return. He was showing signs of nervousness for the first time, and Richardson was glad to finally see a modicum of normality in him. This was the moment when he was going to find out if he would be spending the better part of the rest of his life in prison, or if he would be going home a free man.

They had received the call from the court clerk while they were waiting in Franklin's office. He sent home for the day the construction workers who were remodeling his new expansion areas to give them some peace and quiet, and Stacy brought in breakfast for the three of them. They spent the morning chatting and goofing around online, each trying to distract himself from thoughts of what a momentous day this was going to be. Franklin spent some time preparing his comments for the media, two different speeches depending on the verdicts. He told Ron he was preparing a speech for a not guilty verdict, but he'd be foolish to be unprepared for some camera time in either scenario.

After they received the call, they high-tailed it straight to the courthouse; Stacy locked up the office so that she could go with them. When they arrived, the bailiff removed the ankle monitoring bracelet that Ron Whittaker had been forced to wear for the last three-and-a-half months. He didn't need it anymore; if he was not guilty he'd be going home free, if he was guilty, he'd be arrested and booked into jail right there on the spot.

Everybody rose as Judge Chapman entered the room, having been notified that both parties were present and waiting. Franklin noticed he looked relaxed and at ease, his responsibilities in this case coming to a close, regardless of the verdict--temporarily if it was a guilty verdict, and permanently if it was a not guilty verdict.

Dana Porter also looked relaxed, Franklin noted. He wondered if that was an act for the press, confidence, or just an acceptance of whichever way this was going to go. He knew the last was the most likely, realizing that this verdict would have very little, if any impact on her or her job. She was a well-respected prosecutor and losing or winning a single case wouldn't matter to her long-term career.

Franklin's career, on the other hand, would be greatly impacted by this decision. A not guilty verdict would rocket him to stardom and ensure him a wave of clients in the near future, cementing his name as a great defense attorney, for the short-term at least. A guilty verdict? Well, he was going to get some press out of it either way, and there is no such thing as bad press.

Chapman instructed the bailiff to bring the jury in, and they filed into the room, every one of them studiously avoiding eye contact with Whittaker, Franklin noticed. This reaction has been studied by numerous people and the results have been somewhat inconclusive, though it was thought to be a good thing for the defense. Often when convicting someone of a major crime, the jurors wanted to see the look on the person's face, a reaction similar to people's inability to look away from the site of a deadly car crash.

"The foreman of the jury has informed me that the jury has reached a unanimous verdict on both of the counts in this matter," Judge Chapman began. "I'll ask the foreman to please hand the verdict sheets to the bailiff so he can bring them to me."

The bailiff, knowing all eyes were on him, carefully took the sheets from the hands of the foreman and walked them up to Chapman on the bench. He studiously kept his eyes from drifting down to the papers as he did so. Franklin could only imagine how difficult that must be, and he thought that if he were a bailiff, on his last day of work he would go out with a bang by reading the verdict as he walked up to the judge and then looking at the defendant and saying, "Wow, you're fucked!!!" It would be even funnier if it was actually a not guilty verdict.

Chapman reviewed the verdict forms, his face completely impassive and his features betraying nothing. He would have made a good poker player, thought Franklin.

"The verdict sheets seem to be in order. Both are signed by the foreman of the jury and dated with today's date. I'll now read the verdicts."

The entire courtroom seemed to collectively lean forward as if that would help them hear better, Chapman's words reaching their ears milliseconds earlier than they otherwise would if they'd remained seated back. Franklin noticed out of the corner of his eye that several of the jurors had turned to look right at Whittaker. He didn't know if that was significant, but he felt himself begin to sweat.

"As to the charges: on the first count, we the jury, find the defendant, Ronald Peter Whittaker, *not guilty* of the charge of first-degree murder."

Franklin jumped as the words came out and looked over at Whittaker who took a deep breath and eased himself slowly back in his chair. Whittaker looked his way and gave him a slight smile. Franklin saw his hands shake slightly as he folded them in his lap.

Chapman continued, "On the second count, we the jury, find the defendant, Ronald Peter Whittaker, *not guilty* of the charge of unlawful imprisonment."

At long last, Whittaker lowered his head and took another deep breath, before looking directly at Franklin and smiling broadly. Franklin stood up and waited for Whittaker to stand as well before he engulfed him in a huge bear hug. Whittaker accepted the hug briefly and then pulled away.

Judge Chapman was thanking the jury for their service when Whittaker leaned over to him. "As soon as we can leave, I want to go back to your office. I need to get my briefcase out of your safe."

Part Three

Chapter 54

Ronnie awoke suddenly in the predawn darkness of his bedroom. He stared for a moment at the ceiling, the fan over his bed turning slowly, barely visible in the dim light. He blinked as his mind focused on the present, clearing the cobwebs of the dream. Suddenly, with a rush, a surge of euphoria, he realized it was over. A huge grin came over his face and he laughed out loud. As he lay in bed, he felt an intoxicating sense of freedom, and a sense of tremendous accomplishment. There was something exhilarating about taking a huge risk and surviving it. *This must be what skydiving feels like,* he thought...*times one hundred.*

Yesterday had been the most stressful day of his life--not only having to sit all day in Franklin's office and make small talk with him and the bimbo, Stacy, but just the waiting in general. The jury took so much time to make their decision. He couldn't understand what could possibly have taken them so long; he'd expected a quick verdict of 'not guilty' from them. They were smart people, and the evidence had been clear, at least in his mind. Or, more accurately, the evidence had been muddy enough that their *decision* should have been clear.

He jumped out of bed and did a little dance on the floor, whistling to himself before going into the bathroom. Running the water until it got hot, he filled the basin and then carefully shaved. He wanted to look and feel good today, a day that was going to be momentous, history making, the culmination of six months of hard work and great risk. After he was cleanly shaven, he got in the shower, the hot spray removing the last vestiges of sleep from his eyes.

Walking out of the house just as the sky was beginning to lighten, dressed in hiking boots, jeans, and a hooded sweatshirt, he placed a large, internal frame backpack onto the back seat of his Range Rover and tossed a jacket next to it. It was likely to be cold where he was headed and he wanted to be prepared. He'd been assured by the salesman at REI when he'd bought the large backpack months earlier that it would hold as much weight as he'd be able to carry.

A smaller backpack containing a couple of sandwiches and protein bars, a bag of trail mix, and several bottles of water went onto the floor of the passenger side of the vehicle. He placed the briefcase he'd retrieved last night from Franklin's safe onto the seat next to him. A thermos of hot coffee slid into the area between the seats, and he was ready to go.

Pulling out of his garage, he worked his way east from his house before merging onto the Boeing Freeway. That took him directly to Interstate 5, and he exited there to head north. A few miles further, he exited to the right onto Highway 2 headed east.

Feeling great and with no concerns whatsoever, he sang along with the radio as he crossed the Highway 2 trestle and passed by the exit for the town of Snohomish.

As he came over a small rise, he could see the mountains of the Cascade Range dead ahead, their peaks still snow-covered, glimmering in the sun on this beautiful day. He finally allowed himself to think about the events of the past few months.

Everything had started nearly a year before when he'd been sitting at home one night just goofing around online, looking at Facebook, of all things. He'd seen a post from someone he didn't even know, a friend of a friend, and he'd clicked on it. It was a newspaper article about a treasure hunt, and Ron, with nothing else to do, read it, at first with reluctance and then with growing interest.

The article was an update of a previous story a magazine had published. Ron had never heard the original story or any of the internet talk that swirled around it. According to the article, nine years earlier a man by the name of Richard Frost had learned he was dying of lung cancer. Frost had started a large software company that had made huge strides in virtual reality technology. The company, *Frost Technologies*, had been purchased by Microsoft a few years before Richard's cancer diagnosis. It was estimated that Frost had personally cleared nearly $500 million from the sale.

A lover of the outdoors, Frost had retired and spent the next couple of years traveling the world, skiing and mountain climbing before being diagnosed with untreatable lung cancer. He'd come back to his home in the Seattle area and prepared to die.

While dealing with and preparing for his death, and in between his radiation treatments, designed merely to slow the spread of the cancer rather than stop it, Frost had looked for some way to create a legacy. The company that had carried his name had been absorbed by Microsoft, the name Frost Technologies disappearing from all but a few mousepads and coffee mugs used by some of the original employees. He'd never made time for a family and he had no wife, no children.

Frost had always donated to charities, but now he doubled and then tripled those donations, giving away tens of millions of dollars, getting his name on plaques on children's hospitals and parks all over the country. His fear of the finality of death was strong, though, and his generous donations were not enough to build the legacy he'd desired. After some time, he came up with another way to make sure he was remembered and also to share his love of the outdoors with the world.

Frost decided to hide a fortune in gold and gems somewhere in his home state of Washington.

After Frost hid the treasure, he returned home and gave interviews to every talk show that would have him. His story garnered the love of the American public, and every talk show host from Ellen to David Letterman wanted to help him tell his story. Frost hadn't just hidden a fortune in treasure out in the wilderness, he'd written a poem that gave clues on how to find it, and he'd sparked the adventurous spirit of his countrymen.

Frost posted the poem on his website, and it instantly garnered a large following of treasure hunters from around the world who tried to solve the clues hidden in the text of the poem. On the talk shows, he mostly refused to give any further clues, insisting that everything needed to solve the puzzle and recover the treasure was right in the poem. It was a mystery that captivated the hordes of people following it, though Ronnie had never heard of it during that time period. A year later, Frost died at the age of 61, and his treasure remained unfound, slowly forgotten by all but the most die-hard treasure hunters who still searched persistently, though fruitlessly, for the riches.

Although Ronnie had never heard this story until coming across the article, he was instantly intrigued. Having a genius IQ and being very good at puzzles, he figured he'd be able to solve the thing pretty quickly. He found the entire poem online and printed it out, and then did some more internet searches to see how far other treasure hunters had gotten in their attempts to solve it.

During all the interviews Frost gave before his death, the only real clue that he'd added was that the treasure was located within the boundaries of Washington State. Everything else needed to solve the riddle and locate the treasure was in the poem itself, and he refused to elaborate, saying only that he wanted people to get out and enjoy nature while they searched for the treasure and remembered him.

Frost wouldn't disclose the full value of the treasure, but he did claim that it was well into the millions of dollars, and that the treasure consisted of a combination of gold and gems. At that time, gold prices were hovering right around $700 an ounce, and they'd nearly doubled in the eight years since then, making the treasure even more valuable today than the day he hid it.

Ronnie spent all of his free time for the next several months studying the poem and trying to work out the clues. There were hundreds of blogs and articles online filled with the conclusions of amateur treasure hunters who felt they'd solved the poem or at least a part of it. Some of those conclusions seemed solid, but many of the findings represented nothing more than hacks really reaching with their interpretations of the clues. Ronnie decided that most of them were complete idiots.

He quickly realized the poem was significantly tougher and more complex than he'd originally thought it would be. Unable to solve it immediately, he'd become an expert on things like cyphers and code-breaking techniques. He pored over maps of Washington State, spent hundreds of hours trying to find likely locations and make them fit the poem. After he was stymied in all the traditional methods to solve it directly, he branched out in his attempts. He decided that perhaps it was more complex than it appeared on the surface, and he began studying code breaking techniques used by the CIA and the NSA. He'd done things like write the poem backwards looking for clues that way, turning the letters into numbers and looking for patterns, and mixing thousands of combinations of words, trying to anagram them or identify cyphers that would change the meanings. He'd gotten nowhere.

Nowhere wasn't quite accurate. He managed to solve a few of the clues in the poem and he narrowed down the location somewhat, or at least he'd thought he had. But he was never close enough to go hunting. Unlike the morons who poured into Washington early on, thinking they could stroll through the woods and stumble upon the treasure, Ronnie harbored no such ridiculous notions. He knew there was no sense in even leaving his house until he knew precisely where the treasure was, or he at least narrowed it down to a very small area. Finally, after months of banging his head against a wall, he decided to mention the story to Ron Conner.

He showed Ron the poem, and they went over all of the efforts he'd put into it. They studied his conclusions, and Ron said he was interested and wanted to try to help solve it. They agreed to split the treasure fifty-fifty if they could find it.

It took Conner less than a month to solve the goddamn thing. He came to Ronnie and told him he'd solved the clues, but that the split they'd originally agreed on wasn't fair. Conner had done all the work, and he thought the split should be more like eighty-twenty in favor of him. Ronnie was outraged, but Ron refused to tell him the solution until he agreed to the unfavorable split and signed a contract that would be drawn up by their attorneys. Ron then told him that the treasure was located in the mountains, well above the snow line and. since it was mid-December, they wouldn't be able to go search for it until the spring time. So Ronnie had lots of time to consider the deal.

Ronnie smiled to himself at the memory of the smug look on Ron's face before he informed him the deal was changing. That pompous and arrogant bastard had always thought he was better than Ronnie, always thought he was smarter and cleverer.

Ronnie entered the city of Monroe and pulled into a gas station, filling up the Range Rover and taking the opportunity to fill a cup from the thermos of coffee near his seat. While he was waiting for his tank to fill, he dialed in the combination of his briefcase, clicked open the locks, and pulled out the piece of paper containing the poem with all of Conner's conclusions on the back. He pushed aside the maps that he'd brought along in case he needed them. He ignored the GPS unit and compass that were in the briefcase, as well as the pistol, snug in its holster. He doubted he would need the pistol, but it made him more comfortable to have it.

Had Ronnie not been so comfortable and happy with himself, he might have paid more attention to his surroundings. He might have noticed the car that had been following him since he'd left home, the car that now pulled into the business next to the gas station. If Ronnie had looked over, he might have seen the driver of that car watching him through binoculars.

Chapter 55

Back on the road, the gas tank topped off and sipping his coffee, Ronnie laid the poem on the center console and glanced down from the road at the first stanza, thinking back to his attempts to solve it.

They say youth's folly is the pursuit of wealth,
It's the theif of that which is not slowed.
The most precious thing you own is your health,
And, you'll need it to recover this lode.

That which is not slowed was clearly a reference to time, and Ronnie was sure the first couple of lines were Richard Frost ruminating about his early death and a youth he'd felt had been wasted on accumulating his vast fortune, a fortune so large he was struggling at the time to give it all away. Ronnie tried to put himself in Richard's mindset, his desire to unload his wealth on charities and on this goofy treasure hunt while his death loomed ever closer. There was no doubt in his mind that Richard was being regretfully nostalgic with the first two lines.

He smiled as he remembered all the time he'd spent on the misspelled word: *thief*, spelled with the *i* and the *e* reversed. He was certain this had to be important, had to be an intentional clue. Even poor spellers remember the grade school spelling memory trick, *i before e, except after c*. This wasn't a firm rule of course; it didn't apply in all cases, but it did work most of the time. Not only that, it worked in this case, and if you were going to make a mistake with that rule, you would make it only because of one of the rare exceptions, not when the rule actually applied to the word you were spelling.

If you knew that Richard Frost was an intelligent man, you wouldn't think him capable of making a mistake that even a third grader would have caught with a single proofread. Frost had put an enormous amount of time, thought, and energy into this poem. It was to be his legacy, a lasting monument to his memory, the poem living on in urban lore long after the treasure had been found. In Ronnie's mind, there was exactly zero percent chance the spelling error was nothing more than a spelling error.

It had to be a clue, and probably an important clue, but he'd been unable to figure out what Richard was trying to convey with that error. What he hadn't ever considered was that the spelling error was a red herring, an intentional vacant clue, designed to waste the treasure hunters' time and distract them. Ron Conner had seen that almost immediately; he'd spent just a few hours on the spelling error and then insisted there was no way it was an actual clue. Frost had been having some fun and nothing more. Ronnie had been pissed off beyond belief with that revelation.

The next two lines, Ronnie had concluded and Ron had agreed, meant that the treasure was located in a spot that wasn't going to be easy to get to. Most of the information from the online treasure-blogging retards had said there wasn't a clue in the entire first stanza. Ronnie hadn't agreed though. Knowing the treasure was located in a spot not easy to reach, a spot that required the searcher to be in good health to reach, meant that a lot of false assumptions and conclusions could be ruled out. That check and balance was just as important to solving the puzzle as any other clue, Ronnie knew.

He passed through the town of Sultan, slowing carefully as he drove past a police car on the side of the road, a speed trap. Not even a speeding ticket could dampen his mood today, but he didn't want anything delaying him. There was a lot to do, and he didn't know what kind of obstacles he might still encounter.

Chapter 56

Your search begins where rocks once grew,
And the music man, he spins through the night.
The pitcher's goal, in his name replaces two,
The Lincoln Logs of life must give him a fright.

The first line had been an easy one, a nice, generous gift that eased the hunter into the meat of the clues contained in the poem. Ronnie could only imagine it was meant to lure the searcher into a sense of comfort. An easy clue to start, designed to suck you in so you wouldn't quit. *Where rocks once grew* could only mean the mountains.

Most of the treasure blog trolls had agreed with this conclusion, with just a few of the morons insisting that mountains didn't *technically* grow, they were shoved upwards. They claimed that rocks only truly grow deep inside the earth's crust in belts of magma. When magma comes to the surface it's called lava, and Washington State has a number of ancient lava flows, technically (according to these trolls) the only real areas *where rocks once grew*.

There are five active volcanos in Washington, all located along the Cascade Range and all currently slumbering peacefully, with the exception of Mount St. Helens which had a major eruption in 1980. Ancient eruptions from all five have produced fields of lava, and every summer for the last eight years, a few foolish searchers from around the country had worn out their shoes scouring the sharp edges of these lava flows, looking for the treasure. This was foolish for a number of reasons, the first being that interpreting this clue as referring to a lava flow didn't fit with the rest of the clues in the poem; the second being that there were dozens of square miles of lava flows, and they contained millions of cracks and crevices and caves. Without narrowing the clues down further, searching vast lava fields was pointless.

Ronnie and Ron were both confident that clue referred solely to a mountain range and not to a lava flow. Washington State has two major mountain ranges, the Cascades and the Olympics. Both are old ranges; their peaks have stopped growing long ago and are now losing height through erosion at the rate of centimeters per year. This made both ranges valid as places where rocks once grew. Of course, that still left thousands of square miles of terrain to narrow down.

Ronnie was sure that *the music man who spins through the night* had meant a DJ, and that the other clues were meant to identify that DJ. A pitcher's goal, of course, was a strikeout, but Ronnie hadn't been able to figure out how that fit with the rest of the clues in the stanza.

He flipped the poem over now and looked at Ron's conclusion on the back. Conner realized that Lincoln Logs were a child's toy and that, generically, they were known simply as building blocks. *The building blocks of life* is a well-known term that refers mostly to organic compounds that contain the element carbon, known by scientists to be the primary element in the formation of all life.

Ronnie was correct about a pitcher's goal being a strikeout, but he hadn't made the next step and realized that strikeouts were also known as *Ks*.

On the Periodic Table, carbon is identified by the letter "C", so Ron had decided the poem referred to a DJ whose name contained two letter "K"s where you would normally find the letter "C". A simple online search of popular DJs, and the name of the very well-known performer, Kaskade, popped right up. A music man who spins through the night and is afraid of the letter C, preferring the letter K instead. Switch the two Ks back to Cs and you get Cascade, the name of the predominant mountain range that runs north/south and splits the State of Washington into west and east.

As Ronnie drove through the small town of Startup, so named because it represented the starting point where Highway 2 begins to climb up to Stevens Pass in the Cascade mountain range, he couldn't help but admire the work Ron Conner had done, even though he hated him and was glad he was dead. It hurt him a little to admit that Ron had been smarter than he was, but it had taken Ron just a few days to solve this part of the poem, a part that had stymied Ronnie for months.

Ron had always held his brains over Ronnie, always showing him up, trying to prove he was smarter and cleverer. It had started back when they'd met in the first grade. Their teacher, Mrs. O'Brien, told them it was going to be confusing having two boys named Ron in the same class and she'd have to call one of them by another name. Ron Conner had immediately jumped up and said that Ron was a family name and that calling him anything else would be an insult to his family. He'd then suggested that they call him Ron, and the other Ron could go by Ronnie.

Ronnie hated his new nickname and, as he grew older, it had stuck and he'd hated it more and more. *Ronnie* sounded like a little kid; what kind of adult went by the name Ronnie? Wherever he went, though, it seemed Ron was there, calling him Ronnie and getting it to stick. They'd gone all through high school together, gone to the University of Washington, and had worked many of the same jobs together, culminating in their employment at Puget Sound Aerospace.

The name thing was only the tip of the iceberg. Everybody assumed that Ron and Ronnie were best friends, and Conner had probably thought they actually were. Ronnie was happy to play along; he had somehow known that Ron would play an important role in his life at some point. In truth, every time they were together, he held a deep-seated contempt for everything Ron did. Ron thought he was so clever. If Ronnie made a mistake, Ron would point it out so everybody would laugh. If Ronnie liked a girl, Ron would go after her himself or, if that wasn't an option, he would point out flaws in the girl that only he could see.

Ron scored better on the SATs, did better in college, and when they took IQ tests as part of their employment at PSA, Ron was quick to tell anybody who would listen that he'd scored four points higher than Ronnie.

Yup, Ronnie hated Ron, but he kept him close, and he kept the fake smile on his face whenever they were together, and he bided his time. When he realized that he couldn't solve the poem on his own, he decided to finally get some benefit out of the "friendship" and see if Ron could solve it. And he had.

Ronnie had never had any intention of sharing the treasure with Ron. He hadn't figured out how he was going to go about screwing him out of the 50% split they'd originally agreed on, but he'd known all along that he would do so in some way--provided they could even find the treasure.

What he hadn't planned on, however, was Ron double-crossing *him* and trying to steal his share. Ron's claim that he'd done all the work was bullshit. He'd put in far less time than Ronnie had and, in fact, he never would have heard of the fucking treasure had Ronnie not brought it to him. He tried but was unsuccessful in convincing Ron that the new eighty-twenty split proposal wasn't fair. Ron told him he had until spring to sign an agreement and after that, Ron was going to find the treasure himself and keep the entire thing.

It was right then that Ronnie decided it was finally time for Ron to die.

Chapter 57

The man with the scar on his face let his car fall back a bit as they passed by the turnoff for the town of Index, well into the Cascade Mountains. He didn't know if Ronnie was paying attention to anything behind him, but he definitely didn't want to get caught.

He eyed his gas gauge warily as the needle indicated just under half a tank. He had no idea where they were going or how long they would be driving. He would have filled up when Ronnie filled up in Monroe, but Ronnie would have seen him and recognized him if he stopped at the same station. He didn't want to lose him by letting him out of his sight to go to a different station and then have Ronnie drive off. So he'd had no opportunity to fill up, and that was worrying him as they climbed steadily into the mountains.

He had no idea what exactly was going on, but nobody goes through the trouble that he'd seen Ronnie go through over the last few months unless there was a major reward at the end. Although he'd been well paid for the small amount of work he'd had to do, he was just too curious and entrepreneurial to settle for peanuts if there was more to be had.

It was possible this was nothing, but the man with the scar on his face trusted his instincts, and those instincts were telling him that this was something big. So for now, he would follow Ronnie for a bit and he'd try to find out what he was up to.

Chapter 58

Ronnie knew he wanted to kill Ron, but he also knew that killing someone and getting away with it was tough to do. His first thought was that he could find a way to kill Ron and frame somebody else for the murder. He'd actually begun planning exactly that before he came to a stunning revelation: this is exactly how every genius rotting in a prison cell plans a murder.

Ronnie knew that the police were good. He knew that forensics and DNA gathering were nearly impossible to beat. Ronnie had two other major problems as well. There were ways to kill Ron and get away with it if he could do it from a distance. Shooting a man with a sniper rifle from a thousand yards away has some problems, but it leaves very little evidence, and if you need to kill somebody, it's a viable option. Ronnie's problem was that he first needed to question Ron to get his solution to the poem, and for that, he needed to get up close and personal.

It's impossible not to leave evidence behind at a crime scene, and it's impossible not to take evidence away from the scene. Ronnie spent time researching this and was very familiar with the theory of transference in forensic DNA analysis. Questioning Ron and then killing him could turn out to be a fool's errand.

The other big problem he had was that he didn't know who, if anyone, Ron might have told about the poem and the treasure hunt and his deal with Ronnie. If he killed Ron and somebody came forward with proof of the treasure hunt and the double-cross, Ronnie would become a suspect. That would be okay for as long as he could deny the allegations and any knowledge of the treasure. As soon as he showed up with the treasure, though, any allegations would become a big problem. Even if he successfully framed somebody else and they were convicted, he could still be a suspect sometime later. There is no law that says a person can't be tried for a crime for which someone else has been convicted. It happens quite often, in truth, when the wrong person is convicted and new evidence comes to light that implicates someone else. Ronnie needed protection against that; he definitely did not want to be worrying for the rest of his life that the police might one day come knocking on his door.

He needed another plan and, after a few days of thinking about it, had finally come up with a great one. Instead of planting evidence that pointed the blame at someone else, what if he planted evidence that pointed the blame directly at *himself?* If he couldn't avoid leaving evidence behind at the crime scene, and he couldn't avoid taking evidence with him, then he might was well do both in abundance.

Making this work required a lot of planning and a few assumptions. The first part of his plan was the compelling need for a charge of first degree murder. Second degree murder wouldn't work because he needed the prosecutor to charge him using the statute on premeditation. First degree murder requires premeditation, and for Ronnie's plan to work, he needed the prosecution to argue that he'd planned the murder in advance. It was his IQ level that was going to flip that argument by the prosecution and make it work in his favor.

If a regular person plans a murder and follows through with it, leaving behind a mountain of evidence that points right at them, nobody thinks twice. They just assume he's an idiot and they're usually correct. If a person with a genius level IQ does it though, people will question how that could happen, especially if the people charged with questioning it are highly intelligent themselves.

The first part of his plan was to leave behind as much evidence as possible, evidence that seemed to point directly at him, but could still be argued away as part of a frame-up. It was quite difficult leaving as much evidence as he'd done, Ronnie thought with a quiet laugh.

Ronnie was sure the prosecutors would go for first degree; they always swung for the fences. First degree required proving premeditation, and he'd made that easy for them. After all, he had premeditated it...he'd planned it for weeks.

He needed to leave enough evidence behind to assure that he would be the obvious and only suspect, but not so much that the prosecutors would be suspicious. In order for his plan to work, he needed to be arrested and charged with first degree murder, and he needed the prosecution to follow through by taking him to trial on that charge. He needed to get to trial quickly, to put enough pressure on them that they would be so busy analyzing the evidence he'd left behind they would neglect to delve too deeply into the underlying meaning behind the things he'd planted.

Snapping himself out of his reverie, Ronnie realized that he was approaching the little town of Skykomish, well into the mountains on the climb to Stevens Pass. He glanced back at the poem and read the next stanza, one that had stumped him completely, along with all the online bloggers who had tried to figure it out.

Smog without air makes no sense at all,
But adding gold makes him mighty and great.
A place such as this, a home he might call,
'Lo he ignore the ghosts of those working the freight.

Even Ron Conner admitted that he'd been lost on this one for a long time. On the night Ronnie killed him, Ron finally told him that it had been pure luck solving this part. He'd been taking a break from working on the poem and had been watching TV, just flipping through the channels. He landed on the movie *The Hobbit,* and he stopped to watch, remembering that he'd read the entire J.R.R. Tolkien *Lord of the Ring* series as a kid and greatly enjoyed it.

The movie had been playing for about an hour when the answer slapped him in the face like a wet towel. Bilbo Baggins and company, in their quest to The Lonely Mountain to recover the treasure stolen from the dwarves, know that they are going to have to defeat the guardian of that treasure, the great and mighty dragon, Smaug.

Ron had immediately hit pause and grabbed the poem, the clues now blatantly obvious. He had solved the riddle in the previous stanza, where Frost had used the letter C from the Periodic Table to represent carbon, and that helped him realize that Frost had pulled the same trick twice.

Air is another way of saying *oxygen,* even though it's not technically accurate. Air is made up of lots of gases of which oxygen is only one. Most people use the two words interchangeably. "We breathe oxygen" is a commonly used phrase; a more accurate phrase might be, "We breathe air, a mixture of gases from which our lungs extract oxygen."

On the Periodic Table, oxygen is represented by the letter "O"; and *smog* without the "O" is indeed nothing at all. It's just *smg*, which is meaningless. But adding gold, symbolized on the Periodic Table as Au, makes the name Smaug, the dragon from *The Hobbit*. The dragon that is both *mighty and great*. Ron told Ronnie he'd laughed like crazy when he'd figured it out. It seemed so simple in retrospect, but he would never have gotten there had he not flipped on the TV, seen the movie, and decided to watch it while he took a break from the riddle.

The rest of the clue was simple once he figured out that the first two lines were referring to the dragon Smaug. In *The Hobbit*, Smaug's home is a huge cavern under the mountain. There are no natural caverns in the Cascades, at least none immense enough to house a tremendous, mythical dragon. Ron knew that there are, however, large, manmade tunnels.

Three train tunnels cross the Cascade Range in Washington State. Only one of them is currently in use; the other two have been abandoned. It seemed likely the poem would be referencing one of the unused tunnels, as an active train tunnel would not be a good home for a dragon. The clue to figuring out which tunnel was the correct one appeared in the final line of that stanza: *'Lo he ignore the ghosts of those working the freight.*

Ghosts working the freight would seem to reference a railroad disaster that had killed some freight workers. Ron did some searching and found that the only major train accident involving any of the tunnels had occurred on March 1st, 1910, and it was a doozy. It happened near the western portal of the old Cascade tunnel. An enormous accumulation of snow had fallen in the area, something like eleven feet in a single day, and the railroad plows had been unable to keep ahead of the fall. Two trains, a westbound passenger train and a mail train also hauling freight, had earlier cleared the tunnel from the east, but had been trapped by the huge snow accumulation at the Wellington Depot, high in the mountains. While the passengers and freight workers all slept on the trains overnight, the snow turned to rain, and a thunderstorm moved in. Eventually a lightning strike caused a huge cornice to break off, creating a tremendous avalanche which came thundering down, striking the two trains that were trapped in the snow and rolling them down into the canyon, killing ninety-six people. It was the worst avalanche disaster in the history of the United States, and sixty-one of the people killed were Great Northern Railway employees, hence the ghosts of those who worked the freight.

Frost had been a clever man, but Ron was equally clever, Ronnie admitted reluctantly. He glanced down to the right side of the road where he was just passing by the modern Cascade rail tunnel, an eight-mile long tunnel that was started almost immediately after the tragic avalanche disaster at the old tunnel, but which had taken nearly twenty years to complete. This one was built at a much lower elevation, placing it below the snowline for a longer segment of the year and protecting trains from the avalanches prevalent at the higher elevations and steeper terrain where the old tunnel had been located.

He was getting close to Stevens Pass, and that's where he'd begin looking for the turnoff that would lead to the old Cascade train

tunnel and the current-day hiking trail where he would begin his
search for the treasure.

Chapter 59

The man with the scar on his face had allowed Ronnie to get out
of sight, knowing there were no turnoffs on this road and worried
about Ronnie noticing him if he followed too closely for too long.
Which is why he almost screwed everything up when Ronnie took
a turn onto a road that the scarred man didn't know existed.

He would have missed Ronnie entirely if he hadn't come around
the corner right near the top of the pass and seen Ronnie's black
Range Rover on the small side road. Cursing at the near disaster,
he pulled over, waited for the car that had been behind him to go
by, then made a U-turn and cautiously turned onto the small
gravel road, noticing the mostly hidden street sign that identified
it as *Tye Road*.

Realizing he absolutely had to stay out of sight on this small gravel
road, he quickly pulled up the maps feature on his phone and
searched the road for any turnoffs. The road appeared to wind its
way back down the valley toward a parking lot and a hiking trail.
What the fuck was Ronnie up to? If this was nothing more than a
hiking trip, the man with the scar was going to be absolutely
furious.

He drove slowly and cautiously, straining to see up ahead of him
and dreading each corner, thinking that he might see Ronnie
stopped on the other side and the game would be over. As he
finally approached the parking lot that appeared on the Google

maps image on his phone, he realized that had to be Ronnie's destination.

Finding a wide spot in the gravel road, he pulled his car over and slumped down in the seat waiting. Ronnie didn't know the car the man with the scar drove, so if he was just turning around and coming back, the man would lay flat and pretend to be napping. As long as Ronnie couldn't see his face, he'd be okay.

After just a couple of minutes, he realized that Ronnie was probably not just turning around and coming back. He started the car again and cautiously inched his way up to the parking lot turnoff, making sure it was all clear. It was a few hundred feet further to the parking lot and he quickly covered the distance, slowing down as he approached the lot. He crept up to the corner and spotted the black Range Rover. Ronnie was just walking away from the truck, his back to the man with the scar, laden with a large backpack.

The man pulled quickly into the lot, parking across the other side, as far as he could get from Ronnie's vehicle. He waited for Ronnie to disappear into the trees, heading toward a marked hiking trail. He then got out and began following Ronnie on foot. He didn't know what the fuck Ronnie was doing up here, but he was carrying a backpack much too large for just a day hike and it had also appeared the pack was empty. That was enough to convince the man with the scar that Ronnie was worth following a while longer.

Chapter 60

After parking his truck in the lot and gathering the items he needed from his briefcase, Ronnie threw everything into his big-frame pack and started for the trailhead, excited to be getting closer. The parking lot was empty, surprising for a sunny Saturday, although he did hear another car pulling in right as he was walking to the designated pathway. He was glad he'd decided to get such an early start. By beating all the other hikers, he was less likely to be seen when he left the trail. He wasn't worried too much about the other car that pulled in after him; he would only be on the actual trail for a short distance, and he had a head start on them. As he walked, he glanced at the next stanza on the sheet he carried.

Protected from the Arctic's wet kiss you'll find,
As you begin the true quest from here.
The stalwart kid of course is kind,
But only trustworthy as far as the mirror.

The Arctic's wet kiss was snow of course, he'd figured that part out himself, early on. He at first thought it might refer to wind and he tried to think of what would protect somebody from the wind. After some thought, he realized that if Frost had been trying to say wind, he'd likely have just said, *the Arctic's kiss*, or *the Arctic's cold kiss*. By using the words *wet kiss*, he had to be referring to snow.

There are many things that might protect one from snow, but once Conner had figured out that the clues in the previous stanza referred to the old Cascade tunnel, this clue's solution had been obvious. He did some research on the area, and he discovered that after the massive avalanche that destroyed the two trains and took ninety-six lives, the Great Northern Railway, knowing the new tunnel they'd begun would take decades to complete, had constructed a series of massive concrete snow sheds over the train tracks here at the old tunnel. These gigantic structures still exist today, and they cover hundreds of yards of the old tracks from the western tunnel portal. These were designed and engineered to literally protect from *the Arctic's wet kiss,* and Ronnie could see the first one coming up as he approached the tunnel entrance where the actual trail began.

Stopping for a moment to look to his right down into the old Cascade train tunnel, he shivered a bit at the sight of the ghostly opening. In June of 2007, right around the time that Richard Frost had hidden his treasure, the roof of this tunnel had partially collapsed, blocking the passage that previously had been a popular trail, and now hikers were warned to stay out. Ronnie would have liked to have been able to hike through the nearly three-mile long tunnel but that apparently would never happen again. He turned his back on the tunnel and began walking to his left, to where the massive snow sheds began.

Awe inspiring in their own way, the structures were built to withstand tons of snow thundering downhill at a hundred miles per hour, striking the concrete roofs of the sheds and falling off the downhill side, protecting the trains as they worked their way through the danger zone. Their engineering was impressive, and Ronnie admired the tomb-like atmosphere they created as he strolled silently through them.

According to the poem, this is where the true quest began and, to Ronnie's knowledge, no treasure seeker had ever made it this far. Thousands of hikers had been here over the last eight years of course, none of them realizing they were very close to millions of dollars in treasure just waiting to be found.

The stalwart kid was a phrase that you could really only figure out once you had solved the rest of the puzzle so far. It was otherwise much too vague, but if you got everything else correct, this clue became obvious and you knew that you were on the right track.

As the numerous signs indicated, the hiking trail Ronnie was currently traversing was called the *Iron Goat Trail*. A baby goat is known as a "kid" and "stalwart" is a synonym for strong, which is also a meaning of iron...strong metal. So, a *stalwart kid* would be a clever way of saying an iron goat. This clue told Ronnie he needed to follow the *Iron Goat Trail,* and the next line of the poem indicated he would do so until he reached the mirror.

As he hiked down the Iron Goat Trail, admiring the cathedral-like snow sheds, he thought about Ron and the night he'd killed him. Ron had talked freely that night, telling Ronnie everything about the poem and how he'd solved it. He'd been duct taped to the chair by that time, of course, a loaded gun pointed at his chest. That did tend to lead to introspection and honesty.

Ronnie was prepared for Ron to lie that night. He'd actually been expecting it, had even been entranced at the prospect. He brought a lot of tools with him to Ron's house, tools designed to make sure Ron talked and that he told the truth, tools that he didn't need to use once Ron realized his life was in danger. Ronnie had been slightly disappointed.

Everything Ron told him that night about the poem and the clues he'd solved was true, Ronnie had no doubt. Ron's explanations and interpretations of things, for instance this last line regarding the mirror, were evidence of his candor.

If he'd been attempting deception that night, he could have simply told Ronnie that along the path of the Iron Goat Trail he would encounter a mirror, or perhaps a post where a mirror had once hung. Ronnie had been fully prepared to make Ron show him the research that led him to his conclusions, but nobody could have fabricated the story Ron told about solving the mirror. It was obvious that Ron thought as long as he told the truth, Ronnie would let him live. He'd clearly been mistaken.

It was apparent from the next stanza that a searcher would need to leave the trail at some point and proceed uphill, but where to leave the trail? Ron Conner admitted that he had struggled with the mirror reference. He'd researched everything he could find about the Great Northern Railway and the Cascade tunnel, and he could find nothing that mentioned a mirror anywhere. He'd searched railroad lingo and old articles and found no reference to any kind of a mirror on this route. Trains often had mirrors, and there were points along the rail where mirrors were occasionally employed, typically at switching stations, but at no point could he find any usage of them on the Cascade route near the tunnels.

After nearly a week of searching for any reference to a mirror, Ron had finally caught a break while he was researching the old Cascade train tunnel itself.

The original Cascade tunnel had been built on a grade. It continued to climb uphill from the western portal, peaking as it exited the eastern portal, more than two-and-a-half miles through the mountain. Not being a train engineer, Ron hadn't completely understood the problem, but apparently the grade of the tunnel being close to the relative grade of the track as it climbed uphill through the tunnel, had created an issue with noxious exhaust fumes from the locomotives as they made their way through the mountain. The tunnel was unable to vent itself, and the engineers were in danger of asphyxiation with every trip, particularly if the train had to stop in the tunnel for any reason.

The solution had been to electrify the tunnel using power from the Wenatchee River on the east side and use electric locomotives to pull the trains through. Switching stations where the steam locomotives would be swapped out for the electric versions were set up on both sides of the tunnel, in Skykomish on the west side and Berne on the eastside. This had all been fascinating, but it hadn't helped him solve the mirror problem.

It wasn't until Ron began to research the actual *process* of electrifying the tunnel that he finally found the reference. As the trains were pulled through the tunnel and began to descend to the switching stations on each side of the route, they needed a signal to notify the switching station that they were approaching. Since the rail line was already electrified, it was a simple matter to set up a sensor on the track that would send an electric pulse through the tunnel and down the line to the opposite depot. These sensors, set up on both sides of the tunnel, about a half mile from the entrances, also let the depot know that a train was entering the tunnel from the other side. Obviously, they wouldn't send in another train from their side. It was a clever safety measure to prevent collisions back in those early days.

Ron found an old article published in the 50s that was written about the life of an engineer on the electric locomotives of the old Cascade route. In the article, the engineer talked about a near collision that occurred on one of his trips when the sensor malfunctioned. His actual quote as printed in the article was, *"something had happened to the mirror on the west side, and the Berne depot didn't realize we were entering the tunnel. They sent the westbound train through, nearly causing a head-on collision that would have jammed up the tunnel for a long while."*

Mirror was apparently little-used engineer parlance for the signal sensor on either side of the tunnel and Ron, trying to confirm it and knowing where to look now, was able to find only one other reference to the term in all his research.

Once he knew what the term meant, Ron dug up old schematics of the sensors to get an idea what they looked like and where they should be located. He searched through hiking and outdoor blogs until he found a picture of the west-side mirror, taken by a hiker who had no idea what it was he was photographing. The mirror was just a small concrete box, normally overlooked by hikers, and mostly hidden in the underbrush that had grown up to the edge of the old trail. It was located at the west end of the first and largest of the snow sheds, and Ronnie was almost there.

Chapter 61

The man with the scar on his face shivered as he cautiously made his way down the trail, trying to keep just out of Ronnie's sight. He was wearing a sweatshirt but wasn't at all prepared for a late spring hike through the mountains.

He felt the gun down at his side and considered catching up to Ronnie and using the gun to get him to talk. He thought he'd heard another hiker behind him, though, just a few minutes before and, although he'd turned around to look and hadn't seen anything, he was worried about a possible witness approaching right when he was in the middle of a kidnapping. He may have been getting slightly paranoid, but he didn't want to be holding Ronnie at gunpoint and have someone else come walking along. That would complicate matters to say the least.

He didn't look as though he belonged on the trail. He was wearing leather boots, dark jeans, and a black sweatshirt. He had no pack or even a bottle of water. He found a baseball cap in his car and put that on, pulling it low to conceal his face, but even so, he didn't like the situation he was in. He knew he would stand out and be remembered should something happen here and a witness get questioned about anything that was unusual. The scar on his face was often a burden for exactly that reason.

Ronnie was walking along at a quick pace and making no effort at stealth, so the man with the scar was able to move along rapidly, staying just out of sight but still able to hear the occasional scrape of Ronnie's boot on the gravel path as he hurried along.

He was becoming more and more concerned that this was nothing more than a simple hike by a man celebrating his newfound freedom, but from everything he knew of Ronnie, a random hike in the mountains was not characteristic.

He rounded a corner just in time to see Ronnie stepping off the trail and climbing up the slope of the mountain at the end of this massive concrete structure they'd been walking through. Flattening himself against the wall of the structure, he watched as Ronnie disappeared into the underbrush and climbed straight up the slope. Ronnie held something in his hand, but the man with the scar was too far away to see what it was.

Wishing he'd had some way to carry water, the man scurried along to the point on the path where Ronnie had left the trail. There was a small concrete box here, mostly buried in the underbrush, but nothing else that he could see. He deduced no obvious reason for Ronnie to have ventured off on a cross-country climb. Listening carefully, the man could hear the snapping of twigs as Ronnie climbed the hillside above him.

Shrugging, the man stepped off the trail and began to follow Ronnie's path. Just as he did so, he thought he caught a flash of movement from the area where he'd just come. He turned in that direction and didn't see anything, the colossal concrete tomb silent and still, save for the numerous rivulets of water trickling down the sides accumulating in the shallow ditch that ran along the base of the uphill wall.

Deciding that the movement must have been a small animal, or perhaps his imagination, the man with the scar on his face turned and began to cautiously climb the hillside. He cocked his head and strained to hear the faint sounds of Ronnie up ahead, and he did his best to match his own footsteps and pauses with those of the man he was pursuing.

Chapter 62

Now a mile is the goal, are your legs burning yet?
Don't worry, you've nearly arrived.
A heavy load, a truly great get,
I was amazed at how they had thrived.

The interesting thing about the rest of the poem, Ronnie thought as he stopped on the steep slope to catch his breath and get a drink of water, was that Ron's conclusions from here on in were all speculation. From here on, there was no way to confirm the information, to find outside sources or evidence that he was on the right track. Ronnie was cutting the brush now, slogging his way up the steep incline, no trail to follow and no pictures or blogs from hikers that showed anything about this area.

Based on interviews Richard Frost had given before his death, Ronnie was sure this was intentional. Frost wanted people to get out into the wilderness, to enjoy nature and to remember him while they did so. He intentionally manipulated the poem so that a searcher could get into the right area without leaving his couch, so to speak, but then he left it vague enough so they had to actually get out into the woods and spend some time there to solve the remainder of the puzzle.

The first line of the next stanza contained two important clues, and they were related. The question, *Are your legs burning yet?*

implied that there was a right turn off the path and more of an uphill climb to follow. Your legs don't burn going downhill, just when ascending. *Now a mile is the goal* could be interpreted two ways. The first would be that one needed to walk for one mile, and the second would be that the *goal* was one mile...referring to one mile of elevation.

Ron was sure, because of the way it was phrased, that Frost meant to climb to an elevation of one mile on a straight perpendicular from the mirror. Thinking about it and using his own common sense, Ronnie agreed.

He looked down at the screen of the handheld GPS he'd purchased along with the pack and his new outdoor clothes. It showed he was at 4200 feet, just a little more than 1000 feet to go to reach the needed mile of altitude. He was starting to see small patches of snow remaining in the shadowed areas of the thickly forested mountain slope.

Ronnie smiled and took another sip of water, then re-shouldered his pack and continued to climb up as he thought back to his decision to kill Ron.

The timing had been perfect. By the time Ron solved the riddle of the poem, it was the start of winter, and climbing up here to begin a search would have been impossible. A dozen feet or more of snow could be covering the ground. He needed to wait until late spring to begin his exploration, and Ron decided to use that time to renegotiate his deal with Ronnie, completely underestimating the caliber of man he'd chosen to screw over.

Reasonable doubt is a concept that's tough to define. In order for a jury to reach a conviction in a criminal case, they have to believe the defendant is guilty "beyond a reasonable doubt." If Ronnie could instill in the minds of the jury members some measure of doubt that he'd committed the murder, they would have to acquit him, even if they thought he *might* have done it. What he needed to make sure they acquitted him was someone else that he could artfully blame. The jury could look at this individual and say, "What about this guy, couldn't he have done it?" He needed a smart person to blame, one potentially capable of planting evidence, and that person was Gerry Gresham.

Ronnie smiled to himself as he remembered the look on Gresham's face when he'd told him about Jessamyn and Ron's affair. It was made up, of course, or at least he didn't know if it was true, but he needed to set Gerry up and make him angry enough to want to testify against him. That almost backfired on him twice: first, that weak fuck almost died of a heart attack right in his office; that would have made things much more difficult. Next Gerry decided to lie on the stand. Ronnie had pushed him too far and wasn't prepared for Gerry to make up lies under oath, lies that almost ruined everything.

Ironically, Franklin Richardson, of all people, came up with a plan to discredit Gerry. The bluff he ran was pretending he would call Anne Fowler to testify, and that had worked beautifully. It made the jury suspect Gerry even more than Ronnie had hoped, solidifying his plan even more.

He'd thought for a long time about the risk he was taking. Anything can happen with a jury, after all. Would they be smart enough to realize that a man with his intelligence, with foresight and planning, would never leave behind that much evidence? Would they realize that someone with his brains would never leave the gun at his house, hidden in a laundry hamper, the expended cartridge next to it, duct tape in the cans outside? The answer was that they might realize that if they were smart enough.

Leaving the duct tape in the cans outside his house was a last-minute stroke of genius on his part. He wanted things to move quickly, and he took the chance that the detectives might search those cans. If they didn't find the duct tape then, he would have to bring the cans back in off the alley so they didn't get picked up by the garbage collection scheduled for the next day. He would have to wait until the search warrant was served and let them find the tape then. Fortunately, it worked out as he hoped when Detective Sodafsky was smart enough to confiscate the garbage from the cans.

The crux of Ronnie's plan revolved around the constitutional protection against double jeopardy. If he was acquitted of Conner's murder, he couldn't be tried again, even if more evidence was discovered later. Not knowing whether Conner told anyone else about the treasure made it necessary for Ronnie to take the risk. If he wanted to claim the treasure for himself, he needed to be able to do it without the danger that somebody would connect it to Conner's murder.

Ronnie knew that he could have simply discovered the treasure, which Richard Frost had said was gold and jewels, and he could have sold it off quietly. He could have hidden the money, and that would have protected him, but that would have been foolish. With inflation and the rising price of gold, plus the knowledge that the treasure was worth "millions" back when Frost hid it, Ronnie estimated the current value of it to be in the neighborhood of five to six million dollars. That was the intrinsic value, the scrap value of the gold and gems. The actual value, considering what a cult following this treasure had generated was probably two to three times that amount. People would pay big bucks for something that was an intact piece of pop culture history. Ronnie wasn't about to settle for a measly five million if he could recognize fifteen million out of the thing.

Once he'd been acquitted of Conner's murder, he was free to announce the treasure find without fear of reprisal. Hell, he could shout from the rooftops that he was guilty of the murder if he wanted to; once he'd been tried and acquitted, he could never be charged again.

The two things he couldn't have as evidence against him, the two things that would have nagged at the jury had they been part of the evidence, were his cell phone or his car at the scene of the crime at the time of the murder. The phone issue was easy to solve; he simply needed to leave it at home. Getting a prepaid phone that was untraceable had been child's play. The prosecutor looked at that piece of evidence and thought it fit well with her concept of a smart killer planning a meticulous crime. The jury looked at it just the way Ronnie had hoped they would: as real evidence that showed he was innocent and being framed.

Ronnie could have found another way to get to Ron's house that night without using his car. Calling a cab was dangerous; someone might remember picking him up or dropping him off. Walking was out of the question since his destination was too far, same for riding a bike. What he'd decided to do instead was scout out the location of every traffic camera, and then take a circuitous route that avoided all of them. He would park his car across the golf course from Conner's house, an acceptably small risk.

Once he'd decided to kill Ron and leave all the evidence pointed at himself, Ronnie knew he needed to prepare everything in advance; he knew things would move quickly once he'd committed the murder. His first step had been to find the perfect attorney.

Franklin Richardson was a moron, but he was the perfect moron for what Ronnie had in mind. His plan required him to retain an attorney who was money hungry enough that he wouldn't fight Ronnie on various things he wanted to do. No attorney in his right mind would be okay with his client rushing this case to trial inside ninety days, or with his client's demand that he not file any motions trying to exclude the evidence. No ordinary attorney would have been okay with letting his client run his own defense to the extent that he couldn't even object to the State's questioning without approval.

Good attorneys also always have a full client load, and those clients require their time and energy. Ronnie needed someone who would have all the time in the world to work on just his case. He needed someone who needed the money badly enough that he would do whatever Ronnie told him to do. Franklin Richardson fit that pattern perfectly.

Ronnie spent some time looking into Franklin's background, learning about him and about what made him tick. He had a private investigator dig into Franklin's financials to make sure he was broke enough to do whatever was required of him without too many questions. He even had the PI break into Franklin's office and snoop around. That private investigator had proven to be invaluable, and Ronnie eventually used him for a few other parts of his plan.

One of the things Ronnie had learned through his research was that some things can void protections against double jeopardy. For instance, if the judge in a case is bribed, a defendant can be charged and tried again, even after an acquittal. Oddly enough, if a *juror* is bribed, a defendant is still protected.

Knowing that information, Ronnie realized that finding a juror to bribe should be a part of his fallback plan, in case the trial didn't go the way he expected. He decided to use the same private investigator he used to dig into Franklin's background for the delicate purpose of preparing to bribe a juror. Bringing in another person was the riskiest part of his plan, but it was a necessary risk. He needed someone to make the 911 call from a prepaid phone, keep tabs on the police and, most importantly, follow through on his bribery plan if required.

The private investigator he chose for this was perfect because he was a criminal himself. He had a nasty scar on his face that he got in a bar fight years ago, a fight that caused him to spend some time in jail. His name was Dean, and he wasn't even a licensed PI, but Ronnie knew he could count on him for one reason and one reason only: Dean hated Ron Conner just as much as Ronnie did.

Ron Conner had stolen Dean's girlfriend years before. That was it; his hatred was not based on anything but pure and simple jealousy over a girl. Nevertheless, it was a hatred that had festered in Dean for a long time. When Ronnie decided Ron had to die, he knew that he could count on Dean to help.

Ronnie didn't divulge any details to Dean about his plan, never even told him he was going to kill Ron Conner. He simply told him he needed Dean to do a few things for him, that he would pay him well, and that the things he needed him to do would make Ron Conner suffer. Dean jumped at the opportunity. He wanted to know more about the plan, but Ronnie refused to tell him. Dean had almost certainly guessed that Ronnie killed Ron, but he couldn't know that for sure.

During the jury selection process, Ronnie chose three jurors who he thought might be susceptible to bribery. His decisions were based on Dean's background checks that revealed some shady financial transactions and some IRS troubles they had all been involved in. He didn't know if the bribes would work; they were meant to only be a last-ditch attempt to save his freedom should the case somehow take a bad turn. Luckily, he hadn't needed to use the bribery angle. Nonetheless, he had Dean in the courtroom for the last portion of the trial each day, ready to give him a prearranged signal should he decide to try the bribery route. He never had to give Dean that signal.

Watching for the signal and then negotiating the bribe with one of the three jury members had been the last task he needed Dean for, and Ronnie happily paid Dean the final portion of his fee after the defense rested. The amount he paid to Dean was a pittance compared to the value he got for his service.

Ronnie took another break from his hike and finished off the remainder of his first bottle of water, breathing hard but feeling good. Hearing a rock roll down the slope behind him, he turned and looked back. He didn't see anything moving and decided perhaps a small animal or gravity had dislodged it.

He pulled out his GPS and took a look at it. He had climbed to just under 5000 feet. Only about 300 feet to climb and he could start searching in earnest for the treasure. Feeling the anticipation and excitement mount, he tossed the empty water bottle aside into the brush and started climbing again, his thoughts drifting back to the trial.

What a shock it was when the prosecutor submitted evidence during pretrial motions showing his car passing by the security camera that monitored a building of a private business near Paine Field. He'd been completely unaware of that camera; he never even considered private cameras that monitored business parking lots. He couldn't believe that bitch prosecutor, Dana Porter, had gone door-to-door to the businesses asking to review their footage from that night. With all the evidence he'd given her, she should have thought she had a slam dunk. Instead she looked for more, and in such an unlikely place too. She almost ruined everything with that little stunt.

Ronnie laughed, remembering the look on Franklin's face when he instructed him to not worry about any of the evidence except that stupid shot of his car driving to Ron's that night. It must have seemed to Franklin like a small sapling in the middle of a forest full of data, but Ronnie had known it was the most important piece of evidence the prosecutor owned. He sweated the hearing where the judge had eventually ruled it wasn't definitive enough to be shown to the jury. His relief at the ruling had been palpable.

Ronnie pulled out his GPS and took a look. Just over 5200 feet elevation. He could see what appeared to be a plateau just up ahead and, ignoring the fire from the lactic acid burning in his legs, he quickened his pace.

Chapter 63

Dean, the man with the scar on his face, stopped and picked up the bottle Ronnie had thrown aside. He shook it in vain, hoping for some water to quench his thirst. Finding none, he scooped a handful of snow from a patch under a tree and ate that instead. He was hurting from the climb, out of breath, thirsty, and pissed off beyond belief. If this bullshit didn't end soon, he was going to end it himself, regardless of his curiosity about what the fuck was happening.

Chapter 64

The evidence of the chopsticks in the food had been one of the toughest things for him to pull off. Ronnie was allergic to peanuts. Ron knew about the allergy of course, it was something that had come up a lot during his youth when it was diagnosed, and in fact was another thing that Ron had held over him all the time, a condition that Ron constantly made fun of.

Ronnie ordered food from Satay Thai the day before and made sure to leave some in the box so it could go into his fridge. The night he killed Ron, he brought the chopsticks he'd used with that order to Ron's house, along with the rest of his equipment. Once there, he suggested they order out for dinner. He made Ron call up the restaurant while he, Ronnie, pretended he was thinking about what to order. Ron gave his name and address and then ordered chicken Pad Thai. Ronnie then asked Ron to hand the phone over saying he had a question he wanted to ask. When Ron handed him the phone with a scowl, he made snide comments under his breath about Ronnie being a "diva." When Ronnie took the phone, he said simply, "Oh, never mind. I'll also have chicken Pad Thai." He then pressed the mute button on the phone and added, "No peanuts with mine, though, please; that's very important." The only person who heard those instructions was Ron.

When the food was delivered and Ron discovered there were peanuts in both orders, he told Ronnie he would call the restaurant back. Ronnie told him not to bother, that he wasn't hungry after all.

After he killed Ron, Ronnie had poured most of his carton of food into a zip lock bag, replacing the unused chopsticks with the ones he brought from home, the ones he used the previous day. He disposed of the bag of food by throwing it out the window of his car and onto the highway where it was run over by the tires of thousands of vehicles. The die was cast for a beautiful setup of a prosecutor who had no way of knowing about Ronnie's deadly peanut allergy.

Looking now at the GPS again, he realized he was cresting the plateau right at 5300 feet of elevation. The land began to slope slightly downhill, and Ronnie looked around, remembering the next clue in the poem.

A heavy load, a truly great get,
I was amazed at how they had thrived.

Ron told him it was impossible to know for sure what this meant, but his best guess was that they'd be looking for a beaver dam. He'd studied satellite photos of the area, and there was a series of tiny lakes or ponds on the plateau, right at the correct elevation.

Ronnie could see those ponds just ahead now, and he hurried down the slight incline, skidding across the patches of snow as he hustled toward the water. As he cleared the last of the trees, he looked to his left and spotted a beautiful sight: a large jam of logs, ends sharpened like a pencil by the teeth of a hard-working beaver.

Ronnie gave a huge whoop of delight and started toward the dam at a run.

Chapter 65

Dean heard the yell from up ahead and quickened his pace. He was approaching the top of the slope, and he had a feeling this chase was finally coming to its conclusion. Out of breath, he paused, partially hidden behind a tree. He saw Ronnie up ahead, running down the hill toward a pond.

Chapter 66

Ronnie skidded to a stop at the edge of the beaver dam, his pulse going crazy from the climb up the hill and the excitement of finishing the trek he'd anticipated for so long. He took a moment to revel in the satisfaction of hard work and great planning all coming to a culmination he'd long been dreaming of.

The beaver or beavers who built this dam had indeed thrived, for a long time based on the size of the construction. The creek they had dammed had been nothing but a small trickle, but the lake they'd created with their amazing feat of engineering was simply spectacular. Ronnie estimated the height of the dam at an impressive eight feet, and he was standing at the top of it, the piled logs and mud falling away to a gorge at his feet. A small stream of water exited the dam near the bottom, probably the same amount that entered the lake from somewhere above, keeping the lake at a constant depth.

Much like Richard Frost had been, Ronnie was amazed at the work the little creatures had done. Looking around, he could see the multitude of stumps they had left behind while doing their construction job.

Although he knew it by heart, he took a moment to look at the second to last stanza, and the last one that really mattered because it contained the final clues to the location of the treasure:

Go quickly now, for the end draws nigh,
All great adventures must come to a close.
The entrance you seek, low and yet dry,
The chest in a trunk, protected by a rose.

He began to climb down the embankment, striving for the bottom of the dam. It was still chilly out here, and he was really glad Frost had not chosen to hide the chest under water or on the other side of the dam. *Low and yet dry* meant he could avoid getting soaking wet and then have to walk all the way back to his car trying to stave off hypothermia.

Chapter 67

Dean stayed hidden behind his tree and watched Ronnie stare at a piece of paper, then shove the paper in his pocket and disappear over the edge of the embankment he'd been standing on. Confused more than ever, he walked quickly down the slope, crawling on his hands and knees as he approached the top. He crept up to the edge, keeping his body out of sight behind some shrubs. Lying flat on his stomach, he peaked over the lip to see Ronnie, his back to Dean, prodding at the logs near the base of the huge beaver dam.

Chapter 68

Ronnie suddenly stopped what he was doing and stared in amazement. He was lying on his stomach peering behind the logs in the base of the dam, looking to find the right trunk mentioned in the poem. He assumed that meant a tree trunk, and there were many, their roots buried in the ground and forming the base of the beaver dam. He was standing on a sturdy shelf, thinking that it would be a good platform for Frost to stand on while he hid the chest. That was when, by pure happenstance, he caught a gleam out of the corner of his eye, the sun's rays striking a shiny object and reflecting the light directly back toward him.

He stood and moved to his left, easily stepping across the light flow of the stream as it exited the base of the dam. Leaning in closely, he spotted the item that had caused the gleam of light.

Pinned into one of the trunks of the horizontal trees that made up the base support was a jeweled brooch. The golden edges of the brooch were dull with age, and the red jewels that made up the design in the center had an accumulation of dust or mud on them that made it so the brooch blended into the wood of the trunk. He reached forward with his thumb, cleaning some of the accumulation off to reveal a beautiful representation of a rose, made up of what appeared to be green emeralds on the stem with rubies making up the petals of the flower itself. The brooch was about the size of a silver dollar, far too small and hidden under the overhang of the dam for anybody to see it accidentally in the unlikely event someone had come all the way up to this isolated spot where there were no trails.

Ronnie had been lucky to spot it, the corner just catching the sun's rays perfectly to reflect back to him. He would have found it eventually, though, as he'd planned to scour every inch of this dam, knowing he was within feet of the millions of dollars in treasure.

Now he stopped, staring at the brooch reverently. This was it, the final moment, and he wanted to take a minute to bask in the glory of his find, to enjoy the sweet surge of adrenaline that was flooding through his bloodstream.

Now, leaning down, he pushed aside several branches that he found were not attached to anything, rather just laying across the fallen logs, wedged into place. As he moved them aside, he spotted an old tree trunk, older than the rest of the logs surrounding it. This tree trunk appeared to have been placed here, not by the furry creatures who carefully built this marvel of natural engineering, but by somebody who came along later, somebody who knew he was placing obstacles in a path that somebody, someday, would follow to its end.

Ronnie reached inside and pushed aside the trunk, uncovering a dull gray chest.

"YESSSSSSSSSSSSSS!" he screamed, throwing his hands in the air and dancing on the edge of the bank, reveling in the glory of the find. Reaching back into the dam, he grabbed hold of the handles on each side of the chest, pulling it toward himself, shocked by the weight of it. Grunting, he pushed with his feet for leverage; the chest slid slowly, skidding across two logs that appeared to have been placed there for that purpose. Now Ronnie could see very old scratch marks on those logs, the marks made when Richard Frost first pushed this chest into this space, eight and a half years earlier.

Chapter 69

Watching curiously from the top of the bank, his body lying flat on the grass, his head behind the thick brush that he could see through just enough to observe Ronnie while remaining hidden, Dean frowned as Ronnie screamed and started dancing around. Burrowing deeper into the shrub, he wondered if Ronnie would spot him as he spun himself around in a circle, clearly excited by something down there.

Dean tried to decide if now was the time to confront Ronnie, to take whatever it was that he was so excited about. He made the decision to wait just a bit longer. There was no sense in tipping his hand prematurely when he didn't know what was going on. Ronnie wasn't going anywhere from here unless Dean allowed that to happen, so there was no need to rush.

He reached back to his right-side waistband and slowly pulled out his pistol, cautiously double checking the red mark on the side of the frame that indicated there was a bullet in the chamber. Cradling the gun in his hand, he leaned forward again, curious to see what was going to happen next.

Chapter 70

Heaving one final time, Ronnie wrenched the box out of the dam and onto the log in front of him. The box was sturdy, a strange gray color that Ronnie suspected was titanium. Approximately eighteen inches on each dimension, it was extremely well built with two large, beefy clasps holding the lid closed. The clasps were built to accept locks, but no locks were present. Taking a deep breath, Ronnie lifted both hinges off the clasps and slowly raised the lid.

The interior of the box was covered in a soft black fabric that appeared to have withstood the weather perfectly. The first thing he noticed was that the lid was fitted with a rubber gasket, designed to keep out any water. It had done its job well, as the items inside appeared to have been placed there just yesterday.

On the top of the items in the box was a large, gallon-sized zip lock bag, a laminated letter inside the bag. Picking it up, Ronnie set it aside to be read later. Under that was another piece of the black fabric; moving it aside, Ronnie saw stacks upon stacks of gold bars.

Reverently, he hefted one of the bars. It was small but dense, precision made and stamped with the words, *FINE GOLD .999* and under that, *NET WT 2400 grams*. Doing some quick math, Ronnie performed the conversion. 1000 grams was a kilogram--2.2 pounds. That made this bar just over five pounds of pure gold. Looking into the box, he counted four stacks of bars, five high, twenty total bars equaling a touch over 100 pounds. At a current price of just under $1400 per ounce (he had checked last night) times 1600 ounces, he had in excess of $2.2 million dollars in gold bars.

Packed around the bars were three bags made of fine fabric, their tops closed with drawstrings. Picking up one at a time, Ronnie carefully opened them. The first contained a large handful of green and blue gems that he suspected were emeralds and sapphires, some cut into perfect shapes, others raw stones. The second bag contained rubies, and the third, diamonds--enough to fill one large hand. There had to be millions of dollars' worth of gems here, at least three or four million, guessing conservatively. All told, the treasure was easily worth $6 or $7 million, not to mention what it might be worth all if sold at auction. He had already calculated it might bring a multiple of two to three times its intrinsic value.

His hands shaking, Ronnie took a moment to say thanks to Richard Frost, wherever he was now. He could hardly believe that it was over, that he'd actually found the treasure. Improbably, his thoughts returned to the last stanza of the poem.

If you're persistent enough to have come this far,
The gold, I bequeath all to you.
A paragon of honor, I have no doubt that you are,
Though if not, this day you shall rue.

He smiled at these words. No clue was present in this part, both he and Ron had agreed on that. Richard Frost had simply been

assuring the world that the finder of the treasure was the owner
of the treasure. Ron had laughed at him though, right before
Ronnie shot him. He'd reminded him of the last line and asked
him if he believed in karma. Ronnie flipped it back to him and
asked Ron if he thought *he* had acted honorably. Ron shrugged,
saying he'd done what he thought was fair. Ronnie answered,
"Me too," and then pulled the trigger. Twice.

Shaking his head and remembering the piece of paper in the zip
lock bag, he picked it up, smoothing the plastic of the bag to read
it. He needed to protect this just as much as the treasure; it was
this document that proved this was indeed Richard Frost's hidden
treasure, and therefore, the document had enormous value on its
own, adding to the intrinsic value of the treasure. He noticed it
was another poem, and he smiled as he read:

If you're reading this note, that means you've found,
The treasure I left here for you.
Spend it for good, be wise and be sound,
My life ends, but yours begins anew.

You're clearly a person persistent and smart,
To have come all this way at such cost.
Now take this bounty, go on and depart,
To your lasting health, Sincerely, Richard Frost.

Sentimental old fool, Ronnie thought as he carefully put the bag
containing the poem back into the box and closed it.
Remembering the brooch, he reached up to the log where it was
pinned and carefully pried it loose. Wiping the remaining dirt off
the face of it, he admired the craftsmanship for a moment and
then reopened the box and slipped the brooch inside, closing the
lid again and fastening the hasps. He would have to grab his
backpack and see if it would hold up to the weight of this thing
like the REI salesman had promised. He didn't know for sure that
he could carry the 110 pounds or so that this thing weighed, but
he was sure going to try. At least it was all downhill.

As he stood up, brushing the dirt from his jeans, his heart suddenly gave a lurch, his knees nearly buckling. Standing on top of the embankment was Dean, a hat pulled down low on his face, trying but failing to hide the ugly scar that marked his right cheek. The scar barely drew his attention though. That was reserved for the large black pistol in Dean's hand, the business end pointed right at Ronnie's head.

Chapter 71

Dean could hardly believe his eyes when Ronnie reached into the log dam and pulled out a large metal box, its sides glinting dully in the morning light. Questions raced through his mind: Had Ronnie hidden some kind of valuable up here in the mountains? Why would he choose to hide something this far out in the middle of nowhere? He watched, intrigued, as Ronnie slowly unclasped the hinges of the box and opened it up.

From where Dean was laying, he couldn't tell what was in the plastic bag that Ronnie pulled off the top of the box and set aside. He sure couldn't mistake what was inside the box, though, especially when Ronnie pulled out one of the bars and held it up, staring at it ardently. It glimmered softly in the light, and though Dean didn't have much experience with fine metals, he knew gold when he saw it.

Hardly able to control his excitement, he slowly and quietly got to his knees, his head rising over the shrub. There was no danger of Ronnie seeing him, he realized; Ronnie's attention was focused solely on the contents of the box. Dean waited a bit as Ronnie pulled out each of the bags and looked inside them. Dean couldn't see the contents from his vantage point, but it was obvious Ronnie was excited about whatever they were. Ronnie put the bags back into the chest and looked for a long moment at whatever was in the plastic bag. As he did so, Dean took the opportunity to stand up and point the gun casually in Ronnie's direction. He watched as Ronnie reached up and pulled something off the log, staring at it a moment before placing it in the box and closing the hasps. He stood up slowly, brushed some dirt off his jeans, and then turned, noticing Dean for the first time.

Dean watched as Ronnie's face lost all color, his mouth open, his eyes agape.

Chapter 72

Getting over his shock at seeing Dean standing there with a gun, and thinking quickly, Ronnie realized he'd left his own gun in the backpack lying next to where Dean was standing on top of the embankment. A list of questions ran through his head, his brain raced trying to connect the dots and figure out how it was possible for Dean to be standing there at this moment. Urgently, he needed to figure out how to get out of the jam he was in.

"What are you doing here, Dean?" he asked.

Dean smiled lazily. "I just thought I'd see what you were up to this morning. Seemed strange for you to be going for a drive so early in the morning after your big day yesterday."

"Well, now you know. You mind telling me why you're pointing a gun at me?"

"I was thinking it was important, you know, just in case you have one yourself. I already saw what you do to people you don't like, and I gotta think you aren't gonna like me much after today. You don't have a gun do you, Ronnie?" he asked, making a circular motion with his own gun, indicating Ronnie should turn around in a circle.

Ronnie slowly lifted his jacket and sweatshirt, spinning a 360-degree circle, showing Dean that he did not have a weapon on him.

"I didn't really see the need for a gun, considering I was just taking a little hike here."

"And you happened to stumble onto something interesting on this hike I see," Dean replied with a smile.

"Well, Dean, as I'm sure you've figured out already, I kind of knew this was here." Ronnie's mind was racing, trying to figure out what to do next. Dean had the gun, and he had the height advantage, standing on the embankment looking down on Ronnie. There was nowhere for him to run, no real cover he could take advantage of, no way out that he could see. He realized that his only advantage right now was his mind. Dean was a simpleton, and Ronnie knew he should be able to outsmart him easily.

"Why don't you go ahead and hump that chest up here, nice and easy like," Dean suggested, pointing the gun at the metal chest.

"It's too heavy. I'll never be able to move it alone; you'll have to come down here and help me."

Dean laughed. "I don't think so, buddy. How were you going to get it up here without me?"

REASONABLE DOUBT | Rick Fuller

Ronnie shrugged. "I was going to use that backpack up there. Why don't you toss it down to me?" He kept his face impassive, hoping Dean would toss the backpack down without noticing the gun inside.

Dean glanced at the backpack and took one step toward it, then stopped. "You know, that box has two nice handles on the sides of it. I'm betting you can carry it. Let's see you try."

Ronnie shook his head. "Look, Dean, there's millions of dollars in gold and jewels in this box. You and I can split it. You don't have to do it this way. There's more than enough here for both of us. Put the gun away, come down here and give me a hand, and we'll carry it out together. What do you say?"

Ronnie held his breath as Dean seemed to consider his options. "How much do you think it weighs," he finally asked thoughtfully, motioning toward the chest.

Ronnie tried not to smile. "Maybe 110 or 120 pounds. You and I together can carry it easily and like I said, there's plenty here for both of us!"

Dean glanced again at the backpack on the top of the bank. "You think this backpack will hold that much weight?" he asked.

Ronnie nodded. "Sure. The guy where I bought it said it would hold as much as I could carry. It's made for packing out deer and elk; they weigh more than this box."

Dean slowly nodded. Ronnie allowed himself a small smile. He knew as soon as he got Dean to help him get the box to the top of the bank, he'd be close to his own gun. He'd be able to talk Dean into letting him hold the pack while Dean, who was bigger and stronger, placed the box inside it. While Dean had his hands full with the box, Ronnie could grab the gun out of the front pouch of

REASONABLE DOUBT | Rick Fuller

the pack and shoot him. He'd push him down into this ravine, break apart the gun and scatter the pieces across the mountain and nobody would be likely to ever find either Dean or the gun.

"Come on down, give me a hand, and we'll get it up there," Ronnie said, smiling up at him.

"I don't guess I need your help. Seems like I can handle that box myself, buddy." Ronnie saw Dean smile. He saw his finger tighten on the trigger of the gun, and then he felt a giant wallop as the bullet hit him in the chest.

Chapter 73

Dean looked through the smoke coming out of the barrel of the gun at the inert form of Ronnie Whittaker lying on the bank, his blood sprayed across the brush behind where his body lay. His head was lying on the bank near the stream running through the beaver dam. His blood began to run in rivulets toward the stream to be washed away as it trickled off down the valley.

Dean holstered the gun and hopped down the embankment. Stepping across the stream, he paused to kick Ronnie's body fully into the water. He figured the body would slowly work its way downstream, moved further into the thick brush than it was. After a week or two, the only sign of it would be the flock of birds that were sure to gather, nature's way of cleaning everything up. After a month or two, there would be nothing but bones, and he was pretty sure nobody was ever going to be coming up here looking for Ronnie.

Ronnie's SUV was another matter, and Dean figured he could pretty easily move it up to the ski area parking lot just a few miles up the road. If he left it there, he could jog back to his own car and any search for Ronnie would be focused on the large Stevens Pass Recreation Area. Even if Ronnie's body was somehow located, there was absolutely no way for anybody to tie his murder to Dean. He would dispose of the gun later.

Realizing that he needed the keys to Ronnie's SUV, he stepped back over the body and began searching through his pockets. In the right pocket of his jeans he found a piece of paper, folded carefully with lots of creases. He pulled it out and found the poem written on it.

As he read the poem, he came to a slow realization that this poem contained the clues to the box that Ronnie had found. He had no idea what any of the lines meant, but the one line was clear:

If you're persistent enough to have come this far,
The gold, I bequeath all to you.

He grinned broadly. Obviously, *The gold* referred to what was in the box Ronnie had found, the culmination of some sort of treasure hunt. Dean shook his head. He couldn't believe that Ronnie had actually found a treasure, and a significant one apparently.

Dropping the poem onto the bank by Ronnie's body, he reached into the other pocket of his jeans and found the keys to his Range Rover. Perhaps he'd take the SUV with him instead of parking it in the ski area lot. He knew plenty of fences where he could get good money for the Range Rover, and it would never be seen again, at least not in this country. He'd have to get a ride back up here to get his own car, but that was workable.

Walking over to the box, he opened it up, stunned at the sight of all the gold bars gleaming in the sunlight. He knelt down and pulled out the cloth bags one at a time. Opening them, he marveled at the gems inside, gems that were easily recognizable by their colors. Ronnie hadn't been lying, there were millions of dollars here.

Closing the box, he hoisted it up onto his shoulder with a grunt. It was heavy, but manageable, just barely. Getting it to the top of the bank was going to take some careful footwork though. He stepped gingerly across the stream and, grunting, tried to work the box to the top of the ledge, his feet slipping in the mud as he scrambled to gain purchase, his arms shaking under the significant weight.

Chapter 74

Ronnie opened his eyes, the frigid water of the small stream nearly taking his breath away. He began to stir slowly, the instinct for life preservation taking control of his movements. He heard the sound of someone grunting with exertion; that sound stopped him cold as he remembered that he'd just been shot.

He could feel the pain in his chest now, dulled somewhat by the ice-cold water pouring over it. The same water that had awakened him was now numbing his pain. Out of the corner of his eye, he could see that the water running down past his head had turned a crimson color, and he knew he was losing blood fast. He needed to get help, needed to get to a doctor. He knew his cell phone was in the pack at the top of the bank, along with his gun. Before he could get to either of those, he was going to have to get past Dean.

He turned his head toward Dean now, careful to not make a splash in the cold stream. Dean was standing with his feet just above Ronnie's head, the box with the gold above his outstretched arms, balanced precariously on the top of the ledge as Dean tried to stabilize it. Ronnie could see that Dean's feet were slipping in the muddy bank as he scrambled for secure footing. As soon as he found it, he would be able to shove the box the rest of the way to the top of the ledge, and then it would be too late for Ronnie. It wasn't just about getting help for himself, he didn't want the gold to get away either.

If he was going to act, it would have to be quick. He wasn't sure if he would be able to react quickly enough, if he would be able to do it soundlessly or in fact to do it at all. He didn't know how long he'd been unconscious, how long he'd been in the stream, or how much blood he'd lost. He didn't even know if his arms would work, but he did know that he needed to try, and he needed to do it now. He had nothing to lose.

Just as Dean took one last lurch, Ronnie shoved himself out of the stream with his arms, the bullet wound in his chest exploding with pain. He screamed, a combination of the pain from the bullet wound, the icy waters of the stream, and anger and frustration at Dean...Dean, the man who'd put Ronnie's master plan in jeopardy. He pitched his body forward, scrambling with his left hand for the foot that was just above his head. He grabbed that foot with his left hand while his right hand came up as well, wrapping around the ankle, his fingers digging in to the fabric of the jeans Dean was wearing. With full concentration and completely focused effort, Ronnie pulled on that foot, letting gravity do the work as he fell back toward the stream.

Chapter 75

Dean almost had the box to the top of the bank. One more push and he'd have it over the top. Unfortunately, the goddamn thing was heavy, just at the limit of his ability to lift it over his head. He managed to shove one corner of the thing onto the top of the bank, and now he was scrambling to get the leverage to give it the last push needed.

His foot slipped in the mud, and he grunted again as he used all his effort to keep the box from toppling back down. Finally getting purchase with his left foot, he lifted his right foot, finding a firm spot in the bank. Gathering all of his core muscles together, he coiled himself for the final shove. The splash of water and the scream of pain from below stopped him cold.

He felt the hand grab at his foot, the other hand wrapping around his ankle, and he looked down to see the pale white hands of Ron Whittaker, fingers digging into his jeans, droplets of water falling off those fingers to land on his shoes. He realized he was losing his grip on the box, and he looked back up, trying desperately to give it the final shove to the top of the bank, but knowing he was fighting a losing battle. He felt the pull of Ron's hands and his foot reacted, falling off its purchase on the bank and down toward the stream. His hands lost their grip on the box and as he fell down and away from the bank, he saw the box falling, too. He suddenly, and for the first time, became aware of the great danger, of the weight of the box that was now several feet above his head and falling fast.

Dean lowered his head, dropped his hands to the bank and tried to push himself off and away from the danger. It was much too late for that, though. Gravity was pulling the box down, and even Ron had stopped helping, his grip on Dean's ankle failing, no longer pulling him away from the danger. Dean started to look back up toward the box just as it struck him on the forehead--110 pounds or more, concentrated on a sharp point of the titanium box, a metal known to be stronger than steel, moving at a speed that was too fast for Dean to react.

The blow to his head was enough to render him unconscious, sparing him knowledge of the full extent of his wound. The box pinned his head to the ground, the sharp corner easily cracking his skull and burrowing into his brain. It stuck for just a moment, sitting up into the air unnaturally, like a nouveau art piece, embedded a full two inches into his cranium. It teetered there a second or two before finally toppling over, releasing from his skull with a sucking noise that was quickly muffled by the blood that came pouring out to run into the stream.

The box finished its fall, landing in the stream uphill from where Dean now lay, its top flopping open, gold bars and bags of jewels tumbling out.

Chapter 76

Ronnie fell back into the stream after he lost his grip on Dean's leg. The pain from the effort nearly rendered him unconscious, but the ice-cold water splashing onto his face saved him from taking another trip into that dreamless darkness. With a groan, he rolled over just in time to see the chest fall, strike Dean in the forehead and burrow its way into his skull. Dean's eyes glazed over as he came to rest in the stream, his legs flopping onto Ron's, his head sitting at an unnatural angle just above the water. The box flopped open and Ron saw the gold bars strewn across the stream.

He knew they would sink, but he could recover them easily; the bags of gems were a different story. They tumbled into the stream as they fell, opening and disgorging their contents. They wouldn't float, of course, but they would also be easily dislodged and eventually be pushed down into the valley where they would never be found. For now, they were being held by Dean's body which was partially blocking the stream, and for that Ron was thankful.

With a great effort, he pushed himself out of the stream and over to the bank. His chest was on fire and his heart was beating much faster than it should. He knew he was losing blood rapidly, his body struggling to keep the diminished quantity flowing to his vital organs. He had no idea where the bullet had struck, whether it had hit anything important or whether it had just gone through. What he did know was that he needed to get help and he needed to get it quickly.

He pushed himself again and managed to get onto his feet, unsteadily taking a step toward the bank, leaning forward to grab at it with his hands, trying to steady himself. The top of the bank was there, in his sight and within his reach, and his backpack with his phone was on top of that bank. He would get up there and he'd call for an emergency airlift. He could certainly afford it. He'd tell his rescuers that the gold was his, he had the poem to prove it; he'd make them gather the gold and gems for him, and he'd offer them money to keep it safe.

He turned his head and looked at Dean's body. His sightless eyes were staring at the sky, the unnatural cavity in his head now leaking gray matter as the pressure in his skull forced his brains through the puncture. Ron no longer had to worry about that threat at least.

Taking an unsteady step, he reached for the top of the bank, intending to use it as leverage to pull himself up. There were roots and footholds in the bank, and he'd be able to use his legs as well as his hands. He'd make it to the top of the bank, and everything would be okay.

As he lifted his foot onto the first root, his fingers grasped at the bushes on top of the bank. He intended to use them to pull himself to the top, but his legs suddenly gave out. With a cry, he fell backwards, landing in the stream, his arms flailing behind him. His left hand grasped something on the opposite bank of the stream, and he pulled it forward, trying to sit up. He no longer had the strength to sit up, though, his heart now hammering audibly in his chest. A searing pain exploded out with every heartbeat, shooting fire through his veins. He screamed again, but the scream cut off as he choked, and his senses began to numb.

He realized that the blood flowing from the wound in his chest had slowed to a trickle, normally a good sign; however, he knew that it was only because his body was nearly empty of its life fluid. With a whimper, he looked down at his left hand, the one grasping whatever had been on the bank. Opening that hand, he realized it was the poem: the poem that he had fought so hard for, planned so carefully for, worked so hard on. It was the poem that had launched this search, launched the entire scheme, a scheme that ended so unexpectedly in mayhem and destruction.

He was losing consciousness, but he struggled to focus, staring at the piece of paper, vitriol toward God and toward Richard Frost finally overwhelming him. The words from the last stanza were what he could see, visible on the small section of paper in his hand. Those words, the ones Ron Conner had warned him about, the ones he'd never truly given even a moment's consideration because they weren't even a goddamn clue. He tried to focus on them, the last thing he would ever see.

A paragon of honor, I have no doubt that you are,
Though if not, this day you shall rue.

The stream, oblivious to the misery and death that had momentarily disrupted its course, bubbled on, carrying with it the last of the blood. A large, brilliant-cut ruby, nearly invisible in the crimson waters, dislodged itself from its impediment and slowly bumped along, passing the two dead bodies and slowly tumbling into the valley below.

THE END

Word-of-mouth is crucial for any author to succeed. If you enjoyed the book, please leave a review on Amazon. Even if it's just a sentence or two. It would make all the difference and would be very much appreciated!

Acknowledgements

The inspiration for this novel came from two places: the fantastic book by Lee Child called, "One Shot" in which a mountain of evidence is found against the suspect who is being framed, and the story of Forrest Fenn and his hidden treasure.

"One Shot" got me thinking about what would happen if a smart person were to commit a crime and leave a mountain of evidence pointed right at himself, and Forrest Fenn got me to thinking about what an unscrupulous person might do to find a famous treasure worth millions.

Reasonable Doubt contains what I like to call "a poor man's version" of the incredible Forrest Fenn poem that describes the resting place of a real treasure. If you haven't heard of Forrest Fenn and his treasure, I suggest you start by going to DalNeitzel.com, and from there, read the wonderful book by Forrest titled, "too far to walk". Dal himself has made more than sixty trips looking for the treasure and his stories are fun to read. As of the publication date of this novel, the treasure has still not been found. Who knows, maybe you can be the one to find it! If you do find it, please make sure you're a person of honor, for *if not, this day you shall rue.*

My books would be poor versions of themselves indeed, were it not for an amazing network of people who encourage, inspire, and help me during my writing. None more so than Toni Tami who tirelessly and patiently edits my words, fixing literally thousands of errors in grammar, word choice, and punctuation. Although she must think me an idiot as she corrects the same mistake for the hundredth time, she constantly encourages and praises my work, inspiring me to continue attempting this task of writing novels.

My parents, Rick and Jackie, are the same. Encouraging, supportive, and loving; I know how lucky I am to have such a great support network. *Reasonable Doubt* originally had a different ending and I knew I didn't like it. My mom is the one who came up with the idea for the ending it has now, making the book much better than it originally was.

I made a lot of mistakes in my original descriptions of the legal scene, and Judge Trish Lyon helped set me straight on a bunch of those. I was also helped by another judge who asked me not to name him, so I'll thank him anonymously as his assistance helped me avoid what would have been embarrassing errors in the manuscript. Despite their advice, I ended up writing a lot of things that are not technically correct with regard to the legal system, taking advantage of literary liberties that will probably make the two judges and any other attorneys out there cringe, but that hopefully just make the book more enjoyable to read. Any mistakes then are mine alone and done in spite of the unselfish and helpful advice from my two friends.

April Whitaker did a great job designing the cover of the book, and many friends and family members read an early copy of the manuscript and offered suggestions, pointed out errors, and helped make the story better, none more so than Tracy Fudge, the girl who supports my writing dreams in many ways.

Follow me on Twitter at @RickFuller, and email me anytime at DetectiveRyanTyler@gmail.com. I love to hear feedback and comments from all my readers!

Printed in Great Britain
by Amazon

34221601R00189